LP FIC Robar

Robards, K.
Her last whisper.

(3593/ke X)

HER LAST WHISPER

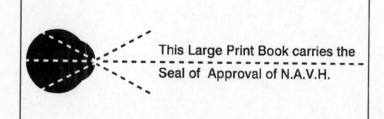

This Large Print Book carries the
Seal of Approval of N.A.V.H.

HER LAST WHISPER

KAREN ROBARDS

WHEELER PUBLISHING
A part of Gale, Cengage Learning

GALE
CENGAGE Learning·

Farmington Hills, Mich • San Francisco • New York • Waterville, Maine
Meriden, Conn • Mason, Ohio • Chicago

GALE
CENGAGE Learning®

Wheeler Publishing Large Print Hardcover.
The text of this Large Print edition is unabridged.
Other aspects of the book may vary from the original edition.
Set in 16 pt. Plantin.

LIBRARY OF CONGRESS CATALOGING-IN-PUBLICATION DATA

Robards, Karen.
   Her last whisper / Karen Robards. — Large type books.
      pages cm-(Wheeler publishing hardcover)
      ISBN 978-1-4104-7371-4 (hardcover) — ISBN 1-4104-7371-6 (hardcover)
   1. United States. Federal Bureau of Investigation—Fiction. 2. Serial murder investigation—Fiction. 3. Women detectives—Fiction. 4. Large type books.
I. Title.
PS3568.O196H47 2014b
813'.54—dc23   2014030081

Published in 2014 by arrangement with The Ballantine Publishing Group, a division of Random House, LLC, a Penguin Random House Company

Printed in Mexico
1 2 3 4 5 6 7 18 17 16 15 14

This book is dedicated to Jack,
with so much love.

Congratulations on your
high school graduation!

CHAPTER ONE

Whoever said that only the good die young had obviously never met Michael Garland.

He was thirty-six years old, sexy as hell, a total badass — and dead as a doornail. Right at that moment, he was also in the process of driving Dr. Charlotte "Charlie" Stone totally around the bend.

"We could be on a beach right now," he groused, referring to the fact that she had elected to return to work rather than take the extended vacation that had been recommended after her most recent death-defying experience. His tone was light. His eyes on her were dark and watchful. He was worried about her, she knew. To tell the truth, she was worried about herself. "Sand. Sun. You in a bikini. Come on, Doc, confess: you've got something against fun."

He only ever called her Doc anymore when he was seriously ticked off at her. Short version: he felt she needed to take

7

some vacation time while she disagreed. At thirty-two years old, Charlie had been in charge of herself since her early teens. She did *not* need a man — ghost, whatever — constantly second-guessing her decisions.

Her brows snapped together.

"Go away," she mouthed at him soundlessly, after a quick glance assured her that her living companion's attention was occupied elsewhere.

Michael snorted. "Not in this life, buttercup." One corner of his mouth quirked up slightly. "Or in this death, either."

Oh, ha, ha. But she didn't — couldn't — say it aloud. If they'd been alone, Charlie would have done more than shoot him an exasperated look. She would have told him to take his fun and stick it up a bodily orifice. Fun was not what life was all about. Life was serious. Purposeful. Sometimes painful. And — well, definitely not fun.

But they weren't alone. In fact, they were even less alone than he thought they were.

"I won't tell." The agonized whisper made Charlie's heart thump. Her fingers tightened around the pen she was holding. The (living) convicted serial killer chained to a seat on the other side of the poured concrete table from her never changed his expression. Neither did the dead convicted serial

killer — that would be Michael, looking as alive as she did herself, in a snug white tee, faded jeans, and boots — who leaned broad shoulders against the beige-painted cinderblock wall to her left as he played self-appointed spectral bodyguard. Which was a complete waste of time, as she had told him when he'd insisted on following her into the interview room rather than waiting outside in the hall as she would have preferred so that she could concentrate fully on her research subject. Number one, there was no need: in this heavily guarded maximum security prison, of all places, she was perfectly safe. And number two, if something were to go wrong, if she were to find herself in danger, there was nothing he could do about it anyway. He was ectoplasm; ether; air. He couldn't so much as swat a fly, because in this earthly plane he no longer existed. In the past, he had occasionally managed to manifest physically for the briefest of moments, but because in typical-for-him aggressive fashion he had pushed the boundaries of that until he had gone a heavenly bridge too far, he had, apparently permanently, rendered himself as insubstantial as a breath. And even if he *could* once again manage to manifest physically, he still couldn't: he'd been warned that if he did, if he once again took on a corporeal aspect, the bond holding him here might very well snap like a rubber band and he would be sucked up into Spookville, as he called the purple twilighty, monster-filled place that was his immediate afterlife destination, possibly never to return.

Therefore, as Charlie had pointed out to him earlier, as a bodyguard Michael was useless.

And even if he wasn't useless, even if he could manifest, there was still nothing he could do to protect her from what was currently disturbing her: the voices.

The voices were all in her head.

Sort of.

At least, she seemed to be the only one who could hear them. Her gift, or curse, depending on how you looked at it, was that she could see/hear/communicate with the spirits of the newly, violently dead (which was how she had found herself saddled with Michael, a former subject of her research who'd been stabbed to death shortly after leaving this very room about six weeks back). But Charlie could only *hear* this woman. Whom she couldn't be completely sure was real. Or dead.

"When's the last time you even took a vacation?" Folding his arms over his chest,

Michael narrowed sky blue eyes at her. At six-foot-three, with tawny blond hair that didn't quite reach his shoulders and a face and body that would make any female between the ages of twelve and ninety drool, he was one of the best-looking men she had ever seen. Too bad he was a total pain in the ass. Not to mention dead. Among other problematic things. He continued, "A real vacation, that didn't involve work, where you just went somewhere sunny and hung out in your bathing suit and relaxed. I'm betting it's been years. Hell, I'm betting you don't even *own* a bikini. Am I right?"

She shot him a look that should have singed his eyeballs. And not just because the only swimsuit she possessed was a five-year-old black one piece.

"I'm right," he concluded with grim satisfaction.

"Where's my candy?" whined the live serial killer she could actually answer without seeming nuts. Her attention instantly redirected toward her job, Charlie pulled from the pocket of her white lab coat the Hershey bar that she had elected to use as a reward (bribe) for this particular subject for responding to her questions, one of which he had answered just before Michael had distracted her. Opening the wrapper, she broke off a section and slid it across the table, then watched her test subject scoop it up and eat it with a great deal of lip-smacking satisfaction. The shackles joining his wrists clanked as he moved. He also had manacles around his ankles securing him to the floor, and a chain around his waist that was fastened to a sturdy metal ring in the wall behind him. It prevented him from rising, or getting close enough to actually put his hands on her.

She might be the goat to his deceptively harmless-looking tiger, but in this controlled environment he was the tethered one.

"You didn't give *me* chocolate," Michael objected. "Hell, I didn't know chocolate was even an option."

Charlie ignored that. She was administering a simplified version of the Myers-Briggs personality test to the hulking, balding fifty-two-year-old convict in front of her. They were alone except for Michael (since he was invisible to everyone except her, she wasn't sure he even counted) and the guard, Johnson, who periodically checked on them through the small glass window in the metal door. Outside the walls of Wallens Ridge State Prison, where they were currently seated in the tiny, windowless room next to her office, her test subject was known as the

Snake River Killer. His given name was Walter Spivey, and he was a hairdresser by trade. He was also notorious as the murderer of fourteen young women whose flesh he had liked, post-mortem, to gnaw from their bones, and he had been on various death rows for the past twelve years. Two months earlier, he had been moved to Wallens Ridge for the express purpose of participating in her government-sponsored study. An apparent anomaly among serial killers, who tended to have higher than average IQs, Spivey was of special interest to her because his IQ of record was 82. Her meetings with him had convinced her that this was an error, or possibly an attempt by some psychiatrist in the pay of Spivey's defense lawyers to circumvent a death sentence, because in many jurisdictions a low IQ was considered a mitigating factor. Whatever, it had been satisfying for her to determine that a serial killer who had at first seemed like the exception to the rule probably was not, after all. He was crazy like a fox — in other words, cunning and manipulative.

A psychiatrist with her own dark personal history with serial killers, Charlie had thought she was immune to the bad vibes that the worst of them emanated.

13

She'd been wrong. With his pale, sweaty skin and loose, damp mouth, Spivey creeped her out. Maybe it had something to do with the fact that she was a slender, pretty brunette like the majority of his victims, whose pictures she had seen in his file, but she didn't really think so. Before — meaning before nearly dying had totally messed her up — being shut up like this with him wouldn't have bothered her at all. She would have regarded Walter Spivey with the clinical detachment of a medical student toward a cadaver.

Now she found that being near him made her skin crawl. The only possible solution? Ignore it. Power through. And hope it went away.

"Again, please just answer yes or no," she said to Spivey. From her calm voice, of which under the circumstances she was justly proud, to the up-twist in which she wore her shoulder-length chestnut hair, to her understated jewelry and the simple blue shirt and black pants beneath her lab coat, Charlie was to all outward appearances unflappably professional. If anxiety had caused her to chew her lipstick off when the voices had started up again just before she'd sat down with Spivey, and if there were shadows resulting from a certain amount of sleeplessness beneath her blue eyes, well, hopefully nobody would notice. "You usually place yourself nearer to the side than the center of a room."

Michael snorted. "You think he's going to answer honestly? Take it from me, by the time you get to death row you've pretty much figured out that I as in introvert is bad, *E* as in *extrovert* is good. So he's going to say no, because everyone knows that preferring the center makes him more of an extrovert, and thus closer to an E than an I. Nobody wants to fry, babe. Everybody you're talking to in here is working every angle they can to avoid it."

Charlie didn't know why she was surprised to discover how much Michael knew about the MBTI personality test. He was highly intelligent. Manipulating the test was something that he was absolutely capable of doing. If he knew that introversion was a mild indicator of a sociopathic personality, then she was pretty confident that he also knew that INTJ — introversion, intuition, thinking, judgment — was the Myers-Briggs personality type most common among serial killers. She spared a minute to try to remember what Michael's type was — she hadn't gotten around to testing him herself before he was killed, although she knew he'd been tested before — and couldn't; when she got back to her office, she would pull his file and check.

"No," Spivey responded with a sunny smile, and as Charlie recorded his answer, he looked pointedly at the Hershey bar. "Can I have my candy?"

"Told ya." Michael's tone was smug as Charlie broke off another section of candy bar and slid it over. The tips of Spivey's fingers just brushed hers. They felt soft and damp. The contact made her stomach tighten, and she quickly pulled her hand back. Michael continued, "And just so you can quit racking your brain, I scored ESFP. And that was without being bribed by chocolate."

The curious thing was, ESFP — extraversion, sensing, feeling, perception — was the exact opposite of INTJ. Absolutely *not* the mark of a serial killer. As far from it as a subject could possibly get, in fact. Charlie's lips twisted. No way had that been an accident. Michael had, no doubt, manipulated the test. As she reached that conclusion, she shot him a condemning look. He grinned, a slow and devilishly charming grin that admitted everything.

And just as easy as that he had her going all marshmallowy inside.

Damn it. She refocused on her test subject with grim determination.

"Please don't do this to me." The disembodied whisper came out of nowhere, snapping her right back into the Amityville Horror that her life was devolving into like a quick plunge into ice water. The terror in the voice sent chills down Charlie's spine. Her instant, instinctive reaction was to glance at Michael, furtively searching his face to see if he'd heard it, too. If the woman she was hearing was present in spirit, even if the timing and circumstances of her death put her beyond the parameters of Charlie's ability to see her, Michael should be able to see her, because as a spirit himself he could see other spirits in his vicinity, just like she was able to see any living, breathing human who might, for example, walk into the room.

But Michael clearly wasn't seeing whoever was connected to the voice. He wasn't hearing her, either.

Okay, deep breath. This was different. This was outside Charlie's experience. This was a whole new facet of the freak show that was her existence. It had been happening to her only since she had died and been brought back.

Either she was cracking up, or — or what? She wasn't sure. Random floaty voices existed in the universe, which she was just now able to access. For the last three weeks, since she had woken up in a hospital bed to learn that she had nearly drowned, she had been hearing the voices at odd moments. The truth was that she didn't know anything about them. Who was speaking. Who they were talking to. If they actually even existed outside of her head. What it meant.

All she knew was that the experience of hearing them was unnerving. And she needed — badly needed — for them to stop.

If they didn't, she was afraid she might start to fall apart.

"More," Spivey demanded, licking his lips. His lashless brown eyes fixed on Charlie's slender fingers as they absently smoothed the foil covering the remaining chocolate.

Charlie shook her head, tucking the candy bar back into her pocket, out of sight. Keeping it visible, she had discovered, was too great a distraction for Spivey. "After you answer the next question," she told him firmly.

"*No*," the unseen woman moaned. Gritting her teeth, Charlie did her best to tune out the voice while glancing blindly down at the papers on the table in front of her. Clairaudience — that's what her sudden ability to hear these disembodied voices was called. Unless they really were all in her head, in which case *crazy* described it better.

"Babe, you just turned a whole nother shade of pale." Michael frowned at her. As she glanced at him, she had to consciously stop herself from taking her lower lip between her teeth, an obvious sign of distress that he would jump on like a duck on a June bug.

Time for Charlie to face the truth: her way-too-close brush with death had done a number on her. In its aftermath, she felt vulnerable in a way that she hadn't in years. It had brought back a host of terrifying memories. It had upset her carefully constructed psychological equilibrium. It had sensitized her in ways that she feared she was only just beginning to discover. It had made her want to curl up in a ball in the middle of her hospital bed and pull the covers over her head and stay there forever, as if that would somehow keep her safe from the evil that she knew — *knew* — existed in the world.

Instead she had coped in the only way she knew: by getting up and getting on with it, and going back to work.

But the voices were unsettling. The voices she didn't need.

"You okay?" Michael's eyes were intent on her face. He suddenly seemed to take up way too much space in the tiny room. Even though, of course, since he had no physical substance and was, in fact, a phantom that only she could see and hear, he took up no actual space at all. "Finish up with this scumbag, and let's head home."

Home. Meaning her house in the nearby town of Big Stone Gap. Hearing Michael call it that felt funny, but . . . good. Since college she'd lived alone and liked it. Now she lived with him. A ghost. *Her* ghost. Her home was *their* home. Six weeks into their association, she was still processing the ramifications of that. Still processing the ramifications of *him.*

Still working hard not to fall in love with a damned — and she was very much afraid that that was the literal truth — ghost.

This was her second day back at Wallens Ridge, and she was tired — way too tired for three p.m. on a Tuesday, when before she had routinely worked until 5:30 five days a week and then had more than enough energy left at the end of the day to go for a long run up the wooded mountain trail behind her house. She'd completed reams of other tasks before getting started with this interview, of course, but still the level of

20

exhaustion she was experiencing was abnormal, and she recognized that. The idea of going home early was enormously appealing. But the work she was doing was important. The stakes were high. If she could figure out a way to identify serial killers in the earliest stages of their development, before they started to kill, countless lives would be saved, as would immeasurable amounts of human suffering.

The suffering she herself had endured being a case in point.

With a quick, barely there shake of her head for Michael, she refocused on the questions in front of her.

"Please answer yes or no." Charlie looked at the chubby-cheeked, harmless-looking man who was watching her expectantly. She felt her stomach tighten. "You prefer meeting in small groups rather than interacting with lots of people."

"No," Spivey answered, so promptly that Charlie wasn't entirely sure whether he was answering the question or just responding at random, as he sometimes did.

"Again, answer yes or no: You prefer interacting with lots of people?" She reworded the question in an attempt to verify his answer.

"I want candy," he said.

"You can have candy after you answer," she told him, and repeated the question.

"No," he said.

She looked at him for a second — he was leaning slightly forward, staring in the general direction of her pocket where the candy bar waited, although she knew he couldn't see it from where he sat. In her judgment, his attention had wandered, rendering his response unreliable. With an inward sigh, she tapped the end of her pen against the questionnaire without recording a response, recognizing that she had gotten as much out of Spivey as she was going to for the day. It was time to end the interview.

"Thank you, Mr. Spivey. We're finished here," she said.

"I want candy," he said again, frowning at her. His round face turned petulant, like that of a giant baby who was about to cry. His eyes batted. He licked his already damp lips.

"All right." Repressing a shiver of revulsion, she retrieved the candy bar from her pocket while Michael straightened away from the wall and muttered, "Hallelujah."

"You've done very well today," she told Spivey as she broke off a piece and pushed it across the table toward him. "We'll meet again next —"

"Please," the woman's voice inside her head screamed, the cry so shrill and full of pain that Charlie lost focus.

She only realized what she had done — that her hand had moved too far across the table, putting it within Spivey's reach — when Spivey grabbed her wrist and yanked her violently toward him.

Her heart leaped. As her stomach slammed into the edge of the table, she tried to stop her forward momentum without success.

"Got you," Spivey crowed with satisfaction a split second before his teeth crunched down on her fingers and Charlie screamed.

"Goddamn it," Michael roared, and dove for Spivey. Charlie felt the brush of a large, solid body hurtling past her, heard the smack of flesh hitting flesh, heard Spivey cry out as his head snapped back. He dropped her hand and she threw herself out of his reach just as Johnson burst through the door.

"Charlie." Michael's voice was no more than a breath of sound as she cradled her wounded hand and fought to regain her composure. Her stomach dropped clear to her toes as she realized that he was nowhere to be seen.

CHAPTER TWO

Michael.

Inside her head, Charlie screamed his name. Over and over. Desperately. Out loud, she urgently whispered it under the cover of the commotion as Spivey was dragged, shouting and fighting, from the room.

Michael didn't answer.

There was nothing from him: no sign, no sound.

Spookville: had he been hurtled into it again? That was the fear that made her go cold all over.

But even if Michael had been yanked away to that horrible netherworld, at this moment, in this place, surrounded by people as she was, there was simply nothing Charlie could do.

The first finger of her right hand was bloody and torn. It burned and throbbed and ached. She was so on edge with mounting anxiety that she barely noticed the pain as she was helped to the infirmary. Nearly every bed in the main ward was filled, and she could feel the eyes of the inmates and guards and orderlies (all of whom were male) following her as she was handed over to Dr. Creason. By the time he had finished treating her, the injury was the least of Charlie's concerns. She was beside herself with anxiety. Her heart hammered. She felt like she was about to jump out of her skin.

And not, as Creason clearly assumed, because she'd just been brutally attacked by a serial killer. She didn't like to think what it said about the screwed-up nature of her existence, but the sad truth was that being attacked by random serial killers was starting to seem like just one more day in her extremely sucky life. At this point, Spivey was of no more importance to her than a mosquito that had bitten her, even if she could still hear him screaming not so far away. Having been strapped down to a stretcher and rushed into a special locked ward just yards from where Charlie now sat on a molded plastic chair in one of the small examination rooms off the main part of the infirmary, Spivey was howling like a werewolf. Clearly the drugs pumping into his veins to sedate him were slow to take effect.

At any other time, Charlie would have found the sounds he made chilling.

Right now, though, she was beyond being chilled by anything the corporeal world could throw at her. She had bigger problems. *Cosmically* bigger problems.

Michael.

She was a quivering bundle of nerves because a good twenty minutes had passed without so much as a glimmer from him. No sound, nothing. She knew there was no way he would have left her like that of his own accord. Through the open door of the treatment room she was in, she watched two inmates in blue trustee jumpsuits mopping the slick gray floor of the admitting area. The trustees were inmates nearing the end of their sentences who had earned the provisional trust of the guards, and thus were given more freedom within the prison, as well as more responsible jobs that required minimal supervision. She watched them mop, listened to Spivey's screaming that all but drowned out other, more ordinary sounds, such as a distant TV and the whir of hospital machinery, and felt the sting of her damaged finger, all without being more than peripherally aware of any of it.

The thought that Michael had been

26

sucked up into the horror that was Spookville, never to return, was becoming all-consuming. If she wasn't careful — if, God forbid, it proved to be true — it would tear her apart inside.

What can I do? The panicked thought fluttered like a trapped bird inside her head. Answer: no clue.

"Your pulse rate is still elevated. Are you sure you're all right?" Creason asked, frowning at her. A small, neat man of forty-six, the prison doctor had thinning brown hair and sharp features. The last time she had seen him, he had been rushing — too late — to join her in trying to save Michael's life. The plastic name tag attached to Creason's white lab coat reminded her that his first name was Phil, and she made a mental note because she had forgotten it. Charlie had her own lab coat off and the short sleeve of her blue shirt pushed up to her shoulder. Having cleaned and bandaged the wound, Creason had just finished giving her an injection of antibiotics. Smoothing her sleeve down over the newly applied Band-Aid that adorned the injection site on her upper arm, Charlie saw that Creason was regarding her with concern. No surprise there: a human bite was ten times more dangerous than a dog bite, and this one went clear to the bone.

She hadn't even noticed that he was checking her pulse until his fingers left her wrist.

"I'm fine." She took a deep breath. Physically, it was true. Psychologically, she was as fragile as blown glass. If Michael couldn't get back . . .

There are things you can do, she told herself fiercely. Even if at the moment she didn't know exactly what. Michael had forbidden her to try to follow him into Spookville again. And the sad truth was, the prospect of once more entering that plane of horrors was terrifying. Plus, getting there was difficult, and tricky, and there was no guarantee the method she had used the last time would work. Or that she could find him even if it did —

"Sure?" Creason persisted.

Charlie nodded. "Yes."

The smell of alcohol was sharp and unpleasant. The institutional green concrete-block walls gave the room a cold feel, or maybe the chill that had taken hold of her was because she was suffering from a little bit of delayed shock; she couldn't be sure. The overhead fluorescent lighting made Creason's skin look too pale, and glinted off the metal examination table and the oversized steel watch that hung loosely around her wrist, which looked far too slender to support it.

With good reason: it was Michael's watch, sized for his powerful forearm. Heavy and warm from her skin, it was inscribed with the Marine Corps motto of *Semper fi,* and it was the only solid piece of evidence supporting his claim of innocence. Maybe it was a foolish feminine failing (the alliteration she'd tagged it with added to the self-mockery she experienced whenever she forced herself to consider the cold hard facts, which overwhelmingly came down on the side of him being guilty as sin), born of an intense attraction to a really hot (dead) guy, but in her heart of hearts she no longer believed he was a serial killer. The watch had gone a long way toward convincing her of what she'd wanted to believe anyway. When it had shown up after his death, Michael had given it to her, he'd said, because she was the only person left in the world who gave a damn about him.

As she instinctively touched the smooth metal bracelet, a hard knot formed in her chest.

Oh, God, where is he? Much as she hated to face it, Spookville was just about the only option. Would he be trapped there? Forever?

29

The fear settled like a concrete block in her stomach.

Creason picked up her injured hand and said, "You want to watch this closely. If it turns red or starts to swell —"

"I know the drill." Pulling her hand from his grasp, Charlie decided that, okay, maybe she was sounding a little abrupt. Creason had been both kind and competent, and didn't deserve to be snapped at. It was just that she was in a hurry to get out of the infirmary, to rush back to the room where Michael had disappeared to see if, perhaps, there was some trace of him there, or some way of making contact. If not — she stopped the thought before it could add to her burgeoning panic, and even managed a quick smile for Creason. "Thanks for taking such good care of me."

He smiled back, his hazel eyes warming on her face. "My pleasure. If you'll stop in tomorrow, I'll change the bandage and —"

Phlatt. Just like that, the lights in the infirmary went out in a quick shower of exploding sparks. Thrown, without warning, into sudden pitch darkness, Charlie gave a start of alarm. She grabbed the flimsy plastic arms of her chair as a way of staying oriented in the complete absence of light. A bubble of nervous dread rose in her throat.

Creason exclaimed, "What on earth?"

From the other room came a tangled burst of shouts and curses from men she could no longer see, and a shattering shriek she thought must have come from Spivey. A loud clatter of metal in the main room was followed by a yell and a heavy *thud,* as if something large had fallen.

A sudden crawling sensation, like a spider running over the back of her neck, made her suck in air. Her shoulders lifted in instinctive self-protection. She looked sharply around. It was too dark: she couldn't see a thing. Making herself as small as possible, she pressed her spine back against the molded chair.

Something wicked this way comes . . . Those were the words that popped unbidden into her head, accompanied by a shiver and the electrifying corollary thought *Michael* — but the energy she was sensing didn't feel anything like his.

This felt — evil.

Then the lights flickered once and came back on as, Charlie presumed, the emergency backup generator system kicked in.

Overreacting much to a power outage? she asked herself derisively. But that, she recognized even as the words formed in her mind, was nothing more than pure bravado. Because whatever had just happened, she was pretty sure it wasn't a simple power outage.

But with the lights on again, everything seemed perfectly fine.

Letting out a breath she hadn't realized she'd been holding, allowing her tense shoulders to slowly relax, Charlie unobtrusively sat up straighter — and found herself looking at a floating wisp of what might have passed for heat shimmer if the room hadn't been cold as ice. The nearly transparent disturbance in the atmosphere drifted until it hovered directly in front of Creason. It hadn't been present before, and she was just telling herself that it must be some sort of vapor from the malfunctioning light fixture, when it surged toward Creason. Purposefully. Like there was consciousness at work there.

What . . . ?

Lips parting with surprise, Charlie was on the verge of calling out a warning. But there was no time — besides, she knew that communicating any of what she was seeing and feeling in terms Creason could grasp would be impossible. All she could do was watch in silent horror as at the last second the energy bunched into a ball that struck Creason right in the middle of his chest and then — disappeared.

Not dissipated. Vanished. Inside him.

She blinked at Creason.

"Babe, we need to get out of here. Right now," Michael growled urgently in her ear. His voice was low and guttural, almost unrecognizably so, but still she did recognize it and practically fell out of her chair in reaction. Her heart had been a poor, frozen thing and she hadn't even realized it until now, as it warmed and throbbed with relief and started to beat properly again. She was so thankful for his presence she barely registered the sense of what he was saying. Instead she turned her head sharply to find him crouched beside her, ephemeral as mist but *there.*

Feeling as if a great weight had been lifted from her shoulders, she barely had time to mutter a worried "You're see-through" at him before he barked, "Leave her alone," in a deep and fearsome voice as he rose to his full, intimidating height. He wasn't talking to her, that was for sure. And even as she glanced around in surprise to see who he *was* talking to, he surged forward to stand protectively in front of her. He seemed to be addressing Creason, who of course couldn't see him — she was *almost* sure. But from what she could see of Creason — and she was looking at him through the shimmery translucence that was Michael, so her vision was admittedly a little compromised — he seemed to be staring at Michael. No, glaring at him. Threateningly.

Which was impossible. Creason couldn't *see* Michael.

Could he?

Unwillingly, she remembered that vanishing ball of shimmering air.

Her pulse drummed in her ears as she realized that there was something off about Creason's face. A distortion of his features, a look in his eyes —

"Charlie. Out the door," Michael ordered in that new, fierce voice without looking around. Coupled with her own shiver-inducing reaction to Creason, Michael's growl had her on her feet and moving toward the door without argument. Whatever was happening — and, though she had no idea what it was, she knew it was something very bad — she was sure that she wanted no part of it.

That it was dangerous.

"Um, I'm going back to work now," she said to Creason, whose eyes rested on her with a chilling expression that was far removed from the doctor's usual benevolent gaze. Creason didn't respond, but his mouth twisted in a way that made her chest tighten.

The question that raised its trembling head was: *why* would Creason look at her like that?

"She's off-limits." Michael's warning was addressed to Creason, and from the doctor's expression Charlie was suddenly positive that he *could* see and hear Michael. Thinking about what that had to mean made her blood run cold.

"Go," Michael barked at her, his eyes never leaving Creason.

Charlie went. As she did, Creason followed. Slowly. Menacingly. Step by surprisingly awkward step.

His gait didn't look right . . .

The hair stood up on the back of Charlie's neck. If Michael hadn't positioned himself between her and the doctor, she would, she feared, have broken into a run before she reached the door. But some instinct told her that would be a mistake, just like running from a snarling dog was a mistake.

Do not show fear.

The last thing she wanted to do was provoke him to attack —

She broke off in mid-thought, aghast: provoke *Creason* to attack?

That's when she consciously acknowledged what she had sensed almost from the moment the ball of vapor had disappeared into the doctor's chest: what was looking at her out of his eyes was not Creason.

That prickle around her hairline? That would be her breaking out in a cold sweat.

"Keep going." Michael's terse directive didn't allow for argument, not that she had any intention of arguing. Getting as far away from Creason as fast as she could was what her every instinct screamed at her to do. As for Michael, she'd already endangered him enough with her carelessness; she couldn't put him any further at risk. As see-through as delicately tinted Saran wrap at the moment, he was in no condition to provide her with any physical protection from anything in this world, and she had no way of knowing if he was psychically strong enough to protect her from anything out of it. And if he was to try to materialize again — Her stomach twisted. One of these days, he would go into Spookville and never come back, just as they had been warned. When it happened — and it would happen, sooner or later — she was afraid she would never recover.

Still, it hadn't happened yet, and having him with her even in his present debilitated state made her feel like she had an army at her back. She must have made some small sound encouraging him to keep pace, because he shot a quick, hard glance at her.

It was then that she noticed with a cold little shiver that his eyes were dead black. Soulless. *That place does things to me* — she remembered him saying that the last time he'd managed to escape from Spookville, radiating brutality, eyes as black and feral as they were now. She'd understood him to mean it did *bad* things to him.

As in, turned him into the lowest, most savage version of himself.

Oh, God. But even the lowest, most savage version of Michael was preferable to no Michael at all.

"Go!" he snarled, and she nodded and went. Her hurried footsteps on the smooth terrazzo sounded very loud to her own ears.

The air itself seemed to pulse with malevolence as she made it through the door and strode out into the infirmary's main room. There she discovered one of the trustees picking himself up off the floor. An overturned bucket disgorging soapy water plus a dropped mop near his feet made her wonder if he had tripped over the bucket when the lights went out. It would explain the sounds she had heard —

"Keep moving." Behind her, Michael kept

himself positioned between her and Creason, who had not said so much as a word. Which, it occurred to Charlie, was creepy as hell. In his new, rough voice, Michael ordered, "Get out into the hall," to her, then snapped, "Stay back," at the now standing trustee in the same threatening tone he had used with Creason.

Which was extra-terrifying, because Michael was perfectly aware that in the ordinary course of things no one besides her could see or hear him. Except it seemed that this particular trustee *could,* because he was regarding Michael with an ugly expression that made Charlie's heart pound. Or was he looking *through* Michael, at her? There was no way for her to know, but she *did* know that his stare was unnerving.

The other trustee and the two orderlies on duty and the single guard she could see and the inmate/patients waiting in beds for treatment seemed totally oblivious to anything extraordinary happening in their midst. They had resumed what they'd been doing before the lights went out.

Of course, unless the universe was throwing a really nasty curveball her way, nothing had changed for them. They were perfectly normal. They couldn't see Michael. When they looked at Creason and the trustee, they saw Creason and the trustee and nothing else. But there was no way she could tell for sure that none of the rest of them had been affected, so she dared not trust appearances.

Stay calm.

Except for Creason and the one trustee, both of whom kept their eyes riveted on her, nobody paid any attention to her as she walked quickly toward the door. Having converged until they were almost shoulder to shoulder now, those two were coming after her and Michael — slowly, thank God! Although — too slowly? As if their bodies didn't quite work properly? Feeling their eyes on her made her want to jump out of her skin.

Were they *chasing* her? Short answer: *I don't want to know.*

"Hurry," Michael growled. And despite the buzz of ordinary-sounding conversation and the resumption of ordinary-seeming activity behind her, Charlie could feel her stomach knotting as she hit the intercom button beside the door.

Hurry, hurry, hurry: the refrain seemed to pulse through her veins.

"What can I do for you?" came the disinterested voice over the intercom.

Trying not to sound as panicky as she was starting to feel, Charlie answered, "Could

39

you let me out, please?"

Security was tight in the prison, and passing from one section to another was not as easy as, say, just walking through a door and strolling down a corridor. After a moment a man's meaty face appeared on the other side of the door's small glass window to check her out, as was routine before unlocking the door. It could not have taken long, but her nerves were so jangled that it seemed like forever; it was all she could do to keep from casting quick, nervous glances over her shoulder the entire time, which she was loath to do because she didn't want to show any more consciousness of something being wrong than she could help. Finally, what seemed like an interminable time later, the door was buzzed open.

"Go," Michael said urgently.

Charlie didn't need to be told twice. She went through that door like a racehorse charging out of the gate, only to find herself trapped inside the cage apparatus that required she be let out through another, separate pair of heavy wire-mesh doors as a security measure.

"Stay away from her," Michael warned behind her, and she didn't need the quick, scared glance she threw over her shoulder to know who he was talking to.

The clang of the infirmary's heavy metal door closing behind her was just about the most welcome thing she had ever heard.

Until it occurred to her that, like herself, Creason had only to say the word and he would be let out of the infirmary, too. As the prison doctor, he actually had access to far more of the facility than she did.

He could hunt her down . . .

Creason? The sheer absurdity of the thought should have stripped it of all its power to terrify. That it didn't spoke volumes.

"The second that damned door opens, move your ass," Michael told her fiercely. "We need to get out of here."

"I can't just run away," Charlie protested under her breath while she waited on pins and needles for the second door to be opened. "I —"

"The hell you can't," Michael interrupted. "Unless you *want* to tangle with Frankendoctor and his buddy back there, that is."

"But —"

"There's no fucking buts about this. You do what I tell you, and *go.*"

"Everything okay, Dr. Stone?" The guard looked up from entering the code that unlocked the airlock-type doors to frown at her. Through the small window behind him, she caught a glimpse of Creason on the other side of the glass walking jerkily toward the infirmary door. The subtle distortion of his face was terrifying. Looking just as abnormal, the trustee was maybe a step behind.

"Yes," Charlie replied to the guard, then changed that to, "No."

"Dr. Stone?" The guard's frown deepened.

"*Not* the time to stand around and chat." The gravelly quality of Michael's voice made her chest tighten. His expression chilled her as he watched through the window as Creason lurched closer to the door. He looked — capable of the most extreme violence. "What part of *move your ass* are you having trouble with?"

Charlie took a deep breath. She might be feeling exceptionally fragile. The other-worldly happenings that she wanted no part of but that kept finding her anyway might seem particularly overwhelming. She might want to run straight for the nearest hidey-hole where she could hunker down and ride out the psychic storm until she got her equilibrium back.

Unfortunately, one of the immutable laws of the universe was: shit happens. Whether she was ready for it or not.

Running would not help.

What she needed to do was get a grip. And do whatever she could to make herself and Michael safer.

Then she could worry about maybe trying to help Creason. And the trustee. And, it sometimes seemed like, the whole fricking world.

Baby steps.

"You need to lock the infirmary down," she told the guard in her best authoritative voice. "I think there may be a dangerous situation developing in there. Dr. Creason . . . was behaving oddly. So were some of the inmates. No one — not anybody in the infirmary — should be let out until more guards are on hand and the cause investigated."

"Whoa." Michael's disconcertingly black eyes were impossible to read as they fixed on her face. He appeared slightly more solid now, thank God, as if the more distance he put between himself and Spookville, the stronger he was growing. Then his mouth twisted slightly, and she realized that it was with approval. "Way to think on your feet, babe. That should slow the fuckers down."

How ridiculous was it under the circumstances that she found his approval warming?

"You sure, Dr. Stone?" Looking worried,

43

the guard glanced back over his shoulder at the infirmary door. "It seems awful quiet in there. And —"

"Yes," Charlie replied as the second door, which was more in the nature of a big wire gate, buzzed open at last. "I'm sure. Something odd is going on. Lock the infirmary down. *Now*. I take full responsibility."

The guard nodded doubtfully. "Yes, ma'am."

As she stepped out into the long expanse of gray-walled corridor, the guard hit the big orange emergency button that sealed the infirmary exits and sounded the alarm that summoned reinforcements. The blast of the siren hurt her eardrums, made Michael wince, echoed off the walls. Even as she started to move away, an odd, metallic rattling sound made her glance back. She saw that Creason had reached the door and was peering through the small glass window at her.

His features seemed blurred. His mouth was twisted. His eyes blazed. The power of his gaze was such that she found it almost impossible to look away.

The intercom buzzed impatiently as Creason signaled the guard that he wanted out. Drawn by the same small metallic sound that she had heard before, Charlie dropped her widening eyes to the doorknob as it rattled and turned.

Creason's voice crackled through the intercom. "Guard, open the door."

CHAPTER THREE

Charlie's heart lurched.

"Move," Michael barked at her.

Jerking her gaze away from that twisting doorknob with an effort, Charlie regained enough of her wits to briskly walk away.

"I'm sorry, Dr. Creason. I can't do that." Behind her, the guard spoke apologetically. "The infirmary's on lockdown. I don't have the power to override it."

Charlie couldn't hear Creason's response to that: Michael was urging her along until she was practically running. He was almost solid-looking again, which was a tremendous relief: in her experience, he only ever turned translucent when he was way too close to disappearing into Spookville. She took his increasing opacity to mean that he was growing more and more firmly anchored to this plane again. Despite the fitful glow of the overhead fluorescents, which were still, she presumed, sputtering along on backup power, the windowless hallway was as gloomy-dark as a tunnel. It smelled, as did most of the rest of the prison, of Pine Sol and urine. About twenty feet ahead, guards in riot gear burst out of an adjacent hallway, heading toward the infirmary with the precision of a military operation.

"Warden Pugh is going to go ballistic about this," she murmured to Michael as the dozen or so heavily armed guards rushed toward her, their booted feet echoing like thunder as they ran toward the infirmary. She was running herself now, only headed in the opposite direction, her bloodstained lab coat slung over one arm, her low-heeled shoes clattering on the hard floor. "But shutting down the infirmary was the only thing I could think of to do."

"That should work." Michael kept pace beside her easily, of course. What worried her was the way he kept glancing back. What was he watching for? As far as she could tell, they were no longer in any immediate danger. The guards who weren't rushing toward the infirmary were clearing the area of inmates. Angry male voices and shuffling footsteps joined the jolting clang of doors closing and locks being thrown, to form a nerve-rattling backdrop to the shrilling alarm. No one paid any attention to her (them) as she hurried past, beyond casting her a few cursory glances. "At least, as long as what we're running away from stays in Creason's body," he added.

Talk about amping up the fear quotient again: Charlie felt an icy rush of horror. "I never thought of that!"

His grunt clearly said, *not surprised.*

Charlie could hear her pulse drumming in her ears. "What is it we're running away from, exactly?"

"Trouble." His voice was hard and clipped. They reached the hallway that led to the nearest exit. When Charlie failed to turn down it he reached out to grab her arm: she felt the mildest of electric tingles as his hand passed right through her flesh and then watched his jaw tighten in frustrated acknowledgment of his physical limitations, which for that one moment he had clearly forgotten. "Damn it. This way."

"I have to get my purse," she said without even breaking stride. He seemed to accept that, because he didn't argue beyond a quick, classically masculine shake of his head that silently condemned women and their purses. She continued, "So you want to tell me what happened to Dr. Creason back there?" Mindful of the security cameras which were everywhere, and the guards, and the inmates, she ducked her head as she spoke so that no one would be able to observe her ostensibly talking to thin air.

"Damned if I know. Nothing good. Come on, babe, speed it up."

Charlie did her best to focus on making sense of what she had just witnessed. "It looked to me like something . . . *possessed* Dr. Creason. And that trustee."

"Looked like it from where I was standing, too," Michael agreed. The pace she was setting had rendered her slightly breathless. He, of course, didn't breathe.

"*What,* though? *What* possessed him?"

"Something I've never seen before. Best I can describe it, an evil spirit. For my money, one got the trustee, too."

She cut her eyes in his direction.

"Oh, my God," she said faintly. "This is all my fault. I should have been more careful with Spivey."

"Ya think? How's your hand, by the way?"

"It's fine."

"I'll just bet it is." His voice was grim. "You want to tell me how that bastard was able to grab ahold of you like he did?"

They were nearing the end of the corridor — a left turn would take them to her office — and most of the commotion was behind them. A quick glance back showed her guards massed by the infirmary entrance.

"Spivey was able to grab me because I got . . . distracted."

"Distracted?" He narrowed his eyes at her. "You were locked in a tiny room with a pervert who gets his kicks torturing and murdering women. What the hell could have —" Breaking off, he swore under his breath. "You were hearing those voices again, weren't you?"

Charlie had told Michael about the voices. He'd been with her in the hospital the whole time as she'd recovered from her near drowning, mostly pacing the room or sprawled out in the chair beside the bed, so it had been only natural to confide in him when the eerie whispers had started. She'd been so shaken up, so tired and confused, and it had been such a comfort to have someone to tell, someone who understood that there was a whole universe of unknowns out there and believed what she told him and didn't think she was insane. When she'd gotten stronger and they'd started arguing about her intention of going back to work what he'd considered way too soon, she'd given him to understand that the voices had gone away.

"What if I was?" she asked, chin in the air.

"You shouldn't be here," he said, hard. The look he gave her practically blistered her eyeballs. "You realize that once Spivey got his hands on you he could have done anything he wanted to you, right? Break your neck, rape you —"

"I know, I know. I'll be more careful in future," she interrupted hurriedly.

"Thank you, Michael, for saving my life. Again." His voice was sardonic.

Okay, she owed him that. "Thank you, Michael, for saving my life. Again." As his unsettling eyes continued to gleam unpleasantly at her, she added, "Can we please just drop it? It's over, and right now we've got bigger fish to fry. For starters, I need you to tell me what happened to you. Everything."

"You mean after that sicko tried snacking on your hand?" His expression promised way more discussion on the topic later, but as she pounded toward the end of the corridor and he floated effortlessly along beside her he responded to her glare by saying, "What do you think? I got torpedoed straight into Spookville. I'm telling you, babe, you gotta stop messing around with serial killers. You're gonna get us both killed."

"*You're* a serial killer," Charlie pointed out acerbically. "At least, you were. Convicted of being one. And I'm messing around with you. Anyway, I can't get you killed because, in case you missed it, you're also already dead."

"I'll give you the already-dead part, but you can't tell me you still think I'm a serial killer."

"Oh, yeah?" Well, truth was, she didn't. At least, she mostly didn't. Every instinct she possessed shrieked that he was innocent of the heinous murders of seven young women for which he had been convicted and sentenced to death. Although the whole legal system, a number of eyewitnesses, and every scrap of physical evidence available said he was guilty. Except for his watch, which she touched now like a talisman. As evidence went, it wasn't much, but it was enough to give her a concrete basis for her growing belief in him.

On the other hand, there was the whole afterlife in Spookville and black-eyed savagery thing to think about.

"Yeah." His lips quirked at her.

She made an impatient sound. "Could you please just finish telling me what happened to you in Spookville?"

"A hunter got me."

He said that in such a matter-of-fact way that it took her a second. Then, as his words penetrated, her eyes widened on his face. "A *hunter* got you?"

Remembering the unblinking yellow eyes of the massive, ten-foot-tall creatures she had glimpsed in the horrible purple fog of Spookville, she shuddered.

"Yep." He grimaced. "First time one's ever caught me. Hurt like hell, too. Actually, when I went through the wall after I jumped on that bastard Spivey I shot right into it, and that's how it was able to grab me. The claws — they've got some kind of poison in them, I think. Once they dug in, I kept getting weaker and weaker until I could hardly move. Fortunately, the . . . things it had been dragging away when I caromed into it took advantage of my bad luck to escape. They got away and it dropped me and went after them. I was so weak I collapsed where I stood. At first all I could do was just lay there on the ground, but I could feel that rubber band thingy we got going on between us tugging at me and after a little bit I managed to get up and stagger away in the direction it was pulling me. Then I saw the hunter coming back and I took a chance and dove at the wall and made it through. Those things that the hunter had when I hit him — they must've been somewhere nearby, because they dove through the wall after me and ended up in that room in the infirmary with us. One of 'em got into Creason. And I'm pretty sure the other one got into that trustee."

"You called them evil spirits. Why?" Charlie asked in a constricted voice as horror dried her throat. The monstrous hunters she had glimpsed still haunted her nightmares; it didn't help that she was pretty sure that their mission was to drag errant souls — an example would be Michael — down to hell.

He shook his head. "All I can tell you is, that's how they struck me. They were shaped like humans, only they were kind of twisted and gray. A blackish, burnt-looking gray, with smoky wisps floating around them and — no faces. No features at all. I don't know what the hell they are, to tell you the truth. I ain't seen nothing like them before. Bottom line, though, is they're not anything you want to mess with. Hell, they're not anything *I* want to mess with. Which is why we're getting out of here just as quick as we can."

Charlie fought to maintain some perspective.

"You know what, I had a fairly uncomplicated life before I met you," she complained. "Aside from a few random encounters with dead people, it was boring. I like boring."

"I was sitting on death row waiting to bite the big one before I met you," he retorted. He was sounding more like himself now. Some of the harshness had left his voice. "You want to talk boring, it doesn't get much more boring than that." That devastating grin of his made another quick appearance. "As far as I'm concerned, though, boring sucks."

As they rounded the corner into the hall where her office was located, Charlie realized that the time for coming clean about what she meant to do was at hand. She shot him a sideways look. "Michael . . . I've got to go back and do what I can to help. I can't just leave poor Dr. Creason to —" She broke off as the guard Johnson emerged from the open doorway to the room where earlier she'd been interviewing Spivey.

"You okay, Dr. Stone?" Johnson called.

"I'm fine." Charlie slowed down to a fast walk. In response to the questioning look Johnson directed at her bandaged hand as she neared him, she held it up for him to see. "All taken care of."

"You were just in the infirmary, weren't you?" Johnson's eyes were bright with curiosity as he looked at her. The ringing of the alarm had stopped abruptly a few seconds before. "What's going on in there?"

he asked.

"I don't know exactly," she replied, working hard to keep her voice sounding normal. "Something's wrong, is all I can tell you. It's been shut down."

"Full moon this week, you know? Inmates are all going crazy." Johnson shook his head. "Hole's already at capacity. Somebody else is acting up, we'll have to start pulling people out to make room. Or we could always just shoot 'em." The wide grin with which Johnson accompanied that told her that it was an attempt at guard humor. "You know how the politicians are always harping on prison overcrowding. That'd be a primo solution."

"Asshole," Michael growled at Johnson, with whom he had been unhappily acquainted while alive.

"Let's hope that the excitement in the infirmary turns out to be nothing." Charlie ignored Michael in favor of replying to the guard. As she passed the open door of the interview room, she glanced inside. The bright yellow vinyl suits and clear face masks worn by the people wiping down the surfaces made her frown. "Who are they?"

"Hazmat team," Johnson replied. Then Charlie understood: they were following protocols for cleaning up blood. Hers, which shouldn't amount to much, and Spivey's. The guards who'd stormed to her rescue hadn't been gentle, and Spivey had been bleeding pretty copiously by the time they'd dragged him out. "Been a hell of a day."

Charlie pushed through the door into her office. This was her world. In here, evil was abstract, researchable, something she could quantify and work toward preventing. As the door closed behind her, some of the dread that gripped her eased. About twice the size of the tiny interview room, her office also had no windows. It held her L-shaped desk with her laptop on it, two plastic chairs opposite the desk, for visitors, and a tall black filing cabinet topped with a crystal vase filled with a dozen red roses (courtesy of FBI Special Agent Tony Bartoli, sent to mark the occasion of her return to work yesterday after she was nearly killed as part of his team; the arrival of the flowers had prompted a derisive snort from Michael, who was no fan of Tony's). A big picture of a sunrise over the Blue Ridge Mountains hung on the wall behind the desk. A dry erase board with the names and some notes about the various serial killers she was currently studying stood on an easel in one corner. Except for a few personal touches (the roses, the picture), the room was institutional and unattractive. Ridiculous as it might be, though, she felt safe in this small space she'd made her own.

Until she considered the fact that the infirmary door almost certainly had been, or was about to be, opened. Of course, the guards might keep Creason inside until an investigation was completed, but she couldn't count on that: if whatever was possessing Creason left his body, all bets were off. Spirits weren't hampered by physical barriers. This one could just appear. Anywhere. Like right here. Right now.

The realization made her go cold all over. It also made her hurry toward her desk, which held her purse, which held a mini mobile version of her Miracle-Go (i.e., spirit banishing) kit. Throwing her lab coat on her chair, she bent toward her desk drawers.

"Grab your stuff. We're out of here." With that stark order, Michael stopped just inside the door. Except for the continuing blackness of his eyes and a certain hardness around his mouth, he was almost back to normal. Which meant that he was looking tall, blond, and surfer-God gorgeous, as well as big and bad enough to take on all comers. The thought that he was choosing flight over fight in this instance was enough to make butterflies take off in big swirling waves in her stomach.

"I can't just go." She snatched open the large bottom drawer of her desk where she kept her purse — actually a big black leather tote bag — and pulled it out as she spoke. Just thinking about Creason's body being invaded by an evil spirit that she had in some part been responsible for bringing into this plane made her shiver. "You know I can't. I have to at least try to get those spirits out of the doctor and trustee's bodies."

"What, you're wanting to play exorcist now?" Those disconcertingly black eyes practically bored a hole through her. "You said yourself that you've never even seen a possession."

He had a point, but — "There's nobody else who can help. It's my responsibility."

"Screw that. No, it's not."

"I'm going to do what I can to rescue Dr. Creason and the trustee."

"No," he said, like that was the last word on the subject.

"You can't tell me *no.*" She met his glower with one of her own as, with a triumphant flourish, she pulled the kit out of her purse.

"I just did." His frown darkened as he eyed the kit, then watched her unzip it. Her quick check of the contents confirmed that everything was there: the sticks of sage incense that were crucial to banishing spirits; her canister of salt — salt created a barrier that spirits were unable to cross, and she had found that loose sea salt worked best; her horseshoe — an old one, solid iron, because iron worked on spirits roughly like Kryptonite worked on Superman. Ah, and there was her jasmine candle, and the small, heavy drinking glass to cap it with, and a lighter . . .

Grabbing an incense stick, she waved it at him. "Remember these? Remember how well they worked?"

His jaw hardened. The memory of how she had driven him from this plane into Spookville in the early days of their acquaintance hung between them. He had fought with every ounce of strength he possessed, and still she had succeeded. From her perspective, that made the incense pretty powerful stuff. The fact that witnessing the pain she had caused him then had taken her to her knees and left her in tears was neither here nor there.

One thing was certain: she wouldn't have that reaction with whatever had taken possession of Creason and the trustee. *Those* spirits she was not going to feel the least bit sorry for.

"You really think you're going to wave that stinky shit at those things and they'll just fold up and go?"

"I think they're going to be forced from the earthly plane. And you needn't bother sneering at me! It worked on you, remember? And you're not the only one, either. In fact, I've never had it *not* work."

"You ever hear *famous last words*?" Far from vanishing, the sneer grew more pronounced. He moved purposefully toward her. "Forget it. I'm not letting you do it."

Tucking the incense sticks back inside the bag, she curled her lip at him. "You're ectoplasm, remember? You can't stop me."

"Try me." He walked right through her desk — he did it to underline the fact that she couldn't get away from him, she was sure — and in response she grabbed her purse and her Miracle-Go kit and, juggling them in her arms, scooted around the side of the desk. He was between her and the door before she even realized he'd changed positions. Damn ghosts and their ability to shift in the blink of an eye anyway!

She stopped, glaring at him. He gave her a sardonic smile.

"Don't think I won't walk right through you," she warned. "Because I totally will."

"Ooh," he said. "You're scaring me."

She started walking purposefully toward him. "Get out of my way."

"You know what's going to happen to me if things go south with your woo-woo shit, right? I'll end up doing whatever I can to save you, which means I'll probably have to materialize to ward off whatever the hell is trying to kill you this time. That'll get me sucked back up into Spookville. You willing to take the chance that I can get out again?"

Since bullying her hadn't done the trick, he was trying another tactic to get her to do what he wanted, and it actually sort of worked. Clutching her purse and the Miracle-Go kit to her chest, Charlie stopped walking to glare at him. Putting Michael in danger was the last thing she wanted to do. As annoying as it was to admit, he mattered to her.

"You —" she began furiously, only to have the rest of what she was going to say lost forever. The heavy metal door to her office flew open with a *bang,* as if blown inward on its hinges by a gigantic burst of wind.

"What — ?" Charlie was so shocked that she jumped back and lost her grip on her purse and the Miracle-Go kit, both of which dropped with a crash, scattering their contents in all directions.

"Holy shit!" Having whirled to face it, Michael stood between her and the door. "Charlie, get back!"

He seemed to be staring up, way up, at — what? There was nothing there. At least, nothing that she could see. Then, squinting past his broad back, she caught the briefest glimpse of what looked like a tall column of heat shimmer surging toward him. Just as she made the connection that — dear God in heaven! — heat shimmer equals evil spirit equals something really bad going down, Michael was snatched off his feet and propelled toward the ceiling as if grabbed and yanked upward by an unseen giant.

"No!" Charlie screamed, while Michael, struggling ferociously, was being shaken like a rat in the jaws of a pitbull by something she couldn't quite see.

"It's a hunter! Stay back!" he yelled.

A *hunter*?! Still processing the enormity of that, she threw herself at Michael, at what was holding him, with the vague plan of disrupting the evil energy attacking him or something, *anything,* that might get him free, only to be knocked backward with a force that lifted her off her feet and slammed her hard to the floor. Her head struck the polished concrete. For the briefest of moments, she saw stars.

"Goddamn it, Charlie! Stay out of this! Keep the fuck away from me!" Michael cried.

"Michael!" Shaking off the blow, she scrambled to her knees, gasping with shock and horror as she watched him fighting for his life with the all-but-invisible hunter. At the same time she realized that she was kneeling amidst the scattered contents of her purse and Miracle-Go kit and realized, too, what she had to do, what his only chance was. Even as she conducted a desperate visual search for her incense sticks or salt or *something* she could use, she spotted the horseshoe peeking out from beneath the overturned tote. Michael screamed, a horrible sound that denoted pure agony. She looked up in terror to see him arching his back and throwing weakening punches and kicks at the air in front of him.

Charlie's heart lurched. Her pulse raced. Pure adrenaline shot like speed through her veins.

Snatching up the horseshoe, she hurled it at the shimmering column with all her strength.

CHAPTER FOUR

Heart pounding, mouth sour with fear, Charlie watched as the horseshoe careened through the barely visible column of heat shimmer, crashed into the wall beyond it, and dropped to the floor with a clatter — but not before it had an effect. The heat shimmer wavered, thinned, and seemed to curl in on itself as, at the same time and apparently flung away by it, Michael came hurtling through the air toward her. He smacked down on the floor, slid right through the plastic chairs without moving them by so much as a hair's breadth, and came to rest in front of her desk.

"Michael!" Shaking with fright, shoving the lightweight plastic chairs out of her way, she scrambled toward him.

Having hit on his side, he writhed and groaned. Reaching him even as she cast a terrified glance over her shoulder — she could see no trace of the heat shimmer, not that that meant anything — she put an unsteady hand on the corded muscle of his upper arm. Of course her hand sank right through; the accompanying electric tingle reminded her that there was no physical substance there.

"Get away from me." His urgent command emerged through lips that barely seemed to move. He shuddered and grimaced even as he looked toward the door — the *hunter* — then started making feeble motions as if he was trying to rise but couldn't quite manage it. His lids were half closed over eyes that were now so black that there was not a trace of white to be seen. His usually bronzed skin had turned a sickly pale shade. His mouth was clamped into a grim line that she thought betokened pain. "Did you hear me? Get back there behind the desk!"

Ignoring that, she cast another panicky glance toward the door. "Where is it?"

"Fuck if I know," he gritted. "I said, get behind the damned desk!"

"Not happening." Just looking at him scared the daylights out of her, but there was no time to spare. She still could see no trace of the heat shimmer — the *hunter* — but what if it had just gone invisible, at least to her eyes? What if it was even now coming for Michael again?

She'd thrown her weapon away.

"Stay still!" she hissed at him, bolting for the horseshoe. As she ran right through where the hunter had been, her heart practically pounded its way out of her chest.

Charlie —" Clearly Michael couldn't get up, because he sure was trying. His eyes were fastened on her.

"Don't move!" Snatching up the horseshoe, she darted back. Flight was clearly out: Michael didn't look like he was going anywhere any time soon. Fight didn't seem all that promising, either, so she was going with Plan C: barricade them in. Having located her canister of salt, she dove for it. Seconds later, ignoring Michael's curses and orders to get away from him, one end of the horseshoe tucked into her waistband so that it would be easy to grab, she was on her hands and knees frantically laying down a line of salt in a circle around them that, hopefully, the hunter couldn't cross.

"You think *salt's* going to keep that thing away?" Michael turned onto his back with a groan. "Jesus H. Christ, when I tell you to go, go! Are you *trying* to get yourself killed?"

"I don't think it can kill me," Charlie said cautiously, throwing another dread-filled look around. "And salt acts as a barrier for all kinds of supernatural beings. Anyway, do you have a better idea?"

No answer. She took that as a resounding *no*. He was gritting his teeth, clenching his fists — and looking around. After a moment in which he seemed to be warily examining every inch of space in the room, he said, "I'm thinking maybe it's gone. If we're lucky."

His voice was hoarse and gravelly again and his lids were once more at half-mast, but at least he was there and making sense. Sending a quick message of thanks winging skyward that it was so, her movements a little awkward because of her bandaged hand, she continued pouring salt for all she was worth.

"Dr. Stone?" At the unexpected sound of Warden Pugh's voice, Charlie nearly jumped out of her skin. Her head came up with a snap. Her eyes went wide as they sought and found him.

"Well, lookee who's here." Michael's gaze found Pugh. "If it ain't The Skunk."

The Skunk — because, oh, ha ha, his name was Pugh — was what Michael called the warden.

Charlie didn't respond to that with so much as a reproving look. Her eyes stayed fixed on Pugh. In his mid-fifties, average height, paunchy and balding, dressed in a rumpled suit with his tie askew, he had stopped short in what seemed to have been a headlong rush to her office. The beads of sweat on his forehead, the puce color of his face, even his still-swinging coattails, all screamed that he'd been moving fast seconds earlier.

Now, standing in the doorway where the hunter had so recently loomed, he peered over the tops of his rimless spectacles at her. Surprise — okay, maybe astonishment was a better word — was apparent in every line of his face.

Still on her knees, frozen in the act of shaking salt out onto the floor, Charlie returned the favor by gaping up at him.

"What are you doing?" Plainly taken aback, Pugh looked from her to the semicircle of sparkling crystals that extended from a few inches in front of her knees around what was actually sprawled-out Michael but must appear to Pugh like an expanse of bare floor littered with the scattered contents of her purse. Fortunately she had only a little more than a yard to go before the barrier was complete. Even as she registered her audience, registered how inexplicable what she was doing must appear, she went back to doing it, because she dared not stop: the hard truth was, they had no idea of where the hunter was, or if it would come back.

"Dr. Stone?" Pugh persevered.

"I, uh, dropped my purse." She started gathering up the closest of her scattered belongings — a lipstick, a pen, her incense — with her free hand even as she continued to pour out a thick line of shimmery salt with the other.

"I . . . see." Pugh's tone made it clear that he didn't. At all.

"At a guess, I'd say he's thinking you're a few French fries short of a Happy Meal," Michael said. The continued raspiness of his voice worried her. His face was tight. One leg moved restlessly until it was bent at the knee and then stretched out again.

"Are you feeling . . . quite well, Dr. Stone?" Pugh asked. "Dr. Creason has apparently fainted in the infirmary, as did a trustee. We're investigating the possibility of some kind of gas leak, or perhaps an accidental exposure to a medication." He was blinking more frequently than was normal as he watched her, which she knew from her training indicated increased anxiety. And no wonder: Charlie felt an almost hysterical urge to laugh as she realized how bizarre her actions must appear. Now would definitely be the time to stop with the salt, she thought, only she couldn't. "You were just with him. Is it possible that you were exposed as well?"

Charlie replied to the part that had given her a fresh thrill of alarm: "Dr. Creason fainted? How — is he?"

Possessed? Unpossessed? Evil? Not? was what she wanted to know, but she could ask none of that. Just considering the possibilities made her mouth go dry.

"He's being evaluated right now." Pugh's expression was troubled as he watched her. It was impossible, she was discovering, to shake salt out onto a floor discreetly. "What I'd like to do is escort you back to the infirmary so that you can be evaluated, too."

The sudden soothing quality in his voice told her that he had, indeed, decided that her Happy Meal was lacking. In the meantime, fear that the hunter might return before the salt was in place had her pulse pounding in her ears and her stomach twisting into a pretzel.

"You can go ahead and admit anytime that you were wrong about coming back to work so soon." The grating undertone to Michael's satiric drawl caused her to shoot him the quickest, most furtive of worried looks. "I won't say I told you so, I promise."

71

"I'm fine," Charlie told Pugh firmly, while still (discreetly) shaking out salt. She finished closing the salt circle, and said a silent *Thank you, God* as she sank back on her heels and put the lid back on the canister.

"That'll convince him," Michael said. "Just so you're aware, to most people, pouring salt on the floor probably doesn't equal fine."

"Dr. Stone." Pugh sounded unhappy. "I'm afraid I'm going to have to insist. I —"

"Charlie?"

The interruption was welcome. The voice was even more so. Head whipping around so fast that she nearly gave herself whiplash, she beheld Tony Bartoli looming in the doorway behind the warden. Johnson and the Hazmat team were visible behind them — drawn, she guessed, by the commotion, which she could only hope they would assume had resulted from her dropped purse — and even as she glanced in their direction more guards came running up.

"Warden!" one of them cried, drawing Pugh's attention. Pugh turned away to speak to the guards, although he remained in full view, framed by the doorway.

"Tony!" Her surprised greeting blended genuine enthusiasm with relief. Here was an ally just when she needed one most.

He stepped past the warden, stopping just inside her office, which placed him only a few feet away.

"Are you kidding me?" Michael groaned, closing his eyes after taking one look at the newcomer. "Him again? This day just keeps getting better and better."

Special Agent Tony Bartoli was six-one, lean, tanned, not quite as gorgeous as Michael (honestly, who was?) but handsome enough to make most any woman sit up and take notice. Thirty-five years old, with short, well-groomed black hair and coffee brown eyes, he was as impeccably dressed as usual, in a charcoal suit, white shirt, and red power tie. Quite apart from being the guy with whom she had been kinda/sorta trying to form a real, lasting human (as opposed to an impossible, insane, ghostly) relationship, she liked him. A lot. More to the point, he was from the Special Circumstances Division out of Quantico. The division that investigated serial killers. In other words, he was a highly competent, *armed* federal agent, just the kind of man she wanted in her corner when things started going south (like now). Having him here made her feel instantly safer. She'd assisted him and his team with their last two investigations and, in fact, had turned down repeated offers of a permanent job with them to return to her research project here at Wallens Ridge. She'd told Tony no largely, she saw now, because all she had wanted after dealing with the horrors of an active serial killer investigation was to go crawling back into the shelter of her safe research cocoon.

Despite her ability to see the newly, violently created among them, ghosts had been absent from her life for more than a year before she had encountered Michael, and that was because she had deliberately arranged things that way. She still had been using her expertise on serial killers for the greater good, but the serial killers she had dealt with on a regular basis were caged, chained, and closely guarded prisoners.

After years of screwing it up, she'd finally gotten her life just the way she wanted it: under control.

She had her home in Big Stone Gap; she had her job at Wallens Ridge. In the carefully constructed environment she had created for herself, she'd felt secure.

Then Michael had died despite her attempt to save him, and Tony had showed up asking for her help in catching the Boardwalk Killer, and between the two of them all her painstaking efforts to build a peaceful life for herself had gone straight to hell.

"What are you doing here?" she asked, and ignored Michael's muttered, "I'll give you three guesses."

"Would you believe I just happened to be in the neighborhood?" Tony replied with a glimmer of humor.

"No," she answered, giving Tony a level look as she got to her feet. Her chest was tight with anxiety and her heart still beat uncomfortably fast, but with the salt down and the horseshoe tucked into her waistband she had done everything she could.

So breathe.

At her less-than-encouraging response, Tony gave her a rueful smile. He had such a nice smile, she reflected. Sweet and charming and masculine, all at the same time. The kind of smile that *should* make her go all soft and warm inside. Charlie wanted to think that the reason it didn't was because she was shaking in her sensible shoes at the possibility that an invisible, murderous monster could launch a second attack at any moment, but she knew perfectly well that wasn't it.

You have issues, girlfriend, she told herself severely.

"I *am* glad to see you." Tony lowered his

voice. "Way more glad than I should be, probably. I missed you."

"Uh-huh. Go on," she replied with the air of one waiting for the other shoe to drop, while Michael gritted out through teeth that appeared to be clenched with a fresh spasm of pain, "It's been all of two fucking weeks. Guy needs a life."

Reflecting how unfair it was that Tony thought they were having a private conversation — Pugh still being occupied in talking to the guards — while she was acutely conscious of Michael looking sardonic, on his back practically beneath her feet, she resolutely kept her attention on Tony. His eyes slid over her, warm with appreciation. They had the almost certainly unintended consequence of making her acutely aware that her hands were full of her canister of salt and the items she had picked up, which in turn reminded her of how much danger she and Michael were facing and how little Tony knew about what really went on in her life. Which was part of the reason why her and Tony's relationship wasn't evolving quite as well as she had hoped. The other part of the reason was six-foot-three and dead, but she wasn't going there.

Anyway, the last time she'd seen Tony she'd been a day away from being released from the hospital after her near drowning, and he'd stopped by her room to tell her he was leaving because he'd been summoned to appear in court in New York to testify in a case and had to go. He'd kissed her good-bye, a surprisingly thorough kiss that had brought Michael, who'd been sprawled out in the chair beside her bed, to his feet with a growl. Since then, she'd talked to Tony twice on the phone, and he'd sent the roses. As far as she'd known, he was still in New York, and she hadn't expected to see him again for quite a while.

"You're right, I'm here on business," Tony admitted, and Charlie nodded even as her heart sank. She didn't say anything else because she really didn't want to know. Business for them could only mean one thing: a serial killer.

Truth was, she'd had her fill of serial killers.

"I know you haven't had much time to recover," Tony said, "but I need your help. That's why I'm here."

CHAPTER FIVE

"I see." Charlie's voice was flat. She was already formulating a regretful-sounding way of saying no.

"Bullshit." Michael gave a derisive snort. "Like you're the only serial killer expert in the damned country? Dudley" — as in Dudley Do-Right, which was what Michael had taken to mockingly calling Tony after the valiant (and inept) Canadian Mountie — "has got a major case of the hots for you, buttercup. *That's* why he's here."

For a nanosecond her eyes slid in Michael's direction. Other than narrowing them threateningly at him, she ignored his contribution to the conversation as Tony continued with a touch of apology: "I called to tell you I was on my way, but it went straight to voice mail."

"I haven't had my phone with me all afternoon." She'd left it in her desk while she'd conducted the interview with Spivey.

"I guessed that." Tony's eyes seemed to probe hers. Keeping her agitation hidden from Tony, who knew her in a way Pugh and the guards did not, was difficult, and she wasn't sure how well she was succeeding. Catching herself biting her lower lip, she immediately stopped. Her compulsive glances around the room, though, were something she just couldn't help.

Oh, God, how would she explain her actions if the hunter attacked again while Tony and the rest of them were in a position to watch? If she threw the horseshoe or launched herself at it as she had before, she would end up in a padded room somewhere.

On the other hand, leaving Michael to battle it alone was not an option.

Please God let the hunter not come back.

Nervous shivers coursed over her skin from just thinking about it. She was the one who broke eye contact with Tony, ostensibly to look down among the debris on the floor for her phone, but really to keep him from reading anything in her eyes she didn't want him to know.

"Is everything okay?" Tony asked quietly. Since she was carefully not looking at him, she didn't see his frown. Instead she heard it in his voice. She *was* behaving oddly, she acknowledged with resignation, and Tony was well enough acquainted with her to pick up on it.

"Yes, of course." She cast him a fleeting glance just in time to watch his gaze slide down to the floor. His expression turned speculative, and she knew that he was indeed taking in the full glory of the circle of salt.

Feeling more than slightly self-conscious about the line of white crystals that curved just inches in front of her toes, she sought and failed to find a reasonable explanation for it. At the same time, knowing Tony wasn't looking at her, she gave in to the impulse to cast yet another swift, veiled look around the room: still no sign of anything otherworldly except Michael, thank God. The relief she'd felt upon seeing Tony had disappeared as she realized that in the situation in which she currently found herself there was absolutely nothing he could do to help. He investigated/apprehended/shot bad guys. He had no power over things that went bump in the night. Like hunters. Or spirits, evil or otherwise.

He did know, to some small degree, about her ability to see the dead, which she had used to aid his investigations. He didn't know anything like the full extent of what she experienced, or (God forbid!) anything about Michael.

Michael definitely knew about him, though. About how much she liked him. About their kisses. About how close she had come to sleeping with him.

Which absolutely would have happened already if it hadn't been for her own personal thing that went bump in the night.

Tony said, "You seem . . ." He hesitated, and she suspected that he was searching for a tactful way to put it. ". . . distracted."

"You got to give it to Dudley — the dude's perceptive." Michael's sarcasm earned him another narrow-eyed glance. His eyes were open, but his lips were drawn back from his teeth in a way that once again made her think that he was experiencing an attack of severe pain. Her insides curled in sympathy, a reaction that was made worse by the knowledge that there was nothing she could do to help him. Treating injured ghosts was way outside her wheelhouse. Hard on the heels of that thought came another: what would she do if he didn't recover within a reasonable period of time? What would she do if he didn't recover at all?

Ghosts couldn't die — duh! — but she was pretty sure that being sucked into Spookville was only one of many terrible fates that could befall them. Trouble was, never having had a pet ghost before, she wasn't sure exactly what those fates were. She did know, devoutly, that she didn't want to find out.

One problem at a time: for however long Michael was stuck in her office, she was stuck there, too. She wouldn't — couldn't — leave him, not even briefly, not to go to the infirmary at Pugh's behest or anywhere (like, say, the ladies' room) else. She'd been warned that if they were separated by more than about fifty feet, a vortex could open and he could get sucked away just like that, no hunter involvement necessary.

Don't panic.

"I'm looking for my phone," she told Tony. "It was in my purse, but everything scattered when I dropped it."

At least she was being partially truthful: she *was* scanning the floor for her phone. At the same time, she was also keeping an anxious eye on the space around them, and on Michael. Every instinct she possessed screamed that she needed to get him out of her office and away from the prison as quickly as possible, but as he still seemed to be almost completely incapacitated there wasn't much she could do. The last thing she was worried about at the moment was a missed phone call, but checking her phone gave her a ready-made excuse to stay right where she was. Pretty soon either Tony or Pugh was going to want her to accompany them somewhere, and when she wouldn't they were going to wonder why she was refusing to leave her office. Since her brain was apparently in a fear-induced fog it was good to delay having to come up with a reasonable-sounding excuse for as long as possible, and hunting for her phone/ checking her messages provided just such a delay. When she spotted her phone poking out from under her purse she didn't know whether to feel glad or sorry, but she picked it up, which required a little more time-eating maneuvering — she had to snag her purse first, then dump the items she was carrying into it. Bending to retrieve it gave her a chance to mouth a worried "How are you feeling?" at Michael. He answered with a tight-lipped, "Just peachy keen," which besides being obviously untrue didn't provide any helpful information. Her gaze swept him: his eyes were half-closed; the white lines on either side of his mouth came, she thought, from his jaw being clenched so hard. Lying on his back with one knee bent he looked as rigid as if he had been carved from wood.

Not good signs.

She certainly couldn't carry him; she couldn't even touch him. Once again she reminded herself, *There is nothing you can do.* That hard truth set her nerves to jumping all over again. Taking a deep, hopefully calming (hah!) breath, she looked down at her phone and saw that there were two missed calls. One from Tony, and a slightly earlier one from Special Agent Lena Kaminsky, a member of Tony's three-person team. Like Tony, Kaminsky had left a message.

Attention caught by that, she frowned at Tony. "Kaminsky called me."

"Sugar Buns?" Michael's eyes flickered with interest. He was, she was glad to see, beginning to experimentally flex his broad shoulders; both legs were now bent at the knee. Progress? She hoped. Sugar Buns was his nickname for Kaminsky. It never failed to irritate Charlie, which, she knew, was at least one reason he continued to use it. "Since when is she a member of the Charlie Stone fan club?"

Michael might be irritating, but he had a point. A call to her cell from prickly Kaminsky, whom she definitely wasn't on just-phoned-for-a-chat terms, was nothing if not unexpected.

"She told me she called you," Tony said.

"Here's the thing: her sister's disappeared. Kaminsky thinks she might have run afoul of a serial killer."

"What?" She looked at Tony with shock. Lena Kaminsky was not a friend, exactly. As Michael had pointed out, Kaminsky wasn't even a fan of the expertise that Dr. Charlotte Stone, renowned serial killer expert, brought to the investigative table. Raised a Scientologist, Kaminsky didn't believe in psychiatry, for starters. From the beginning she'd made it clear that she was deeply skeptical of every insight Charlie provided the team. Add to that her suspicion of Charlie's occasionally unaccountable behavior (for which Michael and the whole spectrum of the spirit world could largely be thanked) and her disapproval of Charlie's budding friendship (?) with Tony, and their relationship, as the saying went, was complicated. Still, they'd nearly been killed together during their last serial killer hunt, which had had the upside of forging some pretty strong bonds between them. In any case, Charlie could definitely sympathize with Kaminsky over this. She felt cold all over.

"So the first thing Dudley thinks to do is come running straight for you," Michael said with disgust. Charlie tried not to watch too obviously as, grimacing, he managed to sit up. It cost him a lot of effort, she could tell. She let out the breath she hadn't realized she'd been holding as he succeeded, then felt a renewal of worry as he sat there on the floor with his arms resting on his bent knees and his head hanging, as if that small action had sapped every bit of his strength. She'd never known Michael to be anything but whipcord tough, so to see him like that was disconcerting. But still, the fact that he could sit up was a good thing. It was *definitely* progress. She felt a spurt of hope.

Maybe they would make it out of there before the hunter came back, after all.

She asked Tony, "Are you saying her sister's been *murdered*?"

"She's disappeared," Tony repeated, clarifying, "No body's been found. That's one reason Kaminsky's so frantic: she's hoping her sister's still alive and we can locate her in time to save her life."

"Oh, God." What Charlie's every instinct urged her to do was clap her hands over her ears and not listen to another word. The last thing she wanted, the last thing she needed, was to be drawn into another life or death search for a serial killer.

"Not your problem," Michael intoned

without lifting his head.

He's right, she told herself. But her fingers tightened around her phone.

Tony continued, "Apparently the two of them were together in Vegas on vacation."

"See there, Sugar Buns took a vacation, and she wasn't the one who flat-lined." Michael lifted his head at last. His eyes were still eerily black, but the lines around his mouth had relaxed a little and his jaw was not so tight. Except for the ashen cast to his skin, and those disconcerting obsidian eyes, he looked almost back to normal. "Good to know *somebody's* got her priorities in order."

Charlie kept (most of) her attention focused on Tony. "So what makes Kaminsky think her sister is the victim of a serial killer?"

"Listen to her message," Tony recommended.

There was no longer any way to try to avoid the true purpose behind his visit. Throat tightening, Charlie said, "You — *she* — wants me to help find this guy, right?"

"Let's see, didn't you almost die the last time you got mixed up with Dudley and the gang?" Michael's voice had acquired a real edge. "So I'd say your answer needs to be 'a big thanks for thinking of me, but stupid really isn't my middle name.' "

"I came to see if I could take you to Vegas with me," Tony admitted. "Tonight. The plane's waiting at Lonesome Pine Airport right now." Something in her face must have told him that she wasn't exactly jumping for joy at the prospect, because he added, "I know it's a lot to ask."

"Ya think?" Michael demanded savagely, those black eyes glittering as they fixed on Tony. "After you nearly got her killed the last time, jerkoff?" He shot a glance at Charlie. "Your answer's *no*."

Charlie ignored Michael, and pressed the button that allowed her to listen to the first of her cell phone messages.

"Goddamn it." Michael's attention had shifted to Charlie. "They were finding serial killers for a long time before they started dragging you into it."

The phone beeped, and the message started to play.

"I need your help," Kaminsky said without preamble. Her usually brisk voice was low and strained. "My sister's missing. We're in Las Vegas, at the Conquistador, and she didn't come back to our room Saturday night. I thought maybe she met somebody, so I didn't start getting really worried until Sunday night, when I called the police and got the local office involved. By Monday I was running the details of her disappearance through the FBI computer system. I got a match with three other women who vanished in Las Vegas over the past year. I did some more checking and there are actually seventeen over two years. *Seventeen.* Attractive young women who went out on the town and never came back. Some of them are officially listed as missing persons and some of them are in the police records as deadbeats who skipped out on their hotel bills and some of them popped up in the computer because they had roundtrip tickets to Vegas and apparently never used the return part. There are so many similarities in the cases that I think we're dealing with an active serial killer at work. I called Bartoli. He and Crane are coming." Kaminsky's voice wobbled. "Please come. I know I haven't always been —" Her voice broke off. When it resumed it was fierce: "It doesn't matter. I have to do everything I can to find her. She's my *sister.*"

As Kaminsky clicked off, Charlie could feel the other woman's anguish so strongly that it seemed to be seeping through her pores into her bloodstream. A large part of her *wanted* to rush to Kaminsky's side just as fast as she could. But —

Charlie realized that the message had been loud enough to be overheard only when Michael growled, "I'd be crying my eyes out here, except she's got the whole damned FBI to help her find her sister. She doesn't need *you*."

Having turned away from the guards, Pugh moved to stand beside Tony. "Dr. Stone, I was told that you were the one who ordered the infirmary shut down." He frowned at Charlie. "Is that correct?"

"Yes," Charlie replied, trying to keep her attention focused on Pugh rather than letting it be diverted by Michael, who was planting his booted feet and bracing his hands on his blue-jeaned knees and giving every indication that he was preparing to try to stand. She was sure that, as the hunter's prey, he was as conscious of their continued vulnerability as she was. Even if the salt worked, they couldn't stay where they were forever. He knew they needed to leave her office, and the prison, as soon as possible. Best case scenario, before the damned thing came back.

But there was Michael. And the whole I-hear-disembodied-voices thing she had going on. And then there was her growing aversion to the idea of ever putting herself anywhere near an active serial killer again.

90

Because, Charlie had discovered, she really, truly didn't want to die. Once was enough: even though she didn't remember much about it, what she had taken away from her recent near-death experience was the un-shakable conviction that she never wanted it to happen again. Eternity was something she just wasn't ready for.

She might learn slowly, but by God, she apparently learned.

"Why was that?" Pugh looked at her prob-ingly. "What was it that made you suspect something was amiss in the infirmary?"

Michael said, "Get your stuff together, babe. I'm going to be on my feet here in a minute and when I am we want to be able to make tracks."

Shooting a hooded, anxious glance at him, Charlie responded with a barely perceptible nod of acknowledgment.

Stepping over to her desk with the inten-tion of retrieving her laptop, which had all her files on it and which she really didn't want to leave behind, she forced herself to focus on Pugh. "While Dr. Creason was treating my hand, I noticed that he was behaving oddly." As she spoke, Charlie thrust her laptop into her purse, then began hurriedly gathering up the rest of her spilled belongings and stuffing them in there, too, skirting Michael, who gave her a sardonic look, as she bobbed and weaved around him snagging items from the floor. "It's possible, as you suggested, that he was experiencing a reaction to a medication, or a gas, or something of that nature. I also noticed that one of the trustees was behaving oddly. I don't know what was happening to make them behave as they were. I only know that I was convinced that something out of the ordinary was occurring, and needed to be contained until it could be evaluated."

She didn't *know* that the hunter couldn't track Michael like a bloodhound anywhere they went, but she was hoping it couldn't. She did know that it knew where he was right now, and *that* gave her the willies.

Tony was looking at her hand. "I noticed the bandage. You hurt yourself on the job today? What happened?"

"She was attacked by an inmate," Pugh told him. "We're already re-evaluating our security procedures."

"A subject I was interviewing grabbed my hand and bit me," Charlie said shortly. "It's nothing."

"See, that's the thing about them serial killers," Michael's drawl was pronounced as he fixed Tony with a hard look. "They're downright dangerous. That's why most of us like to keep our women away from them."

That was sexist, possessive, and otherwise offensive on so many levels that Charlie didn't even know where to start to bristle. Unfortunately, beyond shooting Michael the most fleeting of dirty looks, there wasn't any response she could make.

"I'm sorry that happened to you," Tony said with such genuine sincerity that she rewarded him with a smile. Moving nearer, he started gathering up her dropped items and handing them to her. The pink and flowery case of her Miracle-Go kit looked ridiculously feminine in his very masculine hand as he passed it over. Their fingers brushed: his felt solid and warm. "Let me help you with that."

"Fucking Boy Scout," Michael muttered, seemingly to no one in particular. Then, to Charlie, he added, "What do you want to bet missionary is the only position he knows?"

"You made the right call about the infirmary, Dr. Stone," Pugh said to her at almost the same moment, which allowed her to pretend that she hadn't heard Michael's last remark at all, which actually was a far more effective way of dealing with him than glaring, as she had learned from experience. Pugh then asked, "And how did *you* feel while you were in the infirmary? Other than your hand, I mean? Headachey? Short of breath? Any kind of physical symptoms?"

"I had a headache," Charlie replied slowly, as if giving careful consideration to her answer, while she continued to scoop up her belongings. After all, what had happened in the infirmary had to be explained away somehow, and the truth just wasn't going to cut it. The kind of scenario Pugh seemed to be suggesting worked for her. She decided to go with it. "And I was a little nauseous, now that I think about it."

Pugh said, "Ah," but before he could expand on that another guard came rushing up.

"Warden!" There was a whole boatload of urgency in his tone. His voice lowered as Pugh turned to look at him. "Something you ought to know!"

CHAPTER SIX

"What is it now?" Sounding testy, Pugh once more moved away to deal with whatever dire matter was being brought to his attention. Since it didn't involve a hunter swooping down out of nowhere or some fresh crisis relating to Michael, Charlie didn't even try to listen. She was, in fact, relieved to no longer be the object of his scrutiny. She lied when she had to, which, thanks to Michael and her ongoing ghost problem was more often than she would have liked, but she wasn't all that good at it. She always felt uncomfortable, and sometimes it showed.

"What's with the salt anyway?" Tony asked, low-voiced, when, as he thought, no one else could hear.

"Ants." Desperate, Charlie managed to latch onto something halfway plausible. Maybe. Anyway, it couldn't sound even a fraction as insane as the truth. "There were dozens of them in here earlier, and I hate ants. My purse had candy in it. When it fell they started swarming and" — okay, she was babbling; cut it short — "haven't you ever heard that salt wards off ants?"

"Ants," Tony repeated. To his credit, he sounded only faintly dubious. "No, I hadn't heard that." He glanced around. "I don't see any now."

"That's because it worked," Charlie answered. The note of triumph in her voice sounded genuine because it was genuine: she was proud of herself for coming up with such a fast and unassailable rebuttal. There were indeed no ants anywhere in sight: Tony couldn't argue with that.

Michael gave a grunt of laughter. "You know that sounded nuts, right?"

Even as she flicked Michael the briefest of withering looks, she picked up a few coins and Tony handed her a couple of receipts and a nail file and that was it: the contents of her purse were once again back in her purse. The contents of her Miracle-Go kit were in there, too. Along with her laptop. The fact that everything was a jumbled mess and her purse was bulging and filled to overflowing was something she would deal with later. She did like things organized, but at the moment she had more urgent problems, like a giant murderous monster that could reappear at any second.

"Thank you." She smiled at Tony, then wasn't able to stop her expression from changing as, with a look of grim determination, Michael surged to his feet. That brought him so close that she found herself staring at the T-shirt-covered center of his wide chest before automatically adjusting her gaze upward, over his square jaw and beautifully carved mouth and straight nose and chiseled cheekbones to his eyes. For the most fleeting of moments their eyes connected; his were still terrifyingly black. If she hadn't known him, she would have taken an instant, instinctive step back: only the damned should have eyes like that. As it was, though, she took in the soulless eyes right along with the handsome, hard-planed face and the tall, powerful body, sweeping all of them with the kind of anxious glance a mother would throw over an injured child. He might be on his feet, but he was far from recovered. She got the impression that simply remaining upright was costing him every bit of strength he had.

"Something wrong?" Tony asked with a frown, apparently correctly interpreting her changing face without any inkling as to the cause. He slid a supportive hand around her upper arm. It felt large and warm and comforting against her chilled flesh, but she was too jittery to do more than register it in passing.

"N-no," Charlie answered, already busy scraping salt out of the way with a hopefully discreet foot to make a path that would allow Michael to escape. From this point, everything needed to happen fast: once the circle was open, the hunter could pounce without anything to even slow it down. Barely repressing a shiver, she refused to let her thoughts go there. Both men were looking at her, and for a moment her attention was torn between them. Tall, dark, and handsome, stalwart and gainfully employed in a respected profession that required him to wear a suit and tie (her mother's criteria for the kind of man Charlie should be on the hunt for), her perfect dream man, in fact, if only she had the sense to realize it, Tony watched her with concern. Taller, more powerfully built, gorgeous, golden (dead) Michael, with not one thing in his favor except that he was pure sex on the hoof and she genuinely liked him almost as much as she wanted to sleep with him, fixed her with an inimical gaze.

So unsteady on his feet that he was swaying slightly, Michael shifted his eyes from her face to frown down at Tony's hand on her arm, then looked at Tony in a way that would have been forbidding even if his eyes weren't as black as night. Tony, of course, had no idea that Michael was even there. His focus was all on her.

"This is hopeless. I'll let the janitorial staff deal with it," she said lightly, seeing that Tony was looking down at her busy foot even as she nudged the last few grains of salt aside.

"Good idea," Tony replied. "So, are you coming with me to Vegas?"

Charlie's eyes flew to his face. The thought of Kaminsky's pain made her want to say yes, but there were so many factors to consider. "I —"

"Let's go." Michael stepped through the opening she had made for him. "Chop-chop."

Instead of rushing for safety as she would have wished, he stopped just outside the circle to wait for her.

This is no time to be gentlemanly! The hunter can't hurt me, she wanted to scream at him, but of course she didn't. Although he could only get ahead of her by about fifty feet, in these circumstances a fifty-foot head start was not to be despised. It would at least get him out of her office, where the hunter knew to look for him.

"— am thinking about it," she concluded quickly, pulling her arm free of Tony's hold and hurrying past Michael toward the door. She added over her shoulder in as normal a tone as she could manage, "I'm just going to go outside. I'm feeling a little dizzy and I really need some fresh air."

"Charlie —" Tony sounded perturbed. She didn't look back or even slow down. She was already edging through the crowd at the door. Her fingers curled around the cool hard curve of the horseshoe. Pulling it free of her waistband, she thrust it out of sight into her pants pocket, then kept a firm grip on it. If the hunter came back, she wanted to be ready.

A shiver slid down her spine at the prospect.

Please don't let it come back.

Pugh looked sharply at her as Charlie murmured "Excuse me" to get past him. Michael (being noncorporeal had its plus side) had already made it through the knot of men standing in and around the doorway and was once again waiting for her to catch up. Pugh automatically stepped out of her way, but then came after her as she speed-walked away from him, rushing down the corridor with Michael at her side. Tony was perhaps half a step behind Pugh. With thoughts in mind of how vulnerable Michael was to the hunter, she would have kicked up her pace to a flat-out run except she was afraid of attracting too much attention. Plus, the last thing she wanted to do was overtax Michael's strength. It was clear that whatever the hunter had done to him had left him in a severely weakened state.

Pugh said loudly, "Dr. Stone, wait! Did I understand you to say you're feeling ill?"

"A little light-headed. Nothing some fresh air won't help," Charlie threw back at him. The route to the nearest elevator bank required her to go to the end of the hallway where her office was located and then walk a short distance along the corridor that led to the infirmary — both places, she judged, where there was a better than average likelihood of encountering the hunter — before turning down the hallway that led to the elevator banks. Michael stayed beside her, matching his pace to hers even though his gait was growing unsteady. From that, and his increasingly ashen complexion, she knew that he was having real difficulty. A moment later, he gave up walking and went into what she called the ghost-glide, with his boots floating an inch or so above the floor.

He must have been able to read her worry

for him in her face, because he gave her a crooked half-smile. "No need to get that sexy little blue thong you're wearing in a twist, babe. I'll make it."

That made her eyes widen. There was outrage in the look she threw at him.

Did you watch me getting dressed?

She barely managed to stop herself from saying it aloud. Because a sexy little blue thong exactly described her underwear. And she'd put them on, along with the rest of her clothes, in her bathroom, in which she now dressed because of *him,* which he was forbidden to enter without an invitation.

His eyes raked her face, and his smile widened into a devilish grin. "Just so you know, I saw you getting them out of your dresser. Before you locked yourself in the bathroom to get dressed. Jesus, you have a dirty mind."

That would have totally infuriated her if his voice hadn't been so raspy it sounded like somebody had taken sandpaper to his vocal cords.

What she wanted to do was wrap an arm around his muscular waist and have him lean on her. She couldn't.

Except for tightening her hold on the horseshoe and keeping a wary eye out, there wasn't a thing she could do to help him.

She couldn't even slow down, or manufacture a reason for a rest stop. Reaching a safe place had to be the priority. If there *was* such a thing as a safe place, but that was too terrifying to contemplate.

Getting outside the prison was neither quick nor simple: they had to pass through a guard station with its requisite barred doors before reaching the elevators, then pass through another guard station before being allowed to exit. All she could do was continue moving as fast as she reasonably could while keeping an eye on Michael and a watch out for the hunter.

Knowing that it could swoop down upon them at any time made her pulse pound.

"This place is a damned rabbit warren," Tony said behind her. "Is this the fastest way outside?" He was talking to Pugh.

"I'm afraid so," Pugh replied.

"What the hell do you do in case of fire?" Tony demanded.

"We have an emergency evacuation protocol in place."

Michael snorted. "Think anybody gives a damn if a bunch of convicts burn?"

"Dr. Stone —" Pugh called. They were nearing the end of the corridor, and she (and Michael) had outdistanced the other two by quite a bit. She could hear Pugh's quickening footsteps behind her. Ignoring him, she walked a little faster; she was way too antsy to deal with the warden, or try to think up more lies in answer to whatever questions he was bound to ask.

A rumble of unfamiliar noise grew steadily louder as they approached the junction of the corridors. It told Charlie that a great deal of activity was occurring just out of her sight; hearing it and speculating on its cause upped her anxiety level so much that her chest felt tight.

Once again Michael must have been able to read her face, because he said, "Steady. We got this, babe."

Despite her best efforts, Pugh caught up with her. "In your opinion, Dr. Stone, could we be dealing with some kind of contagion issue in the infirmary? A virus or some other type of disease?"

Charlie saw that his face was freshly lined with worry. Behind him, Tony was also looking worried, but unlike Pugh's she was pretty sure that Tony's worry was strictly on her behalf.

From his and Pugh's point of view, of course, she was alone, racing away from them toward the elevators, claiming to be dizzy and in need of fresh air. Everything she had done from the time they had first seen her in her office had been (face it) bizarre. Her behavior must be setting off all kinds of red flags.

She ought to be glad that Pugh was inquiring about possible medical issues. At least that gave her a cover story she could embrace.

"Why do you ask?" She cast a fleeting glance at Pugh. "Is there something I should know?"

"There's been a death in the infirmary," Pugh announced heavily. "I was just told of it."

Oh, no.

"Dr. Creason?" It was all she could do to keep the wobble out of her voice.

"Fuck," Michael said.

"No." Pugh shook his head. "We're in the process of having Dr. Creason transported to Lonesome Pine Hospital for evaluation. What I'd like you to do if you feel up to it is take a look at him while he's still here in the prison. I would really value an in-house opinion on his condition. If whatever caused this is contagious, Wallens Ridge is looking at a visit by the CDC. Maybe even quarantine. Even if it's not, unless the death is by natural causes, the Bureau of Prisons will have to be notified and will probably investigate. If we could get out in front of it,

identify the cause of the illnesses and death
—"

So much was happening in this new corridor that Charlie's step momentarily faltered. She missed the rest of what Pugh had to say as everything assaulted her senses at once.

"Would you look at this," Michael muttered, and Charlie did even as she picked up the pace again. Noise, confusion, way more people and activity than there should be.

The kaleidoscope of images resolved itself into what, among other things, was clearly the emergency medical evacuation Pugh had spoken of, in progress.

In the foreground, two stretchers raced toward her — which meant that they were really racing toward the turnoff to an adjacent hallway that held the elevator banks. That turnoff was located about a quarter of the way up the hall from her end and was the goal of her little party, too. The rattling of the stretchers' wheels formed a frantic counterpoint to the barked exchanges of the orderlies pushing them and the paramedics running alongside. A quartet of guards ran with the stretchers, too. More guards in riot gear stood shoulder to shoulder in front of the infirmary doors, barring outside access. A third stretcher, being pushed far more slowly than the first two, was just emerging from the infirmary through the line of guards. A blue body bag lay on that one, and Charlie realized that she had to be looking at the fatality.

She was shaken by the thought that an inmate might have died from having a spirit enter his body. Although Michael had only said something about *two* spirits coming through with him . . .

Alarmed, senses on high alert as her attention switched back to the pair of stretchers that were now just a few yards away and barreling ever closer, she got her first good look at the face of the victim strapped to the stretcher that was out in front. She had just affirmatively identified the unconscious-looking figure as Creason when it happened.

The voices inside her head returned.

Please don't do this to me, the woman begged, making Charlie miss a step and instinctively clutch at Michael — fat lot of good that did — for support. She stumbled a little as her hands went right through him, and barely noticed the accompanying electric tingle that was all that physical contact with him amounted to as he, in turn, grabbed at her in a useless attempt to catch and steady her.

She was too tightly focused on what was happening in her head. It was the same voice she'd heard in the interview room with Spivey. A woman's voice, terrified.

Everything else went a little out of focus. She could hear her pulse pounding in thick, fast strokes in her ears. Charlie shook her head, trying to clear it.

Not now, she pleaded with the universe silently. She couldn't deal with the voices *now.*

"Charlie —" Michael's voice was hard with fear for her. "What's wrong?"

I won't tell, the anguished woman promised, and it was all Charlie could do not to clutch her head with both hands. The episode was so vivid that she experienced instant vertigo. She felt a rush of cold sweat.

Please, the woman screamed, just like she had before, and Charlie closed her eyes and stopped dead and shuddered.

"Damn it, Charlie, what's happening? Talk to me." Michael's exclamation was what penetrated, what had her opening her eyes and looking up at him in mute distress. He loomed over her, familiar and safe, and she concentrated on him, mentally anchoring herself to him as a boat in a storm might cast its anchor to a rock. She heard Pugh and Tony saying something, too, but she couldn't understand them and was only vaguely aware that they were there, or of where she was or what was going on or anything else because the woman's terrified scream was echoing through her head and shredding her insides clear down to the bone.

As it died away she had an instant of clarity in which she became aware of many things at once: a man's — Tony's — sturdy arm was around her shoulders: he was asking "Charlie, are you all right?"; Michael, cursing and vividly present as he leaned close, unable to touch her because of what he was; Pugh saying something, too, that she completely missed; the two nearest stretchers rumbling over the concrete floor not far away now from where her party had been stopped in their tracks by what was happening to her. Charlie watched as the stretchers with their accompanying retinue turned the corner into the other corridor, the one with the elevator banks, and disappeared from view.

She even had time to draw a single deep breath.

Then another scream, a window-rattling shriek from the direction of the infirmary, pierced the air. It was so loud and harrowing that it caused her heart to jump and her insides to clench and her blood to turn to ice. Her gaze jerked toward the sound as she made a frantic attempt to identify the source.

It wasn't a voice inside her head this time. It wasn't a woman at all. It was a man.

But she was once again the only living creature who could hear it.

Because the man was dead.

Even as she registered that, she saw him.

Pale and wild-eyed, his mouth stretched wide as his ungodly scream built until it echoed from the ceiling and walls and Charlie thought her eardrums must burst from the sheer shrill volume of it, Walter Spivey pounded down the hall toward her. His big, flabby body was bare to the waist and shiny with sweat. He had one arm extended in front of him. He was, Charlie saw with a burst of horror, clutching a gleaming silver scalpel in his fist. As she watched, he slashed the air savagely with it.

She knew the instant he saw her, the instant he recognized her. His eyes widened. The scream mutated into a roar.

"You! Dr. Bitch! *You* did this to me! I'm going to kill you," he bellowed, and came galloping toward her.

CHAPTER SEVEN

Charlie almost lost it. She flinched instinctively, and probably would have leaped backwards if Tony's protective arm hadn't been around her shoulders holding her steady. She deduced instantly that Spivey had to be the fatality in the infirmary that Pugh had spoken of. She was all but certain that it was his body that lay in the blue body bag on the slow-moving stretcher that trundled its unhurried way down the hall, far behind the Spivey that was charging her in his maddened state. She knew that what she was seeing was Spivey's phantom, knew that it (almost certainly) couldn't hurt her, knew that what was menacing her was (probably) no more solid or dangerous than a puff of air, but she was so unnerved by everything that had happened, so absolutely not herself, so unsure of the true parameters of the supernatural world that she'd thought she knew, it was all she could do not to react as any normal woman would when being charged by a scalpel-wielding serial killer and scream her head off.

Only years of experience with the violent dead enabled her to keep silent and hold her ground. Squaring her shoulders, stiffening her spine, reminding herself that this was her world and she knew how to deal with it, she was preparing herself to withstand the imminent onslaught when Spivey shrieked, "I'm going to cut you up, bitch!" and launched himself at her.

She could feel his terrible energy in the air, tangible as an electric field. Spivey's face was contorted with rage and hate. The blade in his hand gleamed vividly like any real one as it sliced the air. She couldn't help it: her breath caught. Her pulse jumped. Of course the scalpel would pass harmlessly through her. She *knew* that, but . . .

Michael leaped in front of her, all big and bad and aggressive as he planted himself between her and Spivey.

"How about trying for a piece of *me,* motherfucker?" he roared.

Charlie had less than a split second to remember what Michael was, to take comfort in knowing that he'd heard Spivey's screams, that he could see Spivey, too, that even if all the rules of ghost-world that she had lived by for so long turned out to be wrong or incomplete and there was a whole universe of terrible things out there that she'd had no clue even existed *he was in that world with her,* when it hit her: Michael was dead just like Spivey. He and Spivey were on the same side of the divide.

Spivey might not be able to hurt her, *but he could hurt Michael.*

Charlie's heart leaped into her throat. *Get out of his way,* she wanted to scream at Michael. *He can't hurt* me!

But she couldn't. The words stuck in her throat. She had maintained her façade of normality for so long that her instinct to stay silent in the face of anything the supernatural threw at her kicked in to choke off all utterance.

Anyway, it was too late.

Spivey was in mid-leap, almost on top of Michael, scalpel flashing, his bulky body flying through the air like it weighed nothing at all — because it didn't.

"Bastard!" Spivey screamed at Michael.

Eyes wide with horror, pulse pounding, Charlie watched Michael bracing to meet the attack —

Then Spivey screamed again, a totally different sound than before, a hoarse, terrible cry so full of fear and pain that she felt every tiny hair on her body catapult upright in reaction. Her breath caught as Spivey, writhing and screaming, shot straight toward the ceiling as though he was in the grip of —

The hunter!

Heart hammering, Charlie barely had time to register the immense column of shimmering air surging behind Spivey before he vanished.

The shimmer vanished, too.

Spivey's scream was cut off like someone had slammed a soundproof door on it.

The place where Spivey and the hunter had been was eerily calm, eerily silent. Nothing but empty air.

Charlie's chest was so tight that she could scarcely breathe. Her heart pounded unmercifully. The attack of nausea that always accompanied her close encounters with unfamiliar spirits slammed her like a fist to the stomach. Swallowing in an attempt to control it, she felt the rough edge of metal digging into her sweat-dampened palm. Glancing down, she saw that her subconscious had been quicker to recognize the danger than her conscious mind: without even being aware that she was doing it, she had pulled the horseshoe out of her pocket and was gripping it for all she was worth.

"Jesus Christ." Sounding shaken himself,

Michael took an unsteady step back, then turned sharply toward Charlie. Their eyes met for a charged instant. They both knew what had happened: the hunter had grabbed Spivey.

They both knew that the thing could return at any time.

For Michael.

"If it comes back, stay the hell out of the way," Michael growled.

Tamping down on the nausea — now was definitely not the time — Charlie curled her lip at him. Silent message, *when pigs fly.*

"I *will* look at Dr. Creason for you," Charlie said to the others in a voice that was so strong and calm in the face of how bad she felt and the rampant fear that was surging through her that she surprised herself. She was already pulling free of Tony's supportive arm and casting a commanding look at Pugh as she brushed past him. Both men regarded her with surprise mixed with consternation but she didn't care. Didn't have time to care. Her whole focus was on keeping Michael safe. Moving away from them, she threw over her shoulder, "On the way down in the elevators. Let's see if we can catch the stretchers, shall we?"

This time she flat-out ran. Michael had obviously gotten a burst of whatever worked as ghost adrenaline from that second unexpected encounter with the hunter, because he was still exuding a dangerous energy as he caught up with her.

"What happened to you back there? Before the hunter?" he demanded. Those unnerving black eyes were intent on her face.

Dear Lord, she had almost forgotten about that. *That* was how terrified for him she was.

Telling him that she'd heard the voices again was potentially way too fraught a conversation to be as one-sided as it would have to be in these circumstances, or to be conducted while they ran for their lives. She gave a slight shake of her head: *later.*

Wingtips slapping the concrete, Tony caught up with her next. His cheekbones were flushed, his mouth was tight, and his tie and coattails were flying. He looked at her with a frown. "Charlie, hold up! What was that back there? I thought you were about to pass out."

Tony's inquiry, almost identical to Michael's, called for a totally different response: a lie, in fact.

"I had a sudden, terrible headache. Almost like a migraine. It's gone now."

Running alongside her, Tony threw her an exasperated look. "Would you stop? Pugh might be right: you may need medical attention."

He was a runner just like she was. Despite the pace she was setting, he didn't sound even faintly breathless. She would have been equally impressed with Michael's conditioning, except he didn't breathe.

Go along to get along: it was another of her alcoholic mother's famous axioms, and it sprang into her mind then. Tony's words dovetailed so well with her needs that, instead of arguing, she appropriated them into her cover story. After all, who was the doctor here? That's right: she was. Tony and Pugh were in no position to contradict any supposed medical assessment she made.

She shook her head. "What I need is fresh air. I think I may have been exposed to an anesthetic or some other type of toxic gas. I'll know more once I get a look at Dr. Creason and the other victim. But the best thing I can do for myself is to get outside right away."

That produced a huff of laughter from Michael. "Way to lie, babe."

That he could laugh at all under the circumstances was beyond mystifying to her. She was sick to her stomach, scared out of her mind, and doing her best to save *his* ass. Nothing funny about any of that, as far as she could see.

She shot a sideways glare at him.

Tony looked unconvinced. "Are you sure?"

"Yes," she said, and played her trump card. "I *am* a doctor, remember. I know when I need medical attention."

That seemed to settle it. There were no more protests about rushing for the elevators from him.

With Tony running along on one side of her, Michael on the other, and Pugh panting as he brought up the rear, they overtook the stretchers bearing Creason and, she presumed, the trustee just as the stretchers cleared the air-lock type security doors and were about to be loaded onto the service elevator beyond them. Besides fighting back against the very real possibility that she could lose her lunch at any moment, Charlie was so afraid that the hunter would reappear that she could hardly stand still. Her skin crawled in terrible anticipation. If she could have shoved Michael ahead of her and onto that elevator, she would've.

Because the warden was with them, they made it through the security doors in record time. With two stretchers and the accompanying paramedics, orderlies, and guards, the service elevator, which was the size of a small room, was a tight fit even before Charlie, Tony, and Pugh (and Michael, who took up no appreciable space) crowded aboard. Had Pugh not been with them, they wouldn't have been allowed on.

For that matter, if it hadn't been for the threat posed by the hunter, Charlie wouldn't have *gotten* on. Just thinking about how badly wrong this could go sent cold dread pumping through her veins. If the hunter returned now, they had no chance of running, no room to fight. Plus, there was the whole where-are-the-evil-spirits thing.

The memory of how Creason and the trustee had behaved in the infirmary remained all too vivid. If the evil spirits were still present inside their bodies, she really didn't want to find out while she was locked in a metal box with them.

But under the circumstances there was no choice. The elevator was the fastest — the only fast — way out of the prison.

Michael must have been having similar misgivings, because the look he gave Charlie as he settled into place beside her was grim. "If something goes wrong, you leave it to me to handle," he ordered her.

Yeah, right.

Of course, she couldn't say it out loud, but she gave him a look that she was pretty sure he understood, because he said, "I

119

mean it, damn it."

The doors were closing behind them. Just before they clanged shut, Charlie caught a glimpse of the third stretcher, the one carrying Spivey's body, as it came down the hall toward the security doors. With the next run of the service elevator it would be taken to the basement, which housed the prison morgue, for autopsy, she knew.

She shivered.

Then she thought about what had happened to the real Walter Spivey, the part of him that still existed, his soul, and shivered even more. Spookville was a horrible place. What waited for Spivey beyond it was, she felt sure, even more horrible.

She had no idea if the hunter would come back for Michael, or how far it could track him if it did. All she knew was that the more distance they could put between him and it, the safer she would feel.

"How's the headache?" Tony asked her under cover of a conversation Pugh was having with the guards, and she looked at him and answered, "Better."

"You might want to sheathe your weapon, Van Helsing," Michael said drily, nodding at her clenched fist, which, she only then remembered, still had a death grip on the horseshoe, which was perfectly visible at her side. It took her a second, but then she recalled that Van Helsing was a monster hunter from the Dracula movies and realized that he was comparing her to that fearsome warrior. Despite everything, she almost succumbed to a smile. "Dudley's been giving it the eye."

Charlie was reluctant to let go of it, but examining Creason required that she have her uninjured hand free. With a quick glance at Tony — he wasn't looking at the horseshoe right then, if he ever had been, but had instead been drawn into the conversation between Pugh and the guards — she shoved the horseshoe back into her pocket, making sure it was positioned so that she could grab it again easily if necessary, which she prayed it wouldn't be. Then she pushed her jitters over the possible return of the hunter to the back of her mind — she had to if she was to remain objective — and turned her attention to the victims as the elevator began its descent with a lurch and a groan. It moved slowly, with a grinding sound that might have been worrisome under other circumstances. The only thing that Charlie cared about at the moment was its nerve-racking lack of speed, but that was out of her control.

Both stretchers came equipped with IV

poles. The liquid in the bags attached to them, which Charlie guessed to be saline, sloshed as they moved; a steady drip ran down the plastic tubing into each patient's arm. The trustee lay as motionless as Creason, but it was Creason's stretcher that she was wedged in beside and Creason who was her primary focus. Charlie glanced at his blood pressure monitor: the numbers were low, but high enough to perfuse the brain and other vital organs.

"What killed Walter Spivey?" Charlie asked Pugh, breaking in on his conversation without preamble.

As she glanced at the warden, her gaze encountered Tony's. He was frowning thoughtfully at her. She had no idea why, and no time to question it.

"That's what I'm hoping you can tell me. The same thing that sickened these men, I presume." Pugh gestured at Creason and the trustee. "After the infirmary was shut down, a guard found Spivey dead in bed in the locked room they put him in after he attacked you. He was still in restraints. So what we've got to account for is two unconscious, one dead — it has to be from the same cause."

The thing was, she only saw the newly, *violently* dead. Ergo, whatever had killed

Spivey had involved an act of violence. Exactly what, she had no idea.

"Not necessarily." Charlie was finally able to bring herself to look directly at Creason. He seemed smaller than he did when he was up walking around, and infinitely frailer. His eyes were closed. His sharp-featured face was utterly white, as if all the blood had leached from it. The impression he gave was that of a husk, from which a vital inner component was missing. He was breathing, lightly and rapidly, through parted lips that were tinged with blue.

Cyanosis. She glanced quickly at his hands, which rested on top of the blanket that was tucked beneath his armpits. There was evidence of low blood saturation of oxygen there as well: the tips of his fingers were slightly blue.

That her unfailingly kind colleague should be lying there like that made her feel sick. And afraid. Very, very afraid. Spirit possession of human beings was something that she had never before encountered. The mere thought was horrible; the consequences to the victims were, she feared, catastrophic.

A blood-chilling thought occurred: If Michael had not intervened, would she have shared her fellow physician's fate? Would the second spirit have invaded her body instead of the trustee's? She had been closer . . .

She was suddenly, icily sure that she had barely missed sharing Creason's fate.

I'm so sorry, she said to Creason silently. Guilt over what had happened to him washed over her in a wave. *If I hadn't been distracted by the voices in my head; if I hadn't gone to the infirmary . . .*

"Not your fault," Michael told her, and as she glanced at him in quick surprise she realized that he was once again reading her thoughts in her face. "You aren't responsible for the whole damned universe, you know."

Under the circumstances there was nothing she could say to that, so she didn't. Instead, she started to lay a cautious hand on Creason's arm — it was bare, his lab coat and shirt having been removed, she presumed to allow for a medical examination in the infirmary after he had fainted — but the paramedic at his side blocked her access with an outflung arm.

"I'm sorry, ma'am, but until we know what's wrong with them —"

"This is Dr. Stone. She's going to be taking a look at these men for me," Pugh said curtly, and the paramedic stood down.

"If it's something contagious —" Tony objected.

"I'm almost certain it's not," Charlie replied.

This time she was able to put her hand on Creason's arm. She did it cautiously, because part of her was terrified that his eyes would pop open and he would once again be the terrifying zombie-esque creature that had come after her in the infirmary.

But he didn't move or respond to her touch in any way. He wasn't a muscular man, but the biceps beneath her hand felt almost unnaturally flaccid. His skin was cold: *cold as a corpse's* was the analogy that popped into her mind. She barely managed to repress a shudder. Her stomach gave a threatening heave, and this time it wasn't only because of her recent too-close encounter with an unfamiliar spirit.

His pulse, like his breathing, was fast and shallow.

Leaning over the stretcher — "You want to be careful there, babe," Michael warned, and she knew he harbored the same fear she did: that the evil spirit was still there, to be roused at any time — she pinched Creason's earlobe to assess motor response to a pain stimuli. He didn't so much as twitch an eyelash. Then, half-afraid of what she might see, she slowly, carefully, opened an eyelid. The pupils were dilated and fixed.

Not good.

"Could I borrow your stethoscope, please?" Charlie asked the closest paramedic, in a voice so calm, so controlled, that no one would ever guess that her stomach was now roiling and her knees were as shaky as Jell-O. The paramedic passed the stethoscope over, and Charlie draped it around her own neck.

When she listened to the heart, she frowned.

This was light-years beyond a faint.

"Well?" Pugh asked impatiently.

"It's not a disease, and it's not contagious." Charlie handed the stethoscope back to the paramedic, to whom she said, "He needs to get to the hospital as quickly as possible. Tell whoever's on duty" — it was just after five o'clock, when the hospital dealt with a changing of shifts that could sometimes result in treatment delays — "that these patients need an MRI of the head and chest area as soon as possible."

The paramedic nodded. Charlie glanced at the numbered buttons by the door, which lit up one by one as they progressed downward: they were on the second floor, with just one more to go.

"Then what's wrong with him?" Pugh demanded.

"I can't say for sure. My best guess is, again, some kind of anesthetic or toxic gas such as carbon monoxide. We'll know more when we get the results of the MRI. And the toxicology reports, but of course they take weeks."

"You must have been exposed to the same thing." Tony was looking at her intently.

"You have been behaving very oddly, Dr. Stone," Pugh chimed in. He glanced around the elevator, and she got the feeling that he didn't want to be too specific in front of the paramedics, etc. "What you were doing in your office when I came in — it was unusual, to say the least."

"The ants you thought you saw." Tony's tone was carefully neutral. "Might have been a hallucination."

"This is where you ask 'em, 'Do you believe in ghosts?'" Michael said.

"In retrospect, I suppose it's possible." Ignoring Michael, Charlie replied to Tony, then glanced at Pugh to include him in the rest of her response. "If I was exposed to anything, I was unaware of it happening and I can't tell you the source."

"You *were* in the infirmary with the other victims, at approximately the same time they were affected." Tony said it as if he was seeking confirmation.

Charlie nodded. "Yes."

Pugh said sharply to the guards, "We're going to be evacuating the infirmary. Only one of you travels to the hospital with the prisoner. The others . . ."

"How bad a shape is he in?" Michael asked, nodding at Creason, and Charlie quit listening to the general conversation to focus on him. Meeting his eyes, she gave a slight shake of her head. Truth was, she had no idea what the prognosis was for a human being who had suffered possession by an evil spirit. Going by the physical signs she had just observed, it wasn't good.

She didn't know if Creason would survive. She didn't know to what degree he might be impaired. She did know that there was nothing she could do for him. Even an exorcism — supposing she knew how to perform one perfectly and could do it there in the elevator with the meager tools she had on hand — wouldn't work: she was as certain as it was possible to be that the evil spirit was no longer inside him. What she had just examined was the damaged vessel the spirit had left behind. She could only hope that it was strong enough to heal.

"I'm guessing that the hunter took the spirits that were in these two before he came for me," Michael said thoughtfully. "That would account for their fainting, and the state they're in."

Charlie's brow crinkled. She couldn't ask the question that scenario planted in her mind: *So then the hunter went back and killed Spivey? Because something, or someone, did.*

The elevator reached the ground floor.

Following the stretchers, which had priority clearance through the metal detectors and heavy steel doors, it took just a few minutes to get outside. It was a beautiful late September day, and even in the covered loading-dock area where the ambulances waited, the crisp smell of autumn drifted through the heavier scent of exhaust fumes. She still felt like vomiting from her close encounter with Spivey, but she was managing to control the impulse — *practice makes perfect* — and she thought she had it under control. Refusing Tony's suggestion that she go in the ambulance with the victims to be examined at the hospital herself, casting a wary glance all around as she stepped briskly out from beneath the overhang just in case the cloudless blue sky should harbor a terrible surprise — i.e., the hunter — Charlie headed across the gleaming black asphalt toward her car. Feeling hideously exposed now that they were out in the open air, she hunched her shoulders a little in instinctive self-defense. Then she tried to convince herself that there was no way a hunter would attack in broad daylight in such a public spot, but almost instantly gave up: the hard truth was, she had no way of knowing the parameters of what a monster from another dimension might do. For Tony's benefit, she took a few ostentatiously deep breaths to clear out whatever noxious substance she had supposedly been exposed to as she beelined for her car.

Wallens Ridge was a huge complex, a level six maximum security private prison with 700 inmates and about half that number of guards. Eight modern, multi-story buildings that looked almost white in the bright sunshine squatted on the blasted-off top of a mountain, where they were ringed by multiple chain-link fences and rows of shiny silver razor wire. Fortunately, her office was in the same building as the infirmary, so she was able to exit with the stretchers and be close to her car. The west parking lot — that was where she parked — was the overflow lot. Today it was full, and busy. Tuesday was visiting day, visiting hours were just about over, and vehicles of all descriptions were backing out of spaces and chugging toward the exits.

"You feeling better?" Tony asked cautiously after a moment. He was keeping pace beside her, escorting her to her car. She'd been a little short with him after he'd tried to insist that she go in the ambulance to the hospital to get checked out. But she had been so distressed over what had happened to Creason and the others, so unnerved by the continuing threat posed by the hunter, so frightened for Michael, to say nothing of how bad she felt from the physical symptoms associated with Spivey's appearance and the voices, that patience had momentarily deserted her and she'd ended by snapping out a flat, "I'm not going to the hospital," thus ending the conversation.

Even now, she couldn't escape the extra layer of anxiety that Tony's presence added. The time was at hand: she had to decide whether she was going with him or not, whether she was going to answer Kaminsky's call for help or not. Just thinking about the pain Kaminsky must be in made Charlie's heart shiver. If she could help stop a madman and find Kaminsky's sister then that was what she absolutely needed to do. But the thought of getting too close to another active serial killer made it suddenly hard to breathe. And she had to factor in Michael's injuries . . .

"Yes, thanks. I told you, I just needed

some fresh air. If I was exposed to something, it's out of my system now." She really liked Tony so much; if only she could get some of the complications in her life straightened out, there was real potential in their relationship. He was exactly the kind of man she had always wanted, the kind of man a woman could build a future with. "I'm sorry if I was cross earlier. It's been a difficult day."

"That's all right." He grinned unexpectedly. With his lean dark face and twinkling eyes, he looked so handsome that Charlie couldn't help but return his smile. "You're cute when you're cranky."

"That was just fucking lame," the number one complication in her life observed with disgust. "He's trying to get in your pants, and that's the best line he can come up with?"

He was walking beside her, too. Since they'd exited the elevators he hadn't said a word: like her, she thought, he'd been busy keeping an eye out for the hunter. She cast him a withering glance, and then her gaze lingered, arrested. It was only now that she got a good look at him in unforgiving daylight that she became aware that he really looked pretty rough. For a man (ghost) with what was ordinarily a healthy tan, the grayish pallor of his face was alarming. So were the new lines around his mouth of what she thought had to be pain, and the deepening shadows beneath his eyes. He looked almost . . . haggard. The beautiful bone structure of his face was all the more apparent because his skin seemed to be pulled tight over it. His lips were pale. And his eyes were still that disconcerting fathomless black.

A fresh thrill of fear ran down her spine. For the first time it occurred to her that, even if the hunter didn't return, there was no guarantee that Michael would be all right.

"You keep looking at me all big-eyed and worried like that, and I'm going to start thinking you're crazy in love with me," he drawled, then as she stiffened in outrage he nodded at Tony. "There Dudley is, waiting for you to say something. You know, about how cute you look when you're cranky."

For so many reasons — *crazy in love with him, my ass!* — that shifted Charlie's attention instantly back to Tony. She wouldn't even give the infuriating creature the satisfaction of glaring at him.

"Thanks — I think," Charlie said to Tony, perfectly composed. She'd been fishing around in her disorganized mess of a purse for her keys, and found them just as they reached her car. She pulled them out with a triumphant jingle.

"Anyway, when you snapped back at Dudley like that, you weren't cute," said Michael. "You were damned hot. That's what he ought to be telling you."

Charlie didn't acknowledge that by so much as a flicker of an eyelash.

What she said as she stopped beside her blue Camry was, "Here's my car," and clicked the button on the key ring that unlocked the doors.

"I hate to put pressure on you after what you've just been through." Tony gave her an apologetic look. "But the plane's scheduled to take off at seven. Crane's meeting us at the airport. That is, if you're coming with me."

"Hell, no, she's not." Squaring around to face him, Michael radiated aggression in a way that should have made the other man step back a pace. Except that, of course, Tony couldn't see him.

"I am coming with you." Charlie's lips firmed as Michael's eyes shot to her face. She'd made her decision in the last couple of seconds, after sifting through the options about a thousand times and finally coming to the conclusion that going with Tony to

Kaminsky's aid was something she had to do. She knew Michael was going to (to put it politely) disagree with her decision, and their upcoming discussion wasn't going to be pretty, but there wasn't any other choice she could make. "I just need to stop by my house to pack a bag."

CHAPTER EIGHT

"What the hell was that?" Michael's tone was deceptively mild. Charlie only knew how really, truly ticked off he was from the tightness around his mouth and eyes. He hadn't said a word from the moment she'd told Tony that she was going to Las Vegas with him until now, when she and Michael were driving out of the prison after having been waved through the last checkpoint by a sunglasses-wearing guard with a shotgun riding on his shoulder. She was behind the wheel, seatbelted in, physically feeling a whole lot better since the Tums she'd dug out of her purse as soon as she'd gotten in the car had kicked in. Michael had watched her crunching the (multiple) tablets in broody silence. She'd expected a caustic remark about it, but nothing. Since then, the tension in the air had risen with every swish of the wheels on pavement, until by the time he finally spoke she was so on edge that she was sitting bolt upright in the driver's seat and scowling at the beat-up red pickup in front of them. Michael slouched in the bucket seat beside her, his tall, broad-shouldered frame looking too big for the compact car. Those black eyes glinted dangerously as they fixed on her: a sideways glance at his face was enough to persuade her that she'd do better to focus her attention on the road if she wanted to keep her own cool. He looked like a fight waiting to happen, and she wasn't about to play into that. Couples quarreled, but she and her resident ghost were emphatically *not* a couple. After his *You're crazy in love with me* crack, she wanted to underline that fact to herself as well as to him. Tony was somewhere behind them, in the car he'd driven to the prison. They'd arranged to meet at her house, and he would drive her from there to Lonesome Pine Airport, where the team's private plane waited.

"Kaminsky needs me. Her sister's missing. I can't leave her in the lurch." That was the short answer, simple and quick and true. By leaving it at that, Charlie felt that she was taking the high road.

"Oh, yes you can."

"I'm not going to."

"I thought we decided that you were

137

gonna tell Dudley no."

"You may have decided that. I didn't." In the interests of not escalating the "discussion," instead of focusing the glare she felt coming on on its rightful target, she frowned out the window at the gang of orange-jumpsuit-wearing inmates mowing the grass around the outside of the prison under the supervision of a quartet of armed guards. The single road that curled down the mountain had quite a bit of traffic on it at the moment as the prison disgorged its visitors and the guards changed shifts: the Ridge's version of rush hour. She was still behind the red pickup, and would be until they reached town. The thought that the hunter might be circling in the sky overhead like an invisible version of the Wicked Witch in *The Wizard of Oz* sent a prickle of unease over her skin. The need to get as far away from the prison as fast as possible had her nerves jumping. Speeding away from the epicenter of danger wasn't going to happen, however. She was stuck going thirty-five miles an hour, and unless a whole line of traffic got blasted out of her way, nothing was going to change. Her hands tightened on the wheel. She did not curse, not even under her breath.

"That's a load of crap." Michael's fingers

tightened around the edge of the console between the seats. Slanting sunlight bathed his powerful forearm in golden light: the muscles of his upper arm looked hard and sleek below the sleeve of his T-shirt. His arm, she was glad to see, had none of the grayish tinge that she found so worrying when she looked at his face. Not that she was going to let him see her worrying about him again anytime soon. "This Vegas trip is a cluster-fuck waiting to happen, and you know it as well as I do. When we get home, you need to tell Dudley that you changed your mind and can't go."

"No," Charlie said, flicking Michael a cool but by no means nasty sideways look. Come to think of it, she liked that word *no* a whole lot. It was short and sweet, and got the job done.

His lips compressed. "You were hearing those creepy voices of yours back there, weren't you? In the hall right before that psycho freak charged you?"

It was clear from his expression that he already knew the answer.

"So what if I was?" she countered.

"In sports, injured players lay out until they're healed. Consider yourself an injured player, and sit this one out."

"This isn't sports, and I'm not injured.

And Kaminsky needs me."

"You're hearing fucking voices in your head, and they're causing you to spaz out. If that isn't injured, I don't know what is. To say nothing of the fact that a damned murderous lunatic bit you today, and you're chowing down on Tums by the handful because being attacked by his ghost made you want to puke."

He knew way too much about her. "So what am I supposed to do, lock myself in my house until I'm all better?"

"Yes." His answer was uncompromising.

"No." So was hers.

"Damn it, we're not going to Vegas."

"I'm surprised you're not chomping at the bit to go to Las Vegas. They have casinos there, remember? Bright lights, big city! Lots of things to do. Aren't you the one who likes going to bars, hanging out with strippers and hookers, and all that?"

"Being dead kind of takes the fun out of that stuff. Particularly the hookers."

"Oh, ha, ha."

"Look, babe: do us both a favor and forget Vegas."

"You know what? You're a big boy. You can stay home if you want."

"Funny. Especially when we both know you won't leave me."

"Watch me."

"You trying to convince yourself or me?"

"I don't have to convince you. All I have to do is get on that plane."

"What happens next time you hear the voices and spaz out around somebody who wants to hurt you — like, say, I don't know, a serial killer?"

"I'll deal with it," she snapped. "Anyway, the voices are bound to go away at some point."

"Let's just hope it's not after you're dead."

"Hey, Casper, anybody ever tell you that you have a tendency to be controlling?" Charlie gave up entirely on the failing attempt at keeping her cool and glared at him. "It's a little alarming — or at least it would be if I felt I had to listen to you. Luckily, I don't. I do what I want."

"So I'm controlling, huh? You going all shrinky on me now, Doc?"

"I'm pretty sure *shrinky*'s not a word."

"You should know. You're the one with all them fancy degrees." The smile he gave her was tigerish. "Shame they don't come with common sense."

"Are you really going to talk to *me* about common sense?" She let loose a derisive laugh. "If you'd had the *common sense* to keep your pants zipped once in a while, you

141

probably wouldn't have been arrested for being a serial killer, and you wouldn't have ended up on death row."

"Yeah, well, if *you'd* had the common sense to stay away from serial killers, you wouldn't have been messing with a guy on death row the day I got killed, and you and I wouldn't be having this conversation now." The tiniest pause. "Anyway, what's it to you whether or not I keep — kept — my pants zipped?"

"Not a thing in the world, believe me."

"Don't worry, babe: you got nothing to be jealous of. I'm all yours."

Charlie practically sputtered. "Like that's a good thing?" By the skin of her teeth she managed to swallow the angry addendum *you man-whore* before it left her lips and then did her best to dial the whole thing back by taking a deep breath before continuing. "I'm not going to argue with you. I've decided to go to Las Vegas and help Kaminsky find her sister. You can come or not. End of story."

"You wish." His tone made it quite clear that as far as he was concerned the conversation was by no means over. "I thought we decided that serial killers are dangerous. Because, see, a couple of them have tried real hard to kill you already and one actually succeeded. Remember that? Remember dying? I was there: you didn't like it."

She actually didn't remember very much about it. And what little she did remember she tried not to: an explosion of emotions all wrapped up in darkness.

"That was one time."

He hooted. "Well, golly gee, you got me there! The thing is, though, one time's all most of us get. I vote you cut your losses, and thank your lucky stars you got another chance."

Maybe he had a point, but there was a bigger picture. As the Camry chugged around one more S-curve in a long series of them, she deliberately let her gaze linger on the spectacular reds and golds of the autumn foliage out the window as mountain after tree-covered mountain fell away into the distance. The beauty of the Blue Ridge at this time of the year was incomparable. Just looking at it soothed her.

"You know, you should be eager to go," she pointed out reasonably. "I want to help Kaminsky save her sister and bring a monster to justice if I can. I also want to get you as far away from that hunter as it's possible to get. That's the part *you* should keep in mind."

His brows snapped together. "Fuck that.

You're not putting yourself at risk for me."

"Let's see: earlier today I threw a horse-shoe at a ten-foot-tall scary monster. I think that means I already did." Her gaze flicked over him. "By the way, I haven't heard a *thank you* yet."

"Thank you."

"You're welcome."

They pulled up in front of the traffic light at the base of the mountain. The small mining town of Big Stone Gap sparkled in the golden light of the late afternoon sun. It was a Tuesday, near suppertime. Most folks were either at home or heading there, which meant there were more cars on the roads in town, too. Glancing in her rearview mirror, Charlie saw no sign of Tony in the cars lined up behind her. But he was back there somewhere, and he knew his way to her house. He'd be there soon enough: Tony was as reliable as the sunset. And that, she told herself, was one more very positive attribute to add to his side of the scale.

Not that she was comparing him with anybody or anything.

"Besides," Michael said as she pulled through the intersection and accelerated. "How do we know the hunter won't show up in Vegas? Or anywhere?"

That got her attention. She could feel a

fresh burst of agitation bubbling through her veins. "Why would it? It's never come after you before."

"Maybe I just now got on its radar. Maybe it only just now figured out I escaped Spookville."

"Oh, God." Luckily, the way home was imprinted in her brain, because she drove there, past the drugstore and the grocery and the little church on the corner where Michael was buried, without even being aware of any of it while she tried to get her mind around the implications of that. "I don't think it will. I don't think it can. Hunters are not rampaging around this plane on a regular basis, or I would have known about them long before I got mixed up with you," was the conclusion she finally came to. "That one coming through today was an anomaly. It had to be."

"Calling something a big word don't make it true." She could feel his eyes on her profile. "We don't know shit about what a hunter can do. I'm thinking this one might have killed that scumbag who bit you."

"Spivey?" Charlie's breath caught.

He shrugged. "*Something* killed him. He was just fine when he was grabbing you. And if you could see him after he died, then he suffered a violent death."

She'd registered the violent death thing, too, about the time she'd seen Spivey's shade rushing at her, and had pushed it into her mental file labeled *stuff to think about later.* "You're right, he had to have died violently, but I don't think the hunter did it. It didn't kill *me.* I never felt like it could. When it flung me away — it felt more like I hit its energy field or something than it actually attacked me."

"Babe, you're not its natural prey. In fact, you're probably about as far from its natural prey as it's possible to get."

"So what do you think is its natural prey?"

"Evil. I think it can smell evil like a bloodhound tracking a scent."

Which, given his history with hunters, meant that he considered himself part of what he called their natural prey: in a word, evil.

"*You're* not evil." She hadn't meant to say it aloud, especially with such conviction. Because she had, she scowled at him.

He smiled at her, a slow-dawning smile that did embarrassing things to places she refused to think about. "You know what? I think that's just about the nicest thing you've ever said to me. When I wasn't driving you out of your mind in bed, that is."

"You are such a *jackass,*" she snapped,

knowing that her face was pinkening from the unwelcome (blistering hot) memories that conjured up, which, infuriatingly, only made his smile widen. To change the subject, she said, "If we stay here, I have to go to work. At the prison. Tomorrow. Because, you know, I have bills to pay if I want to have a house to live in and food and all that. And in my opinion going back to the prison is just too dangerous right now. If the hunter's lurking around anywhere, that's where it will be." She glanced at him, remembered the adage about flies and honey, and in the interests of not having to put up with having him in a pissy mood all the way to Las Vegas, decided to try it. Also, although she hadn't liked the direction the conversation had subsequently taken, her assertion that she didn't think he was evil had definitely improved his mood. Conclusion: buttering him up worked.

"I don't want anything to happen to you," she said, and had to quell the urge to bat her eyelashes at him.

"I appreciate the thought, buttercup, but in case you missed it, something already did: I'm dead." His voice was dry.

She looked impatient. "You know what I mean."

"Yeah, I do. And just for the record, you're

not sweet-talking me into going to Vegas."

She bristled. "I wasn't trying to *sweet-talk* you."

"No? Well, then, if what you're trying to do in some typical roundabout chick way is tell me you're crazy in love with me, that's a whole different conversation." He folded his arms over his chest. "I'm waiting. Go ahead."

"I am not trying to tell you —" She broke off. So much for honey: this particular aggravating fly deserved to be whacked over the head. "You know damned well that's not what I meant."

He smiled. After the first unwary glance made her heart skip a beat, she refused to look, choosing to concentrate on getting them where they were going instead.

Having reached the two-story white clapboard farmhouse on the neat little street that was her home, she pulled the car into the detached garage and parked. She and Michael got out at the same time and headed inside, through the back gate because that way was closer. A pair of the neighbor's prize hens was in her backyard, rooting around among the sunflowers. She looked for Pumpkin, her other neighbor's orange tabby, which spent much of his time stalking the hens, but didn't see him. Which was just as well: she didn't have time to deal with animal wars at the moment.

They went in through the kitchen.

"You know, you don't have to go in to work tomorrow. You could take some vacation days, like you should've in the first place. Or call in sick," Michael said as he trailed her into the front hall. Because the day was heading on toward twilight, the house was shadowy inside, but she didn't bother to turn on any lights as she headed for her second-floor bedroom, where she meant to pack a bag as quickly as she could, and thus hopefully be ready to go before Tony even arrived. "We could still find a beach, and you could still rock that bikini. The one that you're so repressed, and such a damned workaholic, you don't even own."

She narrowed her eyes at him over her shoulder as she climbed the stairs. "I am not repressed" — well, maybe she was, a little — "and I am not a workaholic" — maybe she was a little bit of that, too, not that it was a bad thing — "and we've been over this."

He was right behind her. "So let's go over it one more time. Why the hell would you even think of putting yourself in danger again, especially when you're not operating at one hundred percent capacity?"

"Because I'm an expert at what I do. And because Kaminsky needs my expertise enough to have asked for it," Charlie growled as she reached the landing and marched into her bedroom. "Anyway, I can stay out of the field and concentrate on profiling and analysis and be perfectly safe." It was a large room, serene, with white walls and a dark hardwood floor and two long windows that looked out over her backyard and the wooded mountain rising into the clouds beyond it. Between the windows was an ornate fireplace with a painting of a waterfall above it. Her big brass bed with its spotless white covers took pride of place in the center of the room: just looking at it made her body quicken. Which reaction was both ridiculous and infuriating: she'd owned that bed for months now, and she'd had steamy, mind-blowing sex in it precisely once. And yes, that sex had been with Michael, when she'd found herself on the same side of the life/death divide as he was one stormy night not long after he'd walked into her life. Probably the sex had been a mistake — no, it definitely had been a mistake — but she couldn't regret it. Just like she couldn't regret repeating the error in a hotel room in Charlotte right before she'd wound up in the hospital. Truth was, the sex had been phenomenal. The problem was the source.

As a result of what she could only consider some weird chemical alchemy, Michael could make her burn hotter than any other man she had ever met. The problem lay in what he was: a ghost. In the living world, in her experience, ghosts had short shelf lives.

In other words, no long-term potential there. They were two different species now: the living and the dead. They had as much chance of being together as a dog and a cat.

He stopped to lean a broad shoulder against the door frame and watch as she dropped her purse on the dresser, opened the closet, dragged a suitcase out, plopped it open on that way-too-disturbing bed, then headed back to her dresser to start retrieving clothes.

Michael snorted. "I'll believe that when I see it."

She shot him an unfriendly look. "Believe whatever you like."

"Charlie, baby, you ever consider that because your mom's an alcoholic, and she wasn't willing or able to be the mother she should have been, and you pretty much had to take care of *her*, you've been trying to take care of everybody around you for most of your life?" The fact that his voice was now incredibly gentle should have robbed his words of any sting. It didn't: each one flicked her on the raw. Her lips parted in shock as they hit. "You've even been doing your best to take care of *me,* which is just about as sweet as it is stupid. Maybe you want to start thinking about taking care of yourself."

Straightening with a neatly folded pile of undergarments in her hands, she slewed around to glare at him as she honed in on the part of that speech that really struck a nerve. A few times, when she'd been feeling particularly vulnerable in the hospital and elsewhere, she'd told him little bits and pieces about her background. She'd definitely mentioned her mother, but she'd never told him *that* about her. That her mother was an alcoholic — she never talked about it to anyone.

Loyalty ran deep. Deeper even than the pain her mother's drinking had caused.

"I never said my mother was an alcoholic." Her voice was sharp. Stepping over to the bed, she deposited the underwear in the suitcase and turned back to glare at him all over again.

"I'm good at reading between the lines." He wasn't smiling. "You ain't the first shrink I've ever seen, you know. Since I got arrested, they've had shrinks coming at me every time I turned around. I heard about adult children of alcoholics until I wanted to put my fist through a wall. That my damned bastard of a stepfather was a drunk was supposed to be a mitigating factor for me being a serial killer. My defense lawyers used it at my sentencing, to try to get me life in prison. Didn't work out, but I learned a lot."

"My mother is none of your business!" Shoulders rigid with anger, she returned to the dresser to jerk open another drawer and extract her running gear.

"Maybe not, but I think she's the reason behind this savior complex you've got going on, and that *is* my business. It's liable to get you killed."

She turned from depositing her running gear in the suitcase to march toward the closet, glaring at him some more on the way. "You know what? When you get your medical degree, I'll consider your opinion. Until then, I have to tell you that you're full of shit."

"I'm trying to look out for you here."

Heading back toward the suitcase with her arms full of clothes, she gave an angry snort and shot bullets at him with her eyes. "You're trying to manipulate me, you mean.

To get what you want, which is to not go to Las Vegas."

"Hey, you tried sweet-talking me." His voice was still mild. He was looking at her with the barest suggestion of a smile, which she found infuriating. Actually, she found *him* infuriating. Times ten. "I'd say that makes us even."

"I'm not talking to you about this anymore." Dropping the clothes in the suitcase — she was so mad she didn't even bother to fold them — she turned her back on him and stalked toward the bathroom. It was en suite, with the door on the same wall as the bed, all white tiles with a big, claw-foot tub and separate shower. Once inside it, she flipped on the light, caught a quick glimpse of herself in the mirror — her hair had fallen from its loose knot to hang in disordered chestnut waves around her shoulders and she hadn't even noticed; her lipstick was gone; and her eyes blazed as deeply blue as her shirt — yanked open the medicine cabinet, and started pulling out the toiletries she was going to need.

"Charlie." He was there in the bathroom doorway, looking at her. She was actually surprised it had taken him so long to get there. "Do us both a favor: forget Vegas."

She shot him a sizzling look through the

mirror — which, damn it, was way less effective than it should have been because, since he was a ghost, she couldn't actually *see* him in the mirror. Turning around, she gripped the edges of the sink behind her with both hands as she glared at him. In the confined space of the bathroom, his tall, muscular form seemed to take up way more than its fair share of space.

"What part of *I'm not talking to you about this anymore* did you miss?"

"The part where you still think we're going to Vegas."

She was usually pretty even-tempered, really she was. Calm and controlled in the face of all kinds of extreme situations, that was her. But now she was mad.

The look she gave him could have lasered through a wall. "The good news for me is that you don't get to make this decision. I do. You're attached to me, not the other way around. And I'm going to Las Vegas. You can do what you want, except, oh, wait, if you get more than fifty feet away from me, you'll be sucked into Spookville and the scary monsters will get you. So I guess that means you're going to Las Vegas, too."

His lips thinned. Those disturbingly black eyes raked her. "So you're going to put your life at risk just to prove you can?"

"It's my life. I can if I want to."

"Babe, you need a keeper."

"I suppose you think that should be you?"

"At least I'm not as irrational as a teenage girl lately."

"You," she said through her teeth, "are a sexist jerk."

His lips thinned. "Yeah, well, I'd rather be a sexist jerk than a brainiac with her head up her ass."

"A *what*?"

"You heard me."

Charlie clamped her lips together. She fumed. She seethed. She would have told him to drop dead, except, guess what, he already was. Telling him to go to hell was a waste of breath, too. She could already hear his reply: *been there, done that.* Complete with accompanying smirk.

She was just opening her mouth to verbally lay him out with none of the above when he folded his arms over his chest. Something about the movement, something about all those brawny flexing muscles and corded, rippling sinews caught her eye. She looked — and her heart stopped.

"Oh, my God," she said in a voice that didn't even sound like hers. Her eyes collided with the disconcerting jet black of his. *"Take off your shirt."*

CHAPTER NINE

"I know you want me bad." Michael lifted his eyebrows at her mockingly. "But are you really gonna jump me in the bathroom?"

Ordinarily, given how she'd been feeling about him until just about half a heartbeat previously, the drawling insolence of that would have been the flame to her already smoldering dynamite. But under the circumstances she didn't even care. Shoving away from the sink, she all but leaped toward him.

"Look at your arm." She always forgot how tall he was until she was standing right in front of him. The top of her head didn't reach much higher than his shoulders. She glanced up, met his eyes. The soullessness of those newly black eyes suddenly held a terrifying significance for her. Her heart was beating again, in hard, fast strokes like she'd been running for miles.

He looked down at his arm, and she followed his gaze.

His left arm, from the hard muscle bulging out beneath the edge of his sleeve to below his elbow, was a deep charcoal gray. More gray ran in streaks down his forearm. If the streaks had been red instead of gray, she would have immediately suspected blood poisoning.

"Jesus," Michael said.

"Take off your shirt." This time, although it shivered with urgency, her voice was scarcely louder than a whisper.

He met her eyes without saying anything. Then he reached down, grabbed the hem of his shirt, and pulled it over his head. The white tee dropped to the floor.

"Oh," she breathed on a distressed note as she looked at him, the word so quiet as to be barely audible. His broad shoulders, heavy with muscle, were where her gaze rested first. A sliver of the green and black cobra tattoo that adorned his right biceps caught her attention. Then her focus shifted to his chest, his beautiful, wide, muscular chest, which she knew from personal experience was sleek and firm to the touch. It was still as ripped as ever, he was still every bit the eye candy he'd always been — except for the area just below his left shoulder. A mark in the shape of a large, jagged C appeared to have been seared into his flesh. It was deep and black, with charred-looking edges. Above it, radiating across the edge of his shoulder and down the top of his left arm, the skin was blackish and burnt-looking. From that point to just past his elbow the color faded gradually to a charcoal gray; the shade, she thought, of overdone meat.

Streaks of the same color extended down his forearm almost to his wrist. She had looked at his arm in the prison as well as in the car on the way home: they'd been casual glances, directed at him as a whole and not at his arm in particular, but if any of the visible flesh had been gray she was sure she would have noticed. The discoloration was spreading: if nothing was done, pretty soon his whole arm would be the same horrible, charred blackish-gray as the area around the injury. Then what? How far could it/ would it spread?

Just thinking about that made her go cold all over.

"Fuck," Michael said. As she flicked a look at his handsome, chiseled face Charlie saw that he was still slightly ashen, with shadows beneath his eyes and a drawn look that was doubly frightening now that she had seen his chest and arm. He was staring at the injury with obvious dismay.

"Does it hurt?" she asked in a constricted voice.

He shook his head.

What she did next came from a place of pure instinct: forgetting what he was, she reached out to gently touch his bare chest, the uninjured part just beside the burnt-looking C. Part of the reason was to check for unnatural heat in what appeared to be firm, tanned skin. The other part of the reason was, well, because he was hurt and she wanted to comfort him. Of course the second her fingers made contact with him, they passed right through. At the now-familiar electric tingle, she drew back a little, then carefully repositioned her hand so that it lay flat against the sleek muscle. The smooth warmth of his hard flesh beneath her hand — that wasn't real: she knew perfectly well that she could only see rather than feel him, because he had no more substance than air. This time the electric tingle was more of a gentle pulsing against the palm of her hand. She'd gotten used to the sensation, she thought: it no longer felt alien.

It felt like Michael.

His hand closed around her wrist as though he would hold hers in place against him; she saw the long, strong fingers wrapping around her slender bones, but that, too, she only felt as a kind of pulsing.

His flesh beneath her hand was no more real than a mirage, an illusion with no physicality behind it to back it up, and she knew it. But for all that, the sensation of touching him was so vivid that she could almost feel the hard resilience of his muscles, the smooth texture of his skin. Deep inside, her body tightened and began to quake.

"Charlie." His voice was low and husky. Breathless, she looked up at him.

For a moment their eyes met. The fathomless black of his made no difference to the wordless exchange between them: it was a moment charged with sensuality. But there was also a sense of profound connection, a depth of feeling, an unspoken acknowledgment: *You matter to me.*

He bent his head and, still holding her hand against his chest, touched his lips to her mouth.

Her lips parted. Her heart lurched. Her body went up in flames.

She closed her eyes as her bones turned to water. The merest whisper of heat fanned her lips. She felt it clear down to her toes.

She wanted to kiss him so badly that she

felt like she would die if she didn't.

It was impossible. Impossible to press her lips to his and slide her tongue inside his mouth and kiss him like she wanted to. Impossible to wrap her arms around his neck and mold her body to his and let the fire that was building between them rage in any kind of a natural way. And that would be because, no matter how solid he looked to her, there was nothing physical of him there.

He was a ghost; he did not belong in her world.

That knowledge was what gave her the strength to open her eyes.

He was still kissing her. He was watching her at the same time, studying her face as his lips moved carefully, gently on hers, and as she looked into the stygian depths of his eyes she was reminded, abruptly, of the harsh reality of the situation they were in.

There was no future for them. She was a fool to have allowed this thing between them to go as far as it had.

Too late to do anything about that, but she didn't have to compound the error by totally losing her too-stupid-to-live heart to him.

Pulling her mouth away from his, taking a step back, she took a deep breath and let the hand he'd been holding drop to her side. There was no resistance. Why? Because as strong and powerful as he looked, he couldn't have kept his hold on her wrist if he'd tried.

His eyes slid over her face. "Charlie . . ."

His voice was husky.

I can't let this happen. She beat back the sense of near panic that accompanied the thought of how close she was to falling head-over-brain-dead-heels in love with him by focusing ruthlessly on the disaster at hand.

"That wound on your chest," she said, very calm. "The hunter did that to you, didn't it?"

"Yep."

From the brevity of his response, she knew that he, too, was still experiencing emotional fallout from that almost kiss.

"When?" She was trying to calculate how long it had taken the discoloration to spread to its present degree.

"In your office."

Like her, he was pulling back, putting emotional space between them. She could feel it in the change in the atmosphere, see it in the tightening of his face, hear it in his voice.

"What did it do?" Thinking of the shape

of the injury, she had a sudden, dreadful thought. "Did it bite you, or . . . ?"

"Dug its claws into me. For a minute there, I thought it was going to rip out my heart." He smiled faintly at her, and she knew that whatever heartburnings he'd been experiencing — always assuming that his emotions bore any similarity to her own — had been put behind him. "Then you went all Van Helsing on it."

"You said you thought its claws might hold poison."

"As bad as I felt both times it got hold of me? Only thing that makes sense."

Charlie felt a knot forming in her chest as she faced what she feared was the hideous truth. "The evil spirits that possessed Creason and the trustee — you said they were a burnt-looking gray."

"Yeah." From the rueful tone of that, she realized that he'd made the same connection she had.

"They were spirits who wound up in Spookville just like you." She could hardly get the words out. Suddenly she felt so cold inside that it was a wonder she wasn't shivering. "The hunter caught them. That's what it does. Turns them into those *things*."

Her eyes clung to his, practically begging him to point out where her reasoning had gone wrong. As black as his eyes were, she couldn't read anything, any emotion, in them at all. But his mouth was grim. It told her all she needed to know.

"Given this," he glanced down at his arm, "that'd be my guess."

"If we can't stop it, that's what's going to happen to you." Horror shook her voice.

Even in this moment of extremis, he gave her another one of those faint smiles. This one struck at her heart. "Time to break out the woo-woo, Doc."

"I don't know anything that'll fix this." Her voice sounded raw to her own ears. *Get a grip,* she told herself sternly. Wallowing in terror was useless. There had to be a way to save him. Determination straightened her spine, squared her shoulders. "Get out of my way. I'm going to call Tam."

Tam being Tamsyn Green, who, besides being her good friend, was also a psychic medium and the New Orleans–bred daughter of a notorious voodoo practitioner. Unlike Charlie, whose interaction with the dead was involuntary, unwelcome, and thankfully somewhat limited, Tam embraced her abilities with enthusiasm: she made her living from it, and was currently based in California giving readings to movie stars. Having been brought up in a household where the occult was as unremarkable as table salt, Tam was possessed of vast knowledge about the things that go bump in the night. Before the advent of Michael into her life, Charlie had rarely needed to call on her for help. Since Michael's arrival, she'd spoken to Tam on the phone more often than she had to anyone else in years.

"The voodoo priestess?" Sounding less than enthused, Michael followed her as she rushed past him. He was still bare-chested; he'd picked up his shirt and it dangled from his hand. Ordinarily she would have enjoyed the view, but under the circumstances all her eyes could focus on was that horrible, spreading gray. "Do we really need to bring her into this?"

Charlie was already at the dresser snatching her phone out of her purse. Michael was, she knew, remembering the other times Tam had intervened on his behalf. Both times had ended up causing him considerable pain — but Tam's prescriptions had worked. She threw a look over her shoulder at him even as she found Tam's name in her list of contacts and hit the call button.

"Depends on how you feel about turning into one of those things," she answered. As the phone rang once, twice, she tried to calculate the time in California: she was too on edge to do much in the way of math, but bottom line was that Tam should be up and about by now.

"Cherie! I was just thinking about you," Tam greeted her cheerfully. Tam was the most upbeat person Charlie knew, and she felt better just hearing her voice. "What's going on?"

Charlie told her. Everything.

"Are we talking about that same ghost you've been helping to stay earthbound? The one from the Dark Place?" Tam's disapproval oozed through the phone. "Tell me you've let him return to where he belongs by now."

Having put his shirt back on, Michael was leaning a shoulder against the wall beside the dresser and looking dour, and Charlie realized that he could hear both sides of the conversation. Even with his shirt on, he was a distraction she didn't need. She turned her back on him.

"Can you help us?" Charlie asked, disregarding both Tam's questions and disapproval. Anyway, responding wasn't necessary: she knew Tam already knew the answers.

"*Us?*" Tam's voice went up an octave. "You and he, *us*? That isn't good, cherie."

"Tam . . ."

"Listen to me," Tam said forcefully. "First, you need to understand that you are messing with the laws of the universe. That is just wrong. Second, those evil spirits you say came out of the Dark Place?" That, Charlie remembered, was what Tam called Spookville. "They are souls who were in the process of being terminated: that's why they were all gray and burnt-looking. A little longer, and they'll turn to ash and *poof* out of existence. And your ghost? If he's turning gray, he's in the process of being terminated, too. The same thing will happen to him: *poof* and he will be no more. And if he's from the Dark Place, you need to let it happen. *There is a reason.*"

"Oh, no," Charlie said faintly, turning to look at Michael. He'd straightened away from the wall and was looking grim. She spoke to Tam, "There has to be a way to stop it. Tam, please."

"To help you wouldn't be doing you a favor, Charlie."

Charlie realized how serious Tam was by her use of her name: Tam almost never called her Charlie. She also realized that Tam knew of something that would help: otherwise she would have said she knew of nothing that could be done.

"Do you remember when you brought

that girl to me whose arm had been sliced open in a voodoo ritual of your mother's?" Charlie's voice was fierce. "Do you remember the kid with the high fever that you were afraid to take to the hospital because you thought your mother caused it? I treated both of them for you. Remember that?"

"Yes." Tam's reply was grudging.

"I'm asking for that kind of favor from you now. Tam, please."

"It's a mistake," Tam warned.

"I don't care."

"What can be done must be done within twelve hours. How long ago did the *abaissement* begin?"

Charlie roughly translated *abaissement* to mean decrease or melting away, and felt her chest tighten.

"About two hours ago."

"You are at home? I don't think I can reach you in time. I must go to the airport, catch a flight —"

"I'm getting ready to leave for Las Vegas," Charlie broke in. The ringing of the doorbell made her jump: Tony had arrived. Michael, who'd been listening intently to the conversation, grimaced. "I should be there by midnight or a little later." That gave them a window of only about two and a half hours. "Tam —"

169

"I can meet you there." Tam's tone was faintly grudging. "For me, it's about a four and a half hour drive. Where are you staying?"

"I don't know. I'll text you on the way," she said, mindful of Tony at the door. "Tam. Thank you."

"Don't thank me. I'm doing you a disservice, not a favor."

"Thank you anyway."

"You're welcome. Remember, though, if we get past the twelve-hour window, nothing can be done."

With another quick word of farewell, Charlie disconnected and looked at Michael.

"You heard." It wasn't a question.

"Yeah." His tone was sour. "What can I say? Viva Las Vegas."

CHAPTER TEN

The doorbell peeled again as Charlie ran for the bathroom. Gathering up her toiletries, she hurried back to her suitcase, crammed them inside it, and zipped the whole thing up, not without considerable difficulty because she'd thrown everything in haphazardly and the small suitcase was overstuffed as a result. The big, muscular guy who just stood there and watched as she wrestled with the zipper then flung her hot mess of a purse over one arm before lugging the suitcase down the stairs was worse than useless, as she told him.

She didn't get so much as a grimace in reply.

By the time Charlie opened the front door, Tony was already knocking on it and she was hot, flustered, and so worried about the broody ghost behind her that she had barely a glance to spare for the handsome dark-haired man on her doorstep.

"Hey," Tony said, and smiled at her. God, it was an attractive smile. The sad thing about it was that, right at the moment anyway, it left her cold.

"I'm ready." Instead of inviting Tony in, she stepped out onto the small front porch, dragging her suitcase behind her. What with everything, she didn't want to waste a single minute. "Sorry I took so long opening the door."

He was looking at her a little strangely. Probably, she thought, she was not giving off the most together of vibes. Her emotions were in a tangle, just like her hair, which she had not yet taken the time to brush. With a quick gesture, she tossed it back, then tucked it behind her ears.

"I thought the bell might be broken."

"No," she replied.

Tony took her suitcase from her and put it in the trunk while she got into the front passenger seat of the big black Lincoln, a rental. Her shoulders were tense as she glanced quickly around for any sign of the hunter, but there was nothing and she shoved the ongoing threat to the back of her mind. The possibility of another attack had just been thrust into also-ran status in the *Terrible Things That Could Happen* sweepstakes. For all kinds of reasons, she was supremely aware of Michael's silent presence in the backseat as Tony got behind the wheel and they headed toward the airport.

"How are you feeling?" Tony asked after a moment. It was still Indian summer and there was about an hour to go until full dark, but dusk was starting to fall and the few vehicles they passed had their headlights on. The bright beams periodically sliced through the interior of the car, illuminating Tony's classic profile. The road was narrow and curvy, but he drove as competently as he seemed to do everything else.

"I'm recovered," Charlie replied, and forced a smile. "No more headache."

She was slewed a little sideways in her seat, the better to throw occasional glances back at Michael, who was swathed in shadows and uncharacteristically silent. It was too dark to allow her to read his expression, or assess the state of his injured arm, but fear for him was making it hard for her to concentrate on anything else. She was supremely conscious of the passage of time. It was hard not to count each swish of the tires. *Hurry, hurry, hurry,* was the refrain that kept running through her head. It was all she could do not to say it aloud.

"Sure?"

She could see the gleam of Tony's eyes as he glanced at her through the growing darkness. Something in his tone made her look at him more closely. The slash of yet another set of oncoming headlights showed her that he was frowning at her. Thoughtfully.

"Yes," she replied.

"Can I ask you something?"

"Yes." Her tone was cautious. "Of course."

"How did you know that Walter Spivey was the name of the fatality in the infirmary? No one told you."

Charlie had a sudden, vivid memory of herself in the elevator asking Pugh, *What killed Walter Spivey?* Replaying the preceding events in her mind, she saw it: there was no way she could have known the dead man's identity by any ordinary means.

Well, she'd always known that Tony was quick.

She hesitated only briefly. It occurred to her to lie, telling him that she had deduced as much because it was Spivey who had bitten her and he'd been displaying distressing symptoms as he was dragged off to the infirmary, *blah blah blah.* But if she was to have any chance of forming a real, true relationship with Tony, some honesty was called for. He already knew that she could communicate with the dead. It was time to expand on that a little.

"I saw him," she said, and waited.

"You *saw* him?" Tony threw a startled glance at her. "This would be — after he was dead? Like, his ghost?"

"Yes." Charlie looked at him steadily.

It didn't take him long to make the connection. "In the hall, when you got sick."

"Yes."

Tony drew an audible breath. In it, she could hear all kinds of mental gears shifting. "Obviously he didn't tell you what killed him or you wouldn't have asked Pugh."

"No," Charlie agreed. "He just screamed and lunged at me. Then he vanished. I have no idea what killed him. I only know that if I saw him he died violently, because I can only see the recently, violently dead."

"Okay." Tony didn't draw the word out skeptically. In fact, he sounded almost matter-of-fact, like he wasn't having any trouble processing what she was telling him, like he took her at her word. After a moment he glanced at her again. "The salt on the floor — it wasn't about ants, was it?"

"No."

"It was about ghosts?"

Actually, one ghost in particular. But *that* she wasn't going to tell him. "Yes."

There was a pause. "You're an interesting woman, Charlie Stone."

That was so unexpected that her face relaxed a little, into what almost felt like a smile. "That's certainly one way of looking at it."

"Hey, your abilities have added a lot to our last two investigations. I'm not one to look a gift horse in the mouth."

This time she really did smile at him. "You're one of the few."

"You know you can tell me anything, right?" His tone was unexpectedly earnest.

Really? Like there's a dead guy in the backseat with whom I may or may not be, to quote him, crazy in love, who's currently atrophying from some supernatural poison injected into him by a giant monster from the bad section of the Great Beyond and who, if we don't get to Las Vegas in time and if the efforts of the psychic daughter of a voodoo priestess who is meeting us there don't work, will abruptly cease to exist, thus very possibly shattering my heart into a million pieces?

She didn't even have to think about it: *Yeah. No.*

"I'll keep that in mind," she said, and managed another smile.

They had reached the airport by then, and Tony drove up to the hangar that handled the private planes. The team's Citation 500 gleamed white through the encroaching darkness as Tony parked near it. The small windows in the streamlined fuselage gleamed with light. The steps were already down.

Tony cut the lights and turned off the engine but made no move to get out. Instead he turned in his seat to look at her.

"You know, when I first asked you to come with me, I got the impression that you were going to say no."

"I probably was. I wasn't feeling too excited about anything to do with serial killers at that particular moment." She held up her bandaged hand to illustrate. "One or two bad experiences too many."

His face changed. "Last time — what happened — I feel like I let you down." His voice had gone lower and deeper. He looked at her steadily.

She knew what he was talking about: her near drowning. He'd already apologized in the hospital at least a dozen times, but she supposed that for a man like him, responsible and conscientious, being Special Agent in Charge of the team meant taking the weight of whatever happened on his shoulders.

"It wasn't your fault." She'd said that to

him about a dozen times, too.

"It happened on my watch." His expression was grim as he looked at her through the deepening gloom. "I just want you to know, it won't happen again."

"Good," Charlie responded briskly as her eyes found the dashboard clock: 6:51 p.m. Enough with the chitchat. They needed to get on the plane, and the plane needed to get in the air. Pronto.

Her response surprised a laugh from Tony.

"*Really* interesting," he said. "Fascinating, in fact."

Then to Charlie's surprise, he slid a hand around the side of her neck, leaned over, and kissed her.

It was quick, but extremely thorough. Plenty expert. Lots of tongue.

If it hadn't been for the alarmingly silent ghost undoubtedly watching from the backseat, and the tick of passing seconds in her brain, she probably really could have gotten into it.

As it was, she didn't.

"Welcome back to the team, Dr. Stone," Tony said huskily, smiling at her as he lifted his head. If he noticed anything lacking in her response, she couldn't tell.

Charlie's answering smile was weak, and she cast a wary eye at the large, shadow-shrouded, stone-still figure in the backseat. Under the circumstances, his silence was downright unnerving. Also under the circumstances, making out in the car with Tony just wasn't going to happen.

Tony made a move as though he meant to kiss her again. She reached for the door handle.

"We should go," she said firmly, and opened the door. The smell of jet fuel wafted her way, carried on the quickening autumn breeze. It was too cold now to be without a jacket, but she'd forgotten to grab hers on the way out of her house and as she stepped onto the tarmac she folded her arms over her chest in defense against the rising chill.

Tony got out at the same time she did, and went around to the trunk to retrieve her things. Michael stepped out of the car, too. When he did it, it didn't require opening a door. He slid through the metal to stand beside her.

She shot him an anxious look. It was too dark to allow her to read his face, or even monitor the progress of discoloration along his arm. The deepening twilight and the purr of the plane's engine were enough to give them privacy.

"So say something already," she hissed,

with a wary eye on the open trunk. "You're worrying me."

"You kissed Dudley." He slanted a look down at her. "What do you want me to say?"

He'd had plenty to say on the subject previously. His reticence only increased her apprehension about him.

"He kissed *me,"* she clarified.

"Okay." His tone acknowledged the truth of that. "He still don't do it for you, babe. If something happens to me, you might want to keep that in mind."

"Oh, my God, nothing's going to happen to you." Panic tried digging tiny little claws into her heart, but she fought it off. "Tam's going to fix you and —"

"She might — or might not — be able to fix what's wrong with me now, but we both know that sooner or later, one way or another, I'm going to be gone."

He was looking at her, just looking at her, and she felt her heart start to beat faster and her pulse start to race. Where they were standing was only a few steps beyond the reach of the airport lights. The plane's headlights cut through the darkness away from them. In the shadows, Michael looked tall and broad-shouldered and solid as a rock. Every instinct she possessed urged her to turn in to his arms. She would have,

180

instantly, except — Oh, wait, she couldn't. The knowledge made her throat go tight.

"You're the best thing that's happened to me in a long time," he said. "I want you to know that." The merest hint of a smile touched his mouth. "Without you, being dead would've been hell."

"Cute." Her heart felt like it was being squeezed in a vise. If he was actually going to go, leave this plane, cease to exist as Tam had suggested, there was so much she wanted to say to him that the words crowded together as they fought to get out. But pure self-defense kept her silent. Besides, she had faith in Tam: if her friend couldn't do anything to save him, she wouldn't be driving to Las Vegas. "Who's sweet-talking who now?"

He shook his head. "I mean it. I've been contemplating mortality, babe. First time I've really done that since I died. Where I am, there's no coming back from, and where I'm going —" He broke off, grimacing. "I thought hell was bad, and as you know I've been doing my damnedest to avoid it, but turns out that the idea of nothingness — just ceasing to exist — is worse."

Her heart turned over. "Michael —"

"Ready?" Tony came up, pulling her

suitcase behind him. Charlie was so focused on Michael that she hadn't seen, or heard, him close the trunk, or heard the rattle of the small wheels on pavement, or noticed his approach at all.

"Yes," Charlie replied, and added strongly, for Michael's benefit, "Let's go get the job done."

"Kaminsky's waiting on pins and needles," Tony agreed, or at least thought he was agreeing with her, while Michael muttered something that sounded like, "From your lips to God's ears."

The three of them crossed the tarmac and got on the plane. Already on board was Buzz — Special Agent Buzz Crane, thirty-two years old, a slightly built five-ten with curly brown hair and a thin, sharp-featured face dominated by a pair of black-rimmed glasses, the classic nerd to Tony's hottie. Buzz and Charlie were good friends, he and Kaminsky had a supposedly secret romance going on that was complicated by the fact that he had once been engaged to Kaminsky's missing sister, and he and Tony were friends beyond their boss/subordinate relationship.

Buzz greeted Tony with a handshake and Charlie with a quick hug. They took their seats and strapped in, and the plane raced down the runway and lifted into the air.

"Lena's not answering her phone," Buzz told Tony as the plane leveled off. They were flying west, so as they reached cruising altitude Charlie could see the last orange and purple streaks of the fading sunset as the sky finished up turning a deep indigo. Tiny pinpricks of stars started popping up everywhere like mushrooms after a rain. Below them, the airport lights quickly faded away. With the nearest big city still hundreds of miles in the distance, the ground looked blacker than the sky.

As she spotted the frosty crescent moon rising up behind them, Charlie had a momentary vision of the hunter dive-bombing the small plane, and shuddered.

"What do you mean, she's not answering her phone? I've been talking to her all day," Tony replied as, deliberately turning her back on the night, Charlie swiveled to face them. The beige leather chairs in this luxurious aircraft could be configured so that four seats in the middle of the plane faced one another, with a small table that could be raised or lowered to the desired height between them. Opposite them, across the narrow aisle against the other side of the plane, was a matching couch. Charlie, Tony, and Buzz were in the chairs. With no need for a seatbelt, Michael sprawled on his back on the couch. His head rested on the rolled arm, his eyes were closed, his arms were folded over his chest, and his booted feet were crossed at the ankles.

She might have thought he was sleeping if she hadn't known that he no longer slept. The discoloration, Charlie was dismayed to see, had spread as far down as his wrist. A glance at his other arm was reassuring, but only slightly. No hint of charcoal gray marred the tanned muscles, but she feared — knew — that it was only a matter of time. Charlie couldn't help but wonder what was going on beneath his shirt. Was the gray spreading where she couldn't see?

Answer: of course it was.

Anxiety gnawed at her. She had never felt so helpless in her life.

CHAPTER ELEVEN

"Then it's me. She's not talking to me. I thought that might be it." Buzz slumped dispiritedly in his seat. His suit coat was off, and the sleeves of his blue shirt were rolled up to his elbows. He ran a hand through his Brillo pad curls.

"Getting involved with sisters never ends well," Tony told him. "Live and learn." He glanced at Charlie. "Are you feeling recovered enough to do some work?"

"Certainly," Charlie replied with a cool she was far from feeling, while Buzz glanced down at her bandaged hand and then looked a question at her. She told him, "A research subject bit me earlier. I'm fine."

Buzz nodded (if she needed anything to confirm how upset he was, his lack of interest in the particulars of her injury would be it) and said to Tony, "Like I meant to get involved with sisters. I've known them both since high school. I just didn't figure out which one I really wanted until I was about to marry the other one."

"Bad timing," Tony observed.

Buzz groaned. "Tell me about it. Lena hasn't spoken to me since she decided to go to Vegas. I asked her if she wanted me to come with, and she said no. She was going to meet up with Giselle, celebrate Giselle's birthday — it was Saturday — with her, just the two of them. No problem, I said. Truth is, I'd rather go swimming in a piranha tank than be in the same room with the two of them together right now. So I went to that ComicCon convention I'd been wanting to go to instead. But I called her a couple of times, and she didn't answer. Now Giselle's gone missing, and it's a damned emergency and they need me and Lena still isn't answering. I don't believe it." His gaze locked on Charlie. "You're a woman: that means she's like super-mad at me, right?"

"Give the man a cigar," Michael muttered. A quick glance at him showed Charlie that his eyes were open now: he was frowning up at the ceiling.

"I don't have a sister," Charlie told Buzz apologetically, "so I can only speak from a professional standpoint. The bond between sisters is one of the strongest there is. I'd say that Kaminsky — Lena — is demonstrating her loyalty to her sister by breaking off contact with you."

"You know her sister — Giselle," Tony said to Buzz. "Do you think it's possible that she just left on her own?"

"I've been asking myself that." Buzz drummed his fingers on the table in front of him. "I don't think so. She's softer than Lena — in personality, I mean" — he shot quick defensive looks at Tony and Charlie — "and more — way more — of a party girl. Guys like her, she likes them. When she said she'd go out with me I thought I'd won the lottery. What I've been wondering is, did she maybe meet some guy and take off with him? Because she's kind of the type that might do that: impulsive and — well, impulsive. But since she was in Vegas with Lena, I don't think she would. Not without giving Lena a heads-up."

"If Lena is convinced her sister is a crime victim, then she probably is." Charlie gave the two of them trenchant looks. "Her instincts have always seemed to me to be right on the money."

"If Lena's right —" Buzz's voice cracked. "I'm having a hard time letting myself think about that."

"I'd say you're too close to the victim to be on the case, but Kaminsky's even closer,"

Tony said. "Even if we could get another team out here, it would take some time, which Giselle Kaminsky may not have. And if it turns out we are looking for a serial killer, we're the best there is at it."

"You couldn't get me off this case if you fired me," Buzz said fiercely. "Lena, either. We'll investigate on our own if we have to."

"That's what I thought," Tony said. "Okay, let's get cracking. Kaminsky sent me some files. Let's see if we can get as much of the preliminary stuff out of the way as possible before we get on the ground."

For just about the first time in her life when it came to anything involving her work, Charlie had trouble concentrating as she read over the information e-mailed by Kaminsky — oh, hell, *Lena;* the Special Agent wasn't a fan of being called by her first name, but the whole Kaminsky bit was stupid considering that they'd worked two cases together now and, in the last one, nearly died together; and anyway, calling her Lena made it easier to differentiate her from her missing sister. Charlie made up her mind there and then that she was just going to do it, and Kaminsky — *Lena* — could stuff it if she didn't like it. She caught herself sneaking glances at Michael, worrying about the hunter, imagining worst-case scenarios in which Tam had a car crash or something on the way to meet them, and only managed to get herself back on track by grimly reminding herself that Giselle Kaminsky's life could be on the line here. That brought to the surface the underlying issue she hadn't wanted to face: the thought that she now might very well be involved in another active serial killer case filled her with absolute icy dread.

Borderline PTSD, she diagnosed herself impatiently. Her recent near drowning plus her exposure as a teenager to the serial killer who had killed her friend Holly and her way too close second encounter with the Boardwalk Killer had done a number on her: she was actively experiencing symptoms of avoidance, difficulty concentrating, and fear.

If a patient had come to her with those symptoms, she would have prescribed a regimen of cognitive–behavioral therapy and possibly medication until the symptoms abated.

For herself, under current conditions, she had a simpler and far more brutal recommendation: *Get over it. Suck it up. Do what you're trained to do.*

So, grimly, that's what she did.

There wasn't a lot of available information: the Las Vegas Police Department file, consisting of precisely two pages and officially describing Giselle Kaminsky as a missing person, which, because of the victim's age, would have made it a low-priority investigation had her sister not been an FBI agent. Adults taking off, which was the default assumption in most such cases, was not a crime. There were also files on seventeen other young women who had also gone missing in Las Vegas. At least half of those were one or two pages as well.

Tony summed up the information. "They're all attractive brunettes under thirty-five. They all went to Vegas and disappeared. There are no signs of foul play, and no bodies have been found."

"That's not much to go on." Charlie looked up from studying Giselle Kaminsky's picture. It was a shot taken beside a swimming pool: Giselle was wearing a gauzy black cover-up that reached halfway down her slim thighs and a carefree smile. Her resemblance to Lena was strong, but she looked happier and more approachable — possibly because she was laughing and holding in her hand a cocktail with a little pink parasol in it. From the background, Charlie thought that the shot had been snapped in Las Vegas, probably on this trip, and wondered if Lena had taken it. Like Lena,

Giselle had black hair, an olive complexion, and eyes that were dark enough brown to look almost black. Both were exotically pretty, and both were curvy. At thirty-one and five-feet-four inches, Giselle was two years older and two inches taller than her sister. Unlike Lena, who had a businesslike chin-length cut, Giselle's hair hung in a sleek, straight fall to just past her shoulders.

"Ten of them are listed as missing persons. Seven of them were never even reported missing." Tony looked at Buzz. "From what Kaminsky has let fall in the past, I gather that her relationship with her sister can be a little rocky. You know Giselle Kaminsky. Is it possible that she just took off somewhere without telling Kaminsky?"

"She and Lena fight a lot," Buzz admitted. He was chewing a thumbnail as he stared at his laptop's screen. He'd been engaged to Giselle before breaking it off just two weeks before their wedding this past spring. Since then, he and Lena had sparred around before hooking up romantically — at least, Charlie was 99.99 percent sure they had hooked up romantically — during the team's last case. "But Giselle wouldn't just leave without letting somebody know. She's fairly responsible. And she'd know Lena would go nuts."

"Tell us everything you know about Giselle Kaminsky," Tony said, and Buzz did. The short version was that, after having been raised in California as Scientologists, Giselle and Lena had arrived in Maryland at ages fourteen and sixteen when their mother, Libby, had left her husband, state, and religion behind to start a new life and had taken the girls with her. Public schools had led to degrees from the University of Maryland. Where Lena had become a cop, Giselle, an aspiring artist, had taken a job in an art gallery. She'd been manager of the Lotus Gallery, which sold high-end pieces of original art, at the time of her disappearance.

"I'm having a background check run on Giselle." Tony held up a hand to silence the protest Buzz had obviously been about to make. "Just in case her disappearance is about something other than a serial killer. It should be available by the time we land."

While they worked on the case, Charlie carefully monitored Michael. He was restless, up and down, walking the aisles, looking out the windows, even disappearing into the cockpit a couple of times. He leaned over her laptop occasionally to check out what she was doing, and once, when the pictures of the missing women were lined up side by side on her screen, even added a helpful comment: "Hot chicks. The other white meat."

At the look Charlie gave him he added hastily, "I was *joking.* Jesus."

A moment later he said, "The ones you can see enough of to tell, they all got something else in common, babe."

He then made a completely male gesture that left her in no doubt of his meaning: the missing women whose pictures were more than just head shots were all noticeably full-chested, which was how she put it when she repeated Michael's observation to Tony and Buzz, and then by consensus added that fact to the things the alleged victims had in common.

"Which makes me think that these killings, if they are indeed killings and are the work of a serial killer, are sexually motivated," Tony said, looking at Charlie. "What do you think?"

"Lust killers tend to have very specific criteria in mind when choosing a victim." Charlie looked back at the pictures on the screen thoughtfully. "These women appear to be similar in coloring, age, and certain physical attributes. But his primary motivation may not be sexual, which it is if he is a lust killer. He could be a thrill killer, which describes someone who simply enjoys the experience of killing: it gives him a high. Or he could be a power-seeker killer, who is motivated by the pleasure it gives him to have total power over his victims. There are other types of serial killers, too, but those three seem the most likely from what we know of this case so far."

"What's the difference?" Buzz asked impatiently.

"Motivation," Charlie replied. "Which affects how he selects his victims. A lust killer, for example, might fixate on women with full chests. A thrill killer picks his victims by opportunity and is much less likely to fixate on a particular trait: with him it's more random, more about having the opportunity to grab someone. He'll have favored hunting grounds, and I would expect to discover that his victims were taken from a specific handful of locations. A power-seeker killer might target women who've offended him for punishment."

"So how does this help us find him?" Buzz drummed his fingers on the table in frustration. His tension was obvious, and if Charlie had been a more demonstrative person she would have reached out and patted his knee. As it was, she simply did her best to answer his question.

"It helps us find him because it helps us identify places he might look for his next victim," she said. "If he's a lust killer, we look for him around locations where he can easily assess women's bodies, like a swimming pool, for example. If he's a thrill killer, he'll tend to go back to sites where he's had success before, so if we can determine where the victims were taken and stake those places out, sooner or later he'll come back to them and we'll have a far better chance of catching him. If he's a power-seeker killer, then we look at any arguments the victims had in the weeks before they went missing. All these labels that we put on these predators are simply tools that help us narrow down the search. The theory is, if we successfully apply enough labels, if we narrow down the search enough, we'll catch him."

"If you eliminate the impossible . . ." Michael muttered. He was leaning over her shoulder again, and Charlie shot him a sharp-eyed look. She recognized the quote as being from Sherlock Holmes, and finished it in her own mind: *whatever remains, no matter how improbable, must be the truth.* She didn't know why it always surprised her to be reminded of how well read he was: as he'd told her, there hadn't been a lot to do in prison.

"Which is what we're going to do," Tony said to Buzz. "Catch him. Unless we get there and find out it's all a big misunderstanding, of course."

Buzz took a deep breath and said, "I hope to God it is."

"According to victim facilitation study criteria, Giselle would be at low risk for coming into contact with a serial killer," Charlie offered. Tony and Buzz stared at her. She frowned at them. "The theory posits that certain types of people are more likely to come into contact with serial killers and, thus, are more at risk from them. Hitchhikers, transients, and sex workers, for example, are statistically at high risk."

"Good to know," Tony said, while Michael leaned over to murmur in Charlie's ear, "Did I ever tell you how much hearing you talk shrink turns me on?"

Four hours later, after they'd gone over everything they knew for what felt like the dozenth time and had come to the conclusion that they were no closer to any answers than they had been when the plane took off, they took a break to eat. Because they were in flight, Charlie hadn't been able to communicate with Tam since she'd texted her that they would be staying at the Con-

quistador. She could only trust that everything was on track at Tam's end for a
rendezvous in the hotel lobby shortly after
the plane was scheduled to touch down.
Given the half hour or so that she calculated
it would take them to deplane and reach
the hotel, that still gave them a two-hour-
plus window — plenty of time, she told
herself stoutly, which didn't stop her at all
from worrying. Over the course of the flight,
Michael's other arm had inexorably turned
that terrible burnt gray, and Charlie had
little doubt that the discoloration had
spread even farther.

After they'd eaten — she was so anxious
that she wasn't able to swallow more than a
mouthful of food — and reviewed the files
one more time to see if there was anything
they'd missed — there wasn't — she
dragged Michael off to the lavatory with
her. Like any airplane restroom, this one
was tiny and designed for function rather
than luxury. When she'd made use of it on
her own earlier she'd had just about enough
room to freshen up. As large as Michael
was, with him in it, too, she found herself
practically perched on the narrow stainless
steel ledge beside the sink so as not to have
a body part protruding into him as he lifted
up his shirt at her command.

It was all she could do not to make a dismayed sound as she observed that the charred black area around the wound looked larger and angrier, and the gray discoloration now covered his chest from the base of his throat to his washboard abs. It undoubtedly had spread elsewhere, too, although her view was blocked by the waistband of his jeans.

"I always wanted to be a member of the mile-high club," he said with a suggestive quirk of his lips while she anxiously examined his torso, having declined his offer to shuck his jeans if she felt the need to check out the rest of him. "How about we try it?"

"Get real," Charlie answered, doing her best to maintain a façade of normalcy while fighting off a fresh attack of cold panic. Besides spreading, the discoloration was darkening. "You're not up for it."

The suggestive quirk deepened. "Oh, I'm up for it."

She settled that with a glance down at his admittedly impressively bulging crotch accompanied by two ego-depressing words: "Ectoplasm, Casper."

"You could pull up your shirt for me."

"No."

"You're no fun." Those black eyes gleamed at her. God, what she wouldn't give to see them restored to their normal sky blue! So far, the gray hadn't reached his face. He was a little ashen, a little haggard, but still the same way-too-handsome Michael.

At the idea that soon he might not be, she shivered inwardly.

Hadn't he said that the things had no faces?

He said, "I'd ask if you've ever done it in an airplane bathroom, but I've got a pretty good idea of the answer: no."

"Turn around," Charlie instructed without replying. He was right, of course, not that she saw any reason to admit it. He grimaced but obeyed. Her throat was already tight from looking at his discolored chest. The sight of the broad, flat planes of his shoulder blades and the long, smooth muscles of his back turned the same terrifying gray made her stomach drop clear to her toes.

Although she tried her best not to, tried her best to keep from letting him know just how frightened for him she was, she must have made some small sound because he let his shirt fall, turned around, and looked at her.

"You just chewed off all your lipstick. You need to quit biting your lip," he said, and she realized that she was, indeed, biting her lower lip with distress and had almost certainly, as he had said, chewed off the lipstick she had freshly applied when she had washed her face and hands and brushed her hair earlier. She instantly stopped worrying her lip.

"It's a bad habit," she replied, because she didn't want him to think she was worried out of her mind about him, which she was.

"You do it when you're stressed." He was crowding her, moving in toward her so that she scooted away until her back was pressed tight up against the mirror and he loomed over her. "And this is stressing you out so much because you're crazy in love with me. Come on, Doc, admit it."

Was she? Even considering the possibility was dangerous. She refused: whatever happened, she had the rest of her life to think about.

"You're delusional," she said, trying to squirm farther away from him and not succeeding, because there was no more room.

"*You* are beautiful." His hands rested against the mirror on either side of her, and she had to tilt her face up to look at him. The strong jaw, the beautifully cut mouth, the chiseled features, were achingly dear to her now. Her heart was beating way too fast, and her blood was heating, and at the same time she was dying inside from fear for him.

"If I was myself again, I'd be getting you naked about now. And then I'd pick you up and wrap your legs around my waist and we'd be joining that mile-high club. And you'd like it. You'd come."

She caught her breath. He hadn't even touched her — he couldn't even touch her — and yet her body burned and her back arched so that her breasts were lifting toward him invitingly and her lips were parting for the kiss he couldn't give her. She was so turned on that if he'd been alive, if there'd been any way, she would have been letting him take off her clothes and do her right there in that cramped bathroom, with Tony and Buzz just outside the door.

"Baby, you've got *fuck me* written all over your face right now," he said in a low, husky murmur that made her go all melty inside and turned the air around them to steam. "Do you have any idea how hot you're making me from just looking at you?"

Her lips parted and her breathing quickened and she felt like her bones could dissolve at any second. So, yes, she did, because she was hopelessly, helplessly, burning in the same fire.

At least she had enough good sense left not to answer that.

He was still crowding her, still leaning

toward her, still had his hands planted on either side of her. Her eyes locked on the sensuous curve of his mouth and her hands tightened around the smooth coolness of the metal ledge and she instinctively did just what she would have done if he were alive: she parted her legs to let him settle in between them and lifted her mouth toward his.

The voice over the loudspeaker made her jump. "Special Agent Bartoli, we'll be touching down at Henderson Executive Airport in just a few minutes. Everybody needs to return to their seats and buckle up at this time."

Michael had raised his head when the announcement boomed. He looked down at her for a second with those terrifying, totally unreadable black eyes, then dropped his mouth to her lips, a brief, brushing kiss that felt like the feathery touch of electrified wings. Even as her lips fluttered under that charged contact, he lifted his head and stepped back.

"If this doesn't work, if I end up going *poof* like the voodoo priestess said, I want you to know that I don't regret a damned thing. Except leaving you."

Her heart turned over. "Michael —"

There was a knock on the door. "Charlie,

is everything okay in there? We're getting ready to land."

Tony.

"Yes," Charlie called back around the lump that had formed in her throat. "I'm coming."

Michael grinned wickedly. "That information really something you want to share with Dudley?"

As Charlie got it, then gave him a *ha-ha* look, Michael stepped back enough to allow her access to the door.

Once again words crowded her lips. There was so much she wanted to say to him. But then the loudspeaker came to life once more: "Please return to your seats immediately and buckle your seatbelts. We're starting our descent into the greater Clark County area at this time."

"Go," Michael said, and she went, exiting the bathroom, walking past Tony almost blindly, heading back to her seat, fastening her seatbelt without any real awareness of doing any of those things.

She felt raw inside.

It wasn't until they landed, until they'd driven the few miles to the Conquistador and turned the rental car over to the valet and the luggage to the bellhop and were walking past the famous dancing fountains into the brightly lit lobby, and she dodged a laughing trio of drunks and Michael got in front of her, that she noticed that he was having trouble with locomotion. He twisted to one side as he moved, awkwardly hunching his shoulders as if, she thought with a thrill of horror, his body was starting to curl in on itself.

She remembered how he had described the evil spirits as awful twisty things, and her insides froze.

Then he looked around at her, and her stomach slid up into her throat.

The gray was now creeping over his face, and his features — his perfectly carved, drop-dead handsome features — seemed to have flattened and blurred. Even his hair was streaked with that same lifeless gray.

She sucked in air. It was the merest whisper of sound, but Michael heard, and he lifted eyebrows that had turned the color of tarnished silver at her questioningly. Not wanting him to read her terror for him in her face, she jerked her eyes from his and turned away to scan the hotel's huge, glittering lobby for Tam.

CHAPTER TWELVE

"Lena's still not answering my damned calls. She's not answering Tony's now, either," Buzz said. Clutching her phone in her hand, Charlie was desperately looking for Tam, having just texted her to let her know that they'd arrived. She had almost bumped into Buzz when he stopped abruptly as they were crossing the lobby, and at the moment had little attention to spare for him. "She's staying in the same room she shared with Giselle. I've got the room number. I'm going to go on up and see if she's there."

Charlie nodded, preoccupied. Her own increasingly urgent emergency was occupying her thoughts to the exclusion of almost everything else. Lena was undoubtedly feeling desperate, her sister's life might be on the line, and rushing to her side was something that Charlie was definitely going to do, but not now. Now what happened to

Michael mattered to her more. More, she realized unwillingly, than just about anything in the world. Michael was beside her, and she glanced at him to assess his condition: verdict, not good.

Buzz strode away, heading, presumably, for the elevators. The lobby was enormous, with eighteen-foot ceilings and marble floors and a magnificent chandelier composed of what looked like thousands of brilliantly colored blown glass flowers. It was ten p.m. Vegas time, although her body clock persisted in thinking it was one a.m., which it would have been in Virginia. She was physically exhausted but at the same time her burgeoning fear for Michael had her absolutely wired. The lobby was busy and noisy, with a pianist in one corner tinkling out show tunes and live birds twittering in a giant gilded cage in another and chattering tourists dressed in everything from jeans to tuxes and sparkling evening dresses flitting about all over the place. Tony, she saw at a glance, was at the reception desk, presumably waiting to check in.

"Cherie!"

Charlie whirled at the familiar voice.

"Tam!" She was immediately engulfed in a warm cloud of bright colors and expensive perfume as Tam greeted her with a hug.

"*This* is the voodoo priestess?" Michael asked as the women separated. It was the first thing he'd said since they'd left the plane, and Charlie was beyond dismayed by how hoarse and croaky his voice sounded. She could tell from his tone that Tam was not what he'd been expecting. At thirty-five, Tam looked years younger. She was eye-catchingly glamorous, with long legs, slim hips, and a tiny waist topped by large, shapely breasts proudly displayed in a clingy, tangerine-colored silk tee with a scoop neckline designed to show maximum cleavage. Her snug-fitting slacks were a stretchy print in which red, yellow, and tangerine vied for dominance. In her chic, kitten-heeled gold sandals she was a little taller than Charlie, and she continued the gold accessories with hoop earrings and an armful of bangles that clinked whenever she moved. She had a slim, attractive face with prominent cheekbones, a full mouth en-hanced by her signature scarlet lipstick, an aquiline nose, and artfully made up brown eyes. Her skin was milk white, and her hair hung past her shoulders in deep red waves. Michael finished the inevitable male once-over with, "Hel*lo,* Jessica Rabbit."

Charlie threw him a reproving look. "She can hear you. *And* see you."

"Really?" His eyes ran over Tam again. Tam was looking him over, too, critically, and it was obvious from her expression that she *could* see and hear him and equally obvious (Michael at this point being far from his usual handsome self) that she was not impressed. He tried for a smile which didn't quite work. Charlie realized that the spreading discoloration was affecting even the structure of his face, and felt a fresh spurt of fear.

"It was a compliment," he added. The rasp made his voice sound almost sinister.

"Tamsyn Green, meet Michael Garland." Charlie had to work to stay outwardly calm.

"He's not in good shape. The *abaissement* is far advanced." Tam's words were addressed to Charlie. What Tam was seeing was a gray and twisted version of Michael. A blurred, muted, and, yes, scary version. "Soon it will start affecting his mind, and not long after that he will be gone. Like this." She snapped her fingers. Her expression was serious as she took Charlie's hand and, with a hard look and a quick order for Michael — "Stay there, spirit!" — pulled her a little aside. "Cherie, I've been thinking about this ever since we spoke, and now that I see him I'm sure of it. It would be best not to interfere, to just let him go."

Her voice dropped to an urgent whisper. "He's from the *Dark Place*. I don't think you understand what that means."

"I don't *care* what that means." Charlie fixed her with a fierce look. "You *owe* me."

"You're making a mistake," Tam said unhappily, then as Charlie pulled her hand free and glared she added with a sigh, "All right, then. I'll try my best, but I can't promise it will work." Her gaze shifted back to Michael. "I've gotten a room, and I have everything prepared. If you're sure, let's go up. We need to get started. Cherie, are you *sure* you're sure?"

"Yes." Charlie beckoned to Michael as they began to move toward the elevators. "I'll reimburse you for the room, by the way. And all your other costs. Just let me know how much."

Tam waved a dismissive hand. "What are friends for? My problem isn't with what this is going to cost me, it's with doing it at all. If he's being terminated, *he did something terrible.* Are you hearing me, cherie?"

At Tam's words, Charlie felt a shiver run down her spine. Michael had consistently denied being the serial killer he'd been sentenced to death as, but he'd also told her that he'd never said he didn't deserve Spookville. Right there and then, Charlie resolved to get Michael to tell her exactly what he'd done to find himself on the highway to hell — just as soon as she saved him from total oblivion. Having caught up with them, Michael must have heard at least the last part of what Tam had said. It was now impossible to read anything at all in his face, but from the way he was looking at her, Charlie had little doubt that *he* could read *her* face.

Doubt and fear and resolve had to be all mixed up in her expression.

"I don't care," she told Tam again, and got the impression that Michael relaxed infinitesimally. "Just save him."

With Tam looking perturbed and Michael invisible to anyone except the two of them, they reached the elevator bank. As they waited for one to arrive Charlie remembered to text Tony — *I'm going to look around, I'll pick my key up at the desk when I get back* — and then they were in an elevator shooting skyward toward Tam's room on the twenty-ninth floor. Other people were in the elevator with them, laughing and chatting away, and an obviously amorous couple got out when they did, so nothing more was said until they were inside Tam's room.

The light was off, and Tam made no attempt to turn it on. Once the door to the hall was closed, the room was shadowy but not completely dark. The whisper of the air-conditioning was the only sound.

As they walked farther inside the room, Charlie set her purse down on the coffee table and glanced around. She'd never been inside the Conquistador, never been to Las Vegas before, in fact, and she was impressed with how large and nice the rooms were. This one had a king-sized bed, a seating area with an armchair, couch and the coffee table, and the requisite armoire with a TV. The room was decorated in beige and blue, and the large window — the curtains were open — offered a glittering view of the city at night. The only odd note about the room was that the bed had been stripped. Blankets and pillows lay in a heap in the middle of the bare mattress.

Oh, and the smell. Charlie couldn't quite put her finger on what it was, but it was faintly putrid in a way that did not say "expensive hotel room."

"I need your full name," Tam said to Michael — who, of course, being Michael, asked why.

"Names have power," Tam replied impatiently. "This is going to take all the power I can muster."

"Michael Allen Garland," Michael replied.

"That's your true full name? No junior? Not an alias?"

"That's the only name I know." His answer was short.

"He may have had another birth name. He was adopted," Charlie put in, and Tam grimaced in a way that said as plainly as words could have that this was a complication. Michael turned his face toward Charlie, but it was now impossible to read his expression. Still, she got the impression that he was not pleased to have such personal information revealed.

Her silent response to that? *Too bad.*

"Go into the bathroom," Tam told Michael, nodding toward an open door through which Charlie could just see the edge of what looked like a large tub. The bathroom light, which was on, beckoned warmly. Coupled with the glow of the city through the window, it was the reason the room wasn't pitch black.

"Charlie," Michael growled. Stopping just outside the rectangle of light that spilled across the bedroom carpet from the open bathroom door, Michael turned to look at her again. The guttural quality of his voice was almost as terrifying as the change in his face and form. But what really moved her was the note in his voice of — was it fear?

Quite possibly: he would be a fool if he weren't afraid. "If I don't come out of this, lay off the serial killers. Hear?"

"We'll talk about it later," Charlie replied. She was jittery with fear herself, and trying her best not to let it show.

"I may not have a later. Promise me."

"Fine. I promise."

"You're lying."

"I'm not going to argue with you about it right now."

"Goddamn it."

"Look, can we just concentrate on *this*?"

Tam was looking from one to the other of them with a gathering frown. Charlie realized that the nature of the exchange revealed an intimacy between them that Tam was bound to have noticed, and disapprove of.

Michael said, "I want to make sure you're going to be all right if I wind up not being around to save your ass."

"I don't need you to save my ass." An instant's reflection amended that to, "Usually. Would you let me worry about me and just *go into the bathroom*?"

Tam said in a warning tone, "Time is short."

Michael turned and went into the bathroom. Charlie followed, with Tam bringing up the rear and closing the door behind them.

The first thing Charlie noticed was that there were a number of tall, fat black candles waiting unlit beside an open gym bag in the middle of the floor. Looking past them, she saw that the bathroom was large, at least ten by twelve feet, all tiled in earth-toned marble, with the big soaking tub Charlie had glimpsed through the open doorway, a roomy glass-walled shower, a toilet, and a long marble counter with twin sinks. It was the type of setup that came complete with a huge mirror covering the entire wall above the sinks. Charlie knew the mirror was there even though she couldn't see it.

And the reason she couldn't see it was that the missing sheets had been duct-taped over the mirror so that not so much as a sliver of glass showed.

Charlie looked a question at Tam.

"Mirrors can be used as a portal," Tam said. "What I am going to try to do here could attract the wrong sort of attention. I don't want to give any *esprit malin* the chance to come through."

Charlie immediately thought of the hunter, and shivered.

"You've done this before, right?" Michael

sounded distinctly uneasy as he looked around.

Tam shook her head. "The spell is my mother's. Ordinarily I never go near the dark side. *Maman* tells me I'm too sensitive, but I prefer it that way."

"Fantastic."

Tam's brows snapped together. "You say that like you have an alternative."

"You can trust Tam," Charlie intervened, watching as her friend bent over the gym bag. "She's the real thing."

"Get into the bathtub," Tam told Michael as she withdrew a package wrapped in layers of clear plastic from the gym bag and set it on the shelflike rim of the tub. It was, Charlie realized as she looked at it with a mixture of fascination and revulsion, the source of the putrid smell. It was also dripping blood. Dark red drops ran down the tub's tan marble side.

"What the hell?" Staring at the package, Michael asked the question before Charlie could.

"A chicken heart and entrails. From a creature killed fresh today. I picked them up at a butcher shop I know as I left L.A. Probably I should have put them in a cooler, but I didn't have time." Tam pulled out a couple of small containers and set them on the edge of the tub, too. Charlie couldn't tell what was in them. She wasn't sure she wanted to know. "My mother would have actually sacrificed a chicken as she did the spell, so you should feel fortunate that I'm choosing to use a substitute."

Thank goodness was Charlie's heartfelt response to that as she was assaulted by an instant, horrified mental picture of Tam slicing open a live chicken in front of them, but she didn't say it aloud.

"Jesus," Michael said.

Tam looked at him with a glint in her eyes. "Would you get into the bathtub?"

"Why the tub?" Michael asked warily.

"Because it makes the cleanup easier." Tam sounded on the verge of losing her patience.

"This is some voodoo shit you're throwing down, right? If it goes wrong, am I going to be turned into a zombie or something?" Michael's deteriorating voice grated on Charlie's ears like sandpaper. The suspicion in it was unmistakable.

"If it goes wrong, you will not *be* at all." Tam frowned at him as she popped the lid off the Tupperware-like containers. "Do you want me to try or not?"

"He does," Charlie answered before Michael could say anything else. She glared at

Michael. "For somebody who's a *ghost,* for God's sake, the amount of skepticism you still harbor about everything to do with the supernatural is ridiculous."

"Yeah, well, if you'd started telling me about all this shit two months ago I would have said you were nuts. I'm still adjusting."

"So adjust already," she snapped.

"Would you get into the bathtub?" Tam said to Michael, not patiently at all now, and with a long look at Charlie, who pointed an admonishing finger at him, Michael did as he was asked.

CHAPTER THIRTEEN

"Oh, and strip," Tam added on a milder note.

"What?" From the middle of the large tub, Michael turned to stare at her.

"Your clothes are a barrier. For the *abaissement* to be stopped, the spell must be able to hit the target."

Michael's clothes were as gray and burnt-looking as he was.

"So if this works I'm just supposed to run around naked afterward?"

"Drop your clothes in the tub. Maybe the spell will work on them, maybe it won't." Tam shot an exasperated glance at Charlie. "This would go faster if the spirit were co-operative."

"Would you just *do it*?" Charlie hissed at Michael as Tam positioned the candles on the ledge surrounding the tub, with one on each corner at either side of the faucets, one on each side of the ledge about three quarters of the way up the tub, and one all by itself in the center of the ledge on the far end.

"Ah, hell," Michael muttered. It was, Charlie knew, surrender. Despite everything, she almost had to smile as, standing inside the tub now, he turned his back and started to pull his shirt over his head. Under some circumstances, it seemed, her big, bad ghost was surprisingly modest. Her smile quickly died as she saw how withered and discolored his usually breathtaking body was. What was happening to him was starting to remind her of — it came to her in an instant — the fate of Gollum, the corrupted creature from the *Lord of the Rings* books.

The comparison terrified her anew.

With the candles in place, Tam opened one of the containers and started sprinkling a substance — salt, Charlie saw — between the candles.

Now that she really looked at them, she realized that the candles had been set out in the shape of a classic pentagram and the salt would link them. When Tam finished, Michael would be imprisoned behind the barrier she was creating.

Charlie's heart started beating faster. Like Tam, she'd always tried to distance herself from the darker edges of the supernatural world. Practicing voodoo with dead chicken parts and pentagrams in a hotel room was a pretty good step beyond the boundaries of what she was comfortable with.

"That salt?" Michael inquired of Tam. Of course he knew what the salt was for.

"Yes." Tam's tone wasn't encouraging.

"There a reason you're locking me into this here tub?"

"There is. The barrier is there in case anything goes wrong. In case the pain is so bad you try to flee. In case something else comes through, so that it cannot get out into the room. In case you should lose your mind and try to attack me."

"Shit," Michael said, his eyes seeking Charlie.

"It's the only way," she told him. "It'll work."

It has to. But she said that only to herself.

"Would you turn off the light, please?" Tam asked, before her gaze swung back toward Michael. "And you, spirit, finish undressing. Quickly."

"Shit," Michael said again.

A small orange flame appearing out of nowhere captured Charlie's attention even as she turned off the light and plunged the room into total darkness. Having apparently just dug a cigarette lighter out of the bag,

Tam had flicked it to life and was at that moment touching it to the candle nearest her. Long shadows leaped up the walls and danced across the floor as the wick lit.

Charlie felt her insides twist. Her mouth went dry, and she swallowed hard.

Tam was about to begin the spell. Charlie couldn't even let herself think about what would happen if it didn't work. Maybe it was wrong to pray for an apparently damned soul, but —

This was Michael. *Please God* —

"Babe. One more thing: you need to pack up your stuff and get the hell out of the Ridge and stay out of it." Michael was talking fast again as he pulled off his boots; it was clear from the urgency of his tone that what he was telling her was something he thought she might need to know if he was no longer around. "There was Hendricks, then me, then Spivey today. That's three death row inmates dying violently in less than four months. Something ain't right about that, and you don't want any part of it. You hear me?"

Charlie only linked the three deaths as he spoke, and then the wrongness of it hit her like a thunderclap. Ordinarily, she thought, she would have noticed sooner, but then, she'd been distracted. By Michael. Which she still was. Which made the deaths at the Ridge just that much more material to be shoved into her mental *stuff to think about later* file.

"I hear you." At this point, she was prepared to agree with anything he said.

"Death row inmate?" Having finished lighting the third candle, Tam straightened to frown at Charlie. "The spirit was on death row?"

"Does it matter?" By this time, Charlie was so anxious that she was practically chewing her nails. She realized from Tam's tone that the news ratcheted up the other woman's misgivings about what she was about to do to a whole new level, and groaned inwardly. "He isn't guilty of what he was charged with, okay?"

"There you go," Michael said in an approving tone. "That's what I've been waiting to hear."

Except for throwing an exasperated glance his way — it was too shadowy to see much more of him than a large shape, but she didn't think he'd yet shucked the jeans — Charlie ignored that. Instead, she concentrated on Tam.

Tam, who was now frowning heavily, had just let the flame on the lighter die. Even as the scent of lilac from the burning candles started to fill the air, Charlie knew that Tam's cooperation hung in the balance.

"Cherie," Tam said in a low, earnest voice. "This spell, if it works, may increase the darkness in him. Sometimes those who are evil grow in strength from it. Please, I'm asking you, let him go."

"He doesn't deserve what's happening to him," she told Tam fiercely. "I know him. I vouch for him. He is — was — a good man."

Michael said, "Babe, I'm touched. You just made my heart go pitter-pat."

"Shut up," Charlie snapped as Tam threw him a doubting look. "You're not helping. And take off your pants."

She didn't watch to see if he obeyed. Her attention was all on Tam.

"I've forgotten something," Tam said. Her fingers curled tightly around the unlit lighter. "For this to succeed, I have to have something of his — a personal item. Hair, fingernail clippings, a favored possession. Something that was his in life."

Charlie held Tam's gaze. She knew her friend well. A direct refusal to help would never be Tam's way. Just as she preferred to avoid the dark areas of the supernatural world, she preferred to avoid the unpleasant facets of the human one, such as open confrontation. Tam's expression told Charlie as plainly as words could have that this supposed hitch in the plan was, in fact, a last-ditch effort on Tam's part to save Charlie from herself.

"We're in luck," Charlie said. "I have his watch."

Tam's lips compressed as Charlie slipped the heavy metal bracelet off her arm and held it out. From the other woman's expression, Charlie knew that she'd been right. Tam looked at the watch, but didn't take it.

"He's important to me," Charlie said quietly, and waited for Michael to say something jokey. He didn't, and she didn't so much as glance in his direction. Instead she held Tam's gaze. "If he gets destroyed in this way, it will break my heart."

Tam looked at her for an instant, then made a face. "We women, we are all of us fools," she muttered with disgust, and took the watch. Then she flicked the lighter back on, and turned to light the remaining candles.

Charlie let out an inner sigh of relief.

"I saw the white light you're always talking about, when you drowned," Michael said as Tam lit the fifth candle. His admission surprised her: Michael had never believed in the existence of the white light that greeted most souls when they died, and for him to have seen it was surprising enough to overcome her reluctance to look at him. Still, Charlie met those black, soulless eyes almost unwillingly. Admitting emotion never came easily to her, and admitting how she felt about him to Michael seemed about as smart as playing Russian roulette with a fully loaded gun. He'd managed to jackhammer his way into her heart because of his looks, she told herself firmly, because he was gorgeous and for some reason he was apparently her particular brand of sexual catnip; and by an inexplicable quirk of chemistry, sex with him was absolutely phenomenal. *That's all it is, an intense physical attraction.* Then she looked at him standing there in the tub. Naked now and barely veiled by shadows, he looked so unlike himself, so *not* the tawny-gold Greek god–looking guy who'd spent the last six weeks or so rocking her world, that she should have had at least an instant of clarity, an instant of revulsion where the truth of what he actually meant to her became glaringly apparent, but she didn't. He was scary and burnt and damaged, and his voice was so hoarse and changed that it was almost unrecognizable, and his eyes burned like they were looking at her straight out of the bowels of hell, and still she trembled on the brink of losing her heart to him.

Taking a deep breath, she tried to push the knowledge out of her mind. Some things it was better not to face.

She could smell the scent of lilacs, feel the energy, palpable as a rising wind, building in the room.

Michael was still talking to her. His voice was low and rough, and his words were hurried, as if he feared they were running out of time, which they were.

"The light came for you, not for me," Michael said. "You tried to get me to walk into it with you, before you went back to your body. After you left, it was still there. I could feel it beckoning at me. I thought about trying it out, seeing if it would take me to wherever. You know why I didn't? I didn't want to leave you."

Charlie's heart pounded like it was trying to beat its way out of her chest. She looked at him, and she couldn't breathe. She knew what he wasn't saying to her: the same thing she wasn't saying to him.

I think I've fallen in love with you.

It was the last thing she'd ever wanted to happen. The last thing she'd ever dreamed could happen. But in that moment, she found the certainty that she was striding full-steam ahead into disaster just didn't matter.

All that mattered was him.

"Michael —" Her heart was in her voice.

"Oh, my God, are you really going to play out this Romeo and Juliet thing with him *now*? There is no *time.*" Tam's exasperation as she rounded on Charlie was palpable. "You need to leave us. Go on. *Shoo.*"

"But —" Charlie protested, while Michael said, "Wait."

"I need to concentrate." Tam interrupted them both ruthlessly. Taking Charlie's arm, she walked her to the door. "You'll just be a distraction."

Panicking slightly, Charlie looked back over her shoulder. "Michael —"

"I'll be all right. Babe, I —"

"If I screw this up he'll be toast," Tam told her grimly, opening the door.

"— don't regret a thing," Michael finished. "Whatever happens, it's all good."

"Go," Tam ordered, and thrust her through the door.

"I'll be right outside," she told Michael as Tam closed it on her. Charlie heard the *click* as Tam locked it.

For a moment she just stood there looking at the closed door. She could almost hear the *throm* of the spell gathering on the other side. (And yes, as she had learned from her association with Tam and her mother, spells make their own sound.) Her heart reached out to Michael, her fingers closed around the doorknob, and then she accepted the fact that whatever happened was out of her hands, that there was nothing she could do.

She had no idea how long she stood there in the starlit bedroom, one hand on the knob, her cheek resting against the smooth wooden panel, watching hazy fingers of orange candlelight reaching through the crack under the door. She heard Tam say, "Michael Allen Garland," sharply. A deep, guttural groan — Michael? — followed that. Then Tam's voice began rising in a chant. Even though she listened intently, Charlie was only able to hear the words in intermittent bursts.

"*Spiritus anime mei*," Tam intoned, and then, a little later and far more loudly, "*Flamma, aqua, terra, aeris*, quintessence."

That last was accompanied by a muffled *boom*, and a bright flash of light that was visible as a red sunburst flaring out from under the door. It was followed seconds later by the strong, unmistakable odor of sulfur.

Charlie caught her breath. She felt her

blood drain toward her toes. That smell, for her, was irretrievably associated with the weeks she'd spent years ago visiting Tam in New Orleans, when Tam several times had taken her out to the murky reaches of some swamp or another to watch her mother at work. In the instance Charlie remembered best, it had been midnight, full moon, the whole foggy, spooky swamp deal, and Madame Zora, as everyone except Tam called her mother, had been engaged in what Tam had explained in a whisper was casting a demon back into hell. There had certainly been something trapped in the center of the fiery circle Madame Zora had created, something that snarled and growled and finally shrieked as it vanished in a puff of malodorous smoke. That malodorous scent had been sulfur, and even as Charlie made the connection Michael screamed.

The sound cut through the night like a knife. It was so loud it seemed to explode through the walls, and anguished enough to make the hair stand up on the back of Charlie's neck. It should have brought half the hotel running, except she and Tam were the only people who could hear it.

"Michael," she cried, trying the doorknob uselessly, listening in helpless terror as the last echoes of his scream died away. After that, there was nothing. The bathroom, as far as she could tell, was now dead silent. The candles seemed to have been extinguished. The red glow was gone. Darkness was all that could be seen in the crack under the door. Only the scent of sulfur remained.

The air was suddenly heavy with what felt like static electricity.

"Tam?" Charlie tried, rattling the doorknob. There was no response to that, either.

Goose bumps swept over her in a wave. Her heart pounded like she had been running. Her breathing came shallow and fast.

Then the doorknob turned beneath her hand.

Heart in her throat, Charlie stepped back.

CHAPTER FOURTEEN

Tam walked out of the bathroom. Actually, stumbled was a better word. She moved past Charlie as if her legs had been turned to jelly. Her always pale face was shiny with sweat. Her hair looked like it had been caught in a whirlwind: it was tangled in a bright nimbus around her head.

Charlie's breathing suspended as her eyes riveted on Tam. She was so painfully afraid of what the answer was going to be that she couldn't put into words the question that was tearing at her heart.

Michael?

"I did what I could," Tam said in response to the look on Charlie's face, then moved on across the room to sink down heavily on the couch. Bending at the waist, she rested her head on her knees and wrapped her arms around her legs. The moonlight streaming through the window glinted on the silver of Michael's watch; it dangled from Tam's fingers.

Charlie froze. Her stomach turned inside out and her blood congealed in her veins and her ears started to ring. For a moment she thought her knees would give out. Then the bathroom door pushed open more and Michael walked out.

Michael, with his tawny blond hair and too-handsome-for-his-own-good face and drool-worthy body. Michael, with all six-foot-three muscular golden inches dressed in jeans and tee and boots, looking like himself again.

"Hey," he said. His voice was husky but *his,* the same honeyed drawl that had been doing its best to seduce her from the first time she'd ever heard it. He smiled at her, a crooked twist of his lips that stole the breath from her body.

Relief made Charlie dizzy.

Even as the dark room revolved around her, even as the floor tilted and the stars and moon and city lights outside the window spun into a single sparkling pinwheel, Charlie did what every instinct she possessed urged her to do. She walked straight into his arms, grabbed two desperate fistfuls of his shirt, rested her forehead against his chest, and closed her eyes.

And breathed.

His arms came around her, hugged her close.

The faint scent of lilacs clung to him. It was as real, as tangible, as he was.

So overwhelmed was she that it took her a second to realize that he *was* tangible: she was actually *in* his arms. She could feel him. He was as firm and substantial against her as any living, breathing man. Her breasts were nestled against a sturdy wall of muscle. The arms holding her were hard and strong. Her hands were twined in cool, smooth cotton.

He was *there.* Physically.

Her lips parted with astonishment. Looking up to make sure, she met a blaze of sky blue eyes.

"Michael." His name came out on a shaken breath.

"Charlie." His hold on her tightened until she could feel every rock-solid inch of him.

"Oh, my God." She threw her arms around his neck even as he bent his head to kiss her.

His lips were warm and dry and unmistakably male and just as unmistakably *there.* They slanted over hers, brushing against the soft curves of her mouth before hardening with a carnality that sent heat shooting through her. She closed her eyes. Her lips parted for him. He licked into her mouth, and she instantly went all soft and shivery inside. Then they were kissing, really kissing, deep and hot and hungry for each other. He kissed her like he was starving for the taste of her, like he could never get enough of her, and she kissed him back the same way. Her heart pounded. Her pulse raced. His hands splayed over her back. She could feel the size and shape and *warmth* of them through her thin blouse. She could feel all of him, the powerful length of his legs, his narrow, muscled hips, his broad shoulders beneath her arms. Greedily she touched the warm smooth skin of his nape, threaded her fingers through his hair. Her breasts tightened and tingled with pleasure as they pressed against the unyielding wall of his chest, and she made a little wordless sound of wanting into his mouth. She could feel his response in the rigidity of his arms around her, in the super-heated insistence of his kiss, in the hard, urgent mound beneath his jeans as he rocked into her a little.

If they had been alone, she would have started ripping off his clothes — and hers. She ached for him. She burned for him.

Then all of a sudden he wasn't there.

Her eyes flew open. He *was* there, still

tight up against her, lifting his head from their kiss with the same glazed and hungry and yet slightly bewildered look in his eyes that she knew must be present in hers, staring down at her with the same dawning realization that she was experiencing as it burst on her that his physicality had been a temporary state, that they were once again on different sides of the barrier, that he was spirit and she was human flesh and never the twain shall meet.

She didn't need to step back from his arms. She could no longer feel them around her. Her hands fell down through his body, just fell of their own weight without the wide shelf of his shoulders to support them. The electric tingle that was all she felt now when touching him was suddenly as horrifying as anything she had ever experienced.

Because it meant that they were once again impossible. Two different kinds of creatures, with no future that they could share.

"What the *hell*?" His voice was a growl as he took a step back from her. The note of frustrated anger in it echoed her own sudden devastation.

"Oh, my God, for a few minutes there I thought you were alive," she told him. Her gaze swung to Tam, who was still bent almost double on the couch, although Tam's head was up now as she watched them with a troubled expression that was just discernible in the starlight. "I thought you'd somehow managed to bring him back to *life.*"

Her tone was a mixture of anguish and pleading.

Tam shook her head. "That can't be done. The dead cannot be brought back to life. Don't hope for it, cherie, because it can never happen."

Charlie knew that, *knew* that, had known it all along and had never before even questioned it, but still that moment of wild hope and joy when he had emerged from Tam's spell feeling as warm and solid as any living, breathing man refused to release its grip on her, and Tam's words felt like a knife twisting in her heart.

Looking at Michael, Tam said, "You understand, spirit. You cannot be made alive again under any circumstances. The spell doesn't exist that can do that."

"I never thought it did." Michael's voice was wry. "Miracles are kind of thin on the ground where I come from."

Charlie must have made a wordless sound of distress, because he looked down at her with a gathering frown.

"Babe —" he said, reaching for her. Like

her, he was obviously having trouble re-membering that he was once again in a non-corporeal state.

Even as his hands brushed her arms, even as the too-familiar electric tingle made her heart ache, Charlie shook her head at him. She wasn't done with Tam.

"Then what *was* that?" she demanded. Pain still shivered in her voice. "The only times I've managed to break through to his side of the barrier I've had to fall asleep first. And he — he gets thrown into Spookville — the Dark Place — whenever he manifests, but here he still is. So what just happened?"

"You must understand, it's all about vibra-tion," Tam said. "These planes — the plane of the living, the plane of the dead — oper-ate on different frequencies, like radio chan-nels. The spirit said you drowned, that the white light came for you. If that's true, then your frequency must have been altered by the experience: you're closer to the Afterlife now, and you're vibrating at a higher fre-quency because of it. Intense emotion like what I just saw from you would send your vibrations higher still. The spirit's vibration was probably temporarily lowered by the spell I cast. You were briefly able to meet at the same level. But it was only temporary.

He had to return to his plane, to go back to vibrating at a higher frequency, and your extreme emotion leveled out, and so you're once again on different frequencies."

"In other words," Michael said drily, "we're just two metaphysical ships who happened to pass in the night."

"That's right." Tam sounded pleased that he understood.

Welcome back to cold, hard reality. The words popped into Charlie's head like a slap in the face.

"You okay?" Michael asked her. His eyes — thank God they were back to their normal sky blue! — searched hers. Suddenly the memory of the things they had said — *if he gets destroyed it will break my heart; I didn't want to leave you* — hung in the air between them. She could see that he was remembering them, too, in the deepening intensity of his gaze, the tightening of his lips. The air between them surged with — something. Whatever it was, the depth of emotion she was experiencing scared her. *You can't love him,* she told herself fiercely, and broke eye contact, looking away. A second later, he was speaking to Tam.

"So what you're saying is that she's permanently stuck on a higher vibration than she was before, because she nearly died,"

Michael said. Internally, Charlie was still a quivering mess. That he was able to pick that one detail out of everything Tam had said, to hone in on that, when she was still raw and bleeding inside, surprised her. He sounded, and looked, so calm and together that she didn't know whether to be impressed or affronted. But wishing things were different or railing against the cruelties of the universe was useless, as she had learned long since, so she pulled herself together instead and locked her emotions down and looked at Tam, who was shaking her head.

"Not permanently. I'm almost certain that any alteration would be temporary."

"Would it be the kind of thing that would let her hear voices that nobody else — me included, and keeping in mind that I'm on the other side of the line — can hear?" Michael asked. Charlie looked at him with dawning respect: affronted now definitely took a backseat to impressed. She would not have thought of that. At least not right now, as shaken and off-kilter as she was.

"Is that what she's doing?" Tam sounded interested. She was still leaning forward, but her forearms were resting on her thighs now and she looked altogether more alert.

Michael nodded. "Since she woke up in

the hospital after she almost died."

"And that would be how long ago?"

"About three weeks."

Charlie frowned: the experience of having herself discussed as if she weren't even present by two people (if Michael even qualified as a person) who meant about as much to her as anybody in the world was new. She wasn't sure she liked it.

"I've been experiencing clairaudience," she told Tam, claiming ownership of her own symptoms with a withering glance at Michael. "I hear voices inside my head now. I'm almost positive that they're real voices and not hallucinations. From the dead, I think. Michael can't hear them, or see whoever's talking, so the voices don't belong to spirits who are around me that I just can't see. I have no idea who's speaking or where the voices are coming from. It's only intermittent, and it seems to happen pretty much at random."

"And at damned inconvenient times," Michael added, and Charlie was reminded of her bandaged hand.

Tam's expression as she looked at Charlie was one of almost clinical appraisal. "If that's only been happening since your near death experience, then I'd say it's probably because you're vibrating at a higher frequency now. It will go away in time. I am almost —"

She was interrupted by the ringing of Charlie's cell phone. The sound was so unexpected, so cheery and normal in that heavy atmosphere, Charlie jumped a little with surprise. She knew immediately what it was, of course, and glanced toward her purse, which was on the coffee table where she had left it.

"— sure," Tam concluded, and looked at the purse, which was right in front of her. "It's important, cherie."

Charlie didn't even question how Tam could know that the incoming call was important: over the years, she had learned that the psychic part of Tam just did. Given the time on the East Coast, the caller almost had to be Tony, or possibly Buzz or Lena, wondering where she was. Charlie had no idea how long she'd been gone, but the bottom line was, too long. Now that Michael was restored to himself again and that particular crisis was past, she needed to concentrate on the job she had come to Las Vegas to do: helping to find Lena's sister.

"Excuse me," she murmured, and dug her phone out of her purse. A glance at the caller ID told her that it was indeed Tony. "I need to take this."

"Where are you?" Tony asked without preamble when she answered. His voice sounded blessedly normal, an antidote to all the craziness she'd been experiencing. Michael's sardonic expression told her that he recognized the caller's voice as soon as she did. He could hear both sides of the conversation, she knew. She narrowed her eyes at him. He kept on listening unashamedly.

"I ran into a friend," Charlie replied, which was perfectly true. "I'm still here, in the hotel."

"We finally tracked Kaminsky down. She's at the morgue, says she thinks she has a lead. Crane and I are heading there now. Are you coming?"

The instinctive shiver that ran down her spine was, she hoped, visible to no one else. She hated morgues. They were worse even than hospitals for someone with her particular sensitivities.

"Yes," she said. The thing about it was, though, that if there was something in the morgue that might help Lena's sister, Charlie was the best person to pick up on it: morgues tended to be full of the recently, violently dead. The good news about morgues was, there weren't likely to be any serial killers in them. At least, not live ones.

"Meet us in the lobby in front of the reception desk in ten minutes," Tony said, and when Charlie agreed he disconnected.

"You sure you're up to this?" Michael asked quietly as Charlie picked up her purse and tucked the phone back into it. "It's been a long day."

"I should be asking you that. You're the one who nearly got obliterated."

"If I say I'm not up to it, will you forget about heading out to a damned morgue tonight?"

"No, but I'll feel really bad about dragging you with me."

"In that case, I bounce back fast."

Charlie looked at Tam, who was watching them with an expression that was very nearly sour, and said, "I have to go. Are you heading home tomorrow?"

Tam nodded and held Michael's watch out to her. Charlie took it, glanced at the time — she was shocked to see that only about half an hour had passed since she'd met Tam in the lobby; it had felt like multiple lifetimes — and slid it back into its accustomed place on her arm.

"I told you about the hunter," Charlie said to Tam, barely repressing a shudder as she remembered. "How much danger are we in from it, do you think?"

"He" — Tam put an emphasis on the pronoun — "should be in no danger here. *Executeurs* almost never come through to the earth plane. The walls must be especially thin where you were. Concentrations of evil, which I have to imagine your prison contains, do occasionally serve as portals, though. He should probably stay away from them."

"Good to know," Michael said, with a significant look at Charlie. She barely repressed a sigh. She was more thankful than she could say to have Michael restored to himself again, but she didn't look forward to ongoing arguments about continuing her work at the prison.

"Want to do lunch before I head back?" Tam asked.

Charlie thought about how intense the team's investigations tended to be. They went flat out, with only the bare minimum of time carved out for sleep and food, because lives were inevitably on the line. With Lena's sister involved, the stakes would be even higher. But she hadn't seen Tam in forever, and she had no idea how long it would be before she saw her again. And her role in the investigation was less boots on the ground than the others', especially now that she'd taken active serial killers in serious aversion and meant to deliberately pull back from the fieldwork as much as she could as a result. Doing her best for Lena and her sister meant using her special ability when it could make a difference, like, possibly, at the morgue tonight, and using every bit of her training and expertise to provide a forensic analysis of the psychological facets of the case.

In other words, she should be able to fit in one nonwork-related meal.

"How does breakfast sound instead? At, say, eight?" Charlie slung her purse over her shoulder. "That's the only time tomorrow I'm almost sure I can get away."

Tam made a face at the early-for-her time, then nodded with resignation. "Eight it is."

"I'll meet you at the buffet downstairs. And Tam — thanks for coming to our rescue tonight." Charlie's last words were heartfelt.

"Yeah, thank you," Michael echoed as, with a quick smile at her friend, Charlie headed toward the door. "I owe you one."

Glancing over her shoulder, Charlie saw that Tam was on her feet, no doubt meaning to follow them to the door and lock it behind them. She watched Michael smile at Tam — full-on charm offensive from a guy guaranteed to knock just about any woman's socks off when he just stood there and breathed — and Tam frown in response.

"You're welcome." Tam directed her words to Charlie. Michael got a long cool look in response to that smile. "Although I'm still not sure I did you a favor."

CHAPTER FIFTEEN

Once they were in the hall Michael said, "I don't think the voodoo priestess likes me very much."

"You're a ghost." They reached the elevators and Charlie hit the down button. "Tam thinks they have their place, which isn't here in the earthly plane following me around."

The elevator arrived and they got on. Of course, when she could really use some company to keep from having a one-on-one conversation she didn't feel ready for, there was no one else in the car. Charlie punched L for lobby.

"Lucky for me you don't agree." Michael was studying her. Charlie could feel his gaze on her averted face, but she resolutely kept her eyes on the changing numbers over the door. She'd felt too much as she'd fought to save him, and what was worse was she'd let him see it. Now she was pulling back emotionally like a turtle retreating into its shell when danger threatens. It was an instinctive reaction, one no doubt honed by years of psychological issues she wasn't ready to delve into, and it was also, she recognized even as it was happening, the only sane thing to do.

"What makes you think I don't agree?" She still wasn't looking at him. Her reflection in the brass doors reminded her of what he was, because there was no reflection of him standing beside her. It also showed her that her hair was a mess and her lipstick was gone. Those were the matters she chose to concentrate on. "Just because I didn't want to see you get turned into a crispy critter and then go *poof* into oblivion doesn't mean I like having you here following me around."

"Let's see, I think it was you saying something along the lines of *If he dies, it will break my heart* that made me think that. Or maybe it was the way you kissed me."

"What I said was, *gets destroyed,* not dies," Charlie pointed out with far more composure than she was feeling as she pulled her brush from her purse and ran it through her hair. The advantage of having lived with the man (ghost) for six weeks or so now was that she'd gotten used to him watching her groom, so having his eyes on her as she made repairs to her appearance no longer bothered her. "For the record, I said that because I was trying to persuade Tam to save you."

Having finished with her hair, she took advantage of the shiny brass to reapply her lipstick.

"And you kissed me like I was holding water and you were dying of thirst because . . . ?"

"You're a hot guy." As she finished up with the lipstick and restored it to her purse, she deliberately kept her voice light. "I didn't say I wasn't attracted to you."

"Are you really going to do this?" Michael said after a moment in which his eyes never left her. She, on the other hand, was religiously watching the descending floor numbers. Thank goodness they were on number three, with only two to go!

"Do what?" Her tone was short. She really, really did not want to have this conversation. Not until she'd had time to get her thoughts together and regroup. Not until she felt less vulnerable.

"Give me the cold shoulder because you're scared to admit you're crazy in love with me. After all we've been through?"

That snapped her head around. She glared at him. He smiled beguilingly at her.

"I am not giving you the cold shoulder," she clarified, refusing to be beguiled. "I'm just getting on with the next item on today's extremely full to-do list."

"Does that mean you're not denying that you're scared to admit you're crazy in love with me?"

"That means I'm not in love with you." She cut right to the chase. Now that he wasn't in imminent danger of disappearing forever and she wasn't going nuts over the possibility, her mind rejected the idea as if it were a snake trying to slither through her front door. Her heart, on the other hand, gave an odd little throb, which she absolutely refused to so much as acknowledge.

The elevator stopped and the doors opened. Charlie didn't think she'd ever been so glad to walk out into a crowded, noisy hotel lobby in her life.

"You can keep fighting it all you want." His voice in her ear was maddening. "Thanks to you, I'll still be here when you get tired of denying it."

Charlie's lips compressed. Her spine straightened. Resolutely ignoring he-who-was-once-again-the-bane-of-her-existence, she strode across the lobby in search of Tony.

He was waiting with Buzz, right where he

said he'd be. Reliable: she liked that in a man. Almost as much as she liked *alive.*

"Ready?" His eyes assessed her as she joined them. He was looking tired, as she had no doubt she was herself. But on Tony tired looked good. The faint lines around his mouth and eyes gave him a certain gravitas. "Get all caught up with your friend?"

She nodded. "She's staying here. When I left her, she was heading for bed."

"She?" he asked with a lift of his brows, as Buzz greeted her with an abstracted wave. Buzz's curly hair bore evidence of his having run his hands through it multiple times: it looked like he was wearing a frizzy brown dandelion on his head. Instead of tired, he looked wired. He was all but bouncing from foot to foot.

Charlie nodded again, as Tony's tone reminded her of how complicated her life was becoming. Good guy FBI agent versus bad boy ghost shouldn't even have been a contest. The unfortunate thing about it was, at the moment it really wasn't.

Michael gave Tony a narrow-eyed look, but didn't say anything.

Nobody said much as they headed for the front entrance, where the valet had the car waiting. The Conquistador's spectacular fountains were shooting toward the night sky, forming a colorful wall of water that pulsated in time to Celene Dion's "My Heart Will Go On." That the tune held a certain irony under the circumstances didn't escape Charlie, but she refused to dwell on it. Given that it was September, which wasn't a big tourist month, she was surprised at the size of the crowd watching the water show. The area in front of the hotel was packed with people of all sizes, shapes, and descriptions.

"She told *you* she's found something. Hasn't said word one to me." Buzz was obviously continuing a conversation he and Tony had been having as they piled into the white Lexus that had been provided for them at the airport, courtesy of the local field office. Tony drove, Charlie was in the front passenger seat, and Buzz sat in the back behind Tony. Michael was behind Charlie. He was being so silent that she would have pulled down her visor and flipped open the makeup mirror to check on him, except — oh, wait — that was pointless because she wouldn't be able to see his reflection in the mirror.

"I *am* her boss." Tony's voice was dry. "She was returning my call."

"Yeah." Buzz's tone clearly said that he knew that wasn't the reason. "I must have called her a dozen times since we got here. She hasn't returned any of them."

"She's probably trying to distance herself a little bit from you right now." Charlie turned sideways in her seat to look at Buzz. She could also — funny how that worked out — see Michael. He was looking out the window at the bright blaze of light that was Las Vegas. Broodingly. She frowned. "If I were you, I would concentrate on being her helpful colleague rather than her boyfriend for a bit."

"How about we just concentrate on finding her sister?" Tony suggested pointedly.

"Did Lena say anything specifically about the lead she found?" Charlie asked.

"No." Tony shook his head. "Only that it was the first solid thing she's turned up."

"I keep hoping this is all a mistake." Buzz's voice sounded hollow. He was cracking his knuckles and jiggling one leg as he spoke. "But it's not, is it?"

"It's not looking that way," Tony said.

They rehashed what they knew about certain aspects of the case — the time Giselle was last seen (exiting the Conquistador around midnight Saturday), the characteristics she shared with the other possible victims (attractive, busty brunette under thirty-five), other scenarios for her disappearance that did not involve a serial killer (leaving voluntarily; accident; abduction by someone who was not a serial killer) — until they arrived at the Clark County Coroner's Office, better known as the Las Vegas morgue. Charlie was surprised to see that the building looked like a church, complete with a stained-glass window set into a wall.

"It's a church?" Buzz asked, clearly as surprised as Charlie.

"It *was* a church. It's been remodeled." It was obvious that Tony had been there before. A few minutes later they were inside being greeted by Coroner Investigator Kevin Jones. He looked to be around thirty-five, average looks, height and weight, with dark brown hair worn in a military-style cut, mild blue eyes, and a pasty complexion. He wore a short-sleeved white shirt with multiple pens and a small flashlight in his chest pocket, and black pants with his badge on his belt.

"Your agent is downstairs," Jones told them after Tony made the introductions. The smell of death was strong even in these well-kept outer offices. Charlie got busy trying to convince herself the sickish-sweet scent wasn't already making her stomach start to act up as, at Jones's gesture, they followed him past the glass-walled work cubicles, which were largely empty at that hour, and into an elevator. "I was the one who gave her a call when I started cataloging the victim's personal possessions. She'd stopped by yesterday, left a photo of the woman you're looking for and a list of what she was wearing, and this fit the bill."

"Giselle Kaminsky — is that the name of the victim?" Buzz's voice went high and reedy. His face turned absolutely white.

"Haven't ID'd her yet," Jones said cheerfully as the elevator stopped and the doors opened. A rush of cold air immediately enveloped them. Charlie shivered inwardly as they walked out into a small corridor. She was starting to hear a humming sound in her ears, and she could feel the cold and smell the stench of death on what was almost an organic level. The grayish-white light cast by the fluorescent fixtures overhead suddenly grew way too bright. Even as she squinted in reaction, she realized that her senses were heightening.

Which meant, of course, that the dead were near. This was how they always affected her.

If they were in the morgue, they would be the newly, violently dead. She would be able to see them.

She could hear the thumping of her own

heart, feel the warm rush of blood through her veins. The familiar miasma with its sense of being part of two worlds enveloped her. Reality took on a whole new dimension.

I hate this. Oh, God, why did you visit this ability on me?

"You're turning kind of green around the gills," Michael said grimly.

"Kaminsky wouldn't have said she had a lead if she'd found her sister's body." Tony gripped Buzz's arm in a way that was clearly meant to be steadying.

"Oh. Right." Buzz still looked pale. Then Jones pushed one of two brushed-steel double doors at the end of the corridor open and stood back with a gesture inviting them to precede him. They walked into a large, low-ceilinged, white-walled room with multiple ventilation fans rattling away in boxlike aluminum housing. The temperature would have done a refrigerator proud, and the reason for that was immediately apparent: six bodies in blue plastic body bags were lined up on gurneys against the far wall. At least three of them had already been autopsied. Charlie could tell because of the clear plastic bags containing their organs that were stored neatly in open bins attached to the gurneys.

Although the room was scrupulously

clean, the smell was intense.

The queasiness that Charlie had been resolutely ignoring was now refusing to be ignored.

Dressed in a tan skirt and a white polo beneath a black blazer (the better to hide her shoulder holster with) instead of one of her signature curve-hugging suits, Lena stood over the farthermost gurney, her head bent so that her black, chin-length bob swung forward to hide her face. At five-two, she was sensitive about her height, and as a result had a thing for killer heels: tonight's were black, with platforms that gave her at least four additional inches. The sultry, exotic kind of prettiness that she shared with her sister was totally at odds with her aggressive personality. The determined jut of her chin was the only visible indication of that as she snapped pictures of the corpse with her phone.

"There she is," Tony said as they headed toward her and the heavy door swung shut behind them with a *swoosh*.

Lena immediately looked up. Charlie just had time to register her red-rimmed eyes and the tight set to her mouth and hear her tell Tony, "This woman was wearing my sister's bracelet," without a greeting or any other preamble, before the onslaught hit.

A blond teen with Alice in Wonderland hair and big, lost eyes appeared out of nowhere. Gaze fixing on Charlie from across the room, she cried, "Can you tell me what time it is? My mom's going to kill me if I miss my curfew."

As Charlie registered that the girl's jeans and tee were soaked with blood, a heavyset gray-haired woman in a pink-flowered housedress sat bolt upright on one of the gurneys, her upper body emerging right through the blue plastic bag that contained it. She blinked, looked around, and moaned, "The TV's broken. Oh, no, what am I going to do?" Sliding off the gurney, she started walking toward Charlie. That's when the knife protruding from the side of her neck became visible, as did the blood that covered her entire left side.

A thin young man with a gray hoodie and long, stringy black hair paced up and down along the far side of the room. He said nothing, just stared into space with a vacant look in his eyes. In the middle of his forehead was a dime-sized black hole. Over in the corner, another young man, this one with short brown hair who was wearing jeans and a tee like the girl, crouched with his head bent. There was no mark on him that she could see. Until he looked up: then she saw that the left side of his face was smashed in, enough so that an eyeball dangled and she could see the white of his shattered cheek-bone and jawbone amidst the gore. What she had thought at first glance was a graphic on his shirt wasn't a graphic at all, she discovered after a second look: it was splotches and smears of blood. An elderly man and woman, holding hands, stepped through a wall, walked across the room, and disappeared through another, but not before Charlie saw the bullet hole between the woman's eyes and the gaping wound in the man's temple.

This convergence of the dead produced an energy field that hit Charlie like a wave. Her stomach gave a warning heave. Swallowing, she stopped walking. It was all she could do not to take a couple of steps back.

Forget queasiness. What she was experiencing now was full-on, stomach-churning nausea. She stuck her hand in her purse, fumbling blindly for the Tums.

"I think I dropped my keys," a bald, florid-faced man told Charlie confidingly even as her fingers closed around the life-saving plastic bottle. At the same time, she visually tracked a tow-headed little boy on a tricycle pedaling furiously down the center of the floor. Flipping open the lid with a practiced thumb, she popped several of the lemony tablets into her mouth while at the same time watching both child and tricycle disappear into one of the tall metal cabinets lining the far side of the room. As she chewed, swallowed, and stuck the bottle back down in her purse, the bald man continued to walk toward her. Now only a few yards away, he was looking at her while he thoughtfully patted down the pockets of a light blue uniform that had *Terry Hale, mechanic* embroidered on the chest pocket. "I can't seem to find them anywhere."

It was only as she took a second look that she saw blood trickling from his mouth and nose and the black smudges of a tire track running diagonally across his abdomen, from which his intestines spilled in bloody loops.

"Can you help me?" he asked, and kept on coming.

CHAPTER SIXTEEN

For someone like her, Charlie reflected, morgues were the worst. They *teemed* with the spirits of the newly, violently dead. Not all bodies showed up in the morgue with their spirits attached, but many did, and a good number of those spirits stayed even after the bodies were processed and sent elsewhere. If she could see them, they'd died within the last seven days or so. Many, many more were around that didn't fit those parameters that she couldn't see, she knew. That was why the atmosphere was so charged.

"Jesus." Michael was beside her, interposing himself between her and the bewildered mechanic, Terry Hale. Ignoring her dangerously unsettled stomach as well as the cold prickles that ran over her skin, she did her best to look past the importunate dead toward where Tony and Buzz were making a beeline for Lena, who stood beside the last gurney in the row. With so many living people in the vicinity, Charlie couldn't react to the things she was able to hear and see that they could not. Fortunately, she had gotten used to remaining largely impassive in the face of spirit bombardment.

Heading toward her now, Alice in Wonderland cried, "It's after midnight and —"

Gray-haired woman spoke over her: "The game's on in twenty minutes! I have to —"

Blocked by Michael, Terry Hale had stopped walking. He frowned at Charlie and said, "Must have dropped 'em when —"

Alice continued, "— she'll kill me if —"

Woman said, "— fix it before he —"

Terry Hale concluded with, "I got out of the truck."

The girl, the woman, and Hale, clearly not yet having realized they were dead, were all talking at the same time, confusion in their eyes. They could see her, Charlie knew, which wasn't the case with all spirits, including, she thought, the young man pacing the floor over by the wall. The boy crouched in the corner could see her, she was fairly certain, but instead of heading toward her he stayed where he was, wariness apparent in what was left of his face. Spirits seemed able to sense those who could see them and tended to be drawn to such people like moths to a light, which was why Alice, the woman, and Hale were now closing in on her so inexorably. Normally the living were invisible to the dead, just as ghosts were normally invisible to the living.

Unfortunately, in this matter Charlie wasn't normal.

"What is this, Cirque du Spook?" Michael asked. He was looking around with an expression that made her think that he was seeing everything she was and then some.

"— I'm not home by twelve. But I don't know where I *am*. Can you help me? Please?" As Alice neared, she reached toward Charlie with pale, beseeching hands. Michael stepped between them, grabbing the teen's wrists before she could make contact.

"Don't touch her," he told the girl, and swept a warning glance around at the others.

"They can't hurt me," Charlie murmured just loudly enough for Michael to hear. Overprotectiveness seemed to be built into his DNA, however, and she was starting to get the feeling that fighting it was a waste of time.

"You got any guarantee of that?" was his response, thrown at her over his shoulder as the girl looked up at him and said, "Who are you?"

Her voice was squeaky with fright. Charlie couldn't blame her: he towered over the teen, a foot taller, his shoulders more than twice the breadth of hers. Anybody with a lick of sense would have found his sheer size intimidating, and from what she could see of his face, his expression was equally so. His hands were tanned and strong-looking as they gripped Alice's fragile wrists.

"My name's Michael." To Charlie he said, "I got this, babe. Go do your thing."

She didn't reply. It was too risky to keep talking to him, with Tony and Buzz and Lena and the coroner's investigator so near. But she felt as if a burden she hadn't even realized she'd been carrying had been lifted, just a little, from her shoulders. As if he'd taken some of the weight of it on to his.

I'm not in this alone anymore.

As she looked past Michael, past the apparitions that were now focused on him, she saw that there was a new one, a sweet-faced woman of about thirty that stood at Lena's shoulder, quietly weeping. Tears ran in silvery tracks down her soft round cheeks. Casually dressed in khakis and a short-sleeved green camp shirt, she was attractive, with even features; soft, full lips; and shoulder-length nut brown hair that curled up at her shoulders. Except for the blood that soaked her clothes from her waist to her knees, she looked like a Midwestern schoolteacher on vacation.

"All of you, shut up," she heard Michael say to the clamoring shades as she moved past him. Tact in dealing with the phantoms that beset her was not his strong suit, as she had previously learned, but she left him to it, glad that she was able to do so. The weeping woman was standing beside Lena looking down at the body on the gurney. The zipper had been pulled down to reveal the corpse's face. As Charlie reached the end of the gurney, she saw that the toe tag was attached to a slender, pink-pedicured, well-kept female foot. Then, looking farther up the bag to the waxy, blue-lipped face the open zipper revealed, she confirmed what she had suspected: the weeping shade was looking down at her own corpse.

"— sure it's the same one?" Tony was asking.

Lena clutched a clear plastic bag that contained what looked like a silver bracelet. She all but thrust it in Tony's face.

"Of course I'm sure," she said fiercely, shaking the bag at him. "I gave it to her. For her birthday. It has spikes on it, see?" Lena touched one of them through the plastic. The bracelet interspersed heavy silver links with what looked like shark's teeth, also in gleaming silver. Half a dozen of the curved, inches-long barbs dangled from the chain. She took a breath. "We were joking that if she ever got attacked, she could use it as a weapon. You know, like some women walking to their cars at night will use keys gripped between their fingers. As soon as I saw it, I knew it was hers." She took a breath, and her eyes flicked to Charlie in silent acknowledgment of her presence before refocusing on Tony. "So I had to come down here and check, make sure the body wasn't her."

A subtle tightening in Lena's face was the only indication of how hard that had been on her.

"Do you have an ID on the victim yet?" Tony asked Jones.

"No, sir. No, we don't," Jones replied. "The police department's trying to ID her now."

Tony nodded.

"Maybe this woman just happened to have the same bracelet. They can't be that uncommon," Buzz said. There was naked pain in his eyes as he looked at Lena, but his voice had lost the reedy thinness that had characterized it when he'd thought Giselle was the victim and was now steady.

Lena shook her head. Her eyes were hard as glass as she met Buzz's gaze. "No. I bought it at a jewelry store near my condo before I came. There's no way that a dead woman in Las Vegas has the same one." She looked at Tony. "This woman's been violently attacked. Beaten and stabbed. She was found in a drainage ditch just outside the city limits when the sun came up this morning. There was a storm yesterday, a downpour. The police think it washed her out of a storm drain where she'd been lying unconscious. Probably since early Sunday morning, according to the coroner's report. She was still alive when they found her, but she died in an ambulance on the way to the hospital, so they brought her here." Her nostrils flared. Charlie thought it was with the effort to keep from showing too much emotion. "Saturday night is when Giselle disappeared. A murdered woman who had my sister's bracelet in her possession and was attacked at around the same time she went missing? There is no way that's a coincidence."

"It doesn't sound like it," Tony agreed, and looked at Jones. "Do you have her clothes and other personal items here?"

Jones nodded. "Yes, sir. Bagged and

tagged, just like her."

"Would you get them together? Everything she had. We're going to be taking them with us." With a glance at the three of them, Tony added, "We'll send them off to the lab first thing in the morning. See what they can tell us."

Buzz said, "I'll take care of it."

The woman's clothes and other possessions would be sent to the FBI lab in Quantico for rush analysis. Charlie had been with the team long enough to know that their cases got priority treatment.

Buzz looked at Lena. "We'll need to send the bracelet, too." His voice had gentled. Lena's eyes met his, and for an unguarded moment her fear for her sister blazed out, visible to them all. What the lab would be looking for was, among other things, blood.

"I hope she was able to use it to scratch the bastard." Lena's voice had a vicious edge as she handed the plastic bag with the bracelet in it to Buzz.

"The victim was just brought in today?" Tony was talking to Jones. "Do you have an official cause of death?"

"Yes, sir, and stabbing." Unbidden, Jones unzipped the body bag and pulled the edges apart to reveal the corpse's thin bare torso. Charlie tried not to see too much: death had no dignity, as she had learned long since, but still the act of looking at a dead person's nakedness seemed like a gross invasion of privacy.

"She has a tattoo." Tony pointed to a small bird inked onto the woman's upper arm. "That should help identify her."

Lena positioned her phone, took a picture.

"There're already pictures in the file," Jones told her.

Lena took another one.

Charlie, meanwhile, focused on the details that were germane to the woman's death. The large Y-shaped incision that ran from her collarbone down past her sternum was the result of the autopsy, so Charlie disregarded that. Her lower rib cage had suffered extensive bruising, she saw at a glance, but what Jones pointed to almost with pride were the four deep slash wounds that laid open her abdomen. "That's what killed —"

Charlie didn't hear the rest because the weeping shade, looking down at her corpse, began to scream.

Charlie almost jumped. Only years of conditioning kept her still as the woman shrieked like she'd just been stabbed in the stomach — as, in the woman's mind, no doubt she had been. Charlie realized that what she was watching was a loop, or a replay of things that had already happened. Usually, like now, it was a re-enactment of what had led to the spirit's death. Screaming, the murdered woman doubled over, clutched her abdomen, and stumbled backward.

"No! No! What are you doing? Stop!" The woman gasped between screams as blood poured through the spread fingers she had pressed against her abdomen. "Joe, *why?*" she cried, looking up in horror at something Charlie couldn't see as she fell back through the wall.

"What the fuck?" Michael landed beside Charlie as the woman disappeared, staring after the phantom just as, she realized, she was doing herself. She couldn't answer him, but then, there really wasn't much she could say other than the obvious: screaming dead woman bleeds and vanishes.

Another round of nausea hit her. Taking more Tums was probably a bad idea: she didn't know if it was possible to overdose, but she felt that she was perilously close to finding out. Though if she didn't do something . . .

Do not throw up.

She tried deep breathing instead.

"Nana! Michael, look, my grandmother's here!"

Charlie looked around to see that Alice was beaming beatifically at something at the far end of the room that Charlie couldn't see.

"There's your ticket, then. Go on," Michael told her. Alice paused just long enough to give him a dazzling smile before running across the room with her arms outstretched and promptly disappearing.

"Dara was killed in a car accident a few hours ago," Michael answered Charlie's look. "She was fucking sixteen." He grimaced. "Death's one hell of a fickle bitch."

"Michael," Hale called. He was once again pacing the room, patting his pockets even as he frowned at Michael. "I can't go home without my keys. How will I get in?"

"This gig ain't what I signed on for," Michael told Charlie with disgust, and, dodging the child on the tricycle, he headed for the mechanic. Under better conditions, watching her big, bad, tough guy ghost deal with a gaggle of needy spirits would have made her smile. But the atmosphere in the room was so heavy with grief and loss, and Lena's situation was so heartrending, that she didn't think she could have smiled if she'd tried.

Her stomach heaved again, and she clenched her teeth.

Breathe.

"How about we ask our eminent psychiatrist what she thinks?" The barbed voice belonged to Lena. The reference to *our eminent psychiatrist* — that could only mean her.

Jerking her gaze back to her live companions, hoping no one had noticed her lapse — fat chance, they were all looking at her — Charlie was just about to ask Lena what she was talking about when Tony rescued her.

"It's possible that we're dealing with a serial killer, but I don't think we ought to jump to conclusions just yet," Tony said, then looked at Jones. "We're done here, Investigator. Agent Crane will pick up the victim's clothes and personal belongings on our way out. We'll have someone get you a court order as soon as possible, but in the meantime we need this body to be held as possible evidence."

"Yes, sir." Jones's tone was the equivalent of a salute.

"This woman makes eighteen. Nineteen if you count Giselle. It's so *obvious*. How can you not see it?" Lena demanded of Tony. Charlie had had the other woman's sharp tone and snapping eyes directed at her before, but she had never seen Lena being less than respectful of the man who was, after all, her boss.

"I'm not saying it's not a serial killer, I'm just saying that at this point we need to keep an open mind." Tony's reply was surprisingly soothing. "We'll find your sister, I promise." His gaze slid to Buzz and Charlie. There was a veiled message in his eyes, but by this point Charlie was too nauseated and headachey and wired and tired to even try to decipher it. She was also past trying to talk to the spirit of the dead woman on the loop if she should appear again, or dealing with any other stray spirits, or doing much of anything else. Basically, she just wanted to throw up and sleep, in that order. Besides, she'd spotted Michael down on one knee beside the little boy on the tricycle, who he had apparently somehow induced to stop to talk to him, and that was a distraction worth paying attention to. With a nod at Jones, Tony turned away from the gurney, concluding with, "Come on, we're leaving."

"No, I —" Kaminsky started to protest, as Jones grabbed the body bag's zipper and began yanking it up again. Charlie averted her gaze from the poor pale corpse as the zipper pulled the plastic closed around it.

Tony said, "*Walk,* Kaminsky," in a tone

that made it an order, and Buzz started to take Lena's arm, only to be angrily shaken off. Nevertheless, they both followed Tony. Charlie was getting ready to fall in behind them when a whisper, the softest whisper, curled through her head.

"I don't want to die." It was a woman's voice, terrified and pleading.

She'd never heard the voice before. No spirit was there to produce it. Her first thought — that it belonged to the woman in the body bag — was wrong. The voices were not the same. This one had the smallest suggestion of an accent. Was it — Spanish? Yes, she thought it was.

"Oh, please," the voice begged, louder now. Charlie felt cold all over as everything went a little out of focus. Her heart began to slam in hard, fast strokes. Suddenly dizzy, barely aware of where she was or what she was doing, she grasped the edge of the gurney for support. She retained just enough clarity to understand what was happening: it was one of the voices that existed only in her head. One of those that Tam had said she was able to hear as a result of having nearly died. The voice went high and shaky as it continued. "I'll do anything. Anything you want."

"Charlie?" Michael was beside her.

"What's up?"

She heard him, she saw him — but not clearly. It was as if she was at the bottom of a swimming pool looking up through gallons of greenish water: he and his voice were distorted and indistinct. Just like everything else around her that was, or should have been, solid and real was distorted and indistinct.

"Please don't kill me! Please don't kill me!" the voice cried. The words were followed by a shriek. A shriek that was so shrill and full of fear and pain that it felt like a knife stabbing through her brain. Charlie shuddered as every tiny hair on her body catapulted upright. Then there was a horrible gurgling sound. She knew what death sounded like when she heard it, and it was like that. Cold sweat poured over her in a wave.

It suddenly became crystal clear that what she was hearing was some poor woman's dying moments. The only question was, was it something that had really happened? A higher vibration — Tam had said that she was picking up the voices because she was operating at a higher vibration. That meant that the voice was real; that the horrible little snippet she'd just heard of a woman's dying pleas was *real*.

Charlie couldn't help it: she gave a little moan of distress as her knees wobbled and threatened to give way.

"Babe, I'm right here." Michael grabbed for her as she swayed. She felt the electric tingle of his hands passing through her arms, heard his growled curse.

She would have sunk to the floor right there and then, with the echoes of that terrifying death sound still swirling through her mind, if a hard arm hadn't wrapped around her shoulders, supporting her, helping her to stay upright.

It was Michael who had his arm around her. Or at least, she thought it was Michael: she could see him, hear his voice, and she clung to his presence like a lifeline. Then she frowned in confusion. It couldn't be Michael. He had no substance. The arm around her, the solid, firm, supportive arm, belonged to Tony. He was there, too, at her side, she realized. She could feel his warmth, and his strength. The solid support of a flesh-and-blood man.

"Charlie?" Worry for her darkened Tony's eyes. Oh, God, he was coming into better focus: she could actually see him frowning at her, see the tension in his face. Having obviously stepped aside to make way for Tony, Michael was frowning at her, too. His hands hung, fingers flexing, at his sides. The electric tingle she'd felt — he'd tried to grab her and failed.

"You hearing voices again? Is that it?" Michael demanded.

In a desperate bid to get a handle on the worst of her symptoms, Charlie took a deep breath, and gave him an abbreviated nod. She was unable to pretend that nothing was wrong. The sense of vertigo that she was experiencing was just too strong.

"What happened?"

"Is she sick?"

Buzz and Lena had returned, to frown at her. Even Lena looked concerned.

"Goddamn it to hell anyway," Michael said. "You can't keep going through this."

"Should I call 911?" That was Jones. He was, Charlie was glad she was able to see, hovering around, too, although he was keeping a discreet distance.

Charlie dug down deep. After all, she'd been dealing with spirits for most of her life. The voices — they were no more than a new wrinkle in an old experience. She was just going to have to learn to deal.

"No. I got a little dizzy suddenly is all," she achieved, and managed to straighten her spine so that she wasn't leaning so heavily against Tony anymore. At the same time, she made an embarrassed grimace at Lena and Buzz. "It's just . . . it's been a long day."

"It has been. For all of us," Tony agreed as he squeezed her shoulder comfortingly. Charlie would have pulled away from him, except her head still swam and her knees still felt weak. Fortunately, he didn't seem inclined to let her go just yet. "Which is why we're going back to the hotel and grabbing some sleep." When Kaminsky looked like she was prepared to argue, he said, "*Now.* You're not doing your sister any good by working until you can't think straight. The local office is on it, and everything that can be done is being done. We'll start fresh in the morning."

Lena still looked inclined to argue, but she didn't, and Charlie suspected that Tony had given her a look that had sealed the deal.

"You okay to walk to the car?" he asked Charlie quietly, and when she replied with "Yes, of course," in as strong a tone as she could muster, his arm dropped away from her shoulders. Instead his hand curled, warm and strong, around her upper arm. She found that she was glad of the support as they headed for the elevators. Michael, on her other side, gave her and Tony a long, hard look, but didn't say a word.

It wasn't until they were all in the elevator heading up that her vision cleared enough to allow her to see that Michael's expression was bleak.

CHAPTER SEVENTEEN

By the time they walked out of the morgue, Tony was no longer holding her arm. Her dizziness and nausea had receded enough so that, as they'd stepped off the elevator, Charlie was able to pull away from him with a quick smile that thanked him for his support. She kept shooting lightning glances at Michael, who moved silently at her side, his expression now impossible to read. Crossing the shadowy parking lot toward the white Lexus, Charlie took a few deep breaths of the dry, faintly chilly night air and revived sufficiently to remember the one solid bit of evidence that she, personally, had gleaned.

"I'm fairly certain that whoever killed that woman is named Joe," she told Tony. "If he isn't the actual murderer, then someone named Joe was definitely involved in her death."

Having stopped to collect the victim's

belongings, Buzz was behind them, trailing Lena, who had arrived in her own rental car and was cutting across the parking lot toward it. Tony had already directed Buzz to drive Lena back to the hotel — *straight to the hotel, Kaminsky,* was how he'd put it. Lena hadn't argued, but from her brisk pace as she strode across the parking lot Charlie got the feeling that losing Buzz was up next on her agenda.

Tony frowned. "You have one of your psychic experiences back there?"

Charlie cut a quick glance at Michael, fully expecting a caustic comment. But still he said nothing. From the remote look on his face he was thinking about something else entirely.

"Yes." Charlie saw no need to elaborate.

"You actually saw her? The dead woman?"

"Yes."

Tony's eyes slid over her face. "And she told you her killer's name was Joe." Again, there was no apparent skepticism in his voice. He was merely probing for facts.

"More or less."

"She tell you her name?"

"She said, 'No, what are you doing, stop,' and 'Joe, why,' " Charlie said flatly. "Then she disappeared."

Tony knew more about what she saw than

did most of the living with whom she came into contact, and if their relationship, professional or otherwise, was to be at all worthwhile it was important that he know the truth. She reflected on that for a second and amended it to some of the truth. Spookville and hunters and sacrificial chicken innards and morgues full of uneasy spirits and inexplicable voices in her head — that might be pushing it. And Michael. Telling him about Michael was definitely out. If ever one of those tell-me-about-your-exes conversations came up between Tony and her, the fact that she was saddled with a studly ghost who was her sometimes lover was definitely something that she was going to fail to mention.

"Did she tell you anything else?" Tony asked as they reached the Lexus, and Charlie smiled at him. See, that's why she liked him: since she'd known him, he'd taken everything she'd thrown at him in stride.

"Nope," she said, glad to slide inside the car. She was still sick in her stomach, and her head still ached. Plus, she was so tired she was practically wilting. Too tired to worry about a silent ghost who sprawled in the backseat with an abstracted look on his face.

They were backing out of the parking

space when a couple of sharp bangs on the rear driver's-side window made Charlie start and look around. Buzz's curly head was framed by the starlit sky. He was frowning, his mouth was tight, and his glasses were crooked. All in all, he was the picture of frustration.

"Open up," Buzz mouthed, pointing at the lock.

Having already hit the brakes, Tony popped the lock and Buzz, still carrying the bagged evidence, got in.

"She wouldn't let me in the car," Buzz said bitterly as he slammed the door. "Told me to either catch you, call a cab, or hitchhike, she didn't care which."

"It's a form of transference," Charlie told him in an attempt to provide some comfort. "She's not really angry at *you.*"

Buzz snorted. "Sure seems like it."

"After this, remind me to institute a rule about fraternization." Tony drove out of the parking lot and headed toward the hotel. "You two are a giant pain in the ass."

"Sorry, boss." Buzz sounded so gloomy that Tony semi-relented.

He said, "It's my own fault. I should have fired one or the other of you after the last case."

That was the end of the conversation until

they reached the bright neon glow of the Strip. It was the middle of the night, and the four-mile stretch of Las Vegas Boulevard was packed with cars driving in both directions and pedestrians crowding the sidewalks on either side of the street. Charlie was fascinated by, in turn, an erupting volcano, gondolas in a Venetian lagoon, a Disney-esque castle, and a miniature New York skyline. She was just eyeing the brilliantly lit replica of the Eiffel Tower when Buzz said, "If that woman had Giselle's bracelet, that means she was picked up by the same perp as Giselle, *after* Giselle, right? Anybody have any thoughts about why a perp would grab two women so close together?"

"You're thinking Giselle might have escaped and he was forced to find a replacement," Tony answered flatly, responding to the faint note of hope in Buzz's voice. "It's possible, but it's way too soon in the investigation to know."

"What do you think?" Buzz directed that to Charlie.

"I agree with Tony: it's too early to come to any conclusions," she replied.

What she didn't do was share her own thought: *Or maybe it means that Giselle was killed before the perp could act out the fantasy that spurs most serial killers to commit the crimes they do, which was why he needed a replacement.*

That was something she would save for tomorrow, when Buzz, like the rest of them, wasn't so tired and on edge.

"You know, it's always possible that Giselle just dropped that bracelet somewhere and the victim picked it up," she added.

Tony and Buzz both said a version of *"Nah,"* at approximately the same time, effectively eliminating that theory. Well, Charlie hadn't really believed in it anyway. It was way too big a coincidence. She'd already learned that a mantra of murder investigations was *there's no such thing as coincidence.*

When they reached the enormous, theatrically lit crescent that was the hotel, it was well after one a.m. The fountains still danced, the crowd still watched, and the air of over-the-top luxury still dazzled. As she got out of the car Charlie spared a brief moment of regret for the early hour of her scheduled breakfast with Tam, but then, if she wasn't meeting Tam she would have been up doing something else by then: the nature of the work the team did meant little time for sleep or anything not related to the case.

The Conquistador's lobby was busier than ever, with a great deal of noise and laughter and activity as hordes of people came and went from the casino and the various restaurants and shows and other resort attractions. In addition, the motorized walkways connecting the hotel to other nearby hotels brought in a constant, never-ending stream of new visitors. Buzz went off to take care of shipment of the evidence while Tony (and Michael) waited as Charlie collected her key. It had been arranged for their rooms to be on the sixteenth floor, alongside the one Lena had shared with her sister and was still staying in. The elevator was crowded, and two champagne flute–carrying couples, the guys in tuxes, the women in sparkly cocktail dresses, got off on their floor with them.

If Charlie hadn't been so tired, she would have felt like she was seriously slumming it as she and Tony followed them down the dimly lit, plushly carpeted hall.

When they reached their quartet of rooms, Tony said, "Let me make sure Kaminsky made it back," and paused to rap on her door, calling to her through it.

A moment later, Lena yanked the door open. She'd taken off her shoes, which made her look surprisingly small, and her

286

jacket, but had not yet gotten around to removing her shoulder holster. Its black straps and the businesslike weapon it contained formed a stark contrast to her curves. Coupled with her unaccustomed paleness and her red-rimmed eyes, her lack of height would have made her look vulnerable if it hadn't been for her gun — and the fierceness of her expression.

"What?" She glowered at them.

"I wanted to make sure you made it back all right," Tony said.

She brushed her hair back from her face and gave him a sharp look. "You don't have to babysit me, Bartoli. I'm fine."

"I know."

"If you need anything, or want some company, I'm right next door," Charlie offered, a glance at the room numbers having confirmed it. Personal relationships did not come easily to her, and she did not consider Lena a friend, exactly. Their association was more prickly and tentative than that. But she knew what the terror of waiting to find out the fate of someone you cared about felt like, and everything about Lena from her appearance to her even more intense than usual reaction to things spoke of a heightened emotional state.

"And *you* don't have to try to play psychiatrist with me."

"I wasn't," Charlie protested.

"Yeah." Lena drew the word out. "Like I said, I'm fine."

Tony nodded. "Okay. We'll see you in the morning, then. Get some sleep."

"That's the plan." Lena looked from one to the other of them. "Thanks for coming," she added abruptly, and shut the door.

"In your professional opinion, Dr. Stone, should I pull her from the case?" Tony asked with a grimace as he escorted Charlie the few feet to her own door.

Charlie gave him a wry glance. "Like Buzz said, she wouldn't go, and you trying to make her would only upset her more. Besides, she's really good at what she does, and if one thing's more certain than anything else it's that she's going to pull out all the stops on this one. And I think her sister needs her. However this plays out."

The sobering thought that Giselle might well be dead hung unspoken in the air between them. The grim truth was that if victims of abductions were not found within forty-eight hours they were usually not found alive. But the forty-eight-hour window was already past, and they still had no real idea of what they were dealing with. It might not be an abduction. It might not even be a crime. At this point, the best thing they could do was assume that Giselle was alive and throw every bit of expertise they could muster into finding her. Hoping for the best, which was that she had left under her own power and simply failed to check in with anyone, while preparing for the worst.

Tony nodded. "That's what I thought."

They reached her door and stopped. A thought had been percolating in Charlie's mind for a while, and she finally made a decision about it. Looking and/or sounding like a flake was a bad thing for her professionally; but then, she'd already gone so far down that road with Tony that she didn't have a lot more of her calm, rational scientist façade left to lose.

"My friend — the one who's here in the hotel — is a psychic medium," Charlie told him. "I don't know if she *can* help, and I don't know if she'll agree to help, but if she will I think it would be a good idea to see if she can pick up anything that might lead us to Giselle."

"Your friend's a psychic medium." At the expression on Tony's face, he was having to work to process that. Michael leaned a shoulder against the wall beside her door, crossed his arms over his chest, and looked sardonic. Whatever had been occupying his thoughts earlier, he was clearly paying attention now.

"Yes," Charlie answered defiantly. "She's very gifted. She makes her living at it."

"I'll take any help we can get," Tony said after only the slightest of hesitations. As a general rule the FBI, she knew, wasn't a big believer in leads generated by psychics. Tony was going out on a limb here. "And I'm confident Kaminsky will say the same."

"I'm meeting Tam for breakfast at eight. I'll ask her then." She grimaced. "She doesn't generally like to get involved in anything involving murder investigations, but I think she'll do this as a favor to me."

"If I never told you what an asset I think you are to the team, let me go on record as saying it now." Tony was looking at her with a smile in his eyes. His lean, dark face was shadowed by stubble and marked by fresh lines of exhaustion around his eyes. It was obvious that he needed sleep as much as she did.

Such a good-looking guy, Charlie thought wistfully. Sweet and upstanding and, basically, just what she'd always wanted. How messed up was she that she wasn't doing her best to snap him up?

"Thank you," she replied.

With Michael standing not two feet away, the last thing Charlie wanted to do was enact a protracted good-night scene with Tony, so she kept her reply short and brisk. Turning, she slid her key card through the lock, and when the door opened she looked back at him to say good night. Before she could, Tony forestalled her by stepping up beside her, sliding a hand along the side of her face, bending his head, and kissing her.

The kiss was lingering, coaxing. A lot of heat on his part, several degrees less on hers. Horribly, annoyingly conscious of Michael watching even as she closed her eyes and tried to get into it, Charlie was grumpily aware that her response was lacking and was just getting ready to disengage when suddenly Tony's lips hardened. His arm wrapped around her waist and the hand cradling her face tightened and angled her jaw up so that he could deepen the kiss. He pulled her fully against him, flattening her breasts against the solid wall of his chest.

The very unexpectedness of it kept her from reacting for those first few surprised seconds. Then his hot, wet invasion of her mouth caught her up in its urgent demand, sending an electric thrill of excitement surging through her. His kiss was suddenly way more practiced, expert, thrilling. His other arm went around her, too, and his hand slid down to cup her bottom, possessively caressing the tender curves, rocking her against him in a way that left her in no doubt about exactly what he had in mind.

She shivered with pleasure. Her body clenched deep inside in instinctive response. Her breasts swelled against his chest, her hips moved sensuously against his hardness, and suddenly heat poured over her in a wave, extinguishing the instant shock she had experienced at his sudden aggressiveness. Just as quick as that, he had her craving sex like an addict craves meth. She was burning inside, throbbing inside, melting like microwaved plastic.

Tony. Festooned with surprise, his name was the one coherent thought that managed to surface through the steam that fogged her brain. Along with, *Oh my God, who would have thought he could get me so hot so fast?*

Sliding her arms around his neck, Charlie kissed him with the blazing desire that she'd been hoping all along would ignite between them. He kissed her back with such blatant carnality that she was rendered temporarily blind, deaf, and mindless to everything except the way he was making her feel.

An elevator full of noisy celebrants that

disgorged its occupants into the hall interrupted them. Charlie pulled her mouth from his and looked around almost dazedly. Before she had time to focus on the revelers or locate (shudder) Michael or even process so much as a complete thought, both Tony's arms locked around her waist and he picked her straight up so that her feet no longer touched the floor and shouldered through her unlocked door.

As the laughing crowd passed by, he closed the door on them with his foot, put her down in the dark little hallway just inside the door, and started kissing her again.

Still so blown away by this unexpected explosion of passion between them that she couldn't do anything except respond, Charlie wrapped her arms around his neck and kissed him like she was dying to get naked with him, like she was ready to push him down on the king-sized bed with which the room was furnished and have her wicked way with him. Like she was on fire for him, which she was.

He had her pressed up against the wall and his mouth was crawling down the side of her neck and his hand was caressing her breast through the thin layers of her blouse and bra when a measure of sanity returned to her.

Michael. Ridiculous to feel like she was cheating on a dead man, but . . .

"Tony, stop." Her voice was low and breathless.

"You don't want me to." He cupped her breast and bent his head to nibble at the aroused peak. Fire shot clear down to her toes.

Oh, my.

His hand slid up under her shirt —

This wasn't the time. It wasn't the place. She needed to think. Dear God, somewhere nearby Michael had to be going nuts. Charlie pushed against Tony's shoulders. "I said, stop."

— and found her breast. Her slinky little bra was all that lay between them as he caressed her, squeezed. His mouth was hot against the sensitive spot right below her ear. He ran his thumb back and forth over her eager nipple.

Her bones liquefied. She wanted him so much that she was dizzy with it.

From somewhere she mustered the strength. *"Stop."*

He didn't. Instead he kissed her ear, drew the lobe into his mouth. "It's all right, babe. It's me."

Her eyes blinked open, angled sideways, and she got as good a look at him as she could. Well-developed shoulders in a suit coat. Crisp black hair. Leanly muscled build. She frowned, not entirely sure she'd understood.

"What?"

"You really think Dudley could get you this hot?" His lips slid across her cheek toward her mouth.

She froze. *"Michael?"*

Delving inside her bra, he fondled her breast.

"I love how warm and soft your tits feel."

The blatant masculinity of his hand caressing her bare breast was mind-blowing — or at least it would have been if her mind hadn't already been blown by the realization that had just clobbered her over the head like a baseball bat.

"What the hell are you *doing*?" It was a yelp, and the shove to his shoulders that accompanied it sent him staggering backward. He tripped over something — her small suitcase, she saw as she squinted at it through the darkness, which the bellboy must have dropped off — and, swearing, went down heavily.

His head struck the wooden framing around the closet with a *thud.*

Charlie was so flabbergasted that all she could do was stare down at the dark shape of Tony's body lying unmoving against the pale carpet. He was on his back, stretched out at an angle that practically filled the narrow space between the bathroom and closet. The curtains were open, so with the streaming starlight beaming in through the large window as illumination she had no trouble whatsoever seeing what happened next.

A tall, strongly built, tawny-haired shadow rose like pale mist out of the figure on the floor, hovered for a second, then surged upward to solidify beside the fallen man with a muttered, *"Fuck."*

CHAPTER EIGHTEEN

"What did you *do*?" Aghast, Charlie glared at Michael even as she dropped to her knees beside Tony. Towering over them both, Michael looked perfectly fine; Tony, on the other hand, was now as pale as any self-respecting ghost ought to be. His eyes were closed. She touched him to discover that his skin was warm, and he was still breathing, which relieved her mind of its first, most terrible fear, which was that Michael, in possessing him, had killed him. Tony was not dead. He was, however, definitely unconscious.

Michael frowned down at the two of them as she checked Tony's pulse, which was a little elevated.

"I borrowed his body."

"You can't just borrow a body! Especially not *Tony's* body!" Charlie practically screeched it at him. Having checked Tony's pulse, she let his arm go: it was totally limp, totally flaccid as it dropped to the carpet. She had to fight against complete panic: who knew what spirit possession did to someone? And how the hell was she supposed to treat it? She shot a furious look at Michael. "How could you do such a thing?"

"He was kissing you, and doing a half-ass job of it, too." Michael shoved his hands in his pockets, rocked back on his heels, and watched as she frantically loosened Tony's tie and unbuttoned the top few buttons on his shirt to make it easier for him to breathe.

"That's your *excuse*? Look at him!"

"Yeah, well, watching him kiss you pissed me off." He had the grace to sound a little ashamed of himself, at least. "It's not like I did it on purpose. I was standing there watching him slobber all over you, and I remembered how you almost passed out there at the morgue and I tried to grab you and I couldn't but he could, and then I thought about how those spirits took over Creason and the trustee. Next thing I knew, *whoosh,* I did it. It was easier than I thought. Dudley didn't even put up a fight." She didn't have to look at him to see the quick lightening of his expression: she could hear what was going on with him in the sudden note of humor in his voice as he added, "FYI, that was me grabbing your ass."

They both knew that shortly before that, actually precisely when Michael had taken over Tony's body, which she was pretty sure she could pinpoint to the nanosecond, was when the kiss had caught fire. Not that Charlie was ever going to admit it. And the fact that he could find even a trace of amusement in what he'd done? Not cool.

The glance she threw at him should have blasted him into eternity. "You know what? I figured that out." She paused, considered how he might take that, conceited thing that he was, and added with a sniff, "*Tony* would never do something that crude."

"You liked it."

"Don't flatter yourself."

She was busy running her fingers through Tony's hair, feeling every inch of his skull. The injury was in the hairline just above his right temple. There was a definite bump, but no blood, as far as she could tell. His head must have hit the edge of the door frame. Scrambling to her feet, she dived for the nearest light switch. As light flooded the room, she glared at Michael then returned to crouch beside Tony. He was definitely pale, but everything else about him seemed normal to her anxious examination. The bump above his temple, however, was rapidly swelling. It was approaching the size of a small egg.

"He should be fine," Michael said, sounding almost sulky. "I was only in there for a few minutes."

"You remember what happened to Creason and the trustee, right? Being possessed almost killed them! For all we know, it still might." With yet another glare for Michael, she jumped to her feet, ran to the bathroom, grabbed a towel, and headed for the door. There was an ice machine down the hall. In her professional opinion, that bump needed ice.

"I'm pretty sure the hunter did that. When it yanked the evil spirits that were inside them out." Michael followed her into the hall.

"You don't know that." By this time Charlie was so mad at him she was practically sputtering. Scooping a ladle full of ice cubes out of the machine, she dropped them into the towel, wrapped it around them, and rushed back toward the room. A trio of middle-aged women passed her, clearly on the way to their rooms: the looks they gave her as they heard her apparently yelling at herself would have totally shut her up at any other time. Right at that moment, though, she barely noticed and didn't care. She added nastily, "I'm only surprised you got out when you did. I know it wasn't because you had an attack of conscience."

"You're right about that." They were back inside her room. "I got knocked out of him when he hit his damned head. Otherwise, babe, you and I'd be in bed right now."

"Oh, no, we would not be." She glared at him one more time as she crouched beside Tony again and applied her makeshift ice pack to his head. "Once I knew that was you? Take it from me, Casper: sex wasn't happening."

"Easy for you to say *now*. I was there, remember?"

"Just so we're clear, it was Tony I was kissing, not you."

"It was me who was getting you hot."

"Under false pretenses!" To Charlie's relief, Tony began to stir.

"See there, he's not hurt."

"If he's not, it's no thanks to you," Charlie said fiercely, then clamped her lips together as Tony groaned and opened his eyes.

"What happened?" He blinked at her uncomprehendingly for a moment, and reached up to touch the ice pack that she was holding to the bump on his head.

Oh, God. How to explain?

She said, "You tripped over my suitcase

and hit your head."

"What do you know? That's even the truth," Michael marveled. "Sort of."

With Tony's eyes on her, Charlie couldn't even shoot her own personal evil spirit a blistering look.

Tony frowned, then made a face. "Ouch."

"I imagine it's a little tender."

"I can't remember coming into your room. Last thing I remember" — Tony's probing fingers slid beneath the ice pack and encountered the bump. He winced, grimaced, and then, to Charlie's distress, sat up — "we were out in the hall. I kissed you good night, right?"

Charlie nodded. She was still holding the ice pack in place and he was looking at her quizzically, their faces just inches apart.

"Then what happened?" Tony asked.

"Um, well . . ." Charlie's voice trailed off as the instant, unbidden memory of his hand on her bare breast surfaced, unexpectedly flustering her. Of course, while the hand had technically belonged to Tony, the memory did not: that belonged to Michael. Thinking back, Charlie realized to her chagrin that somewhere deep in her screwed-up psyche she must have recognized Michael from the moment he'd entered Tony's body. Only Michael had ever been able to turn her on like that.

You have some real issues, she told herself.

"Things were heating up, huh?" One corner of Tony's mouth quirked wryly. "Then I had to go and trip over a damned suitcase. I can't believe I don't remember."

"A blow to the head will do that sometimes."

"You're getting good at this," Michael approved. "Of course, you're still doing that thing with your tongue that you do. You know, kind of sexily wetting your lips whenever you tell a lie. Like I said before, it's a dead tell."

Had she really saved him from total annihilation just a couple of hours previously? Charlie asked herself wrathfully.

What was I thinking?

"I'm not usually so clumsy." Sounding rueful, Tony reached up and took the ice pack away from her, then gingerly felt his head. His eyes cut to her face. "Quit looking so worried. I'll live."

"I'm glad." Her incautious response was so heartfelt that Tony gave her a slow smile while Michael snorted derisively and said, "There you go getting his hopes up all over again."

"I'm actually pretty hard to kill," Tony told

her. Still holding the ice pack, he got to his feet, pulling her up beside him even as she protested, "You should probably stay sitting for a while."

"Except for a little bit of a headache, I'm fine." His grip on her hand tightened, and he leaned toward her, his intention to kiss her again impossible to mistake. "No harm, no foul."

Okay, so he obviously wasn't suffering any severe ill effects.

"You know, I could get to liking this," Michael observed from behind her. "He and I fit together like a hand in a glove."

"It's late," Charlie demurred, speaking to Tony as she freed her hand and took a step back. "I know you have to be as exhausted as I am, and now you've got that bump on your head. Let me get you some Tylenol and walk you to your room."

Tony looked at her for a fraction of a second without saying anything, while comprehension flickered in his eyes.

"By golly, I think he just figured out that he's not getting any," Michael said. "Smart guy."

Tony, meanwhile, shook his head and turned toward the door. "I've got some Tylenol in my room. I'll take some if I need it."

Charlie followed him anxiously. "Are you sure you're going to be all right?"

"I'm sure." Opening the door, he stepped out into the hall, saying over his shoulder to her, "I'll see you in the morning."

Grabbing the door in turn, Charlie moved into the open doorway. "Keep that ice pack on the bump. It'll bring the swelling down."

"Will do." But he was focused on something behind her, his expression turning slightly wry. Charlie followed his gaze to discover Buzz there in the hall staring at them. Buzz was, in fact, standing in front of Lena's door, which was open just enough so that Charlie could see Lena, clad in what looked like men's pale blue cotton pajamas, looking at them, too. Both Lena and Buzz were wide-eyed with interest, and Charlie realized that Tony, with his hair all mussed from her fingers running through it and his tie askew and his shirt partly unbuttoned, looked like he'd been getting busy. So did she, probably.

No way was she even going to try to explain this to Buzz and Lena, was the lightning conclusion she came to. Not tonight. Maybe not ever.

"Good night," she said to the three of them with what she hoped was at least a modicum of dignity. Then she stepped back inside her room, closed her door, and turned to glare for what felt like at least the hundredth time in the last fifteen minutes at Michael.

"Let's see, what was it Dudley said? Oh, yeah, I got it: you're cute when you're cranky." The bane of her existence was unwise enough to give her a slow grin. "Now I see what he meant."

"You are a —" Charlie broke off, swallowed what she had been going to say, and finished with a fierce, "I'm not talking to you right now. I'm dead tired, and I'm going to bed."

"Jesus, babe, it wasn't that big a deal."

"Not — talking." Rigid with anger, she grabbed her suitcase, unzipped it, yanked a nightgown and her toiletry kit out of it, and stomped to the bathroom, saying over her shoulder, "If you dare to come in here, I'll have Tam *summon* a hunter to get you, I swear."

Before he could reply, she shut (did not slam, although it was a close run thing) the bathroom door. Then, seething, she washed her face, brushed her teeth, got into her nightgown, and made damned sure to turn the bathroom light and the room light off (both switches were outside the bathroom door) before stalking back into the main part of the room. The last thing she intended to do was give him an eyeful, which was what he'd get if he could see her properly, because she tended to like pretty, feminine lingerie to the point that it was all she possessed.

Enough light glimmered in through the window to allow her to see him. He was sitting in the armchair in the corner, his hands locked behind his head, his long legs stretched comfortably out in front of him, his booted feet crossed at the ankles.

Unfortunately, she realized that if she could see him so well it meant that there was also enough light to allow him to see *her* in significant detail.

His gaze tracked her. "You wearing that sexy pink lace thing you know I like?"

She seethed. She fumed. Her thigh-high pink floaty chiffon nightgown was lavished with lace, and, indeed, the last time she'd worn it he'd expressed his extreme approval of it.

Item number one on her shopping list, she decided savagely: flannel granny gowns. And granny panties. And granny bras.

Hah!

Turning a deaf ear to every other infuriating comment the maddening creature made, she marched across the room in the starlit darkness, yanked the curtains closed, and tumbled into bed. Ostentatiously turning her back on him, she pulled the covers up around her ears.

And then, despite her exhaustion, she lay scowling into the darkness.

"You awake?" he asked after a few minutes.

Clearly he knew she was. She stiffened, but didn't reply.

"I'm sorry, okay?" he said, and that was enough of a surprise to make her roll onto her back and look suspiciously in his direction. She couldn't see him: the room was now too dark. But she could tell from his voice where he was: still in that armchair in the corner. "I just thought" — he hesitated; she thought she could hear a shrug in his voice — "it might be a way out."

That did it: he had her. She was still mad at him, but she couldn't resist asking, "A way out?"

"I want my life back. I want you. I want — a lot of things. I thought, if I could get a new body . . ." His voice trailed off. "It was a way out."

A whole host of emotions hit her. They were varied and tangled, but they swept the hard knot of her anger away. She sat up in bed.

"Michael." She hesitated, then added gently, "I don't think there is a way out of being dead."

"If there was, everybody'd be doing it, right?" The wry humor in his voice wrung her heart. "I got it. I'm a fucking ghost. I don't have to like it, but there it is."

Sugarcoating the hard truth would do him no good.

"Pretty much," she said.

"Yeah." It was acceptance. "Go on to sleep, babe. I'll still be sitting here dead when you wake up."

That made her smile. The fact that he could make her smile when he was in such obvious pain brought a lump to her throat. He didn't say anything else, and she didn't, either: really, what was there to say? After a moment she lay back down and curled onto her side, but this time she was facing him. At some point her eyes must have closed because finally, against all odds, she slept.

Chapter Nineteen

In the morning, Michael was flickering. Solid one moment, see-through the next. Having lived with ghosts in her life for what felt like millennia now, and with this ghost in particular for a little more than six weeks, Charlie knew the signs: flickering meant trouble. Flickering meant a spirit was on its way out.

Her heart was in her throat from the moment she woke up, glanced at him stretched out on the bed beside her, and saw what was happening to him.

"Holy crap!" were the first words out of her mouth as she sat bolt upright in bed and stared at him by the dim gray light filtering in around the curtains. To which he replied with a quick quirk of his lips, "I'm pretty sure holy's got nothing to do with it." At the same time, his eyes were sliding over her (the covers having dropped to puddle around her waist) and he added, "Looking good, babe."

She almost screeched it. "You're *flickering.*"

"I caught that."

Bottom line was, he hadn't even tried to do anything about it. Hadn't tried to wake her up so that *she* could try to do something about it. He'd just watched himself flicker and waited to see what would happen.

Que sera sera was what his new attitude seemed to be: what will be, will be.

Which she found almost as alarming as the flickering.

"What are you, a ghost with a death wish now?" she fumed at him as she hurriedly dressed. Then she rushed him down to Tam like a mother whisking an injured child to the emergency room.

"There are no more spells to fix you to earth," Tam told Michael sternly. This morning she wore a figure-hugging hot pink silk jumpsuit with a gold scorpion pendant nestled where it would call the most attention to her ample cleavage. Her outfit should have clashed with her red hair and bright lipstick but somehow didn't: she looked as fresh and vivid as Charlie didn't feel wearing a white blouse and black slacks with only small silver hoop earrings and Michael's heavy silver watch by way of accessories. By that time, Tam and Charlie — with Michael prowling restlessly around the sleek modern table — were finishing up a quick breakfast in the sumptuous, surprisingly-crowded-given-the-early-hour buffet. Charlie had mainlined coffee, and nibbled on a piece of toast, which was a total waste considering the vast quantity of food on offer for a single price. Her appetite clearly unimpaired by this latest crisis, Tam was polishing off the last of a heaping plate of waffles, eggs, and bacon. Looking at Michael, she added, "Last night, when you left me, you were restored. Then you possessed a body!" She shook her head and looked at Charlie, who'd spent breakfast filling her in, with a small number of judicious edits, on everything that had transpired after they'd left her the previous night. "Once a spell is used on an individual, it won't work again on that same individual. It loses its potency."

"So what do we do?" Charlie put down her coffee cup. She needed the caffeine, but the sudden lump in her throat made swallowing difficult.

"There's that *we* again." Tam frowned at her as she ate the last of her waffle. "The first thing you do is put *that* out of your head. You and he — no. Not *we*."

"Tam —" Charlie looked at her friend

impatiently.

"Fine. You want to know what to do?" Tam sipped at her juice. "You hope he's strong enough to recover. It's possible that the grounding spell I used on him last night will have enough lingering aftereffects to keep him here. Possible, but not certain."

Michael's response was flat. "In other words, I either make it or I don't."

"Exactly." Tam nodded, giving him an assessing look. "This has been going on for about six hours?"

"Give or take," Michael agreed.

"Probably you would already be gone if that's what was going to happen," Tam told him grudgingly, and Charlie got the impression that she wouldn't have been entirely sorry if Michael had been sucked away into Spookville during the night. Despite Tam's tone, Charlie instantly felt better: Tam was rarely wrong about anything to do with the spirit world. "Although I can't guarantee it. What I can guarantee is that if you'd done something so stupid without having recently been fixed to this plane by my grounding spell, you would have no hope. You would have been hurtled into The Dark Place the instant you left the mortal body you stole."

"Borrowed," Michael corrected, and Tam made a derisive face.

"He can't just possess a body and expect to live a normal, human life in that body," Charlie said, just to clarify things for Michael — and herself. "Right?"

"Spirits do possess bodies occasionally," Tam replied. "They sometimes even manage to stay in them for considerable periods of time, by which I mean a few days, a few weeks. Usually the body must be empty, which means the spirit must enter at precisely the moment of the previous soul's exit and the body's death, for that to be possible."

"So all I have to do is find a guy who's just died and I'm golden?" Michael looked at Tam with sudden interest.

"Hardly," Tam said. "It's way more complicated than that. Even the mechanics of it are complicated: the body has to be capable of living, for one thing, which if the person just *died,* the body probably isn't. A limited number of the possessed walk among us, indistinguishable from the living, at any given time. They're known as revenants. But that's very rare, and is never permanent. Revenants are considered monsters, and the price they eventually pay for their temerity in trying to cheat death is high." She gave Michael a warning look. "Remember that: there is always a price."

Charlie put the question to Tam that she knew was tearing at Michael. "Is there any way you can think of for him to get any semblance of a human life back?"

"No," Tam said. "There isn't. I thought I made that clear last night. He can stay as he is — a spirit walking the earth plane — for as long as he's able to hang on here, possibly for as long as eternity, although given his proclivity for getting himself into trouble I doubt that'll happen. Or he can go ahead and give in to the inevitable and move on to whatever awaits him in the Beyond."

Michael grimaced. "Now, there's a real win-win situation if I ever heard one."

"He was being terminated." Charlie had given up on even trying to drink her coffee. "I don't think moving on to the Beyond is an option for him."

Tam shrugged. "The *executeurs* can't be everywhere. If he manages to escape their notice, he might continue to exist in the Beyond for a considerable time. Who knows? I can't say for sure. No one can."

"Great," Michael muttered.

"Spirit, listen to me," Tam ordered, and he stopped pacing to look at her, curling his fingers around the top rung on the back of one of the two extra chairs at the table and looking so alive that if Charlie hadn't known for sure that he was dead she wouldn't have believed it. Until he flickered again, that is: in and out, quick as a blink, like a failing lightbulb. "Understand that there are consequences to everything you do. You're like a cat with nine lives. I don't know how many you've used up already. I don't know how many you have left. But I do know this: on the day that you run out of them, there is nothing that I or anyone else can do to save you. You'll go into the Beyond, and you'll face whatever awaits you there. So if you want to stay earthbound, you need to be careful. For starters, no more possessing bodies."

"Got that?" Charlie chimed in, just to be clear. His eyes, very blue and not nearly as troubled as they should have been under the circumstances, met hers, and Charlie frowned at him while Tam added direly, "Unless you *want* to find yourself back in the Dark Place."

Charlie was getting ready to pile on more warnings, but the ringing of her cell phone interrupted.

It was lying on the table beside her plate because she'd been waiting for this call. As part of her summation of last night's happenings, she'd told Tam about Giselle Kaminsky and asked if she would help. Tam had agreed — reluctantly, because she had long made it a rule to focus her abilities only on the light. Shuddering away from Charlie's choice of profession, she had once explained it to her this way: touching on something as dark as murder felt like it left the psychic equivalent of a bloodstain on her soul.

Once Tam had agreed, Charlie had texted Tony, asking him to run it by Lena. This should be his reply.

"It's Tony," Charlie announced as she verified that with a glance at the incoming number, then picked up the phone and said hello. Their conversation was brief. As noisy as the dining room was, she didn't think there was any way Tony's side of the call could have been overheard by the other two, so when she disconnected she looked at Tam and repeated the gist of it. "He said Kaminsky — Lena — would welcome your help. She has Giselle's things up in her room." Tam had told her that it would make it easier if she had something that belonged to Giselle to concentrate on. "Tony's there with her now, if we want to go on up."

Tam nodded, and Charlie signaled for the check. The waiter, a good-looking, thirtyish guy whose name tag read, *Hi, my name is Bob,* came over with it, asking, "Can I get you ladies anything else?"

While Charlie was shaking her head no, Tam, who was infinitely more with it than Charlie this morning, grabbed the check and signed the room charge. With a reproving look for Tam, Charlie counted out the cash needed to cover the bill and tucked it into her friend's purse, then looked up to find that the waiter's gaze had parked itself admiringly on Tam's cleavage.

"Nice necklace. Are you a Scorpio?" Bob asked as Charlie plopped her purse on the table with a *thump* and he tore his eyes away to discover both Charlie and Tam frowning at him. Michael was looking at him, too, with the kind of level look men give each other, but of course he couldn't see that. Charlie had to give Bob credit: the bit about the necklace was a pretty good save.

Tam didn't seem at all perturbed. Rising, she met his eyes. "No, but you are," she told him. "You're also single, from — either Kansas or Kentucky, a state that starts with a *K,* I'm leaning toward Kansas — and you own a big blue motorcycle, which is waiting for you in the parking lot right now. With an expired tag."

Bob's mouth fell open. Taking a stumbling step back, he blinked at her, suddenly google-eyed. "How — how did you know that?"

Tam smiled seraphically at him. "I'm psychic. I know everything about you," she cooed, and swept from the restaurant with Charlie and Michael trailing in her wake. Charlie could feel the waiter's shocked gaze on them all the way out the door.

"Bet that's the last time he lets his eyes wander for a while," Michael murmured to Charlie with a chuckle.

"I told you she was good."

"Spirit, give us a minute," Tam imperiously told Michael as she paused in the opulent hallway to let Charlie catch up.

"Yes, ma'am." There might have been a touch of irony in his voice, but he obediently dropped back, following at enough of a distance to allow them to talk privately as they headed past the in-house theater and gift shops then threaded their way through the busy lobby toward the elevators.

"I can see what you see in him," Tam said, low-voiced. "He's absolutely gorgeous. When my spell restored him and he was all of a sudden standing there naked in my bathtub — well, I have to admit my eyes popped. He's built. And hung. A total stud-muffin if I ever saw one."

Charlie tried not to sound defensive.

319

"That is *not* what I see in him."

Tam gave her a skeptical look. "Cherie, I'm not blind. I see the way you look at him. I've seen the way you two are together. *Muy caliente.*"

Okay, maybe she did sound defensive. She couldn't help it. "So I like him. So sue me."

"Like?" Tam practically snickered. "That's a new word for it. I'd ask if you've managed to have sex with him yet, but the answer's obvious. Was it before he died or have you been practicing up on your astral projection?"

"I'm not that good at astral projection, believe me," Charlie said defensively. Her sex life — especially her sex life with Michael — wasn't up for discussion. Not even with Tam.

"You've got to practice to get good. Like with Kegel exercises. Anytime you get a few minutes, close your eyes, clear your mind, and focus on forcing your vibrations higher. Right now, as close as you apparently still are to the Beyond, you should have an easier time pushing through. Do it while you still can, and have sex with him until your tongue is hanging and get him out of your system. Then you can let him go *poof* with no regrets."

"I'm not going to practice up on astral

projection just so I can have sex with him," Charlie said firmly.

"Your call." Tam shrugged. "Probably for the best. But if he has a hot ghost friend — one who's not a serial killer — send him my way. For a guy who looks like that, *I'll* astral project out the yahoo."

"I told you before, he's not a serial killer." Honesty compelled Charlie to add, "I'm almost certain."

"You told me," Tam agreed with just a hint of derision. "It's the *almost* that has me worried."

"There's evidence that he's innocent." Charlie touched Michael's watch as she spoke: really, it, plus his word and her gut feeling, was all there was, but she wasn't going to tell Tam *that*. "I'm having the DNA test results that were admitted as evidence in his trial rechecked as we speak. The lab should be calling me any day now. There's something wrong somewhere, I know it."

"Mm-hmm." Tam sounded skeptical. "Just keep in mind that the legal system may sometimes be wrong, but the universe never is. He wound up in The Dark Place for a reason. He was being terminated for a reason. And the reason is, he's done something *bad*, cherie. Really bad. Time to wake up and smell the coffee. He's smokin' hot, no doubt about it, but you need to remember what they say about judging a book by its cover: don't."

"I'm not —" Charlie began, only to break off as they reached the elevator banks and Michael caught up. She shot a look at him. He was still flickering, but maybe a little less frequently and he was maybe a little less see-through each time he came back.

"I'm just wondering what your friend did to deserve being sent to the Dark Place." Tam addressed the remark to Charlie so as not to look insane for talking to what, to the small crowd milling around them waiting for the elevators, would look like the empty space beside her. A flicker of Tam's eyes in his direction, however, made it clear that the remark was directed at Michael. Charlie didn't even know why she was surprised: a shrinking violet Tam wasn't. If she wanted to know something, she was going to ask.

"No clue," Charlie responded.

"I think that was meant for me." Michael smiled at Tam. It was his patented charming smile, but there was a hint of something in his face that made Charlie remember the hard-eyed convict she had first met. "You wondering if I'm a stone-cold killer? Is that it? Why don't you make like a psychic and find out for yourself?"

"I would, but I can't read the dead like I can the living," Tam said to Charlie. "I can only go by what they tell me when they show up."

"Well, now, ain't that convenient," Michael drawled. "For a minute there, I was shaking in my boots at the thought that you knew all my secrets."

"If you're that worried, they must be terrible secrets," Tam retorted.

"Maybe." Michael smiled at her again.

"Would you two stop?" Charlie asked him in irritation, forgetting that to any of the roughly two dozen people waiting for the elevators who happened to be paying attention she was talking to the empty space and probably looking nuts because of it. Fortunately the elevator they were waiting for arrived just then, serving, she hoped, as a distraction. As they filed on, she said in a quiet, excusing aside to Tam that she was fairly certain Michael couldn't overhear, "He has a tendency to play into what people think of him. When you act like you think he's a bad guy, he'll do his best to behave like one."

Tam, who was behind her, leaned forward to say in her ear, "What makes you so sure he's *not* one?"

Charlie almost said *I just am,* but that sounded so embarrassingly juvenile that she stopped herself before the words could get out. Besides, obviously Michael had done something to wind up in Spookville, and the question of just exactly what that was was something that she meant to address. With him, in private. When she got the chance. Which was not now.

Thus she maintained a dignified silence until they reached the sixteenth floor, and then spent the few moments until they got to Lena's room giving Tam thumbnail background sketches of the Special Agents she was about to meet.

Tony answered her knock. In a navy suit with a white shirt and blue tie, he was his usual tall, dark, and handsome self. His smile as he greeted her was warmly intimate. Charlie couldn't help it: at the sight of him, the memory of how she'd melted under his hands last night came flooding back. She felt instantly, ridiculously self-conscious. Reminding herself that all *he* remembered was a relatively chaste good-night kiss didn't help.

If they'd been alone, she would have shot Michael a dirty look for so thoroughly muddying up her relationship with Tony.

"Hi," Tony said. Then, "Come on in."

Beyond Tony, she saw that Lena was perched on the edge of the armchair (the room was identical to Charlie's). Buzz stood beside her in front of the window. The curtains were open, and the bright sunlight spilling into the room made a stark contrast to the tension Charlie felt the instant she stepped over the threshold.

CHAPTER TWENTY

"Tam, this is Special Agent Tony Bartoli. Tony, this is Tamsyn Green," Charlie said as Tony closed the door behind them. After Tam and Tony shook hands, Charlie performed the rest of the introductions. At the sight of Tam, the expression on Tony's face — a touch of surprise, coupled with sheer masculine appreciation for a woman so dazzlingly glamorous — was no more or less than what Charlie had expected: men always had that reaction to Tam. Buzz, too, was transparently impressed. Lena, on the other hand, looked Tam over with suspicion.

"I understand that you're a psychic. Can you tell me where my sister is?" Lena asked abruptly as she and Tam finished shaking hands. She looked like she had barely slept: there were dark circles under her eyes. Her hair was still damp from the shower, and slicked straight back from her face. If she wore any makeup beyond a smear of pink lipstick Charlie couldn't tell. She was on her feet now, and while she was fully dressed in a knee-length navy skirt and a grass green tee, her feet were bare, which made her look surprisingly small and vulnerable. Her mouth was tight, but there was so much pain in her eyes that it robbed her tone of any offensiveness.

Tam shook her head. "It doesn't work like that. I get — impressions. Scraps of thoughts and feelings. Fragments of knowledge. Pictures of objects. Snapshots from a life. That kind of thing. I'm not going to be able to give you an address." She glanced around the room, and Charlie followed her gaze: the bed was unmade and the closet door was open, revealing two small suitcases and a few garments on hangers. The remains of a light, mostly untouched room service breakfast took up most of the table beside the chair. The faint smell of coffee from the untouched cup on the tray hung in the air. "If you could give me something of your sister's to hold, I'll see what I can do."

Lena didn't quite roll her eyes, but her expression made her skepticism obvious. Charlie's nerves tightened: she knew Lena, and she also knew that Tam was unlikely to react well to Lena's particular brand of disbelief.

To Tony, Lena said, "I don't have time for this." She looked at Tam, then at Charlie. "I'm sorry, but I just don't." Her gaze swung back to Tony. She was talking a little bit too fast, clasping her hands together hard as she spoke. "I've been going over the hotel security tapes again and there's a guy who might have followed her out the front door. We need to try to identify him. And —"

"I want to give Ms. Green a chance, Kaminsky," Tony interrupted. His tone, his expression, everything about him was steadying. Charlie thought, *This is a man a woman could depend on,* then tucked the thought away to be examined later. "I think it's a shot worth taking," he said.

"She's the real thing," Charlie told Lena earnestly. "I promise."

"It can't hurt," Buzz chimed in. "Believe me, I want to find Giselle, too."

Lena's gaze fastened on him like a hawk sighting prey.

"This might be a good time to trot out that party trick you used downstairs," Michael said to Tam, who was starting to look affronted. He was still flickering, but the flickers were more widely spaced, as if they were slowing down. Charlie was really starting to feel confident that he was going to

328

make it through. "Kaminsky's a hard-ass, but she's suffering here."

Tam frowned at him. Her lips compressed. She gave a not-quite-nod which was directed at Michael. Then she looked at Lena, and her expression changed.

"You grew up in a small house in California." Tam spoke just as Lena, her attention still all on Buzz, opened her mouth, presumably to lambast him. "I see a red tile roof, Spanish tile. A white house. I see a woman who looks like you — Libby? Libby? Yes, Libby — backing out of the driveway in a tan car. The car is loaded with luggage — some is strapped to the roof — and there are two girls in the car, young girls, young teenagers, I can't be sure of the precise ages. The one in the front seat has tears streaming down her face. She is looking back at the house, at the man standing on the front stoop watching the car leave. He is balding, a little tummy on him." Tam made a paunch motion in front of her own stomach. "Paul. His name is Paul." Libby is saying to the weeping girl, "Stop sniveling, Gigi. You're not going to change my mind. The girl in the backseat is not crying. She's a little younger, and she's looking away from the man, from the house. Her expression is set. On her lap is a dog, a small golden dog with long floppy ears, a spaniel of some sort, I think. The name I'm getting is Jiff. Or Jin. A short *J* word. The girl's arms are wrapped tight around the dog. The girl is —"

"All right, stop." Lena's voice sounded strangled. Her widened eyes were fixed on Tam. She sucked in a shuddering breath. "The girl was me. The day you're describing is the day my family broke up and my mother started driving us toward the East Coast. My sister, Giselle, was in the front seat. She always hated being called Gigi, but my mother called her that anyway. And the dog was a cocker spaniel named Jip."

"If that's an unpleasant memory, I'm sorry to have recalled it to your mind," Tam said. Charlie felt a flutter of pride: she'd never known Tam to be wrong, and clearly this wasn't going to be the first time. "I can only report what I see."

"It was accurate." Lena looked shaken. "Accurate's what I'm interested in." Her eyes met Charlie's. "Your friend got everything right." Taking a deep breath, she focused on Tam again. "I have some clothing of my sister's, some jewelry, her toiletries. She left everything except what she was wearing in the room when she disappeared."

"Do you have her hairbrush?" Tam asked. "Yes."

"Does it have her hair in it?"

"Yes, I think so."

"Only her hair? You didn't share it?"

"No."

"If I could have that."

Lena nodded. "It's in the bathroom. I'll get it." She picked up an iPad from the foot of the bed and looked around at all of them. "I took this video of Giselle on Saturday, a few hours before I left for the airport. If you watch it, you can see what she was like."

She pressed the button, handed the iPad to Tony, and then walked into the bathroom as the rest of them gathered around Tony to watch Giselle, clad in a black top with spaghetti straps — all that could be seen of her attire, because from the waist down she was hidden by the table at which she was sitting. Her black hair was twisted into a loose knot on top of her head, and she smiled broadly at the camera. Giselle then looked at the large, white-frosted cupcake with the single flaming candle that was being presented to her on a tray by members of a restaurant's waitstaff. Two waiters and two waitresses in bright yellow uniforms placed it on the table, and began to sing "Happy Birthday."

Giselle joined in, cheerfully off-key: "Happy birthday to me, happy birthday to me, happy birthday dear me-e, happy birth-day to me."

As the singing concluded, Lena's voice could be heard in the background urging, "Blow out the candle!"

Giselle did, the waitstaff faded away, and — still off camera — Lena asked, "Did you make a wish?"

"Yes." Her dark eyes sparkling, Giselle grinned at the camera, or rather, presumably, at Lena, who was behind it. "And I'll never tell what I wished for, so don't even bother to ask."

"I know what you wished for," Lena retorted. "The same thing you've been wishing for on your birthday since you were fifteen: for us all to be one big happy family again."

"Well, you're wrong, Miss Smarty Pants." Giselle playfully stuck out her tongue at Lena. "I've outgrown that."

"Sure you have."

Giselle said, "If you must know, I wished that we could both have our own happy families, so *there*."

Giselle looked, and sounded, so much like Lena — a happier, less snarky version — that Charlie was riveted. Then, still out of sight, Lena went "Aww" at her sister with her trademark snark, and the video ended.

Charlie realized that she had a lump in her throat. She knew that, some eighty-odd hours after Giselle's disappearance, if what had happened to her was anything other than a voluntary leave-taking, there was a strong statistical probability that she was dead. Twenty-four hours was the golden time period in which the recovery of abduction victims alive was still a realistic possibility, and they were well past that.

"Right after that I gave her the bracelet," Lena now said. Charlie hated to meet her gaze for fear Lena might be able to read what she had been thinking in her eyes, but Lena was staring at the iPad and nothing else, and, anyway, Lena knew the score as well as she did. Lena was standing just behind Tony, and it was obvious that she'd been watching the last bit of the video. Her eyes were maybe a little brighter than usual, but other than that indication of a possible quickly banished welling of tears she looked composed. No, determined and focused. Like, say, a pitbull was determined and focused.

"What restaurant was that?" Buzz asked as Tony put the iPad on the table. Lena passed a small hairbrush to Tam, who accepted it with a nod of thanks and began pulling the loose hairs from it.

"The Polo Cafe," Lena replied. "It's downstairs. Coffee, sandwiches, pastries. We just wanted to grab a quick bite." Like the rest of them, Lena was watching Tam set the hairbrush down then slowly roll the hairs she had removed from it into a ball with her fingertips. Tam's abstract expression made it obvious that mentally she was already elsewhere.

"You left for the airport at around five on Saturday, if I correctly remember what you told me," Tony said to Lena. "What did you two do in the time between when this video finished and then?"

Lena shook her head. "Nothing in particular. Played some slot machines at the casino. Shopped. I had to pack, so we came back to the room about four. Giselle was with me. I left her here in this room at five."

There was a stark expression in her eyes that told Charlie how close to the edge Lena was. The fact that she was able to maintain focus and control under such terrible circumstances and concentrate her energies so completely on finding her sister was, Charlie thought, a testament to her strength.

"She thought you weren't coming back," Tony said thoughtfully. It wasn't a question — Lena had been over the sequence of events with him multiple times, Charlie knew — but Lena answered it anyway.

"I was going to fly home. She wasn't scheduled to fly out until Monday morning — there were some local artists whose work she was planning to check out for the gallery. But my flight was canceled, so I came back." Her voice wobbled for just a second. "She wasn't here. I thought she was out doing something, that maybe she was visiting those artists she'd been talking about, or even that she'd met a guy. Oh, God, if only I'd started looking for her *then* —" She broke off. Her lips pressed tightly together. Her jaw clenched. Charlie's heart ached for her.

"You couldn't have known," Buzz said fiercely. "There was no way you could have known."

Lena turned a razor-sharp gaze on him.

"I'm picking up a jumble of images," Tam said, and the rest of them immediately switched their attention to her. "Which ones are related to Giselle, I can't be sure. Someone should be prepared to write them down because afterward I won't remember most of what I say."

"I'll get it on video, if you don't mind." Buzz immediately whipped out his cell phone and started pressing buttons to set up his camera.

Tam nodded. "That's good." She looked at Buzz in a way that seemed to see right through him. "You like video games. You play — Assassin's Creed. When you're alone. All the time."

With all eyes suddenly on him, Buzz turned red. "I'm trying to beat it," he explained defensively. "The game, I mean. It's not that easy."

Tam continued unheedingly: "I'm seeing someone drinking too much. In a bar with an American Eagle over the door. Double saloon doors. Red. Red, white, and blue." Her eyes slid toward Lena. "There's a lot of guilt over an illicit love affair." As Lena's eyes widened, Tam blinked and looked away, toward Tony, her gaze going a little unfocused. "A blond woman. Pretty. Long, silky hair. Screaming *Get out, get out.* She's . . . throwing something. A . . . shoe?"

Tony stiffened.

Tam's hand clenched around the ball of Giselle's hair. She took a deep breath, and her eyes seemed to fix on the wall behind them. Charlie couldn't help it: she had to glance around to check out what Tam was looking at. As she had expected, there wasn't anything but beige patterned wallpaper and the entertainment center within Tam's line of vision. Not that it mattered:

what Tam was seeing was nothing tangible, and it was nothing that the rest of them could see. "I'm getting a strong image of that old TV show with Joan Collins and Linda Evans: *Dynasty*. That's it, that's the name: *Dynasty*. I don't know what it means but that's what I'm getting: *Dynasty*. I'm getting the number fifteen. Dogs barking. Lots of dogs. An old — some kind of sign. A service station sign? I don't know. It's faded. There's a word on it, and a picture: a shell, I think. And birds. A flock of birds. It looks like the surface of the moon." Tam stared intently at the wall. Her voice went quieter, and took on a deeper pitch. Charlie had seen Tam do her psychic thing on many occasions before; still, every time she witnessed it, goose bumps prickled up and down her arms. "I see a small, dark enclosure. A woman stuffed into it. She's . . . limp. Unconscious. It's Giselle. There's movement. Wheels turning. Silver. A sensation of speed. Oh, she's waking. The space feels larger now, but it's still dark. It's hot. It smells bad. *Where am I? What is this place?* There's something over her eyes. *I can't see.* She's not alone. *Who are you? What's happening?* She's panicking. She's being moved again, lifted. There's blood. She can see now and she sees blood. A puddle of blood. Blood everywhere. There's screaming. *She's* screaming. *Oh, God, oh, God —*"

Dropping the ball of hair, Tam spun around. Her eyes were wide, and she was visibly shaking. Michael moved swiftly toward her, and so did Charlie. Michael reached her first, but it was Charlie who put an arm around her because, of the two of them, it was Charlie who could.

Charlie said, "Tam . . ."

Tam blinked. She sucked in air. Her expression changed. It was obvious that she was once again aware of her surroundings, that she was back with them.

Catching the thick fall of her wavy red hair in her hands, she pulled it up away from her neck. A slight sheen of perspiration covered her face and neck. "Is it hot in here? I'm so hot." She looked at Charlie, at the rest of them, then finally at Lena. "I saw Giselle. She's been taken."

"I knew it." Lena's voice was thin. "Is she alive?"

Tam looked troubled. "I can't tell you that. I don't know the answer. I only know what I saw. A slice out of time. I was seeing some things through her eyes, so at that moment she was alive, and in grave danger. I can tell you this, too: there's a murderer out there. It was he who took her."

"Oh, God." Lena closed her eyes. Thrusting his phone into his pocket, Buzz was beside her in an instant, sliding a hand around her upper arm. Such was Lena's state of mind that she didn't even try to shake him off.

"I'm sorry," Tam said.

Lena opened her eyes to look at her. "At least we know she was alive when you saw her, and that she didn't leave on her own or have an accident or something. We can focus one hundred percent on what we do, which is finding her and the bastard who has her. Hopefully we'll be in time."

"Is there anything else you can tell us?" Tony asked Tam, while Lena, apparently having just become aware of Buzz's hand on her arm, pulled away and shot him a poisonous look.

Tam shook her head. "When I see through someone's eyes like that, I get bits and pieces. What they know, what they see. And I can't go back to them. Not for a long time. It's like the window closes." She huffed out a breath. "I can't help you with this anymore." She looked at Charlie. "I have to go."

Charlie nodded. Knowing Tam as well as she did, she knew that the darkness of what she had seen acted on her like frost on a flower. If she didn't get to the figurative sunlight soon, she would start to wilt.

"I'll walk you to your room," she said.

"No." Tam had pulled herself together. She was no longer holding her hair away from her neck, and her distressed look was fading. "There's no need. I'm just going to grab my things and get in my car and head back to L.A. You stay here and help them." A nod indicated the others in the room.

"We're going downstairs anyway," Tony said. "The hotel didn't want us to set up shop on the premises because they were afraid that having an ongoing investigation under their roof might be bad for business. We're partnering with the local FBI on this, and they've given us some space and the promise of full cooperation. So if everyone wants to meet in the lobby in ten minutes, we'll head on over there."

"I'll walk you," Charlie repeated. This time Tam nodded.

"Thank you," Lena said to Tam. Sincerity was in her face, her eyes. Tam had clearly impressed her a lot.

Tam nodded. "You're welcome." Then she nodded in response to the farewell chorus, and slipped through the door with Charlie — and Michael — at her heels.

"Thank you," Charlie repeated as they headed for the elevator. "I know that was hard on you."

"There's a dangerous energy associated with what befell your friend's sister," Tam warned. "It's like a dark storm. It could engulf anyone who gets too close. You should stay away."

"There you go. That's what I've been telling her all along," Michael said.

Tam glanced at Michael with a kind of wary interest. "Have you?" Tam's gaze slid to Charlie. "You should listen. To me, and in this instance to him."

The elevator arrived. Since it was full of people, nothing more was said until they were walking along the hall to Tam's room.

"I appreciate you coming," Charlie said. "I don't know what we would have done without you."

"He" — this was accompanied by a nod at Michael — "would have gone *poof,* and you probably would have been better off." The tartness of Tam's tone was a good indication that she was back to normal.

"If it helps, you might want to try thinking of me as her bodyguard," Michael said. "I'll keep her alive if I can."

Tam frowned at him. Then, seemingly reluctantly, she nodded.

"It does help. A teeny, tiny, smidgen of an amount, because as a spirit there's not a whole lot you can do, but I guess anything's better than nothing. Safety conscious, she's not."

"Tell me about it."

"Hey, guys." Charlie waved a hand in the air. "I'm right here. I can hear you."

"I keep hoping that something — like your friend the real-deal psychic here telling you that there's danger — will make you back off some of this stuff," Michael said to Charlie.

"It won't," Tam told him. "I've tried. She's stubborn." Michael gave a grunt of agreement, Charlie shot them both indignant looks, and Tam's attention shifted to her. "Telling you that you should follow my example and go home, too, is a waste of time, I know. But there is a great deal of danger here. The man who took Giselle — I didn't get a sense of distance. That tells me that he is still right here."

"That tears it," Michael said. "We're out of here."

An inner shiver at the thought of inserting herself into yet another investigation into an active serial killer shook Charlie. The fear was too close to the bone: it had taken root in her psyche, she realized, and getting rid of it permanently was going to require time and possibly therapy, self-administered or otherwise. But there was nothing she could do about it right now except deal. It cost her some effort, but she deliberately closed her mind to it. "No, we're not going anywhere. I can't. Not when it's Lena's sister."

"Death wish," Michael growled. "Savior complex."

"Bite me," Charlie retorted.

"I thought so." Tam's tone was resigned. She told Charlie, "Try to stay out of harm's way as much as possible." As they stopped in front of her door she looked at Michael. "Spirit, you understand that my grounding spell will wear off soon. If you get yourself in trouble again there's little more I can do to help. The least thing could end you. Think of yourself as a bug flying around in a world full of zappers. You get too close to one, and you're gone."

His eyes lighting in sudden amusement, Michael nodded. "Bug. Zapper. Got it."

"I hope you do, because this is not a joke." Tam's tone was severe. "Now go away. I have something to say to Charlie."

Michael and Tam exchanged measuring looks. "Thanks again for everything you've done," Michael said. Then his eyes met Charlie's for the briefest of seconds. "I'll be waiting by the elevators," he told her, and sauntered off. Charlie watched his tall form — all broad shoulders and narrow hips and sexy swagger — striding away, then glanced back at Tam.

Who'd been watching him, too.

"He's hot, I'll give you that," Tam muttered as she fished her key card out of her purse. "Even kind of charming." Flourishing the key triumphantly, she gave Charlie an admonishing look. "That handsome FBI agent — Tony — is interested in you. I can feel the vibes when he looks at you. *That's* who you should be focusing on. Forget Gorgeous Ghost Guy. Believe me, he's bad news. And he'd be bad news even if he weren't dead."

"Thanks for the advice," Charlie replied drily. It was exactly what she'd been telling herself for weeks, so why she should find it annoying she didn't know.

"Which you're going to ignore." Tam gave her a partly fond, partly exasperated look. "Honestly, cherie, how can you be so smart and yet be so stupid about men?"

Tam had seen her through a variety of relationships, so the observation wasn't exactly unfounded.

Charlie made a face at her. "You know

what they say: you have to kiss a lot of frogs."

"Yeah, yeah. Fine, don't listen to me. Did I mention I'm a *psychic*?" Tam retorted good-humoredly, and reached out to enfold Charlie in a hug. She hugged her back, then watched as Tam slid her key through the lock, then turned to point a monitory finger at her. "You take care of yourself. And remember what I said about the dangerous energy around this case. Keep out of its way."

"I'll do my best," Charlie promised. As Tam stepped inside her room she said, "Drive safely. Talk to you soon." Then a thought hit her and she added, "Oh, and, uh, just how sure are you that we don't have to worry about hunters anymore?"

"There's that *we* again." Pulling a face, Tam shook her head. "I'm sure. But then, what do I know? Besides just about everything."

"Love the modesty," Charlie retorted.

Tam grinned, waved, and closed the door. Smiling as she headed for the elevators, Charlie multitasked, making use of her time and her phone to check her e-mail. At what was waiting in her in-box, her eyes flickered with interest. First up, a message from Warden Pugh in response to the one she had sent him asking to be kept in the loop on Dr. Creason's and the trustee's progress: both were still hospitalized, but they were alive and slowly improving, which was a relief. The cause of their collapse was still being investigated. The second message was the one she'd really been waiting for. Quickly reading through it, she frowned, then read it again, more carefully. By the time she reached the elevators, her frown had morphed into a full-blown scowl. Michael was there, alone, arms folded over his chest, one broad shoulder propped against the wall.

He took one look at her expression and said, way too flippantly for her current state of mind, "What's up, buttercup?"

"The DNA results on those women you were convicted of killing," Charlie said as she punched the down button and prepared to wait. "I had them rechecked by a lab I know I can trust. I just got the report back. Want to know what it said?"

CHAPTER TWENTY-ONE

"Not particularly." Michael straightened away from the wall, his eyes on her face. "Whatever it says don't change a thing for me now."

"It says," Charlie told him with precision, "that you're guilty as hell. Your DNA was all over those women. All of them, not just Candace Hartnell."

Of his seven alleged victims, he'd admitted to sleeping with the last one, Candace Hartnell. The others he'd claimed to have never laid eyes on. Problem was, DNA doesn't work like that.

"Crappy lab," Michael said without much apparent interest.

Charlie waited. That was it: nothing else. Nada. Zip.

"Nope." Charlie shook her head. "Not a crappy lab. The best in the business. Want to try a different answer?"

Michael's eyes narrowed. "What do you

want me to say? That I'm guilty? Fine. I'm guilty. Feel better?"

Charlie felt her temper heating. If she'd been wrong about him — the thought made her sick. It made her question her intuition. It made her question her judgment. It made her question — everything.

"You're admitting that you killed those women?" She waited almost painfully for his response. He had nothing to lose if he did admit it. He was well beyond the reach of any kind of human justice now, and the Powers That Be in the Great Beyond for sure knew the truth, whatever it was. As Tam had pointed out, there was no hiding anything from the universe.

He shrugged. "Can't get away with a thing with them fancy-schmancy DNA tests."

The sheer unconcern of that made her downright mad.

"You are so full of shit, you stink," Charlie burst out, then could have bitten her tongue off as the elevator arrived and the door slid open with a *ping* on a car full of people, every one of whom looked out at her with interest. Their interest seemed to intensify when it turned out she was the only one to get in, the only one in sight in an otherwise seemingly empty hallway. Given that they'd apparently caught her in the act of swearing angrily at empty air as the door opened, their covert glances were perfectly understandable, if no less embarrassing.

"Could be." Michael, on the other hand, was not one whit deterred by the presence of the other people in the elevator because *they could neither see nor hear him*. She was stuck in the front of the car and hemmed in by people giving her sidelong looks as she stared stonily at the supposedly empty space in front of her. He lounged comfortably with his back against the door, looking at her. With a smirk. "I guess you're going to have to make that call for yourself, babe. I'm not interested in lab results anymore. At this point, they don't mean a thing."

Charlie could hardly contain herself until they reached the lobby and the elevator emptied. As she (they) made their way across the marble floor she felt comfortable enough that no one was paying attention to her to hiss at him, "They mean something to me."

"Let's see, I seem to recall you telling the voodoo priestess that you were sure I wasn't guilty. That you thought I was a good man. Them DNA results really enough to change your mind?"

"Oh, my God, would you get over that?"

Charlie glowered at him. "As I told you before, I said all that for Tam's benefit."

"So you didn't mean it." He pressed a mocking hand to where his heart would have been if he'd had one, and gave her a not particularly nice smile. "You're breaking my heart here, babe."

"Better than letting you break mine." Muttered half under her breath, that came out before she could stop it.

But he heard, and looked at her, then said in a tight voice that was totally at odds with his previous mocking drawl, "This is the last time I'm ever going to say this: I didn't kill those women."

Unwilling to let herself be convinced by his word alone, which would make her all kinds of gullible fool in the eyes of anyone (like Tam) who learned just exactly what had persuaded her of his innocence, she remembered what in her view was the most damning (literally) piece of evidence against him and shot back, "Then how did you wind up in Spookville?"

He shook his head at her. "Not for that."

"Then why?"

He shrugged.

"Damn it, Michael —"

"Are you looking for us?" Buzz's voice caused her to break off in mid-blast. Her head snapped around. There they were, Buzz and Lena and Tony, standing near the bell captain's desk. She had nearly walked right past them. They were talking to three men in jackets and ties. Two of them had rectangular silver nameplates on their lapels, Charlie saw as she joined the group: hotel employees.

"I was," she admitted, and tried her best to thrust her concern about the test results plus her aggravation with Michael to the back of her mind. Giselle Kaminsky was the priority now. Michael was no longer in danger. He was also dead, and no threat to anyone (except maybe to her, and that would be to her sanity). Whatever he had or hadn't done in life, she could safely postpone her ongoing discussion with him until later.

"Careful, babe. Wouldn't want your face to freeze like that," Michael gibed, and to her annoyance Charlie realized that she was directing the fierce scowl he had prompted at the unknown men.

"This is Dr. Charlotte Stone," Tony said as she hastily rearranged her features into something that she hoped at least approximated pleasant. He introduced the two men with nameplates as Andrew Hagan, the Conquistador's head of security, and

George Bruin, the general manager. The other man was Detective Lance Renfro, Las Vegas Metropolitan Police Department, Missing Persons Detail.

"We're doing everything we can to co-operate with the investigation," Bruin said after the introductions were complete. Average height and slim with short dark hair, he looked to be around forty. "Anything else you need, you only have to ask."

"As Agent Kaminsky requested, we put together a list of all the employees who were working Saturday from noon to midnight, plus a list of that night's guests broken down by floor." Hagan nodded at the manila envelope in Tony's hand. "A hard copy of both lists is in there. I also e-mailed a copy to you." He looked to be in his mid-to-late thirties. About five-ten and stocky, he had a short, light brown brush cut and a round, cherubic face. "I warn you, there's about ten thousand names altogether. I wouldn't want to be the one who had to check them all out."

That would be Lena, Charlie thought, and she would plow through it speedily and with maximum efficiency. At least, ordinarily it would be Lena. Although how much having this be about her sister would change the usual method of operations was still unclear.

Lena was holding it together like a champ, but everything from the brittle note in her voice to her jittery inability to stand still spoke to the tremendous amount of stress she was under.

"I also requested a list of the independent contractors who had staff working for the hotel Saturday night," Lena said to Bruin. She was wearing a loose, short-sleeved green shirt, open like a jacket over her tee: the better to hide her shoulder holster, Charlie knew. In response to Tony's look of inquiry, she explained, "They outsource things like the parking valets, the gardeners and groundskeepers, some of the catering staff, people like that."

"That's included as well," Bruin said. "You should be aware that we do a background check on everyone who works for us, and our contractors are required to do one, too."

"We'll need access to those background checks," Tony said, and Bruin nodded.

"See to it, Hagan," he said.

Hagan said, "I'll have my office e-mail you the files right away. Is there anything else?"

"They've handed over all the relevant security footage?" Tony asked Lena.

"Yes," she said, and looked at Bruin. "Later today we may need to interview more of your employees."

"We'll see that they're available. Just let us know."

"Thank you."

Detective Renfro said, "If you want to get a look at the place where Destiny Sherman was found while it's still roped off and relatively intact, we should probably get a move on. Our guys won't be out there much longer."

"Let's go," Tony said, and with nodded farewells for Bruin and Hagan they headed with Renfro for the door. Charlie's eyes slid over the detective as he stayed half a pace in front of them. He was about six feet tall, attractive, and well built, with thick tobacco brown hair and a square, blunt-featured face.

"Wait a minute." Michael fell into step beside her. "I thought you were going to let the *FBI agents* do the fieldwork while you stayed back somewhere where the bad guy can't get at you and took care of the shrinky analysis part."

That actually had been the plan. *Was* the plan. But things like crime scene details were an important part of the *shrinky analysis part,* as she would have told him if she could have spoken to him. Which she couldn't. So she limited herself to a quick narrowing of her eyes in his direction and turned her attention to things that actually existed in the real world.

Like Tony. And Lena. And Buzz. And the case.

"And here I was thinking that the whole woman's prerogative thing was a cliché," Michael said with a *tsk-tsk* cluck of his tongue.

It took Charlie a second, but then she got the reference: *It's a woman's prerogative to change her mind.*

And shot him a glare — *eat dirt, you sexist pig* — before blocking the now-grinning affliction with which she was cursed out of her mind.

"Destiny Sherman?" Charlie inquired quietly of Tony, who loped along on her other side. The lobby was aswirl with activity: people arriving, people leaving, people heading in all directions. The noise level was high. The scent of lilies from several large floral arrangements being carried past wafted pleasantly beneath her nostrils. She thought she recognized a number of famous faces; she definitely saw a man walking a tiger on a leash.

"The woman in the morgue," Tony clarified. "The one with Giselle Kaminsky's bracelet. Renfro called me about an hour

355

ago to let me know they'd ID'd her."

"How long will the morgue keep her?" Charlie asked. Much as she dreaded the thought, she needed to go back. Destiny Sherman's spirit had been there last night and was probably still there. Ordinarily, with the spirit on a loop re-enacting her last moments alive, Charlie wouldn't have been able to talk to her. She still wouldn't be able to, but there was a slim possibility that Michael could, one spirit to another.

It took her a beat to realize that she was now starting to automatically count on Michael to help her and the investigation. Counting on anybody for anything was something that she had learned relatively early in life not to do, so it was unsettling that she now was relying on *him* to come through for her as unquestioningly as she expected there to be air for her to breathe.

Her chest tightened and she shot a covert look at him. *Oh, God, I'm in way too deep.* Her nails curled into her palms.

"I don't know," Renfro said, overhearing. He glanced around at her and Charlie saw that his eyes were hazel. "I heard the family was pretty eager to claim the body."

"You get that judge's order holding the body, Kaminsky?" Tony asked over his shoulder. Lena and Buzz brought up the rear. From that, Charlie deduced that they had already known the body had been identified. Clearly the others had been working while she'd been breakfasting with Tam, or maybe even earlier than that.

"Yes," Lena replied. "Good to know your department actually investigates *murders*, Detective."

Renfro sighed. "We have over forty million visitors to Vegas every year, Agent Kaminsky. Most of them come and go just fine. But some of them — about two hundred or so *a month* — get reported missing. The majority of those turn up on their own. We don't have the resources to run down every tourist who decides to take a side trip without telling anybody."

"My sister did not decide to take a side trip." Lena's voice was fierce.

"Hold on, now. I never said she did. I just said that adults are allowed to pick up and take off without telling anybody if they want to. We can't mount a full-out search for them all."

"Now that the woman wearing my sister's bracelet has been classified as a homicide, shouldn't there be a *homicide* detective working this case instead of you?" Lena asked in an acidic tone.

"There's a couple of homicide detectives

working the Destiny Sherman case. I'm helping you because your sister is still considered a missing person," Renfro replied.

Before Lena could explode, as Charlie was pretty sure she was about to do judging from the strangled sound Lena made, they reached the big revolving doors at the entrance and emerged into a wall of baking heat leavened with the smell of vehicle exhaust.

A school-bus-yellow Jeep Wrangler with an LVMPD tag propped against the windshield was parked at the curb directly in front of the doors, to the clear inconvenience of the vehicles that were trying to maneuver around it.

"We'll follow you in our car," Tony said after taking one look at the boxy, open-roofed vehicle.

"Suit yourself. We'll be going off-road," Renfro replied, scooping up the tag as he headed around to the driver's side.

Tony grimaced. "Bureau won't like it if they have to pay for a rental car's busted axle." He cast a glance around at the rest of them and added in a resigned tone, "Pile in."

CHAPTER TWENTY-TWO

They did. Charlie barely got a chance to register how busy the wide driveway of the drop-off zone was before the Jeep took off. Renfro pulled away from the curb with a squeal of tires, and the ride got progressively wilder from there. Having declined the front passenger seat in favor of Lena — there were bucket seats in the front and a hard, narrow bench seat in the back — Charlie was wedged in between Tony and Buzz in the rear. The top was off, and Michael sat on top of the roll bar, his booted feet braced against the backs of the front seats, his hands curled around the bar. He looked surprised when the Jeep peeled rubber without warning at the start, then threw a quick "Buckle your seatbelt" over his shoulder at her as they dodged an arriving limo with scant inches to spare. As Charlie complied, then pulled a pair of sunglasses out of her purse and slipped them on, they whizzed past the hotel's dancing fountains and whipped out onto Las Vegas Boulevard in the teeth of oncoming traffic. Charlie caught herself fearing that Michael might be thrown off. Then she realized that the wind of their movement that was lifting her hair from her neck and ruffling Tony's and Buzz's wasn't disturbing Michael's *at all,* and remembered what he was. Being thrown off his insanely reckless perch on top of a speeding car was one of the many things he didn't have to worry about anymore.

His enjoyment of the wild ride was evident, and she remembered him mentioning that he'd once owned a motorcycle; he'd also once been a Marine, although she hadn't yet had the chance to access his military records so that she could go over them in detail (she meant to, because if there was any evidence of psychopathy it should have been showing up by then and there should be clues in the records). The smart money was on the fact that before he'd been sent to prison he'd been extremely physically active, and Charlie found herself reflecting on exactly how miserable the years he'd spent in confinement must have been for him. Then the thought of those lab results stabbed through her like a knife, and she glared at the back of his head with its motionless mane of tawny hair.

In spite of everything, her gut still said he was innocent, but it was entirely possible that her damned gut was one hundred percent wrong.

"What do you know about Destiny Sherman?" Addressing his question to Renfro, Tony practically had to shout to make himself heard as they hurtled through an intersection and then turned onto a wider road identified by a sign as I-15. Charlie pushed Michael out of her thoughts and strained to hear the reply.

"Destiny was a local girl," Renfro shouted back. The Jeep rattled along, weaving in and out of light traffic, the ride bumpy and loud as the hot desert wind whistled through the backseat and the sun blazed down out of the cloudless blue sky. In the distance, the deeper blue of a mountain range stood against the sky like the blade of a serrated knife. Charlie found herself glad that she was wedged in so tightly between Tony and Buzz. With hard-bodied Tony on her right and wiry Buzz on her left, she wasn't going anywhere. They served as human air bags as she was jostled from side to side. She found herself ducking her head against Tony's shoulder more than once to dodge airborne grit. "Lived out in Pahrump.

Twenty-eight years old. No criminal record."

"Boyfriend? Married?" The wind kept Tony's bellow from sounding as loud as Charlie knew it was.

"Not married. No word on a steady boyfriend. She worked out at the Farm."

It took Charlie about half a beat longer than it took Tony to make sense of that. He was already asking, "The Pigeon Farm?" when she made the connection: Renfro had to be referring to one of the better known of the legal brothels that flourished just outside of Las Vegas, prostitution being illegal in Clark County where Las Vegas was situated but not in most of the surrounding counties.

"Destiny Sherman was a hooker?" Buzz blurted in surprise.

Even as Charlie had an instant visual image of the wholesome teacher-type she'd seen in the morgue, it hit her that hooker equaled sex worker: one of those who, according to Victim Facilitation Study criteria, was at relatively high risk of falling victim to a serial killer. Her heart started to beat faster.

"Yep," Renfro yelled back.

"Great," said Lena. "That's going to widen the pool of suspects." It wasn't a shout but the wind carried it perfectly audibly to the backseat. "If we can even identify most of them, that is."

There was a moment of silence. Then Buzz said, "They keep records of their customers at The Pigeon Farm. That should help."

Everybody except the driver looked at him. Lena leaned into the space between the middle of the front seats to frown back at him. Tony shot a quizzical glance his way. Michael turned his head to look down at him with a speculative grin.

"How do you know that?" Lena asked the question the rest of them were thinking. The big round sunglasses she was wearing made it hard to be certain, but Charlie was pretty sure her expression was accusatory.

Buzz's cheeks had reddened under the scrutiny. "Before I joined Special Circumstances, I was a regular old FBI agent, remember? We took part in a racketeering investigation. A few Las Vegas–area brothels were asked to cooperate. They did. The Pigeon Farm was one of them. Turns out, they keep records."

"If that's the case, we can find out who her customers were," Tony said. "That would give us one more place to look."

Charlie quietly told him about Destiny

Sherman's high-risk ratio according to the Victim Facilitation Study criteria. Given the rushing of the wind she didn't think Lena would overhear — no point in increasing her anxiety levels when there was nothing she could do with the information — but Lena did overhear and glanced back just as Tony said, "Yeah, I don't think there's much doubt any longer that we're hunting a serial killer. I got the background check on Giselle Kaminsky this morning and went over it. She had a stable job, an apartment, a cat that she left at a kennel. A number of ex-boyfriends, including Romeo over there on your left, but none that have any record of threatening her. There's nothing in her life that would suggest she took off voluntarily, or that someone she knew wanted to do her harm."

That was actually bad news because it meant the odds that Giselle was dead went way up. Despite the hot blaze of the sun, Charlie felt suddenly cold.

"I can understand why a serial killer might target Destiny Sherman," Lena burst out, and Charlie knew that the same thought must have occurred to her. It was hard to tell with the sunglasses obscuring Lena's eyes, but Charlie got the impression that Lena was looking at *her* like she could provide an answer. "But why Giselle?"

Charlie tried. "There's a connection somewhere. Giselle had to have crossed paths with this guy, and so did Destiny Sherman and all the others."

"But *where*?" Lena's hand, which was resting on the console between the seats, clenched tight in frustration.

Charlie shook her head. "All the women almost had to have encountered him in the same place, or in the same manner. As soon as we find where they intersected, we'll have our suspect. When we get done here, we need to sit down and figure out every single place your sister went while she was in Las Vegas."

"I've been over everything we did." Lena's jaw was tight. "There was nothing out of the ordinary. Nothing."

"Then we look at the ordinary," Charlie said.

"There's a common denominator somewhere." Tony's voice was grim. "There always is."

"We have to cross-reference her movements with the other women's movements as much as possible." Charlie tried not to think about how little they actually knew about the other women's movements before they had disappeared: the trails on most of them were way cold. There were going to be huge gaps in the web they needed to weave, but Lena didn't need to hear that. Charlie said, "We'll get it done."

"We'll find this guy," Buzz told Lena. "We always do."

Left unspoken, the question nevertheless hung in the air: but would they find him in time?

"Hang on, this is where we have some fun," Renfro yelled. Before Charlie quite grasped what was happening they left the highway with a sudden swerve of the wheel and started bouncing over the cracked, uneven surface of the Mojave Desert. The ground was khaki brown, concrete hard, and so rough that she had to keep her jaw clenched to stop her teeth from rattling. Rocks and undersized, scruffy bushes were scattered across the endless small undulations that stretched with few interruptions to the horizon. A number of Joshua trees and spikey cacti dotted the landscape, and the occasional small bluff rose up out of the dirt to interrupt it, but it was mostly flat. Renfro just managed to avoid hitting the larger fissures and car-sized boulders that lay in wait for the unwary, but with each one it seemed it was a close call. Even with her seatbelt on, Charlie was flung around like a stuffed toy.

"Okay?" Tony asked when she slammed into him for what must have been the dozenth time.

"Yes." Charlie unclenched her teeth long enough to reply even as the Jeep hit a rut and went airborne again and she bounced off him and Buzz. With an inarticulate sound of concern Tony wrapped a hard arm around her shoulders and pulled her close to his side. Charlie grabbed onto him, wrapping her own arms around his waist. The firm muscles beneath her hands and even the subtle scent of his body seemed way more familiar than they should have, and for that she knew she had Michael's little stunt to thank. She shot her *bête noir* a dark look, which since his back was turned he didn't see, but as they continued to get rattled around like die in a box she settled into Tony's embrace gratefully. Even so, by the time the Jeep jerked to a halt her tailbone ached from repeatedly being slammed down onto the seat and her head felt like it was about to fall off her shoulders.

"Here we are," Renfro announced with unimpaired cheerfulness, hopping out of the vehicle and gesturing toward the spot at the bottom of an arroyo that had been roped off with yellow crime scene tape. A number of vehicles with off-road capabilities like the Jeep were parked nearby, all of them bearing tags from one official law enforcement agency or another. Down in the arroyo, which began just beyond their front wheels, about half a dozen officers, a couple of uniforms and the rest in plain clothes, walked the length of a drainage channel carved into its bottom toward a big, dark, concrete-lined hole at the base of a twenty-foot-high bluff. Up on their level just inside the crime scene tape a police videographer recorded the scene.

"That's the drainage ditch?" Buzz stared down at the narrow trail of what looked like dried mud at the bottom of the arroyo, as, still rattled from the ride, they all stayed put for a moment. "I had a whole different picture in mind. More concrete, less dirt."

"You must be a city boy," Renfro replied, turning back to wait for them.

Charlie gave Tony a quick smile of thanks as his arm dropped away from her and they, Lena, and Buzz climbed out of the Jeep. Already on the ground, Michael looked from Tony to her with the slightest of frowns as the four of them joined Renfro, but said nothing as they all began to walk toward the crime scene tape.

Renfro continued, "This area is used for

recreational off-roading. You know, ATVs and dirt bikes and that kind of thing. It's prone to sudden, heavy rainfalls. They put in a drainage system to direct the water when that happens so no one is caught in a flash flood."

"How far are we from the nearest road?" Tony asked.

"About four miles," Renfro replied. "And that would be the one we came in on."

"So Destiny Sherman almost certainly didn't walk here," Buzz said, looking around at what was basically a whole lot of nothing as far as the eye could see.

"Not likely," Renfro agreed. "Almost had to have come in on some kind of four-wheel-drive vehicle. Or a dirt bike. Something like that."

"Or a horse," Lena said.

Without the breeze created by the Jeep's movement to stir the air, it was broiling hot. Charlie could actually feel heat radiating up from the ground. Her skin felt like it was coated with dust, and trying to brush some of the grit off with her fingers just made it worse. Out of the corner of her eye she watched a small brown lizard skitter up the side of a knee-high pile of rocks. Thinking of the snakes that might be hidden among all those rock formations, she vowed to be extremely careful where she stepped and put her hands.

"Thing is, no vehicle was found." Renfro cast a quick look at Lena, who appeared untroubled by the thought of snakes if, indeed, it had even occurred to her that they might be present. As always, she was wearing her high heels, but she was striding along with as much confidence as if she'd been walking on a sidewalk. Luckily the ground was hard enough so that her heels weren't sinking in. "And no horse, either. Which our guys are taking to mean that she was brought here by somebody."

"From the preliminary examination that was done of the site after she was picked up, she wasn't attacked here," Lena said.

"So she was attacked elsewhere and brought here. You think the unsub left her for dead?" Buzz asked.

Tony shrugged. "Seems likely."

Renfro made a face. "If so, it was his bad luck that she wasn't. She made it to that drainpipe, where our guys think she holed up deep inside for a couple of days, probably going in and out of consciousness, until that big rain we had Monday night washed her out."

They'd reached the crime scene tape barrier by then, and stopped, looking toward where the officers were picking their way along the sides of the arroyo, taking obvious care to stay off the bottom. Charlie understood: any evidence that had been in the storm drain with Destiny Sherman would probably have been washed down into the silt on the bottom of the creek bed. They didn't want to risk disturbing it any more than it already had been. Now that the case was officially classified as a homicide, they would be sifting through that silt for clues.

"Hey, Gregg, I brought company," Renfro cupped a hand around his mouth to yell, and one of the plainclothes officers looked up at them and waved in answer.

"Let's go." Tony ducked under the crime scene tape.

Renfro, Buzz, and Lena followed. Charlie would have followed, too, except Michael stopped her.

"Hold up a minute," he said. "I need to ask you something."

Looking at him, she was reminded that he didn't sweat. He didn't get covered in dust, either. He looked tanned and healthy and Marlboro-man handsome and more alive than she felt, standing there with the blazing sun beating down on him. It occurred to her that she hadn't seen him flicker in a while, which at least eased one worry that had been taking up real estate in her mind.

Because she was still ticked at him, and also majorly conflicted, her reply was terse. "What? I don't have time to chat right now."

He narrowed his eyes at her. "Much as I enjoyed watching you getting all cuddly with Dudley, this ain't personal. Look toward the south."

He nodded toward an expanse of rocky, uneven terrain that stretched away toward a high mesa in the distance.

"So?" Following his gaze, Charlie was just thinking that the land in front of her looked as bleak and inhospitable as the surface of the moon, when she remembered Tam's words and registered the import of that thought with a tingle of sudden interest.

Michael said, "You see anything around those rocks over there?"

Charlie frowned some more in the direction he indicated. Then she pushed her sunglasses up on top of her head, squinted against the sunlight, and tried again. Nothing but rocks, desert, and sky. "No."

He sighed. "I was afraid of that. Babe, we got us a ghost."

Chapter Twenty-Three

Charlie stared futilely toward the knee-high pile of rocks Michael had brought to her attention for a moment longer: still nothing. "What kind of ghost?"

He grimaced. "A woman. She's sitting on the rocks."

"Oh, my God." Mindful of her own limitations, Charlie didn't doubt him. Being a spirit himself, Michael could see any spirit who happened to be in his vicinity.

"Yeah." His voice was flat. "You better give Dudley a shout."

She looked at him with a frown. "Why?"

" 'Cause I think I recognize her. I think she's one of those missing women we're hunting for."

"Really?" Charlie sucked in air, stared harder at what to her was an empty tract of land, then started walking purposefully toward the rock formation he'd pointed out. If what Michael was looking at was indeed one of the missing women, the case might be about to break wide open. The ghost could even be the link that led them to Giselle Kaminsky.

Her heart started to beat faster.

"What the hell are you doing?" Michael sounded exasperated.

"Come on," she said over her shoulder to him. "I want you to talk to her."

"Wait, damn it." He caught up, frowning at her as she kept walking. "I told you, you need to yell for Dudley. In case it's escaped your notice, every other living soul around here is down in that gulley. Going over there alone's a bad idea. I'm ectoplasm, remember? Something bad starts going down, I don't know how much use I'll be."

"I can't tell Tony that there's a ghost I can't even see sitting on a pile of rocks." Her voice was impatient. "At the very least, I need to know more first. She might be some random spirit with nothing to do with the case at all." It occurred to Charlie that whatever Michael might or might not be, he never failed to do his best to make sure that she stayed safe. Acknowledging that made most — not all, but most — of her anger at him fade. She would have been more concerned about her safety if it hadn't been a blazingly bright day, with surroundings open enough to make it unlikely that a serial killer was concealing himself somewhere in the vicinity. She directed a quick look at Michael and a semi-mocking smile at him. "It's sweet of you to worry, though."

"Sweet?" He sounded revolted. "Fuck that. I'm trying to keep you alive here."

"The faster I get some confirmation of who this spirit is and what she's doing here, the faster I'll yell for Tony," she told him as she closed with determination on the rock formation where the ghost was apparently sitting. "Describe her."

The look Michael gave her was dark with aggravation, but he said, "She's a woman. With curly brown hair, an average face, a good bod with a nice rack. She's looking at me right now. She's figuring out that I can see her. Oh, here it comes, she's standing up she's so happy to see me. I'd be real excited, too, except she's covered with fucking blood because she's been slashed to death."

"Poor woman." Charlie shuddered.

"Yeah," Michael said. "She's coming this way."

"What's she wearing?" Charlie wanted to know. Not that she was interested in the ghost's fashion choices: her attire might give them some clue as to where she'd been when she'd encountered her killer.

"A dress."

"Day or evening?"

"How the hell am I supposed to know? It's black. Kinda tight. And short."

"Evening," Charlie decided, as, in a different, gentler tone that Charlie knew wasn't directed at her, he said, "Nevada. Near Las Vegas."

Charlie realized that he was answering a question posed by the spirit, whom she guessed had reached him. In fact, from the look of him he was holding her at arm's length, his hands curved around her upper arms. She nearly smiled: the last time he'd hugged a ghost he'd gotten all wet. She guessed where blood was concerned he didn't want to take the chance.

"Ask her name and —" Charlie's voice trailed off. Beyond the rock formation, the hard, uneven ground began to shift, as though it was less than solid. She frowned, and stared. "The last thing she remembers," she finished almost as an afterthought.

"She says her name's Alicia Dale," Michael reported after repeating the questions, although other than registering that was, indeed, the name of one of the missing women, Charlie wasn't really paying attention anymore. "The last thing she remembers is falling asleep in her hotel room. She doesn't remember anything that happened after that. And she doesn't have any idea where she is."

In several places — one, two, three, the spots popped up in rapid succession like mushrooms after a rain — the landscape began to emit a faint glow. Charlie squinted at them.

"She fell asleep in her hotel room in a short black evening dress?" Charlie frowned abstractedly as she tried to make sense of it. Then possible enlightenment occurred. "Oh, had she been drinking?"

In Las Vegas, coming home and passing out after a night out without bothering to undress was certainly not unheard of.

Michael said something to the spirit, then told Charlie, "She doesn't remember. She says she's been here for a long time."

Charlie's eyes widened as the glowing spots took on color, an individual color for each spot, pastel blue here, soft yellow there, a deep rosy pink near a crevice.

"Michael." Charlie barely managed to get his name out. She nodded toward the glowing spots of earth as he glanced at her inquiringly. "Look."

He did, and said, "Holy shit. They're coming out of the ground."

Charlie felt cold all over.

"What's coming out of the ground?" She watched, transfixed, as the glowing colors crept upward like lazy tendrils of fog reaching toward the sky.

"Women. More women. They're sitting up right through the dirt, like they're coming out of their graves. Three of 'em."

Charlie glanced at him to discover a misty lavender sphere about the size of a basketball hovering at chest level in front of him. Surprised, she realized almost instantly that it could only be the spirit he was talking to. Her eyes shifted back to the field, and it was then that she truly understood what she was seeing: the pockets of glowing colored mist rising from the ground were the dead that were outside the parameters of her gift. Only now she *was* seeing them, both as a kind of mist and, in the case of the one in front of Michael, as a sphere. Perhaps, she thought, their colors were the colors of the auras the spirits had possessed in life. She had never seen such a thing before, and she guessed that she was able to see it now only because the change in the frequency of her vibration was enabling her to tap into more of the supernatural world.

"They're standing up now," said Michael. "You really can't see all these women?"

The soft colors and erratic movements of the tendrils of mist as they swooped and soared reminded her of butterflies. Then each patch of mist started to swirl, and they coalesced into spheres like the one in front of Michael.

Charlie blinked, and realized what she was looking at: orbs. They were orbs. Of course.

"I'm seeing orbs," she told him, glancing at him again just to be sure. "There's one in front of you, by the way. It's lavender."

"Alicia's in front of me," Michael said, confirming for Charlie that the orbs were indeed spirits. "She says she's cold." His tone changed. "We'll get you someplace warm," he promised, and Charlie knew he was talking again to the spirit of the dead woman she couldn't see.

"What are they doing?" she asked him, as the more distant orbs seemed to drift on the wind without any seeming direction. "The ones out there in the field?"

"Just kind of wandering around. Aimlessly. I'm not sure the rest of them see us. Alicia does, though. At least, she sees me."

"Can she see me?" Charlie asked. "Or hear me?" The surprise of having another brand-new supernatural experience was still with her, but she was coming to grips with it, and the urgent need to find Giselle was fast reasserting itself. Any information that could be gleaned from these spirits might make all the difference.

"I don't think so. She seems to be having trouble staying focused on me. I'm not sure how in tune with what's happened to her she is."

"For God's sake, don't tell her she's dead." Charlie had lively memories of him being just that blunt with spirits before, and the last thing she wanted to do was have him freak out any potentially helpful spirit. "Ask her how she came to be here in this field."

Michael did, while Charlie watched the orbs floating over the parched ground with near total fascination. They looked more like airborne Japanese lanterns, she decided, than anything.

"She said she doesn't remember. Hell, she's crying again." His voice changed once more, and she knew he was talking to the spirit, but Charlie had stopped listening.

And that would be because as Michael had spoken she had just happened to glance down, and what she saw riveted her attention to the exclusion of anything else.

Peeking out from beneath the pile of rocks on which the spirit of Alicia Dale had been sitting was a woman's hand. To be specific, the tips of the phalanges bones of three fingers, one with gray slivers of flesh still adhering to it, another with a manicured fingernail semi-attached. They were curled slightly downward like they had been clawing at the dirt that covered the body they were presumably part of when they were stilled forever.

As she absorbed what she was seeing, Charlie's heart lurched.

"Michael." She interrupted whatever he was saying to the spirit, which she was too agitated at the moment to register, without ceremony. "Look down."

After one glance at her face, he did.

"Jesus." He looked up again, swiftly, as he seemed to listen to the spirit. His mouth tightened. His eyes went grim.

"What?" Charlie demanded.

"Alicia says she's here. Under the rocks and dirt. She says others are here, too."

"Dear God." Charlie looked back down at the grotesque fingers. "I think we've found the killer's dumping ground."

By early afternoon, seven bodies had been located. One, Alicia Dale, had already been removed from her grave site, photographed, bagged, and placed in one of several Coroner's vans that were now at the site. The dirt that had covered her was being carefully loaded into sterile containers for processing as well. Two other bodies had been fully uncovered, and were just waiting for the painstaking process of being extracted from their makeshift graves without compromising any of the evidence they or the killer might have left behind. Special equipment that would locate more bodies without digging up the entire field was en route, but Charlie felt fairly confident that most if not all seventeen of the missing women would be found.

The bodies were being uncovered manually — the only way to do it to preserve evidence. The grating sound of shovels digging in the dirt at four sites at once formed a constant, macabre backdrop to the cacophony of voices, footsteps, radio chatter, and arriving and departing vehicles. The chemical smell of the compounds used to preserve organic evidence hung strongly in the air. Dust was everywhere. The area swarmed with law enforcement: on hand was every nearby agency, from the local FBI to the Nevada Bureau of Criminal Investigations to the LVMPD.

None of the bodies, not even Alicia Dale, had been officially identified yet. The ones recovered so far were in such an advanced state of decomposition that a visual identification was impossible.

Charlie called up the case files, which included the missing women's pictures, on her phone. Looking at them, Michael identified the four he could see: Alicia Dale, Mary Bayer, Kimberly Watters, and Jessica French.

"Kimberly is the only one I can get to talk to me, and she kind of goes in and out," Michael reported after trying to get what information he could from the spirits. "She doesn't remember anything about being abducted. She said she was supposed to meet a friend in the casino at her hotel, so she was getting dressed in her room. Next thing she knows she's hanging by her wrists from a ceiling with like a grid in it and being tortured with a knife. She couldn't really see anything because she was blindfolded. She said she was screaming, and then there was this horrible sharp pain in her stomach and she passed out. Next time she woke up she was here." He grimaced. "I figure that pain is when she got killed. Probably stabbed to death. I know what that feels like: hurts like a mother."

Having been there when he'd died, Charlie grimaced, too.

It was too late to save any of the women

buried in the field. That their lives had been ripped away from them in such a way was more than a tragedy: it was an atrocity.

That was the thing about serial killers: none of them, not one that she had ever studied, felt any remorse, or had any feeling at all about the value of another person's life.

Alicia was a thirty-year-old hairdresser from Omaha who left behind two young daughters. Kimberly was a twenty-nine-year-old dental assistant from Grand Rapids who left behind a fiancé. Mary was a thirty-three-year-old homemaker from Des Moines. She left behind a husband and son. Jessica French was a twenty-six-year-old graduate student from the University of Texas. There were still posters of Jessica being handed out on the Strip, courtesy of her frantic parents.

All human beings, all with lives, all taken.

They — and the other victims — had at least one thing in common: they'd all come to Las Vegas for a fun, exciting vacation, and they'd all vanished without a trace.

Victims of a serial killer.

I'm scared. Charlie faced the hard truth of it as she watched the bodies she knew were there under the ground being systematically uncovered. Most people went their whole lives without ever coming face-to-face with the kind of evil that a serial killer represented. But she, she had spent practically her whole life in the shadow of it. She *knew* that monsters walked the earth, monsters who raped and tortured and killed for no other reason than because it was their nature. The knowledge had seeped into her pores, invaded her bloodstream, curled through her brain and her heart, and made her afraid.

"You don't have to do this. You can walk away, right now, and go home." Prompted by whatever he was apparently able to read in her eyes, Michael told her that as she watched Jessica French's remains being lifted from her grave site. The thing was, he was right, even though she shook her head at him: *not happening.* That was another truth. There was nothing binding her to this kind of work. She wasn't a sworn law enforcement officer. She wasn't anything.

Except an expert who maybe can help stop this guy before he hurts anybody else.

The photos of the faces of Alicia, Kimberly, Mary, Jessica, and the other victims of this particular monster were emblazoned in her mind. There were so many more: Holly, her teenage best friend; Raylene Witt; Laura Peters; Bayley Evans. And others.

Countless others.

That was why she wasn't going home. *They* were why she was going to stay and help in the fight. With every bit of expertise she possessed.

Looking away as Alicia's remains, now in a blue body bag, were lifted onto a gurney, she bent her mind to the task of finding a killer.

"Serial killer investigations with a single disposal site for the bodies involve a triangle of locations. What we have now are two points of that triangle. That's why finding this dumping ground is such a good thing for us. It really tells us a lot." Minutes later, she crouched in the shade of a canopy thrown up by one of the agencies and, with a stick, stabbed a point in the dirt. Then she looked up at Tony, Lena, and Buzz, who were standing over her in a circle, looking down. "The first location is the PFE, or point of first encounter with the victim. The second one is the BD, or body dump." Charlie stabbed another point in the dirt. "The KS, or kill site, is the third point in the triangle. So far, that point's unknown, but studies have shown that it will be closer to the PFE than the BD and in the same general direction. The killer — the fact that there's a single body dump tells us he's a local — will live somewhere in the center of the triangle."

"What theory is that?" Tony sounded impressed.

"It's a mathematical model called CGT — Criminal Geographical Targeting." She stood up and pulled her phone from her purse. "I can plot it on my phone, if you'll give me a minute. I just have to get the coordinates of where we are now — the BD — and where we're positing the PFE took place, which for our purposes I'm going to say is the Las Vegas Strip."

"Don't tell me there's an app for that." Michael had returned from another attempt to coax information from the spirits.

"There is" — which was when she remembered that no one else knew he was there, and hastily tacked on for the benefit of the others — "an app for that, believe it or not. It's called Map Expert."

"Seriously?" Michael raised his eyebrows at her.

This time Charlie ignored him.

"I've never heard of it." Lena took a deep breath. Beneath the fine layer of dust that coated her (and everybody's) skin, she was as pale as paper. "But if it helps find Giselle, I'll buy stock in the company."

"Look." Charlie held her phone out to

them. With the coordinates punched in, two areas were shaded in red. "The kill site should be along one of these two lines." She pointed to the far sides of the shaded areas. "Depending on where the kill site is, the killer will live within the shaded areas."

"Can you e-mail that to each of us?" Tony asked, and Charlie nodded and started to do so. "When we get into some kind of an office, we'll blow it up and print it out."

"Done," she said when she'd finished, and looked up. "There's one more thing," she added, remembering the information that Kimberly Watters had passed on via Michael. "The kill site will be relatively isolated. Far enough away from neighbors that screams won't be heard. It won't be in a subdivision."

Tony looked at her, and Charlie thought she saw the knowledge that she must have obtained that information by otherworldly means in his eyes. She smiled at him.

Before anybody could say anything else, Renfro strode into their shelter.

He said, "I thought I'd give you folks a heads-up. A butt-load of TV trucks just rolled in."

CHAPTER TWENTY-FOUR

"What do you want to bet that the body recovery efforts are playing out live on the local channels right now?" His tone rueful, Tony was behind the wheel of Renfro's borrowed Jeep as they whizzed along a black-topped highway through a whole lot of flat, scruffy land. Charlie was beside him, her sunglasses in place, her hair now twisted into a fairly windproof bun, praying that the sunscreen in the moisturizer that she used on a daily basis was up to the task of keeping her skin from cooking to a crisp in the broiling sun. Lena and Buzz were in the back, with Michael between them. There was plenty of room for him, as they were keeping as far away from each other as they could. The group sped down Blue Diamond Road toward the Pigeon Farm, following a pair of LVMPD homicide detectives and a quartet of uniforms in a big black SUV. The detectives considered Destiny Sherman the killer's latest victim because of where she'd been found and were going straight from the body dump site to search her quarters at the Pigeon Farm. Opting to go along, Tony was planning to pull rank once they got there, hoping to get a crack at whatever evidence might be in Destiny Sherman's room before teams of locals tramped through and contaminated everything.

"If the unsub sees it on TV, and if Giselle by some miracle is still alive, will that make him go ahead and kill her immediately, do you think?" The tension in Lena's voice was palpable as she met Charlie's gaze through the rearview mirror. Lena had been reluctant to leave the body dump because, as she had finally admitted to Charlie, she feared Giselle's body might be found there. Charlie was almost certain Giselle wasn't there. None of the graves were fresh enough, Charlie told her, but the overriding reason Charlie felt she wasn't there was because if Giselle had been, given the time frame and the circumstances under which she would have died, Charlie would have been able to see her.

Now, in the Jeep, Charlie met Lena's eyes. "If he's not killing his victims immediately" — which he wasn't, Charlie knew from torture victim Kimberly Watters — "then there's a reason. Probably because he uses them to act out some kind of a ritual. Until he completes his ritual, he'll keep Giselle alive if he can."

"How do you know he's not killing them immediately?"

Trust Lena to instantly hone in on that.

"You ever think I might appreciate getting a little credit here?" Michael drawled. "This ghost whisperer's apprentice thing you've got me doing kind of sucks. I'm feeling like the hired help."

Charlie ignored him. "The use of a separate kill site and body dump argues in favor of it," she said to Lena. "This is a methodical killer. He has everything planned out. I'd be a lot more worried if we were finding that he'd left the bodies all over the place."

Lena took a deep breath. The sense that the clock was ticking down was motivating all of them, and she was clearly feeling the stress most of all. Her eyes were dark and haunted, the skin around her mouth was pinched, and a few minutes ago Charlie had caught a glimpse of her in the rearview mirror chewing her perfectly manicured nails.

Buzz said, "You realize that Ms. Green gave us the number fifteen, and off of I-15 is where Destiny Sherman *and* the other victims' bodies were found, right? Also, she said to look out for a moon landscape, and that's sure what the terrain back there looked like to me."

Charlie nodded, pleased that someone else had made the connection. "I told you, Tam's good."

"Hot, too," Michael added. "Maybe a mite unfriendly."

"I always thought psychics were a load of crap," Lena said. "But I have to say, your friend was amazing."

Lena's eyes met hers once again in the mirror. The message Charlie read in them was one of silent thanks for her contribution.

"So suppose we go over what she told us." Buzz glanced at Lena, then directed a pointed look at the back of Tony's head. "How about we start with that blond woman throwing a shoe at somebody while yelling, 'Get out, get out'? Anybody recognize anything like that?"

Buzz's question was aimed at Tony, and his teasing tone made it clear that he was making an attempt to lighten the atmosphere — for Lena's sake, Charlie knew.

If so, it succeeded. The smallest of smiles touched Lena's lips.

"You know what you can do to yourself, Crane." Tony's response was good-humored. Charlie looked a question at him. Catching the look, he sighed. "My ex-wife has a temper. Toward the end of our marriage, these two came by my house — which I no longer own, because Rachel got it in the divorce — to pick me up because my car was in the shop. It was night, Rachel and I were supposed to have dinner, she didn't want me to leave — she felt I always put my job before our marriage — and when I had to go anyway because something had come up in the case we were working on she totally lost it, threw her shoe at me, and screamed, 'Get out, get out.' " He sighed again. "Which these guys are obviously never going to let me live down." He flicked a glance at Buzz through the rearview mirror. "Of course, *I* don't play Assassin's Creed every chance I get. Now, *that* would be embarrassing."

"I told you, I'm trying to beat the game," Buzz defended himself.

Tony continued, "And as for the illicit love affair Ms. Green mentioned — well, that isn't me, either."

At that pointed remark, Charlie *felt* guilty. A reflexive glance in the rearview mirror at the cause of her guilty feeling — that would be Michael, whom she forgot she couldn't actually see that way because his reflection didn't show up in mirrors — revealed Lena and Buzz exchanging uncomfortable glances.

In other words, in that car, for that moment, there was a whole lot of guilt going around.

"Dudley's talking about Pebbles and Bam-Bam back here, not you and me." Michael's voice was dry. He could see her through the mirror even if she couldn't see him. "Jesus, babe, don't ever play poker."

Oh, right. Of course. Tam wouldn't have mentioned Charlie's personal business in front of anyone else. Tam was a friend, first and foremost.

She was trying to settle her expression into a not-guilty look as they reached the small community of Pahrump.

Minutes later, they'd passed a giant Gold Town sign, a McDonald's, a couple of strip malls, and were pulling up to the Pigeon Farm. The long, low clapboard buildings were painted gray, and there was a gazebo at the edge of the parking lot. A sign out front bore an image of a pair of sexy female legs kicking out of a broken eggshell. Life-sized figures of a cowboy and cowgirl with cut-out openings for customers to put their faces in invited visitors to take a picture. All in all, the ambience was a cross between a mid-range hotel and a Cracker Barrel.

The woman who answered the door was pleasantly plump, gray-haired, and grandmotherly in a pair of pink polyester slacks and a flowered blouse. If she introduced herself Charlie missed it: she was too busy looking around as they stepped inside. The interior was all white walls and leather couches and framed prints — not exactly tasteful, not high end, but except for its large size and an excessive number of couches it could have been a living room in any ordinary suburban house. Hanging in the heavily air-conditioned air was the faintest scent of — potpourri? perfume? If business was being conducted on the premises, there were no apparent signs of it. No gathering of half-dressed females. No nervous johns.

It was not what Charlie had been expecting.

Michael's eyes twinkled at her. "First visit to a whorehouse, eh?"

Charlie shot him a withering look. *Obviously not for you.*

The twinkle morphed into a grin. "Think I'm dumb enough to admit to that?"

With a sniff, Charlie directed her attention elsewhere.

"Looks like we missed the lunchtime

rush," Buzz said in a low voice. He was watching Lena, who was prowling around restlessly. "Mid-afternoon's always slow. Things should start picking up again around five."

Charlie frowned at him. She was just thinking that Buzz of all men didn't seem like the type to possess that much insight into the workings of a brothel when she remembered what he'd said about investigating them as part of a case. Her brow cleared.

Michael chuckled. "If I'd said that, you'd be giving me a dirty look. Him you give the benefit of the doubt. You're supposed to be a woman of science, Doc: where's the fairness in that?"

Her eyes raked him. The obvious answer, that tall, hard-muscled, surfer-god gorgeous Michael exuded sexuality in a way that was unimaginable from smaller, wiry, nerdy-cute Buzz wasn't something that she was going to tell him even if she'd been able to talk to him.

So she gave him a snarky quirk of her lips instead.

By that time Tony had identified himself and explained what they wanted, which was then backed up by one of the detectives proffering a search warrant. Moments later they were escorted along a corridor lined with doors. Most were closed, but some were open, and in some of the open ones attractive young women in skimpy outfits ogled the men as they passed.

"You didn't call us out for a lineup, Mrs. J," one of the girls complained. She was giving Tony in particular a sultry look. "Did you tell them about our discount for cops?"

"They're here about Destiny," Mrs. J replied, which made it clear that everyone knew Destiny was dead. She clapped her hands. "In your rooms, all of you."

The girls all said some variation of "Oh," disappeared inside their rooms, and closed the doors with near simultaneous snaps.

Okay, then.

"We're going to need to talk to them," Tony said.

"They get scared, it's going to be bad for business," Mrs. J replied. "Destiny had the weekend off when she was killed. They don't know anything."

"We're still going to need to talk to them."

Mrs. J's mouth did the sour-lemon thing.

Destiny's room was in an annex accessed by a covered walkway. Six rooms off a central living area, each with its own bath. According to Mrs. J, Destiny had lived there full-time, as did most of the girls. At first glance, her quarters looked pretty much like any bedroom anywhere. A queen-sized four-poster with a pretty pink bedspread — and fur-lined handcuffs attached to the posts. A dresser with a clear glass vase filled with riding crops. A wicker magazine basket overflowing with sex toys. Charlie averted her gaze, only to accidentally get a closer look at the pictures hanging on the walls. They were pretty graphic, and she glanced away.

"You haven't lived till you've tried some of them toys." Michael's grin was positively wicked now. "Or the handcuffs. They're always fun."

Charlie ostentatiously turned her back on him.

"Has anybody used this room since Ms. Sherman was last in here?" Tony asked. The uniforms were all business now, with one of them starting to rummage through dresser drawers while another slid open one of the two closets that took up the far wall. Glancing that way, Charlie thought for a startled moment that severed heads were lined up on an array of shelves built into one side of the closet. Then she realized that what she was seeing were Styrofoam wig forms holding an astonishing array of wigs. The other half of that same closet contained what

Charlie concluded were costumes, from the glimpse she got as the cop riffled through them. The second closet, opened by another uniform, appeared to contain Destiny's own street clothes.

"No." Mrs. J shook her head. "It's been locked. She and I had the only keys."

"From the looks of things, she, um, serviced the S&M crowd?" Only the faint clearing of his throat indicated that Tony might feel a little uncomfortable.

Mrs. J nodded. "She was a specialist. The customers loved her. We billed her as our Kitten with a Whip. There's a brochure with her in it beside the bed."

Lena, who was wearing thin plastic gloves passed out by one of the uniforms, picked up the brochure, which featured a generously endowed topless woman riding a mechanical bull on the cover.

"Yee-haw," Michael murmured, and she saw that he was looking at the brochure, too.

Charlie narrowed her eyes at him. Glancing up, he met her gaze and grinned. "Hey, I'm dead, not blind."

Lena unfolded the brochure to reveal a big, glossy photo of Destiny Sherman in thigh-high black boots, a black bustier with garters and stockings attached, and black kitten ears — and nothing else — holding a whip. Charlie had a momentary flashback to the wholesome-looking young woman whose spirit she had seen in the morgue.

Glancing away, she tuned back in to Tony, who continued with Mrs. J. "She have any regulars?"

"A few. Mostly we get tourists coming through, though. We call 'em one and dones."

"We're going to need a copy of your records. Customers and employees."

Mrs. J frowned. "I don't know —"

"I can have a court order here in half an hour."

"There's no need for that." Mrs. J's response was grudging. "I'll give you what I've got."

Feeling like a voyeur but knowing that it was her job to notice as much as possible, Charlie pulled on her own pair of thin plastic gloves. Then she walked around the bedroom and bathroom, and tried to work up a psychological profile of the woman who had lived in this room.

She was doing her best to integrate a collection of Beanie Babies into everything else she'd seen when one of the detectives turned on the big, boxy, old-fashioned TV that sat on a stand against the wall directly

400

opposite the foot of the bed. Naked, writhing bodies filled the screen. The unmistakable sounds of sex permeated the room. The woman was in dominatrix gear, and the man — Charlie turned away as the sound of a cracking whip and a long, ecstatic groan filled the air.

With her periphery vision Charlie caught a sudden movement, and glanced around in time to watch Lena punch the button that turned off the TV. In that same glance Charlie also discovered that every single man (and ghost) in the room was staring at the screen with interest.

As the TV went dark she and Lena exchanged purely feminine glances fueled by an identical thought: *men are pigs.*

Then Lena hit the button popping the DVD out.

"I can't imagine that she'd watch that for fun," Lena remarked as the TV whirred with the effort to eject the disc. "So my guess is that it was probably part of her last session with a cust—"

She broke off, staring down at the disc as it emerged. She had such an arrested expression on her face that Charlie stepped closer to look, too.

The round paper label at the center of the disc read Dynasty Films.

Tam was right again, only instead of the old TV show this was hard-core porn.

CHAPTER TWENTY-FIVE

A few hours later, the four (five) of them were in a small office on the second floor of the FBI's sleek, modern headquarters in Las Vegas. On their way out of Pahrump the team had grabbed a drive-through lunch at McDonald's, then stopped by the hotel for a quick shower and a change of clothes (to get rid of all the accumulated dust) before heading over to the FBI building. Pictures of the eighteen victims hung on the whiteboard that took up the whole right wall of the room, which was a bland beige rectangle with a big window at the back and a couple of long tables now serving as desks. Michael stood in front of the pictures, studying them. While Lena was getting the computers set up to her liking, Buzz printed out the gridded map that Charlie had e-mailed them. Then he clipped it to the other end of the whiteboard, leaving the center clear. Complete with street names and neighborhoods, the map in theory should have made possible kill sites as well as the unsub's residence easy to locate. But the area involved was way too large to make a lightning-strike-fast, door-to-door search feasible, and any lesser undertaking ran the risk of spooking the unsub without finding what they were looking for. They needed more specific information.

Charlie took a moment to pull Tony aside and tell him the new pieces of information revealed by the spirits of Alicia and Kimberly.

"I've learned that the last memories of both women involved falling asleep in their hotel rooms. Kimberly Watters was hung by her wrists from a ceiling with some kind of grid set into it and tortured with a knife. All the victims probably were, as most serial killers have a killing routine that they follow religiously." She left out the bit about Kimberly being stabbed to death, because upon reflection that had been pure speculation on Michael's part. Cause of death needed to wait for the autopsy. "Kimberly was blindfolded but not gagged, which is why I think the kill site is relatively isolated. The killer wasn't worried about anyone hearing her screams."

As she finished, Tony met her eyes for a

moment, then said quietly, "You got that from talking to their ghosts."

It wasn't a question.

"Yes."

"I'll say one of the detectives told me."

"Thank you." Charlie gave a little shrug. "If word got out that I can see the dead, nobody would take me seriously anymore. I'd lose all professional credibility."

He nodded. "I'm honored that you trust me enough to tell me."

Charlie smiled at him.

Before she could say anything else, John Morris, one of the local FBI agents, stuck his head in the door and said, "Bartoli, you and your guys might want to come out here and look at this."

The four of them exchanged glances, then followed Morris down the hall to a small lounge area. Several agents were standing around a flat-screen TV affixed to the wall. As soon as she stepped through the door, Charlie realized what they were watching: coverage of the dump site. On CNN.

Oh, joy.

". . . at least seventeen young women have been found in a stretch of desert just outside Las Vegas. They came to Sin City as tourists, eager to visit the casinos, enjoy the shows, see the sights, and partake of all the glittering amusements the self-proclaimed Entertainment Capital of the World offers. Then they simply — disappeared. Some of them weren't missed. Some were the subjects of desperate searches by frantic family members. Today all of them were found." The broadcaster, Courtney Bennet, a pretty blonde whose name Charlie knew because of the banner posted beneath her picture as she spoke, paused portentously. "In this barren expanse of scrubby ground that you see behind me, in shallow graves lay the victims of a serial killer who preyed on unsuspecting female vacationers. The authorities are calling him the Cinderella Killer —"

"Wait, we are?" Buzz threw a questioning frown around the room.

Morris shook his head. "We aren't."

Tony shrugged. They weren't, either.

"— because the last sightings of a number of these young women occurred as they left their hotels around midnight, only to vanish forever."

Lena took a deep breath. "How does she *know* that?"

Charlie felt her chest tighten. If the story was on CNN, it was everywhere, and the possibility that the unsub might miss it was remote. That couldn't be good news for the investigation — or, if she was still alive, for

Giselle. "The missing persons files. Remember? Someone must have given them copies."

Lena had gone through the files at least as thoroughly as Charlie had: she knew all the details that were in them.

Lena rounded on the local agents. "Who's been talking to the media?" she demanded fiercely.

"Sure as hell not us." Morris looked alarmed at Lena's vehemence. "Must be somebody at the PD."

"They need to shut up," Lena growled. "Everybody needs to shut up and get to fricking work. Standing around watching TV with our thumbs up our butts isn't going to help us find this guy."

She stomped out. With a frowning glance at the surprised-looking agents who were staring after Lena, Charlie followed her.

"Kaminsky's got a point," she heard Tony say as she hurried from the room. "We need to clamp down hard on the information leakage. There may be a woman still alive out there and at this bastard's mercy."

"She's dead, isn't she?" Lena asked quietly when Charlie caught up to her. "Giselle."

Charlie looked at her with compassion. Lena was wired with anxiety even if she was doing a yeoman's job of holding it together.

"I don't know." She gave Lena the answer she deserved: the truth. "Her body wasn't at the dump site, so not necessarily."

"Just because they didn't find a fresh grave doesn't mean she's not there." The look Lena gave Charlie was stark. "Maybe her grave's hidden. Maybe they haven't come across it yet."

Charlie shook her head. "I would know if she was there," Charlie told her. "Trust me, I would."

Lena frowned at her, but then Tony and Buzz caught up with them, as did Michael, who said, "I thought I'd give you and Sugar Buns some girl time," earning a quick frown for his trouble.

Once everyone was back inside their temporary office, Tony shut the door and turned to look at them.

"Okay, guys." His voice was crisp. "Let's get cracking. What do we know?"

"All the victims except Destiny Sherman were staying in hotels in and around the Strip when they disappeared," Lena said. "Eleven different hotels among seventeen victims. Eighteen victims if you count Giselle." She paced the room, her arms folded, a look of deep concentration on her face.

Tony nodded at Buzz, who wrote *all but*

Destiny — hotels on the whiteboard.

Michael said, "Destiny Sherman was a hooker. It's possible that she was at a hotel the night she ran into this guy. You know, moonlighting."

Charlie slid him an approving look and repeated his observation, prompting Buzz to add a question mark in parenthesis beside Destiny's name.

"I heard from a detective that two of the victims were last known to be asleep in their hotel rooms," Tony said. Charlie waited, but he didn't continue with the information about how the victims were tortured, and she guessed that it was to spare Lena additional distress. At this point, knowing that wouldn't help in the search anyway. It only added to Charlie's profile of the killer.

"The victims share a physical type," Charlie added, "but there is no common pattern to family situation, educational status, or anything like that. So at this point the assumption is that he is choosing them by physical type."

Lena said, "The unsub has access to a four-wheel-drive vehicle. Large and covered enough to carry a body, so we're probably talking about an SUV of some kind."

"He's a local," Buzz said, writing as he spoke. "Most likely a native of the area.

Certainly he's lived here long enough to know it well."

Tony said, "He likes using a knife."

Charlie said, "He's familiar with the dump site. He visits it fairly frequently. He may be watching the body recovery now."

The stipulations came thick and fast. Buzz wrote them down.

"There was a crowd gathered around out at the body dump site last time I talked to someone on the scene, which was about an hour ago," Tony said. "We've got somebody filming everything."

"We'll comb through the footage," Buzz said. "We'll stake the site out."

"We don't have time." Lena's voice was tense. "We've got to figure this thing out *yesterday.*"

There was a moment of silence as the stark reality of that sank in.

"So," Tony said. "What else?"

"He's heterosexual," said Charlie. "Between the ages of twenty-five and forty. White male. He'll have a job, probably something fairly menial. He will not inject himself into this investigation, and will avoid being questioned if possible. He'll blend in to his surroundings. His neighbors would probably describe him as a nice guy. If there is an available parent, it will be a mother —

dominant. He's a sadist — he likes inflicting pain — but it may not be obvious, although he may have killed pets or small animals in the past. There will have been a stresser — a job loss, a divorce, the death of a parent, some kind of trigger — in his life around the time of the first murder." Charlie frowned, thinking hard. "The first seventeen victims were tourists. That tells us that he is careful, methodical. He doesn't want to dirty his nest. The fact that Destiny Sherman was a local tells us that there is something different about her."

"Unless he didn't know she was a local," Michael interjected. "That's possible. Vegas is a big place. If he spotted her around a hotel, he might have thought she was just another tourist."

Good point. Charlie didn't say that aloud, but she repeated Michael's observation, and added, "I think his name or nickname might be Joe."

"We need to consider the information we got from Ms. Green," Tony said. "I think we all agree that what we've been able to confirm of what she said was accurate enough so that the rest should be included."

Everybody nodded, and Buzz played the relevant portion of the recording of Tam's reading so they could all hear it, pausing the recording to repeat the pertinent points and jot them down as necessary.

"The number 15 — which we think was I-15; a moonlike landscape, which we think was the dump site; dogs barking; an old sign with something to do with a shell on it; a flock of birds; a bar with an eagle over the door; red, white, and blue; a small, enclosed space; silver wheels. And a dynasty, which we're thinking is Dynasty Films."

"Anything else?" Tony raised his eyebrows as he looked at them. "What about surveillance video?"

"Only on Giselle," Lena said. "The other cases are too old. And I've watched it a dozen times. Nothing jumps out at me."

Tony said, "All right, that's enough to go on. Here's the plan: Kaminsky, run through the computer employee, guest, subcontractor, whatever, lists of all the hotels the victims were staying at on the night they disappeared. Screen for gender, age, and race, the same name appearing at more than one hotel, for residence within the area Charlie mapped out for us, for priors, for ownership of an SUV, for the name Joe. The more markers that turn up on an individual, the higher he goes on our hit list."

Kaminsky nodded. "Will do."

"Might want to rescreen the girls," Michael said. "Maybe they had more in common than looks. Forget family situation and all that stuff. Maybe they were all into S&M or something."

A good suggestion. Charlie repeated it.

"Not Giselle," Lena and Buzz said in unison. Lena looked daggers at Buzz — the obvious implication was that she wasn't happy about how he knew about her sister's sexual proclivities — who threw up his hands in surrender.

"You know, if I'd married Giselle then figured out how I feel about you, we would be in a mess," he burst out.

Lena's eyes blazed at him. "Keep the personal *out of this,* Crane."

"Damn it —" Buzz began.

Tony cut him off with a snap of his fingers. "Both of you, save it for after this investigation is over. Or I'll put you both off of it."

There was no mistaking that he meant it.

"Sorry, boss," Buzz muttered, while Lena gave a jerky nod.

"Screen the others for something like an S&M connection," Tony directed, continuing as if there'd never been an interruption. "Anything. Maybe they all like to knit. See if they went to any of the same shows, bars, or restaurants. If we find the common denominator, we get our guy."

"I'll also do a cross-match with the names of the johns we got from the Pigeon Farm," Lena said, her demeanor once again totally professional. She grimaced. "This is going to take some time. If I do everything exactly right, and the program works the way it should, maybe the rest of the day. Maybe longer."

"Since Destiny Sherman was the latest victim, and the only local, I think we should concentrate on her," Charlie said. "We know she had some contact with Giselle because of the bracelet. It's possible that Destiny knew the unsub, or encountered him in such a way that she became a danger to him. He may have killed her because she saw him with Giselle, something like that. If we investigate *her* — it might give us a quicker path to the killer."

Tony nodded. "I've got an address for Destiny's mother. Buzz, you're with me. Let's go talk to her, see what we can find out."

After they left, Lena got busy loading names and running programs to screen for the designated criteria, while Charlie went through the victims' files again, futilely looking for any missed connection between them. Then at Lena's suggestion she watched the surveillance video of Giselle,

414

hoping that fresh eyes might discern something new. They didn't. There were several snippets of Giselle in casinos and nightclubs, although not on the night she went missing. The rest was mostly footage of Giselle around the hotel, confirming what they already knew: since coming to Las Vegas, she'd come in, gone out, eaten at some of the restaurants, shopped in the shops. On the night she'd gone missing, there was footage of Lena and Giselle going into their room, then Lena leaving about an hour later. Giselle had stayed in, ordered room service around eight, then left, dressed for a night on the town, at around midnight.

And vanished.

"I'm not picking up anything," Charlie said finally, leaning back in her chair. She was at one table in front of a computer screen. Lena was at the other, also in front of a computer screen. Michael had disappeared when she'd started watching the video for the second time. Not as in, *poof,* gone, disappeared: he'd walked out the door. He'd stopped blinking, so she wasn't worried about him in that way anymore. Wherever he'd gone, it was close by, and he'd be back.

"Big surprise." Lena sounded discouraged.

Charlie looked at her. "Not having any luck with that?"

Lena snorted. "More like, too much luck. So far, those eleven hotels have 682 employees in common, and the search is barely a quarter of the way through. Apparently they share a staffing service. And use some of the same subcontractors."

Checking out as many people as that extrapolated out to be would take weeks, not days, even if they used the entire resources of the local FBI office and the LVMPD.

Charlie tried not to think what that would mean for Giselle.

"While the computer's doing its thing, I'm going to see what I can find out about Dynasty Films," said Lena. For the first time in hours, a hint of a smile tugged at her mouth. "And somebody needs to watch the DVDs to see if anything relevant is on there, like our victims."

"Somebody meaning me, I suppose." Charlie sighed. "Fine. Hand them over."

Lena did.

Charlie was watching the last of the DVDs when Michael returned. There were three of them, each about fifteen minutes long, and because her purpose was to try to identify any of the victims among the performers or anything else that might have some bearing on the case, she couldn't just fast-forward through them. The DVDs were S&M pornography, and the principals were definitely not actors. But they weren't the victims, either, and nothing — setting, props, highly dubbed sexual noises — had anything to do with the case as far as Charlie could tell. Coming up behind her, Michael took one look at the action on the screen, grinned, and settled into a chair slightly behind her. She got the feeling that he was having more fun watching her face than he was watching the film. She would have said *Go away* if she could have. Since she couldn't, she settled for ignoring him. Loudly.

Charlie sat through the credits. They listed everybody involved, but since everybody involved used obviously fake names, like Big John Johnson, the whole exercise was useless. She cast Michael a dark glance.

His grin widened. She was expecting some coarse remark, but instead he said, "FYI, the Scooby gang's all over TV in there. CNN's busy telling the world that Special Agent Anthony Bartoli heads one of ViCAP's crackerjack teams, and they're in Las Vegas right now hunting the Cinderella Killer."

Charlie's eyes widened. "Oh, no," she breathed.

"What?" Lena looked up. "Did you find something? If so, it's more than I did. Dynasty Films makes porn, but there's no obvious connection to the case that I can see. There's a members-only section, but it requires a sign-in and so far I haven't been able to crack it."

"I didn't find anything, either," Charlie said. "Anyway, that's not it. I think I just heard somebody passing by out there in the hall say that we're all over TV."

"You're getting good at this," Michael said. "Probably she won't notice that you couldn't hear anything that was said out there in the hall because the door's closed."

The news made Lena's face tighten. "Bloodsucking scum," she growled, and stood up abruptly.

Charlie assumed that *bloodsucking scum* referred to the TV people.

Before Lena could do whatever it was she meant to do — Charlie guessed it was check out the TV coverage for herself — her cell phone rang.

Its ringtone — *Lena's* ringtone — was "Girls Just Wanna Have Fun."

Michael laughed. "Did *not* see that coming."

"Giselle changed my ringtone," Lena ground out, obviously responding to Charlie's startled expression. She took one look at the number, and answered the phone: "Kaminsky."

Charlie could hear the other side of the conversation well enough to follow it. The caller was the FBI lab technician who had been given the job of checking out Destiny Sherman's clothes and everything else she was in possession of when she died.

"We've identified a substance on the spikes on the bracelet," the technician said. "Blood and skin cells. Belonging to Destiny Sherman."

The bracelet the technician was referring to was Giselle's, Charlie knew.

"That's not surprising," Lena replied. "Destiny Sherman sustained multiple slash wounds. She was bleeding."

"From the way the blood and skin cells were distributed on the metal, the more likely explanation is that she was gouged with the bracelet."

Lena's brows knit. "Really," she said slowly. Then she thanked the technician, disconnected, and looked at Charlie, her expression thoughtful. "I need to go to the morgue."

CHAPTER TWENTY-SIX

"You're a glutton for punishment, you know that?" Michael growled as Charlie followed Lena into the cold storage unit where Destiny Sherman's body was being kept. Because of the court order requiring that it be held, it was stored separately from the other corpses. This was helpful to Charlie: she wasn't facing the onslaught of spirits that had overwhelmed her before.

On the way in, they'd only passed two ghosts, both blood-soaked adult males with what looked like bullet wounds. Neither had paid any attention to her. She'd returned the favor, and so far the nausea that spirits always brought with them hadn't hit her.

She expected that to change the moment Destiny Sherman's spirit put in an appearance. Having argued against Charlie making a return visit to the morgue until the taxi had dropped them at the building's door, Michael was well aware that she wanted him to talk to the spirit, getting as much information as he could. Given that Destiny's spirit was on a loop that might be difficult. Still, Charlie knew that he would try, however grudgingly.

"Unzip the bag, please." Lena made the request of Coroner Investigator Glenn Heinz, who'd preceded them into the room.

The resultant loud zipping sound made Charlie think of a chainsaw. One that was tearing through her head. Her eyes widened at the instant onslaught of pain.

The sudden headache was so bad it made her feel sick. Her stomach churned. The degree of distress she was feeling meant that something was definitely up.

She didn't know what she looked like, but she felt like she'd just turned fifty shades of pale as she lifted a thankfully icy hand and pressed it against her temple.

"I can't catch you if you collapse," Michael warned grimly. His mouth was tight. His eyes slid over her as if he expected her to crumple to the floor at any moment.

Charlie gave him a look that silently ordered him to turn his attention to the *corpse.* She gritted her teeth and got a grip. She was there to help the investigation, not hinder it.

Destiny Sherman's body was naked, and

with the zipper on the body bag in which she lay pulled all the way down, it was fully exposed. As Charlie had observed many times, there was no dignity in death.

The woman's flesh was that particularly corpselike purple-tinged white that dead bodies turned after having been dead for a while. Her lips were blue, and drawn back to reveal glimpses of her teeth. Her eyes were closed; the lids looked sunken and bruised. Her whole body looked sunken and bruised.

The edges of the wounds to her abdomen were crusted and black and horrifying. The other details of what time had done to the corpse were so disturbing that Charlie's mind simply glossed over them. What she was looking for was a scratch or scratches deep enough to draw blood.

"I don't see any injuries that look like they might have been made by Giselle's bracelet," Lena said, and looked to Charlie for confirmation.

Charlie would have shaken her head, but the headache had grown too intense. Instead she held her head still and said, "Me neither."

Michael was looking at her, not the dead woman. "You're white as a damned sheet."

"Turn her over," Lena instructed Heinz.

The corpse had passed beyond rigor mortis, so the coroner's investigator was able to comply without too much difficulty. Charlie tried not to see the limp flop of dead limbs.

As the body was shifted, the rank smell of death combined with formaldehyde fanned through the air, strong enough to make even Lena wrinkle her nose.

Almost as soon as the body was on its stomach Lena said, "Look there," and pointed at four parallel scratches in the center of Destiny's back, just below the nape of her neck. Charlie focused despite the headache and saw that they were about an inch apart, six inches long, and looked deep. They would have hurt — and bled.

"Somebody attacked her with Giselle's bracelet." Lena glanced at Charlie, her voice suffused with suppressed excitement. "How could we have missed it?"

"We weren't looking for injuries that might have been caused by your sister's bracelet," Charlie replied with credible evenness as Lena pulled her phone out of her purse and sent a brief text — Lena had called Tony and Buzz on the way over, and they were on the way, so Charlie presumed the text was to them. Lena started taking pictures. "At the time, we —" Charlie broke off abruptly as the weird, disoriented feeling that she had been experiencing only since she'd died overwhelmed her.

Oh, no.

"The scratches are in the autopsy report," Heinz said, but Charlie barely registered the words. She felt dizzy. She could hear the throb of her own pulse in her ears. The chainsaw headache was back, sawing her brain in half.

"Damn it —" Michael loomed close, but the rest of what he was saying to her was lost.

"I don't want to die." A woman's soft, Spanish-accented voice was terrified and pleading.

Charlie didn't know what she looked like, but Michael said, "Babe," and reached for her. Uselessly, of course. His hands passed right through. She never even felt the tingle, or heard anything else he said, even though she could see his lips moving and knew, in some abstract way, that he was cursing a blue streak. As unobtrusively as possible, Charlie took a couple of steps away from the gurney and pressed her back against the freezing cold wall.

Then the same terrified voice she had heard before whispered through her head.

"Oh, please. I'll do anything! Anything you want." There was a pause, not even long enough for Charlie to sneak in a breath. The high-pitched, frightened voice continued, "Please don't kill me! Please don't kill me!"

A hair-raising shriek followed, then that hideous gurgle Charlie remembered from before: the death gurgle.

Cold sweat broke over her in a wave. The voice was the same one that she'd heard the last time she'd been here. Then she'd wondered where it was coming from. Now she knew: it was attached to Destiny's body. What that meant, exactly, she was too sick and dizzy and disoriented to even try to figure out.

"Charlie." As the horrible gurgling sound faded away, Michael swam into focus. He was leaning over her, his eyes boring down into hers, his face hard with concern. "You're hearing those damned voices again, aren't you?"

Charlie managed a truncated nod, and this time when he cursed she heard it.

She glanced around. If Destiny's spirit had been going to show, it would have done so already. If it had been nearby, Charlie would have been far more nauseated than she was. The spirit was gone, she concluded, claimed by the Great Beyond. Glancing past Michael's shoulder, Charlie saw Lena still taking pictures of the corpse, and felt another wave of dizziness gathering strength.

She really didn't want to hear the voice again.

"I'm going to wait for you upstairs," she told Lena. Without waiting for the other woman's reply, she propelled herself out the door and to the elevator by sheer force of will. She rode up leaning against the wall with her eyes closed. By the time she reached the ground floor the worst of the symptoms had receded, and she was able to find a chair in the reception area and sink down on it and breathe. Michael stood over her, his body tense, his face harsh.

She knew how much he hated the fact that there was nothing he could do to help her.

A moment later Tony and Buzz strode through the door. They checked on seeing her.

"Lena's downstairs. Last door on the left." Charlie was proud of herself: she sounded perfectly normal.

Buzz nodded and strode off without a word.

Tony hesitated, frowning at her. "You okay?" he asked.

"She's just peachy-keen, Dud," Michael answered for her. "Can't you tell?"

"I'm fine. I just needed some air," Charlie

replied, and waved a hand toward where Buzz was holding the elevator. "You go on."

Tony hesitated a split second longer, nodded, and left.

By the time he, Lena, and Buzz returned Charlie had largely recovered. Having delivered himself of his opinion on her continually putting herself in the way of both serial killers and bad psychic experiences, Michael stood with his back to her. He was staring out the window at the fuzzily lit parking lot, and, beyond that, the inky blackness of the night.

"It could have been Giselle who scratched her," Buzz said thoughtfully as they all piled into the rental car. They took their usual places by default: Tony driving, Charlie in the front passenger seat, Lena and Buzz in the back, with Michael between them. Michael was sprawled expansively, with his legs stretched out and his arms spread across the back of the seat behind Lena and Buzz. They had no idea he was there, of course, but Charlie noticed that they tended to hug their respective doors, and that occasionally Buzz would flinch a little if the back of his neck got too close to the electric energy of Michael's arm extended behind it.

"It could have been anybody who scratched her." Tony sounded tired as he drove out of the lot and turned left toward the Strip. "Anybody could have gotten hold of Giselle's bracelet."

"But first they had to get it from Giselle." Lena leaned forward in her seat, her hands clasped together in her lap. The white skirt and short-sleeved jacket she'd changed into after their midday shower made her seem to glow faintly in the dark. In contrast, Charlie wore a silky black sleeveless blouse with her standard black pants and felt like she probably blended into the shadows almost too well. With her hair smoothed back into a low ponytail and her only jewelry her silver earrings and Michael's watch, she felt way too low-key for the flash that was Las Vegas.

"The killer didn't take Giselle's bracelet and scratch Destiny Sherman with it," Charlie said. Since she still wasn't able to make any sense of what the voice that was attached to Destiny's body meant, she tucked that problem away to be worried over later. "It doesn't fit with anything we know about him. In fact, I'm confident in saying that a woman made those scratches."

"But who?" Lena's eyes shone with intensity, making them as easy to see in the dark as her white outfit. "And *why*?"

"Maybe the women were forced into having some kind of cage match," Buzz speculated aloud. "You know, like that last guy we caught pitted victims against each other." He stared thoughtfully out the window with his fingers templed beneath his chin. "Maybe the match was with Giselle, and the loser — say, Destiny Sherman — got dumped."

"If so, she got dumped *alive,*" Tony said. "And she had the bracelet. Doesn't fit."

"Unless she *took* the bracelet, and this guy thought she was dead when he dumped her," Michael put in.

Charlie repeated that.

"We need to go over every moment of Destiny Sherman's day on the day she disappeared," Lena said.

"Crane and I talked to her mother." Tony braked as they hit an intersection, looked both ways, and made another left. City lights were all around them now. The huge Technicolor glow that was the Strip lit up the near horizon like a rainbow among candles. "She said she hadn't seen her daughter for a month. There's a half-sister in town. We'll talk to her tomorrow. Crane, did we get Destiny Sherman's credit card records and bank statements in yet? They ought to help us track her movements that day."

"Yeah, we — Uh, wait." Buzz straightened

in his seat, staring out the window. "Stop. Turn in here. Do you see what the name of that place is?"

They all looked where he was pointing.

A neon sign riding the roof of a long, low, warehouselike building said *Red, White, and Blue Club.* Under the peaked eave that rose above the entrance, a soaring eagle was picked out in deep yellow lights.

"Oh, my God," Lena breathed.

"Tam," Charlie said.

"Hellfire," Michael muttered. A glance back showed Charlie that his arms had left the back of the seat. He was sitting up and frowning out the window just like the rest of them.

"Worth a look." Tony yanked the wheel, and a moment later they were cruising the packed lot for a parking space.

"What is this place?" Lena asked as they got out. Seen up close, the one-story building looked as large as a strip mall.

"Busy," Michael said at the same time as Buzz answered, "No clue."

Two burly bouncers stationed outside the door had a better answer: it was a nightclub for military veterans, or serving military on leave. Tony flashed his credentials and they were allowed in. Raucous music and the smell of barbecue and beer were the first things to hit Charlie's senses. The next thing she registered was that the place was dimly lit and the air-conditioning was cold. In one encompassing glance, she saw couples grinding together on a dance floor in the center of the room, waitresses in red, white, and blue sequined bikinis weaving in among the many dozens of small, candlelit tables set around the dance floor, a buffet, and a bar. Various displays on the walls were highlighted by spotlights, but Charlie was too far away to see what they featured. On top of the bar, g-string-clad women in cowboy hats and boots danced to the music.

Tony stopped a waitress and asked where to find the manager. The waitress pointed, and they all followed Tony to the bar.

It was a classic wooden bar with a mirrored wall behind it, long enough so that it required a dozen bartenders and accommodated half a dozen girls dancing on top of it. Patrons sat on bar stools or leaned up against it, and with Tony taking point they had to wedge their way through the crowd to reach the burly, gray-haired man behind the cash register. He was tall, with ruddy skin, uneven features, and a slight paunch that his tucked-in white shirt and the green apron tied around his waist did nothing to conceal.

Once they reached him, Tony identified himself and showed his credentials.

"You're the manager?" Tony half yelled to be heard over the music.

"*And* owner. Ed McGowan. What can I do for you?"

"I'd like to show you some pictures, ask if you've ever seen any of these women."

McGowan nodded assent, and Tony turned to Lena. "Show him the pictures."

Lena pulled out her cell phone and started showing him the victims' pictures. She clicked through them one at a time, giving him ample time to look. Each time he shook his head.

"You're that serial killer team that's been all over TV today, aren't you?" McGowan asked, his eyes sweeping over them when they were done. "Those the girls who were killed?"

"Yes, to both," Tony answered. "Is there anything you can tell us about them?"

McGowan shook his head. "If they've ever been in here, I've never seen 'em. 'Course, it's a big place, and we get a lot of people coming in and out. A new crowd every night."

"Yeah." Tony pulled out his card and handed it to McGowan. "If you think of something, would you give me a call?"

"Sure will." McGowan tucked the card into his shirt pocket, then waved a hand at the buffet. "We got the best food in town, no joke. You folks are welcome to help yourselves. On the house." He beckoned to a waitress. "Susan. Get them a table. Anything they want, it's free."

"Appreciate it," Tony said. McGowan nodded and turned away to ring up a tab while the waitress, Susan, a pretty blonde with super-sized assets above a tiny waist, beckoned them to follow her and took off, weaving with practiced dexterity among the tables. The sparkle of her sequins made her easy to keep track of despite the gloom. "I was thinking fast food, but this would give us a chance to look around, see if there's anything here we're missing."

"I could eat," Buzz admitted.

Charlie's stomach growled in agreement, and she realized that it was after ten p.m. and her last meal had been a drive-through hamburger hours before.

"We don't have time to eat." Lena's voice was sharp. "We have to keep going."

"We've talked about this, remember? We have to eat, and we have to sleep, or we're not going to be able to do our jobs to the best of our ability," Tony told her patiently. "Keep in mind that we're not the only people working on this. The local agents and the local PD are on it, too. Everything that can be done is being done."

Lena looked at him, then growled, "Fine," and turned to follow the waitress. The rest of them fell in behind her. Susan showed them to a round six-top tucked into a corner, took their drink order, told them to help themselves to the buffet, and left.

The buffet featured down-home Southern food, with chicken wings, pulled pork barbecue, corn on the cob, green beans, and much more. Wishing vainly for a sweater as the brisk air-conditioning slid over her bare arms, Charlie filled a plate, then headed back toward the table. Staying close to her side, Michael was uncharacteristically silent. His face was absolutely unreadable as she sat down and he dropped into the chair next to her. She frowned at him, but before she could say anything Tony joined her. He was still standing, still putting his plate on the table as another arctic blast of air-conditioning hit her and she shivered.

"Cold?" He'd clearly seen her shiver, and she said, "A little."

"Here." Sliding out of his jacket, he walked around behind her and draped it over her shoulders. Glad of its warmth, she tugged the edges of the jacket closer and smiled up at him.

"Thank you."

Feeling the steady regard of a pair of sky blue eyes, she glanced at Michael. His mouth had a sardonic twist to it, but he still didn't say anything.

She frowned.

"Something wrong?" Tony sat down on her other side and looked at her with raised brows. She realized that he was referring to her frown.

"I've got the beginnings of a headache, is all."

"You see something back there in the morgue?"

She shook her head. "I heard something. A woman's voice. It seems to be attached to Destiny Sherman. I think it might belong to one of the victims. She basically says, Please don't kill me, and then she screams."

Tony looked at her for a moment longer as she sipped the iced tea the waitress had brought while they were at the buffet. Then he reached over and took her hand in his, careful to avoid the Band-Aid that protected her injured finger. His felt strong and warm. Hers, she knew, felt icy. *She* felt icy. Icy enough to shiver inside Tony's too big and very warm jacket.

"When we get through with this investigation, I'm going to take you out to dinner to the fanciest place around and we're not going to talk about serial killers or murder victims or anything but how beautiful you are and how much I'm enjoying getting to know you." Tony's voice was low and intimate. He lifted her hand to his mouth and kissed the back of it, then looked at her steadily over it. His lean jaw was dark with five o'clock shadow and his eyes were intent on her face and his shoulders did a nice job of filling out his white shirt and all in all he was looking seriously handsome. Unfortunately, her heart didn't speed up. Her pulse didn't race. The brush of Tony's lips against her skin had been pleasant, but nothing more. The reason, of course, was sprawled in the chair beside her. She felt Michael's eyes on her, but he still wasn't talking and she refused to look at him. If she did, her eyes would probably blaze something like *You are ruining my life* at him. If it weren't for the twist of cosmic fate that had foisted him on her, she absolutely already would have embarked on a romance with Tony, who was just exactly the kind of man she was looking for. "We're going to talk about the weather. About the TV shows you like to watch. About our hobbies." Tony kissed her hand again, sighed, and let it go. "But for now, tell me what the damned voice said. Before Crane and Kaminsky join us."

Charlie did, pretty much word for word, and told him, too, about how the gurgle made her suspect that those might be the woman's dying words. She also cautioned him that she couldn't be sure, that the voice could be anything and might not even be real.

"You think it's real, and I do, too." He glanced up and shut up as Lena and Buzz reached the table. Lena's expression was so stony, and Buzz's was so exasperated, concluding that they'd argued their way through the buffet line was a no-brainer.

"Crane thinks we should go straight back to the hotel after this and go to bed." Lena plopped her plate on the table and flung herself down in her chair. "He says I'm obviously fried."

"I did not say —" Buzz started to sit down in the chair Michael occupied, jumped, frowned, looked at it askance, and moved to another one. The slight smirk on Michael's face was the giveaway, although Charlie had no idea what he'd done.

"Enough," Tony said, biting into a chicken wing with apparent relish. "Kaminsky, fill me in on where we are with our hit list. Any names popping out at you?"

Lena told him about the unfortunate overabundance, and they spent the rest of the meal talking about the case. As they were finishing, Charlie excused herself to go to the restroom. Michael strolled along beside her. He'd been so quiet for so long that she gave him a sharp look and asked tartly, "What is this, your strong, silent side?" the moment she felt that she was out of earshot of the table.

His answering smile was tigerish. "Didn't want to interfere with your lovefest with Dudley."

That was bullshit and she knew it. She was just about to call him on it when her gaze happened to fall on one of the spot-lighted display areas that she was passing. Or, more specifically, on the wall-mounted, framed photos in the spotlighted display area. The center one, a poster-sized image of a young man in a military uniform, meant nothing to her. It was the image beside it, an eleven-by-fourteen framed photo of four young men in uniform standing together in a desert setting, that stopped her in her tracks.

One of the men was Michael.

CHAPTER TWENTY-SEVEN

There was absolutely no doubt in her mind.
"That's you," Charlie said unnecessarily.
The guy in the picture was a lot younger,
probably somewhere around his mid-
twenties, and his tawny hair was cut military
short, but there was no mistaking the square
jaw or the chiseled cheekbones, the straight
nose, the beautifully carved mouth. The eyes
of the man in the picture were narrowed
against the sun, but were still unmistakably
a dazzling sky blue. He was taller than his
companions and broader of shoulder, and
the unbuttoned shirt he wore with well-
worn fatigues revealed his wide, smooth
chest and muscled abs. He was bronzed and
laughing and gorgeous.

In other words, he was Michael.

He didn't say a word. Looking at the
display more closely, she discovered that
one of the guys in the picture with him was
the man in the poster-sized photo in the

center of the display. Framed eight by tens were lined up on either side of it, and her eyes widened as she realized that several of the photos — one taken right here in this bar, showing both men with their arms around nearly naked cowgirls — featured the guy in the poster and Michael.

Then she glanced up at the top of the display and read the caption: A Fallen Hero.

Her breath caught. She looked at Michael.

His eyes were fastened on the poster at the center of the display. His face could have been carved from stone.

"He was a friend of yours." It wasn't a question.

"Yeah," he said, and turned and walked away.

She hesitated, then grabbed her phone from her purse, snapped off a couple of pictures of the display for future reference, and hurried after him.

"Fifty feet," she hissed at him when she caught up, reminding him of the length of the cosmic leash that tethered him to her.

"Fuck it." He'd stopped walking when he reached the bar and was leaning against it, looking longingly at the whiskey being tossed back by the man next to him.

"Talk to me," Charlie said, sliding in on his other side. The lighting was so dim, and there was so much noise and activity going on around them, including bobbing boobs as a pair of red cowboy boots kicked up their heels not six feet away, that nobody was going to notice her having a one-way conversation with air. And from the granite set of his jaw and the hard glint in his eyes, air needed to talk.

"I ain't up for the shrink shit right now, babe."

"You've been in this bar before." There was no denying it. She'd seen the picture, and he knew it.

"Yeah. So?"

"You might have mentioned it."

She thought he wasn't going to answer at all, but finally he said, "So I'm mentioning it. A long time ago I visited a Vegas bar with a friend. Woo-hoo."

"*That's* why you were so dead set against coming to Las Vegas. You have memories here."

He looked at her then and said, "Leave it alone, Charlie."

His eyes were as cold and remote as the moon.

"Michael —"

Before she could say anything more, McGowan loomed in front of her. "Can I get you a drink, young lady?" The owner accompanied the question with a genial smile.

Charlie didn't want one, but on the other hand she couldn't just take up real estate at his bar. "I'll have a beer. Whatever you have on tap."

Michael rolled his eyes. He had a point. She wasn't going to drink it. What she was going to do was use it as a placeholder while she talked to Michael.

Who had other ideas.

"Let's get out of here," he said, pushing back from the bar. But McGowan returned with her beer right at that moment, and as Charlie fumbled in her purse for the money to pay him he said to her, "You're one of those FBI people, right?"

Charlie didn't feel like explaining her exact role with the group, so she simply nodded.

"Thought so." He scooped up her money and dropped it into a pocket in his apron, then nodded at the spotlighted wall she'd just left. "I saw you taking pictures of my son."

"I said, let's go," Michael growled in her ear, but Charlie wasn't about to leave at that point.

"Your son?" Her eyes were riveted on McGowan. He wasn't — couldn't have been

— talking about Michael.

"Sean." The old man's eyes were suddenly bright with pride. "Big picture, middle of the wall over there. First Sergeant Sean McGowan, Marine Force Recon. Killed in action."

At his obvious pain Charlie felt a surge of sympathy. "I'm so sorry for your loss," she said sincerely.

"You were taking a picture. Did you know him?"

"No." Charlie shook her head. "I wish I had." As she spoke she pulled her phone out of her purse and pressed a button. Her copy of the photo of the four young marines filled the small screen, and she pointed at the picture of Michael. "I actually — knew — this guy."

Michael grated, "Damn it, Charlie. Don't do this."

But McGowan was already looking at the picture. "That was the unit. Sean, Captain Ollie Bridgewater, Sergeant First Class Hoop Ferrara, Staff Sergeant Michael Garland." McGowan tapped Michael's picture with a forefinger. "Came here with Sean a couple of times. Kind of a hell-raiser, but my boy always said he was for sure one you wanted on your side in a fight." His voice deepened. "Refused to leave him

443

behind when Sean was mortally wounded. Stayed with him, then carried his body out. I owed him for that. No matter what he did after, I owed him for that."

"What he did after?" Charlie felt her chest tighten. Behind her, she could feel Michael radiating tension.

"Those women. The murder thing. I couldn't believe what they said he'd done. Far as Sean was concerned, Garland was a stand-up guy. 'Course, combat changes a man, and the things they had to do over there were pretty hard-core. Lots of wet work, you know."

The harsh voice behind her growled, "Fifty feet or no fucking fifty feet, I'm walking. Stay if you want."

She sensed rather than saw him moving away. In his present mood, she placed no reliance on his sticking to the fifty-foot limit. "I have to go. It was a pleasure to meet you, Mr. McGowan," she said as she glanced around to find Michael striding straight for the exit. *Yikes.* She concluded swiftly, "I'd like to hear more about Sean. I'll get back in touch, if you don't mind."

"Anytime," McGowan said.

Then she hurried after Michael. A quick glance toward their table showed her that Tony and Buzz were on their feet, and Lena was nowhere in sight. Probably gone to the ladies' room in search of her, Charlie guessed. She tapped out a quick text — *I'm outside getting some air* — to Tony as Michael pushed through the double doors and disappeared from view.

Forget hurrying. She ran. If he got too far away . . .

"Damn it," she exploded as she burst through the exit and found him leaning against a post supporting the overhang, staring out at the night. Relief washed over her; anger followed close on its heels. A quick glance around told her that, while a few people were threading their way through the cars in the parking lot toward the entrance, the porch itself was deserted. She stalked toward him. "Would you stop behaving like a *child*?"

He threw a sideways glance at her. Those blue eyes were glacial.

"Stay the hell out of my past."

Exasperation caused her to fold her arms over her chest. "Guess what, Mr. International Man of Mystery: I have access to your files. I can find out anything I want to know about your past just by reading them."

Those eyes raked her. "Great. Go for it. Knock yourself out."

Clearly whatever he didn't want her to

445

know wasn't in his files. At least, not in the ones she had access to. His military files were less than complete: they consisted of scarcely more than dates of service and his medical records. Everything else had either been redacted or withheld.

"So you were in Force Recon." She'd known that he'd been a staff sergeant — that much was in the files — but not that he'd been in Force Recon. She found herself looking at his profile. The set of it wasn't promising.

He gave a slight shrug. "Not a secret."

"Mr. McGowan said you did wet work." She watched him carefully as she spoke. *Combat changes a man.* Combined with the DNA results, that thought was worrisome.

His jaw tightened. "That means I killed people, babe. Knifed them. Shot them. Broke their necks. Up close and personal. Feel better knowing that?"

Ah. Paradoxically, his being so in-your-face about it calmed her fears considerably. She didn't think that by learning he'd killed in the context of war she'd just been handed any kind of new evidence that he was, indeed, a serial killer. What she did think was that she was getting close to something dark and ugly that he'd been harboring deep in his soul.

"Guilt can be a corrosive emotion, you know," she told him quietly. "Maybe it's time you let go of some of that."

"You just can't stop with the shrink shit, can you?" Michael slanted a hard look at her. "Guess what, Doc? I don't feel any damned guilt."

Charlie's lips compressed. Before she could reply, the sound of the door opening behind her caused her to glance back. A uniformed soldier with his arm around a girl in a mini-skirt came out, followed by Tony, Buzz, and Lena.

"I thought you went to the restroom," Lena greeted her, while Tony met her eyes with a silent question of his own.

"I'm still trying to shake that headache," she answered both of them, while at the same time making a concerted effort not to let her eyes follow Michael, who was already walking down the stairs to the parking lot. "The fresh air helped."

Apparently sometime after she'd left the table, the others had agreed to call it a night. As it was after eleven p.m. by that time, Charlie thought it was a good decision. She was so tired she was having trouble concentrating, and she knew the others had to be equally exhausted. Even

Lena seemed resigned to their need for sleep.

"Did *you* see anything in that bar that might pertain to the case?" Tony asked Charlie as they drove back to the hotel. "Ms. Green was so accurate that I'm afraid we might have missed something."

Charlie had a sudden, electric realization: just like Tam had seen the blond woman for Tony and the illicit romance for Lena and Buzz, she'd seen that bar because it had significance for Michael.

"I didn't see anything," she said, flicking a glance into the backseat. Michael's grim silence was unsettling. He met her eyes expressionlessly, but she was left in no doubt that he'd known exactly what Tam was referring to from the moment she'd said the words red, white, and blue. That bar, and the McGowans, and Las Vegas were all part of his history that he was actively trying to avoid.

"You can't expect her to be totally accurate." Lena slumped tiredly against the passenger door. On some level she and Buzz both seemed able to sense Michael's presence: they were always giving him all the space they could. "I'm impressed that she got as much right as she did."

"At least the food was good," Buzz put in.

Lena responded with, "All you think about is your stomach." Then, fiercely, "Giselle's out there. Don't you even care?"

Buzz practically spluttered, "Of course I care. You know I care. We're all working our butts off to find her. Lena —"

"Don't call me that."

"Guys. Don't make me give you a time-out." Tony said it lightly, but there was a warning in there, too. He pulled into the hotel, and nobody said much of anything until they had reached the hallway outside their rooms.

"Seven a.m. call," Tony reminded them.

Sliding her key card through the lock, Lena nodded.

"And get some sleep." Tony gave her a stern look as the door opened and she stepped inside her room.

Lena sneered at him and closed the door.

Tony sighed.

"Night, all." With a quick glance that encompassed both Charlie and Tony, Buzz, too, went into his room. Charlie's lips tightened. She knew that was Buzz being tactful, in case Tony was going into her room with her.

"Don't stay out too late." With that mocking aside, Michael surprised her by walking through the door into her (their) room while she was still out in the hall with Tony.

Idiotically, the sheer unexpectedness of that flustered her.

She summoned up a smile for Tony, who like the true gentleman he was was waiting to make sure she got safely into her room. The uncomfortable memory of how the last time he'd stood like this in the hallway with her had ended made her glad she already had her key in her hand.

"Good night," she said, and was getting ready to unlock her door and go inside when she remembered that she was still wearing Tony's jacket. She looked back at him. He was watching her with a rueful expression that softened into a smile as she slid the jacket off and held it out to him.

"Thanks for loaning it to me," she said as he took it.

"You're welcome." He met her gaze, grimaced, and added, "I'm a fine one to preach about fraternization, aren't I? But —"

Then he slid a hand around the back of her neck, bent his head, and kissed her with just enough heat and tongue to let her know where he wanted that kiss to go, if she was willing. When she didn't go there, he released her and looked down at her with a kind of grim humor.

"One of these days we're going to have some time," he said. "Then we're going to talk this thing out and you're going to explain to me exactly why it is you aren't sleeping with me."

Charlie looked at him, a little flabbergasted, because, really, what was she going to say to that?

"After the case is over," Tony added, sounding resigned as he made a gesture toward her door. Charlie took advantage of the out he was giving her to smile at him, say good night again, and retreat into her room.

Where the far larger problem in her life was waiting for her. She flicked on the light to find that Michael had flung himself down on the bed. He lay on his back with his arms folded behind his head and his booted feet crossed at the ankles. She looked at him speculatively: if he was still harboring any dark and brooding thoughts about what had transpired in the bar, she couldn't tell it from his demeanor. To all outward appearances, he was back to his normal carefree self.

He watched her walk into the room. "So, when are you going to break it to Dudley that the reason you're not sleeping with him is because you're sleeping with me?"

The bed — the only one in the room — was a king, and he took up way too much of it. Having him share her bed was starting to feel normal, she realized, which was probably — no, definitely — a bad thing. Charlie sent him a reproving look.

"You were listening." Opening the closet door, she bent to retrieve her night things from her suitcase, which she hadn't as yet had a chance to unpack. Her toiletries were already in the bathroom.

"I overheard."

"Just to be clear, sleeping with you doesn't preclude sleeping with him." Charlie smiled sweetly at him as she headed for the bathroom. "There's no reason on earth I can think of that I can't sleep with you both. Hey, I can even sleep with you both at the same time. In retrospect, that two-for-one thing you did the other night was kind of hot."

"Babe, the part that got you hot was all me."

She laughed. "Keep telling yourself that."

"What pretty thing are you planning to wear for me tonight?" he yelled after her by way of retaliation as she shut the bathroom door on him.

Charlie glared at the closed door. Since she hadn't yet had a chance to go shopping at the granny store, all her lingerie was still in the sexy/feminine category. Tonight's sleepwear was a satiny lavender slip that fell to mid-thigh. She knew he'd like it, and she also knew that he wasn't going to see it: she was going to turn off the lights as soon as she emerged from the bathroom. That was the thought that sustained her as she went through her nightly pre-bed ritual at warp speed.

"Looking good, babe," he said as, after clicking off the light, she returned to the bedroom. That made her lips compress: Vegas at night was as bright in its neon way as most places at high noon, and there was just enough light filtering in around the closed curtains so that she could see him, which meant that he could see her, too. He was still on *her* (*not* their) bed, lying on his side with his head propped up on a hand. What had changed was that he'd taken off his shirt and boots.

Even in shadowy silhouette against the curtains, those broad shoulders and sinewy arms were something to see.

Her pulse, which obviously didn't have a clue, picked up the pace a little from just looking at him.

"Of course, if you really want to make my night, you could take that sexy nightie off for me. Give me something to think about while I don't sleep."

She pulled the covers down on her side of the bed.

"Sad to say, I don't want to make your night." She sat down on the edge of the bed, picked up the alarm clock on the night table, and set it for 6:15. Then she slid her legs beneath the covers and lay down with her back to him.

"See how we're different?" He was looming over her, his voice low and husky now as it poured over her like honey. " 'Cause I'd sure like to make yours. I'd start by kissing you all over. I'd kiss your breasts, and take your nipples in my mouth until they got all hot and wet and hard for me —"

She could suddenly feel the slithery satin of her nightgown rubbing against her nipples, which were disgustingly tight and eager for him to do just what he said.

"— and then I'd kiss my way down your stomach until you were making those sweet little moaning sounds you make —"

The hot throbbing between her legs would have been pure pleasure if she hadn't been so outdone with herself for letting him turn her on like that.

"— and then you'd spread your legs for

me and I'd move on down and kiss your
—"

She knew where that was going before he got there, and the blast furnace heat born of the image he conjured up blazed through her and made her body tighten and quake. She *wanted* him to . . .

In sheer self-defense she rolled onto her back and glared up at him.

"Stop," she ordered, and hoped he wouldn't notice that her voice was as husky as his, and her breathing was coming way too fast.

"You know you like that part." He was still lying on his side with his head propped on his hand. Her eyes slid over the sleek muscularity of his chest and his wide shoulders and her mouth went dry. The hot dark gleam in his eyes made her bones melt. "You come for me every time I —"

"You," she said with a precision that cost her a lot to summon, "are just trying to avoid a conversation. Don't think I don't know that."

His eyes narrowed. The hot gleam was still there, but there was wariness in them now, too.

"What I'm trying to do, babe, is make you horny. And you can't tell me I'm not succeeding."

She frowned at him. "You need to talk about what happened with your friend Sean. It's obviously been bothering you for a long time. Believe me, talking helps."

He flung himself onto his back. "Damn it, would you forget about playing shrink? What happened back then don't matter anymore. It's over. It's done. It's in the past. Leave it there."

Now it was Charlie who turned on her side, propped her head on her hand, and looked down at him.

His eyes were closed. His face was hard. No matter what he said, what had happened back then obviously still did matter. To him.

"Mr. McGowan said you stayed with his son when he was mortally wounded, then carried his body out." She said it very gently. "That had to have been a terrible experience for you."

His eyes opened to blaze at her. "All right, Doc, you really want to know what my terrible experience that day was? I didn't just stay with Sean and carry him out. I fucking killed him."

CHAPTER TWENTY-EIGHT

Charlie almost sucked in air. What saved her was her training. During the course of her internship and residency and the research she had undertaken afterward, she had interviewed so many subjects with so many different manifesting symptoms and syndromes and stories that she was pretty sure she was shockproof.

So instead of betraying any kind of surprise or concern, Charlie looked at Michael steadily, mirrored what he had just told her by repeating in a totally nonjudgmental way, "You killed him," then added a low-key, encouraging, "Tell me about it."

He made a sound halfway between a snarl and a growl.

"Hell of a technique, Dr. Stone. Shame it don't work on me." His eyes flamed at her. She could sense his anger, his determined resistance.

She looked into his eyes. Obviously, his

emotions about what had happened were both deep and conflicted. Part of her wanted to stop, now, and leave him alone. But a larger part of her recognized the circumstances surrounding the death of his friend as a defining moment for him, and a traumatic one. Like a boil, the debilitating memories needed to be lanced if he was ever to be free of them. She still thought he was telling the truth about not being a serial killer; it was almost an article of faith for her now that he might behave badly but he wasn't *evil*. And if he *was* telling the truth, then it seemed logical that whatever had happened with Sean played a part in why he had found himself in Spookville. Why Michael thought he deserved Spookville.

"I'm just trying to understand," she said in her best soothing tone. "Hiding from the pain you feel is the worst thing you can do."

"Goddamn it." His voice was savage. His eyes were, too, as they gleamed up at her. One arm was tucked behind his head. The other lay straight down by his side. Charlie watched the powerful muscles in his shoulder and arm ripple as his fist clenched. "I'm not feeling any pain. I got over it a long time ago, believe me. And no, I'm not feeling any goddamned guilt, either."

"The fact that you can't talk about it —"

"I shot him. I shot him in the goddamn heart. Point-blank. Pulled the trigger. On purpose. How's that for talking about it?"

"Michael." If, right now, he was the emotional equivalent of a ship tossing in storm-whipped seas, it was her job to be the anchor that kept him off the rocks. Her tone was calm, steady. "We both know that's not the whole story."

"Who are you, Dr. Pitbull? I told you what happened. Now quit trying to shrink me."

"You're telling me that you murdered your friend." Charlie slowly shook her head, knowing even as she did so that what she was about to say was backed by every ounce of intuition she possessed. "I don't believe it."

He stared up at her. It was dark, but she could see his jaw tighten. He looked overwhelmingly big and masculine lying there on the mattress beside her and the aggression that was coming off of him in waves should have made him feel dangerous. He was far larger and stronger than she was, and if he'd been alive, and wanted to, she knew he could have physically overpowered her without breaking a sweat.

"You should believe it." His voice was very quiet, devoid of any trace of emotion, and all of a sudden Charlie was afraid. Not of

459

him, but of something in the atmosphere around him, some feeling of darkness and latent violence. This wasn't her gorgeous, tawny-haired, drawling Michael. This was a man she didn't know. "Like I told you from the beginning, babe, I've done a lot of bad things."

His eyes had taken on a steely gleam. The set of his beautiful mouth was almost cruel.

She remembered the scary convict she had first met. She remembered the strong wrists linked by chains, and the powerful body in the orange prison jumpsuit, and the deadliness she'd sensed behind those sky blue eyes whenever she'd looked into them.

Then she remembered the man she'd gotten to know in what felt like a lifetime since. She looked at him steadily. "Tell me what happened that day."

Their eyes held for a moment longer. His went dark and hostile. Hers, she hoped, stayed serene. Then his mouth twisted. "You are a pain in my ass."

The crackling sense of menace that had swirled around him faded.

"Right back at you, Casper. So talk to me. Please."

"Fuck. Fine. Whatever it takes to get you off my damned back." He gave her a hard look. Charlie carefully kept her face impassive. When he started talking, his tone was cool, dispassionate. A defense mechanism, she knew. "We were in Afghanistan. A platoon got wiped out up near the Pakistan border. A couple of surviving soldiers were taken prisoner. We — Sean and Hoop and Cap and me — got the order to go in and get them out. We moved in at night. They were being held in a little village at the bottom of a valley, steep mountains all around, no real cover anywhere. We did what we had to do — that means we killed whoever got in our way, just so we're clear — and we recovered the soldiers. We were on this narrow trail on our way out of the valley when all hell broke loose. Damned Taliban crouched behind every bush. It was an ambush and we were outnumbered twenty, twenty-five to one. Ain't no way that's going to end well."

He paused, and his face tightened. For a moment she thought he was going to stop there. She didn't make a sound, just watched him steadily, and finally he continued.

"Sean and I hung back to provide cover fire while Cap and Hoop got the soldiers out of there. They were coming at us like ants at a picnic, hitting us with everything from AK-47s to rocket-propelled grenades.

There was so much ordinance blowing up it looked like Fourth of July. We were hunkered down near this little gnarled tree when Sean took one to the chest." His eyes flickered, and he glanced away. It was, she knew, a classic sign that what he was talking about was causing him distress. Despite her determination to be a neutral vessel into which he could pour his worst memories, the sight of Michael in distress sent a chill rippling through her. "It was a bad one. He was bleeding like a pig, and when I tried to pack the wound and stop the bleeding I could hear it sucking air." He grimaced and looked at her again, and she tried to keep any reaction to what he was telling her from showing on her face. "We were taking fire from everywhere, they had us pinned down, and if we stayed put it was just a matter of time until we got overrun. Plus, I was getting low on ammo. So I lobbed my last damned grenade toward what seemed like the biggest nest of them, hoping to create enough of a distraction so I could get us both out of there. Then I threw Sean over my shoulder and ran like a motherfucker. They spotted us, and opened fire, but the only way I was stopping was if they shot off my legs because I knew if I stopped we were dead. That's when they hit us with a goddamned mortar and knocked us right off the side of the mountain. We fell about eighty feet. I wasn't hurt enough to make any difference. Sean landed about twenty yards away. The way I found him was, he started screaming." Michael looked up at the ceiling. A means of distancing, it was an instinctive reaction to a deeply emotional memory, Charlie knew. "When I got to him he was in a bad way. He'd taken another round to the back, and there was this big ol' branch sticking up right through his gut. He'd landed on it and it had impaled him. When I got there he looked at me and kind of gasped and said, *I'm not going to make it, Mike.* Then he said, *Don't let 'em take us,* because what they did to captured Americans wasn't pretty. About a second later he started screaming again. The enemy was coming down the mountain toward us like a damned bunch of goats by that time and we were getting some gunshots flying overhead but it was obvious they couldn't see us and didn't know exactly where we were. I punched Sean in the jaw to knock him out, and I pulled that damned branch out of him because there wasn't any way he was going anywhere like that. I thought he might bleed out but he didn't. His gut was laid open, though, and it was bad. I looked for a way out but there wasn't one. We were on a damned ledge. There was no way off it except straight up the mountain, right through the middle of the damned Taliban. I couldn't make it on my own, much less hauling Sean. Our only possible chance was to hide. And Sean was in so much pain that the second he woke up he started screaming again."

A muscle worked at the corner of his mouth, and Charlie felt that tiny giveaway all the way down to the bottom of her soul. She didn't realize she was holding her breath until he continued, and she let it slowly escape. "I punched him fast, but not fast enough. We got more gunshots, closer. They were homing in on us. I knew there was no way in hell either one of us was getting out of there alive if he let out another one of those shrieks." Michael was still talking to the ceiling in that cool, impersonal tone, the hardening of his jaw a telltale sign of emotion. His fist stayed clenched. Charlie felt her chest tighten. For him, those were giant markers of suffering. And if he hurt, she discovered, so did she. "I had to make a decision. Our work was supposed to be under the radar, which meant our side-arms had silencers. I drew mine and I pressed it right up against Sean's heart and pulled the trigger." He stopped and she watched his nostrils flare for the briefest, most telling of moments. Other than that, Michael's face was absolutely impassive. She was the one who had to press her lips tightly together to keep back a sound of pain. "After I shot him, I lay down there in the brush with his body for a couple of hours while the Taliban searched right on top of us. Then the rescue Cap and Hoop sent back for us finally showed up. I was pretty glad to see them big ol' Apache helicopters, especially when they opened fire and the bastards went running. I waved and one of the choppers dropped a ladder down to me and I climbed up with Sean's body slung over my shoulder." He made a sound that might have been a short, un-amused laugh, and his tone turned ironic. "We leave no man behind."

He regarded the ceiling unblinkingly for a moment longer, then looked at Charlie. His hard, handsome face was emptied of all expression. His eyes were as unreadable as stone.

"Happy now?" His voice was harsh.

She took a breath and sat up, curling her legs beside her. Her nightgown rode up so that the hem hovered dangerously near the top of her slim thighs but she didn't care.

He was still on his back, close enough so that if he'd been solid she could have laid her hand flat on the center of his wide bare chest. He looked big and dangerous and intensely sexual lying there like that, and her heart broke for him.

"You need to let the guilt go. You had no choice." Despite her best effort to sound clinically dispassionate, her voice was thick.

"Like I said, I don't feel any guilt." He frowned, peering up at her through the darkness. "Jesus. Are you *crying?*"

Charlie fought the urge to sniff. Damn the light coming in around the curtains: it must be hitting on the glimmer of the tears welling in her eyes. She wasn't *crying,* exactly. Her throat was just a little tight and her eyes were just a little wet.

She narrowed her eyes at him. "I never cry."

She said it with conviction, because she never — well, almost never — did.

He sat up, looking at her closer, all powerful muscle and sleek skin just inches away. "The hell you don't." His voice got lower, huskier. "We both know you cry over me."

There wasn't much she could say to that, because it was true. She'd cried twice in the last five or so years, and both times had been over him.

Since there was no hiding it, she did the only thing she could do: she owned it.

"Anybody would cry after hearing *that.*" Her voice was both truculent — and thick with the tears she was refusing to shed. Now that he'd seen them, she gave in to that insistent sniff and at the same time glared at him. "If you weren't totally emotionally stunted, you jackass, you'd be crying yourself."

And how was that for the calm, collected professional she'd vowed to remain at the outset of this?

"Damn it to hell and back anyway." He touched her tears where they trembled on her lower eyelashes. The brush of his long fingers against her skin was so unexpectedly tender that she closed her eyes in case any of those embarrassing tears should actually escape. He sounded almost angry as he added, "You and your damned soft heart."

Then her eyes flew open again as she realized that she could feel his fingers, feel *him,* that he was actually there, all six-foot-three, two hundred some-odd pounds of him, solid and present in her bed. On a note of alarm, she gasped, *"Michael."*

At the same time he, too, must have realized what had happened, because he went statue-still as their eyes locked. With that look, the memory of Tam's warning, the specter of Spookville, the threat of hunters and oblivion passed between them in a thunderclap of shared comprehension.

As it had before, intense emotion had enabled him to materialize. And afterward there would be a price to pay.

"Oh, my God." Charlie stared at him, appalled.

He looked down at himself, looked at her, and said, "Fuck it."

Then he reached for her. His hand slid around behind her head and his fingers threaded through her hair and he pulled her toward him and kissed her, his lips warm and insistent. The kiss was carnal as hell, hungry, demanding. Their chemistry was electric: she was instantly shivery with desire. The inside of his mouth was hot and wet and so real, so earthily male, that she was dazzled. As their tongues met her heart started to pound and her pulse rate skyrocketed. Deep inside, her body tightened urgently. She clutched his shoulders — sleek solid shelves of heavy muscle, warm and strong and *there* — and closed her eyes and kissed him back like she might never have another chance, desperate with the knowledge that this couldn't last, that it was the briefest moment out of time and *there would be consequences.*

No matter how tempted she was, she couldn't let him just shrug off the consequences.

"Michael," she pulled her mouth from his long enough to whisper, meaning to put her warning into words, to point out the risk, to do her best to apply sanity and logic to a situation that had gone way past both in hopes of somehow mitigating what would come after, but he slid his mouth down the side of her neck, his lips and tongue trailing fire over her skin. Suddenly she was so turned on she forgot how to form words.

"Don't talk," he ordered against her skin. His voice was low and faintly hoarse as he pressed his mouth to the sensitive area where her neck and shoulder joined. He still cradled the back of her head, holding her in place, while his free hand came up to fondle her breasts, caressing her through the satin. His hand felt firm and strong, and the sensation of having him touch her like that through the slippery cloth was mind-blowing. Her nipples tightened with need and she swayed closer, loving the feel of his hand on her breasts, loving the feel of *him*. Her pulse thundered in her ears. Her breathing came short and fast. She was touching him, too, delighting in the ability to touch him, running her hands over the hard muscles of his arms, stroking the unyielding wall of his chest, trailing her fingertips across the tightness of his abdomen. His skin was smooth and warm, and his body felt honed and strong and utterly masculine beneath her hands, and she couldn't get enough.

"I want you like hell." Muffled by her skin, his voice was fierce.

She knew she ought to argue that this probably wasn't the moment, to point out that maybe if they got it together and focused they might be able to come up with a way to ward off the consequences before they happened, but then he was kissing her again, kissing her like an eternity in hell was a small price to pay for the taste of her mouth.

And all she could do was cling to him and kiss him back, as the torrid heat of his mouth robbed her of her reason and her caution and everything else except a throbbing, insistent need.

"I want you, too." She sucked in a much-needed breath as his mouth left hers again to find her breast, opening over the sensitive tip through the thin layer of her nightgown. She could feel the wet heat of his mouth practically scalding her through the cloth, and she remembered that he'd done the same thing before. Only he'd done it that time in Tony's body, and the effect hadn't been nearly so intensely sexual. The inexplicable magic that was her and Michael blazed between them, a white-hot conflagration of lust that turned her brain to mush and her body to flame and the air around them to steam. Passion surged like hot sweet liquid through her veins. Deep inside, her body clenched and burned. Her bones melted. Her muscles dissolved. His tongue moved back and forth across her nipple, deliberately tantalizing, and a shaft of pure desire made her tremble. The sensation was incredible enough to make her forget everything except the way he was making her feel. She clutched at his hard biceps and made a tiny moaning sound and pressed her lips to his shoulder. She kissed the broad expanse, openmouthed, loving the salty taste of his skin.

He growled, and tipped her backward on the bed, shoving her nightgown up out of his way with rough hands. The sliver of satin was twisted up under her armpits but she barely noticed and didn't care as he stretched out beside her and his hand slipped between her legs.

"Oh." Scarcely more than an indrawn

breath, it was a sound of surprise — and anticipation. She knew how he could make her feel. She suddenly wanted to feel that way again with an intensity that would have scared the daylights out of her if she'd had even a fraction of her rational mind remaining to her. But she didn't.

His mouth was on her bare breasts, kissing the soft slopes, sucking her nipples. Farther down, he touched her where she burned to be touched, a light, teasing touch at first, making her wordlessly beg for more. Finally he gave it to her, rubbing her, sliding his fingers inside her. She was already all soft and pliant with arousal, but that made her wild.

"Oh." It seemed to be all she could say. He was good at turning women on, good at ramping up the excitement, good at sex: she knew that. But he was just now reminding her exactly how good he was. She was drowning in waves of pleasure, pulsing with need, making small excited sounds as she moved beneath his hand and mouth and he expertly pressed every erotic button she had.

He started kissing his way down her body, hot wet kisses that slid over her skin, and her fingers sank deep into the thick strands of his tawny hair.

By the time he had kissed his way to just

slightly south of her belly button, she was shivery with anticipation. She knew what he was doing: exactly what he earlier had promised her he would do if he got the chance.

She knew where he was going, too.

He lifted his head, and for the briefest of moments their eyes met. The dark restless glitter in his was purely predatory. It made the hot quickening inside her start to spiral out of control.

"Tell me what you want." There was a guttural undertone to his voice now.

"Michael." Hers was a soft, hot breath of protest. A plea.

"Tell me."

So she told him. Then, just as he had foretold, she parted her legs for him. And her heart pounded and her blood raced and she responded with a series of the soft little moans he had praised as he licked her and kissed her until she came in a great undulating burst of ecstasy.

She was still quaking in the aftermath when he shoved his jeans down his legs and covered her body with his. She wrapped her arms around his neck, loving the feel of the sturdy column and of the soft thickness of his hair where it brushed her skin. The strong muscles of his back were bunched and tight beneath her fingertips and she loved the way they felt, too. She loved his weight on her, the feel of him on top of her, the hot urgent nudge of his erection against her.

Even before he bent his head and kissed her she was tightening with arousal again.

She had time for one coherent thought: *This is Michael. This is real.*

Then he pushed inside her and the feel of it was so amazing that she cried out. Senses reeling, she reveled in the sheer pleasure of the physicality of penetration. He was huge and hard with wanting her, the answer to all the erotic fantasies she had ever had, stretching her, filling her to capacity and then some, and she wrapped her legs around him and clung and moved with him in sensuous need. Every sound she made after that was muffled by his mouth as he kissed her, deep lush kisses that made her woozy, and moved inside her, making love to her with a controlled savagery that found its answer in a primitive part of her own nature that she only ever realized existed when she was with him.

It was sex at its rawest, at its most elemental. He kissed her and touched her and drove into her in a relentless rhythm that made her wild as it burned through every inhibition she had ever had. She dug her nails into his back and matched his thrusts with her own and lost herself in the urgency and the heat until she was mindless with passion, writhing with it, burning and quaking and panting with it.

When the dark waves of lust that were rolling off him peaked, she got swept away, too, coming with a shattering intensity. As he thrust deep inside her and found his release, he groaned out her name.

"Michael," she moaned in answer as the wildfire he had ignited inside her consumed them both in its flames. *"Michael."*

Afterward, Charlie spent a moment or so wrapped in his arms while she floated in a state of postcoital bliss. To say he had rocked her world was an understatement. He had rocked her universe, upending it around her in a way she could have never in a million years foreseen.

I just had mind-blowing sex with the hot ghost of one of my serial killer research subjects, was the thought that popped into her head, and the really crazy thing about it was that she didn't regret a thing.

Then reality intruded and she surfaced like an underwater diver coming up for air.

She took a deep breath. Her eyes opened. She got an excellent view of a broad bare shoulder, a strong back, and the curve of a tight, athletic ass. He was collapsed on top of her, hot as a pizza oven, heavy as a steel beam, his face buried in the curve of her shoulder, his arms locked around her like he never meant to let her go. The firm muscularity of his big body, the smooth heat of his skin, the brush of his long legs against hers, were all wonderfully, intoxicatingly real. Greedily, she wanted to savor every second.

Because she knew it couldn't last. Fear speared through her at the thought. But for the moment, he was still in her world, as solid and tangible as she was, and she pressed her hands against the flat, smooth planes of his shoulder blades in an instinctive bid to keep him there.

"Michael."

"Mm?"

"Let me up. I need to call Tam."

That brought his head up. His eyes were heavy-lidded and slumberous, and they gleamed at her through the darkness. His mouth had a sensual look to it that was only slightly marred when he frowned at her.

"You call that pillow talk?" he chided. "How about something like, *That was incredible. Let's do it again.*"

"I'm *serious.*"

"Me too."

He nuzzled the side of her neck while his hand found and fondled her breast. Oh, God, she loved the way —

She thrust the thought aside.

"Would you let me up? I need to call Tam because I want to bring her in on this before whatever is going to happen to you happens. Maybe she can —"

He silenced her by kissing her, a lush sampling of her mouth that would have totally distracted her if she hadn't been terrified of what was coming. As it was, she kissed him back because she just couldn't help it, but briefly. Then she pulled her mouth away.

"Michael." He was too damned big to just push off of her. "Let me up."

"You can be a real buzzkill, you know that?" He shook his head at her. His hand still covered her breast, and she could feel the weight and heat of it clear to her toes. Her nipple was pebbled against his palm. "Forget calling the voodoo priestess. I'd rather spend whatever time I have like —"

Charlie's cell phone started to ring. In that quiet, dark, sex-laden room the sound was startling. They both jumped, and looked toward the source.

As if the shrilling phone had ripped open

the cocoon that had protected them, the atmosphere changed just like that. Charlie felt something that she could only describe as a kind of disturbance in the Force. Like an increase of static electricity in the room, or —

Oh, God.

Her eyes snapped fearfully back to Michael. He felt it, too: she could see it in his face. She locked her arms around him, terrified.

That was all there was time for.

He was swept out of bed and sent hurtling away into darkness so impenetrable that it was impossible to see anything at all.

Charlie knew because she was swept away with him.

CHAPTER TWENTY-NINE

Michael's muttered curses were the next thing Charlie was aware of. His voice sounded furious and desperate and scared, all at the same time. The thought of what it would take to scare Michael brought her eyes fluttering open.

It didn't help. The world was still dark.

Otherworldly dark. That realization hit her along with the smell.

Of rotting things. Of damp.

And it was cold. So very, very cold.

Spookville. It had to be. She shivered. The knowledge frightened her to the marrow of her bones.

"Michael?" Instinct made her whisper. He was carrying her. She could feel his hard arms around her, one behind her shoulders and the other beneath her knees. She could feel the solid warmth of his chest against her body.

"Thank God." His voice was scarcely

louder than hers. His hold on her shifted as he hitched her a little higher against his chest. Her arms instinctively wrapped around his neck. Before, she'd been lying limply in his arms. She was decent, if just barely. Her nightgown covered her to the tops of her thighs. She could hear the faint brush of denim on denim and guessed he'd managed to get his jeans back on. "You okay?"

"Yes." She was, she realized. Whatever had occurred to render her insensible, she was over it now. "What happened?"

"My luck ran out and somehow or another you got taken along with me." His reply was terse. "My guess is, it was because of that vibration thing with you, and because we were so, ah, entwined."

Charlie had a vivid memory of exactly what he meant. They'd been lying all but naked in each other's arms. His hand had been on her breast. He'd still been partially inside her.

"What are we going to do?" Curling tendrils of fear wrapped around her heart.

His reply was grim. "We'll figure something out."

She got the sinking feeling that he'd said that just to reassure her.

Sexy as she found his demonstration of

manly strength, there was no point in him continuing to carry her. "You can put me down."

"Not now. And quit wiggling." The tension in his voice was unmistakable. His arms around her, his chest against which she rested, were taut with it.

Her eyes must have adjusted to the darkness, because she was starting to be able to see a little. What she saw was like nothing she had ever seen in Spookville before: black on black on black, different shades of the color in a curving sky that arched maybe fifty feet over their heads, and walls that rose to meet them maybe thirty feet away on either side. The walls seemed to keep on plunging down, far below the level of the ground over which Michael was moving fast but — delicately. As her eyes adjusted more, she looked down and saw why.

He was carrying her across a terrifyingly narrow stone footbridge that spanned a vast chasm. The walls and ceiling were the rough stone of the inside of a cave. Below them was — nothing. A seemingly bottomless drop.

Her heart seemed to stop. Her arms tightened around his neck. Her knees curled up closer against him. After that instinctive response, she went absolutely motionless.

Quit wiggling, indeed.

"Oh, my God," she breathed.

"Yeah," he acknowledged her reaction a split second before a growl froze her blood. It was low and guttural, loud enough so that she knew it came from the throat of something huge, and behind them. Accompanying it was the scrabbling sound of claws racing over stone.

The hair stood up on the back of her neck.

"Fuck." Michael moved faster, almost running now, balancing carefully on that perilously slender bridge in what felt like an aerialist's race against death. Another growl, more scrabbling sounds, the thud of enormous feet coming after them: it didn't require genius to deduce that they were being chased.

"Is that a hunter?" There was no doing anything about the squeak in her voice.

"Yep." His answer was grim. "We came through at the bottom of a ravine about thirty feet in front of it. I managed to get us away, then ducked into this cavern, but it must have picked up our scent."

The growl came again, louder, closer. Charlie cringed.

There was nothing she could even say.

Her heart pounded. Her mouth went sour with fear. Michael took a last flying jump, and then they were off the bridge and on solid ground. He skidded to a stop on the uneven surface and put her down. A glance around showed Charlie that beyond the giant cavern in which they found themselves, a concentrated area of more intense darkness seemed to indicate a passageway that continued on indefinitely.

"Run," Michael told her urgently the minute her bare feet hit the cold stone.

An earth-shattering roar from the other side of the chasm made Charlie whip around to face it instead.

A huge, terrifying shape blacker than the blackness all around launched itself across the chasm toward them. A hunter: there was no mistaking the enormous bulk, or the glowing yellow eyes. Forget the footbridge: the thing had leaped.

Charlie's blood froze. It was too close: there was no chance that they were getting away.

"I said *run!*" Michael roared at her, shoving her behind him. "It wants me, not you!"

He'd turned to face it, balancing on the balls of his feet in a half-crouched fighter's stance. A baseball-sized rock he'd scooped off the ground was ready in his hand. He was bare to the waist, in stocking feet, big and bad and dangerous in the world they came from but practically helpless in the face of this.

Charlie's heart lodged in her throat. Her pulse raced as panic surged in an icy tide through her veins. The hunter roared again, the cry echoing off the stone. It was almost upon them: without iron, or salt, or anything at all to work with, there was nothing she could do.

"Charlie, *run!*" Michael screamed. The hunter was arcing down toward them, coming in for the kill, its huge bulk blocking out almost everything behind it as if the night itself was falling in on them. Its roar had shrilled and amplified into a hawk's fearsome death screech times about a thousand.

Michael's feet planted as he braced for the impact.

Charlie ran.

Toward him.

"Damn it, get back!" he cried as she wrapped her arms around his waist from behind, ducked her head against him, closed her eyes, and did what he'd told her to do when they'd found themselves in Spookville together once before.

Think of somewhere safe.

She did, with all the fervency of desperate prayer. The air around them seemed to vibrate as the hunter's scream filled her ears. The rush of its big body in passing felt like a million electrified hairs brushing against her skin. Terror stopped her heart even as the ground beneath her feet dropped away. She kept her arms locked around Michael and her head tucked into his back as they were whirled into blackness. An enormous suction almost pulled them apart but she clung to him as if her life depended on it, which in a way she supposed it did. He grabbed her before she could lose her grip, clamping her close as they fell forward through what seemed like an eternity of nothingness. Then the air was suddenly still, and her feet hit solid ground. Michael was there, firm and warm against her. She clung to him as if to the only solid thing in existence as her eyes cautiously opened on darkness. It was a different type of darkness than the Stygian one they'd left: this was illuminated by the faintest of neon glows.

Her hotel room.

Charlie barely had time to recognize it, to go all weak-kneed with relief, before two things struck her simultaneously: she'd obviously astral-projected again, only this time without falling asleep first, because she was looking at her body lying almost naked on the bed. The other thing was, someone was pounding on the hotel room door.

"Babe —" Michael began, but she never heard the rest of it, because just then the room seemed to collapse around her. She felt a whirling sensation, a blast of cold air, and he was gone from her arms as everything went black.

She had the sensation of catapulting through space, then tumbling to a landing on something soft.

Her eyes snapped open on impact, and she discovered that she was lying on her hotel room bed. She realized instantly that she was once again back in her body, that she was to all intents and purposes naked, and that Michael, clad only in his jeans, his big body outlined against the closed curtains, was standing beside the bed.

And someone was still banging on her door.

She sat up, yanked her nightgown back into place, turned on the bedside lamp — the sudden explosion of light made her blink — and got out of bed.

"You okay?" Michael asked. His voice had a gravelly quality to it. His eyes — they were solid black, with the soulless glitter that she'd seen in them before. He looked even more badass than usual, and barely controlled aggression radiated from him in waves. Encounters with Spookville and its denizens had that effect on him, she remembered. Hadn't Tam said something about it turning him evil? Or bringing out the evil that was already in him?

Whatever. She didn't care. He'd once said, "You're mine, Doc" to her. Now her too-stupid-to-live heart was saying it right back: he was hers.

The other half of her very own illicit love affair.

It was a scary thought. One she didn't have time for.

"I'm fine," she said brusquely. "On the other hand, your eyes are black and you look like you eat little children for breakfast."

He gave her a hard look. "Next time I tell you to run, run."

"See, the thing is, I like to use my own judgment on these things."

Bang, bang, bang went the door.

"Charlie." The voice on the other side of it belonged to Lena. A glance at her bedside clock told Charlie that it was almost four a.m. Alarm widened her eyes. The time coupled with Lena's use of her first name — this could mean nothing good.

"Hey," Michael said as she hurried toward the door, and she glanced at him over her shoulder. "Thanks for saving my ass back there. I guess that makes you" — he batted his eyes at her like a bashful girl — "my hero."

She shot him an aren't-you-funny look, and pulled open the door.

Lena was wearing blue men's pajamas and no makeup. She was barefoot, and her fist was raised to bang on the door again. She looked up as Charlie opened the door and snapped, "My God, do you sleep like the dead or what?"

In the hall beyond Lena, Tony, clearly having had his door banged on, too, was leaning out of his room. Charlie couldn't see his lower half, but his black hair was ruffled and his leanly muscled chest was bare. A wedge of black hair tapered down toward his belly button, Charlie saw. Buzz, wrapped in a hotel-issue robe, had just emerged from his room and was walking down the hall toward them.

"What?" Charlie said to Lena.

"You've got to come and look at this, all of you." Lena's voice shook with excitement. "I've found something."

In her hotel room, Lena's laptop sat open on the small table in front of the window. The curtains were closed, the lamps by the bed were on, and they were all gathered around the laptop as Lena ran a thumb over the touchpad to bring the screen to life. Like Buzz, Charlie had pulled on a hotel-issued robe over her nightgown. Tony was clad in the previous day's shirt and pants, half-unbuttoned, untucked, and rumpled. Michael had added his usual tee and boots to his jeans.

"I was on the Dynasty Films site, fooling around with a list of like a thousand computer-generated most likely passwords, trying to get into the members-only section, and I typed *member* into the log-in just because it took six characters. I couldn't believe it: it worked. I got in." Lena looked back over her shoulder at them as the Dynasty Films logo appeared on the screen and warned, "I took it to the end, but still, this is pretty graphic."

Then she tapped the play arrow in the middle of the screen and stepped back.

A naked woman hung by her wrists in front of a scarlet backdrop. Her toes just touched the floor. There were ugly red welts on her thighs that looked like they'd been made by a belt or whip. Blood trickled in thin red lines from maybe half a dozen small cuts around her breasts. The woman was young, shapely, pretty — and hysterical. Her shattering sobs made Charlie's throat tighten. Doing her best to divorce herself from the emotion of it, Charlie worked to take in details: the scarlet seemed to be silk or satin cloth, some kind of draping. The floor was gray and looked like poured concrete. Silver handcuffs glinted around the woman's wrists; the chain was passed through a black metal grid set into the ceiling.

A black metal grid. A full-breasted brunette.

With a thrill of horror, Charlie realized what she had to be looking at a second before the woman began to speak.

"I don't want to die." The woman's soft, Spanish-accented voice was terrified and pleading.

"You have failed to give satisfaction." The man was off camera. His voice was harsh, full of menace. Unaccented. Relatively young?

"Oh, please. I'll do anything! Anything you want." There was a pause, not even long enough for Charlie to sneak in a breath, as the woman struggled wildly within the limitations of her restraints. Her wide eyes focused fearfully on the off-camera man. Then she begged, "Please don't kill me! Please don't kill me!"

A large hand in a black gauntlet streaked

into view. Charlie barely registered that it was wielding a wicked-looking knife before the blade plunged into the woman's stomach and slashed through the vulnerable flesh, slicing her open so that blood spilled like a waterfall.

The woman barely had time to shriek before the knife flashed again, higher this time. It cut her throat in a single swipe. Her eyes went huge, more blood gushed, and then came that hideous sound that had carved its own special niche in Charlie's memory: the death gurgle.

Amidst the gush of blood, the woman's head flopped hideously forward in a way that wouldn't have been possible if she had been alive.

They had just watched a woman die.

Cold sweat broke over Charlie in a wave. The voice was the same one that she'd heard the last time she'd been in the morgue. The one that was attached to Destiny Sherman.

Her knees suddenly felt rubbery, and she took the few steps needed to reach the nearest chair and sank down in it.

"Babe?" Michael crouched beside her, frowning at her with concern. She met his eyes, mouthed, *"Hers was the voice in the morgue,"* then as his eyes flared with comprehension and he said, "Oh, shit," she took a deep breath, and got a grip. This time the voice wasn't in her head, so it didn't make her sick. What made her sick was the knowledge that she'd just watched a woman die live, on camera.

"It's Carmela Lynch." In the moment or so that Charlie had spent collecting herself, Lena had clicked onto a page with all the victims' photos. Lena tapped a picture with her finger. "She went missing six weeks ago, and the video was posted about a week later. She was the last one to disappear" — Lena's voice faltered a little — "before Giselle."

"So was that acting? Was it fake?" Buzz was staring at the screen.

"It was real." Charlie was still so upset by what she'd seen that she just came out with it. "What you just saw — it was real. That woman was killed on camera."

"How do you know?" Lena asked as everyone turned to look at Charlie.

"I know." Charlie looked at Tony. "I *know,* okay?"

Tony stared at her briefly and then nodded. "Good enough." He looked at Lena and Buzz. "It was real," he said.

"We just watched a snuff film." There was an odd note to Buzz's voice, and as Charlie looked at him she was in time to watch the appalled realization come into his eyes. He opened his mouth, shot a quick look at Lena, and closed it again.

Lena got it a moment later. "Oh, my God, *Giselle.*" The stark horror on her face made Charlie's heart ache for her. Lena whirled back to the computer. "That's what he's doing with the victims: the bastard's making *snuff films.*" She clicked a button. "That was the featured film. There are sixteen more tabs on the member site." She was typing furiously as she spoke. "Damn it! Member doesn't work on the rest of them. Each one requires a separate password. But altogether, *there are seventeen films.*" She stared hard at the screen, then looked around at the rest of them. "Does that mean he hasn't killed Giselle yet?"

Her expression was such a pathetic mix of hope and terror that nobody could quite bring themselves to say what Charlie knew that, like her, they had to be thinking: either that, or he just hasn't had time to post the film.

"We're going to assume Giselle's alive," Tony said. "Until we have evidence to the contrary."

And that, Charlie thought, was another reason she liked Tony so much: he was calm and unflappable, a natural leader.

"There's a little pop-up on here that says a new video will be posted tomorrow at ten p.m." Lena's voice was so thin with fear that it didn't even sound like hers. She took an audible breath. "Oh, God, that has to mean they've killed somebody else. It has to be — Giselle."

"They may not have killed her yet." Buzz looked grimmer than Charlie had ever seen him. "It doesn't necessarily mean that."

Lena made a small, strangled sound.

"Everybody go get dressed. We're back to work." Tony's order was brisk. He was already heading toward the door as he spoke. "Fifteen minutes. Let's move, people."

CHAPTER THIRTY

Michael said thoughtfully, "If Carmela Lynch was killed six weeks ago, then how did her voice get attached to Destiny Sherman?"

Eyes widening, Charlie looked at him. They were still within the fifteen-minute window that Tony had given everyone to get dressed, and Michael was leaning a shoulder against the bathroom wall watching her as she finished applying a quick dash of pink lipstick. His eyes were almost back to normal. Since he wasn't flickering and nothing else unusual was happening with him that she had noticed, she was holding on to hope that maybe this time he'd gotten away from Spookville unscathed. Having just taken what felt like the world's fastest shower, she'd dressed in her trademark black pants and a pearl gray sleeveless blouse, secured her still slightly damp hair in a low ponytail, and started applying makeup when he'd called to her that he had a question for her. She'd told him to come in. Which he had, walking right through the door.

"For that to happen, wouldn't Destiny have had to have been there when Carmela died?" Michael continued.

"Yes," Charlie said, as the impossible logistics of that tried to work themselves out in her brain. The bathroom smelled of soap and was still faintly steamy, and she'd had to rub a spot clear so that she could see herself in the mirror. She put the cap back on her lipstick as she thought about it and returned it to her toiletries case. "Yes, she would."

"Destiny Sherman had small tits. Compared to the rest of them, I mean."

Trust Michael to notice something like that. Charlie gave him a reproving look. But when she thought about it she realized it was true, and then she frowned as more anomalies occurred to her.

She enumerated them slowly: "She was a local. She disappeared on the same night Giselle did, the only time in this case that two women went missing on the same night. She had scratches from Giselle's bracelet on her back, which links her to this killer. And she didn't die immediately. If she'd been attacked like Carmela Lynch, there's no way she would have survived long enough to reach the dump site, much less to get away and hide."

Oh. My. God.

It hit her like a blinding flash of light. "Destiny Sherman wasn't one of the victims."

"Ain't looking that way," Michael agreed, following her as she flew to share that revelation with the others.

"So you're saying Destiny was an accomplice." Tony frowned at Charlie as he and Lena and Buzz digested what she'd just told them about her conclusion concerning Destiny Sherman. The bright lights of Vegas lit up the night like the mother and father of all Christmas displays, and cast an ever-changing, multi-colored glow over the inside of the car as they drove toward the FBI office. There'd been people in the hall and the elevator, and the lobby had been busy as it always was even in the wee hours of the morning, so she'd had to save her brilliant flash of insight until they were in the car.

"She's not the primary," Charlie said. "I think she was part of a team. About fifteen percent of serial killers work with an accomplice or partner. I think she had a boyfriend or lover, and I think they had a falling out and he killed her, and I think that's who we're looking for."

"She helped him kidnap Giselle." Lena's tone didn't make it a question. "Giselle must have attacked her with the bracelet."

"That's a good working assumption," Charlie agreed.

"So how did Destiny wind up getting killed? What made her partner turn on her?" Buzz mused.

Nobody had an answer to that.

"The mother said Destiny didn't have a boyfriend." Tony drummed his fingers on the steering wheel. "Maybe the unsub is one of her clients."

"It would have to be a regular," Charlie said. "Most of the time in these cases, it's an abusive relationship with the male being the dominant partner. In order to achieve that kind of control, there would have to be an extended contact."

"She didn't have that many regulars." Lena leaned forward in her seat. There was no missing the tension in her voice. "I have the list."

"Or maybe the mother just didn't know about the boyfriend," Michael pointed out. Charlie repeated that just as they arrived at the FBI office.

A surprising number of agents were working, considering that it was just after five a.m. Some of them, Charlie knew, had been assigned to help out with the investigation; others had their own thing going on. They exchanged early morning greetings (basically grunts) with the people they encountered and grabbed coffee from the break room. Then, while they were walking to their makeshift office, Charlie saw something that made her heart lurch.

Michael flickered.

He was a couple of steps behind her, and she never would have caught it if she hadn't glanced over her shoulder in response to something Buzz, who was behind her, too, said. But she did see it, and the hot coffee she'd just taken a sip of turned cold and tasteless in her mouth and for a second she forgot to breathe.

"I'm just going to stop by the restroom," she told the others, and veered off. Michael, of course, followed. Ordinarily he would have waited in the hall, but when they got there she beckoned him inside. It was a single-person restroom with the usual amenities, and she turned on him the second they were both through the door.

He lifted his eyebrows at her. "What's up,

buttercup?"

"You're flickering." Her voice was tight with anxiety.

"I know."

"You know?" She stared at him, aghast.

"It's been happening since you were in the shower."

"Why didn't you say something?"

He shrugged. "Nothing you can do about it."

And he hadn't wanted to worry her. She knew that as well as she knew her name.

She was already digging through her purse. Her Miracle-Go kit, complete with horseshoe and salt, was in there, but that was useless against this threat. The only thing that might help was her phone. "I'm going to call Tam."

"What is that, your go-to answer for everything? Unless I'm mistaken, the voodoo priestess already said that there's nothing else she can do."

"There's always something she can do." Having snagged her phone, Charlie pushed Tam's contact button. "There has to be something she can do."

"I'm hoping that grounding spell she was talking about's still good."

"It might be." Charlie tried not to sound as worried as she felt while she listened to the phone ring on the other end. "But it might not be, too."

His mouth curved wryly. "That's a helluva bedside manner you've got there, Doc."

She frowned at him as, on the other end, the phone continued to ring, trying to keep her burgeoning fear out of her eyes. He was so outrageously handsome that just looking at him could make her pulse flutter, but the hard knot that lodged in her chest at the thought of possibly never seeing him again had nothing to do with his looks.

Admit it: you're crazy in love with me. He'd said that to her only the day before.

She didn't want to admit it. In fact, she refused to admit it.

That road could only lead to heartbreak.

But she was terribly, horribly afraid it might be true.

When Tam's voice recording answered instead of Tam, she jerked her eyes away from Michael's face — he was way too good at reading her expression — and said into the phone. "Tam, call me back right away, please. It's urgent."

She ended the call. All she could do was pray that Tam got back to her in time, or that Michael wouldn't actually flicker out of existence.

"She'll call me back," Charlie said, which

she knew Tam would as soon as she got the message. Then, because they had a serial killer to catch and there was no time, and because engaging in any kind of heartfelt confession would be counterproductive as well as just plain foolish at that point, she didn't. Instead she moved around Michael and opened the door. But the fear still ate at her, and as she stepped out into the hallway she glanced over her shoulder at him and added a fierce, "Hang on."

"Quit looking so worried. I've been playing chicken with oblivion this long. I think I can win another round or two."

I hope so, Charlie thought, but she didn't say it because there were other people around by then. Instead she pushed her concern for him to the back burner for the moment and got busy doing everything she could to find Giselle Kaminsky. But even as she pulled out all the stops and applied her years of accumulated expertise to the task of identifying a killer, she found herself twisting Michael's too-big watch round and round on her arm as she waited for Tam's return call.

"None of the johns match the criteria." Lena's tone was despairing as she shoved back away from her computer. It was almost lunchtime and they'd been working nonstop. Lena had broken the log-in code to every one of the members-only videos on the Dynasty ("Die-nasty, get it?" was Michael's contribution to that) Films site, and confirmed that they were all snuff films featuring the murder of one of the victims. Buzz had been trying to track down the owners/purveyors of Dynasty Films beyond their Internet identities, which were (of course) fictitious. Charlie had been on Skype reinterviewing the victims' closest relatives before moving on to what she was currently doing. Tony had been on the phone with his contacts at headquarters, getting autopsies on the victims prioritized so that they could have at least some answers that day. Lena continued, "They don't live within the grid, they don't work in any of the hotels or on the Strip, they have no possible connection with any of the victims that I can find. And none of them is named Joe."

"Having a female accomplice tells us that he's a narcissist. A thrill-seeker killer whose secondary motivation is financial gain. Being involved in filmmaking provides him with both an audience and money, which is what he wants," Charlie said, as she paged through the files of all of Destiny Sherman's other known associates. She looked at Lena.

"It's likely we're looking for a failed or relatively unsuccessful performer, so add that to the list. And remember, Joe might not be his legal name. It might be a nickname, or just something she called him."

"Great." Lena rolled in her wheeled chair back to her computer.

"This is Las Vegas. They gamble here. There are all kinds of unexplained deposits in half these bank accounts," Buzz growled in frustration. "I can sort them out, but it's going to take some time."

Nobody said what they were thinking: that time was exactly what they didn't have.

"Did you go through Destiny Sherman's credit card records to try to pinpoint where she went on the day she was killed?" Tony asked Lena.

"If she spent any money the day she died it was cash," Lena replied grimly. "Nothing showed up. I'm actually going back for a month to identify places and areas she frequented. I'm having the computer map it. It'll *ping* me when it's done."

Tony nodded. "See if you can find something that places her within the grid. Any of the hotel staff panning out?"

"Too many of them are panning out is the problem." Lena's voice was tight. She patted a sheaf of paper beside her computer. "I broke it down to the top fifty suspects by using that checklist of Charlie's, but the ones I have here all meet four of the criteria — not necessarily the same four, but four — so fifty is how many we're stuck with. Buzz is checking them out now."

"And a thankless task it is," Buzz muttered, before a rap at the door had them all looking up.

"Somebody order pizza?" one of the local agents stood in the doorway beside a deliveryman in his distinctive red shirt carrying two big boxes. Charlie's stomach gave a gurgle of anticipation as the smell of the hot pies reached her, and she realized that, except for coffee, none of them had eaten all day. With her concentration broken, she glanced at her phone. She'd called Tam twice more, and her friend still hadn't called back.

"So the voodoo priestess is sleeping in," Michael said, correctly interpreting her look. He'd been flickering, not real fast, not real close together, but flickering, all day. She didn't know what to do about it except wait to talk to Tam, but she was growing increasingly anxious. If he were to disappear — she couldn't even finish the thought. "She was probably tired after the drive."

That might be true, but it didn't make

Charlie feel any better.

"I did." Tony paid, and by silent consensus they ate where they were. The television in the break room stayed on CNN, and as none of them wanted to listen to the regular Breaking News bulletins about the bodies still being recovered or any other aspect of what the station was calling, in big bold banner headlines scrolling across the bottom of the screen, The Search for the Cinderella Killer, they kept out of the break room.

After she finished eating, Charlie couldn't stand it anymore. She went to the restroom and, giving up on Tam's cell phone, called her office, which was in a carriage house behind her home and where she saw clients every afternoon. Maria Pelissero, Tam's longtime assistant, answered.

Tam wasn't there.

"Would you mind going into the house and telling her to please call me right away?" Charlie asked. She'd met Maria a number of times, and Maria knew that she was one of Tam's closest friends.

"No, you don't understand. She's not here, not in the office, and not at home. I've already been through the house. She missed both of yesterday's appointments, and she's got another one this afternoon. She *never* misses her appointments." As Maria spoke, Charlie felt an icy hand clutch at her heart. Maria continued, faltering now. "I thought she must still be in Las Vegas with you. There's something wrong, isn't there? Should — should I call the police?"

"The voodoo priestess is missing? Holy shit!" Michael said, while Charlie told Maria, "The police won't accept a missing-person report on an adult for forty-eight hours. I'm working with an FBI team right now: I'll have them look into it. In the meantime, if you hear from her, please call me."

Charlie disconnected, looked at Michael, and tried to keep her voice steady as goose bumps raced over her skin. "This guy's got her. I know it."

Chapter Thirty-One

"I'm sorry about your friend." Lena's eyes were so shadowed with fatigue that it looked like she had dark smudges beneath them. They were all running on just an hour or two of sleep and were exhausted, though the extreme stress Lena was under meant she was showing it the most. "But we can't stop to look for her. You know we can't. If Giselle is still alive, she's running out of time."

"Tam's disappearance has to be connected with this case." Charlie's voice was tight. "It has to be. It's too big a coincidence otherwise."

"There's no such thing as coincidence." Michael and Tony said it at almost exactly the same time. Charlie was too wired to acknowledge either of them, or how ironic it was that both the men in her life were having parallel thoughts. Michael's flickering seemed to be slowing down — she was giving cautious credit to Tam's grounding spell for that — but her fear for Tam was growing by leaps and bounds.

They had confirmed that Tam had completed an online check-out and her car had left the self-pay lot. The hotel had already e-mailed security footage of her car being driven out of the lot. The time stamp said it was 2:06 p.m. the previous day. Checkout was at eleven, so that left a gap of three hours.

The glare of the sun on the window made it impossible to determine who was behind the wheel. If it was Tam, what had she been doing for those missing three hours? And where was she now?

"We've got six singers, four improvisers, four magicians, two clowns, two stand-up comics, an acrobat, a sword-swallower, a flamenco dancer, a knife-thrower, and a guy who makes balloon animals in the restaurants, which I guess counts," Lena reported. "By adding performers to the checklist, that brings our previous fifty down to twenty-three. Which we have identified because they meet certain criteria, not because we have any direct evidence against them."

"That's what criteria do — it winnows the pool." Charlie was reviewing the security footage from Tam's floor the morning she checked out. As she spoke, she fast-forwarded past the part where she walked Tam to her room, hugged her, and then left — no point in having everyone else watch her engaging in what looked like an animated conversation with air (i.e., Michael) — then kept going until Tam left her room. The time stamp said 10:41 a.m.

She was carrying her purse, but didn't have a suitcase with her. Charlie wasn't surprised to see her return to her room at 10:56. Obviously Tam had run a quick errand downstairs. Then at 11:01 a.m. Tam left her room again, this time pulling her small leopard-print (typical Tam, who would never choose something as basic as black) carry-on behind her. Charlie watched her walk to the elevator. Someone inside the elevator must have seen her coming, because they held the door open for her. Tam stepped inside, and the door closed.

"She left her room at check-out time." Tony was looking at the footage over her shoulder. "What did she do for the next three hours?"

"I don't know. I'm going to try to follow her through the hotel." Charlie clicked through the rest of the footage the hotel had sent — basically all their security video for that day — but could find no other image of Tam.

She went back to check the elevator videos, meaning to follow Tam's movements chronologically. Six elevators serviced that floor. She had footage for five of them. There was no video of Tam in the elevator. There was no video of the elevator Tam had gotten into.

Charlie's heart started to beat faster as she reported her finding aloud.

"That ain't good," Michael said.

Tony got on the phone to the Conquistador's security office to see what had happened to the missing footage, while Charlie went back to the video of Tam leaving her room at 11:01, suitcase in tow. Everything about Tam from the soft swing of her red hair to the vibrancy of her pink jumpsuit to her confident stride in her delicate gold sandals looked perfectly normal.

Charlie paused the video just as Tam stepped into the elevator. The angle of the camera made it impossible to see more than a slice of the interior. But what she did see made her frown.

"The camera in elevator six is broken," Tony reported as he ended his call. "It's being replaced, but there hasn't been any footage from it for the last week."

"There's no such thing as coincidence," Michael repeated grimly. "The guy either knew the camera was broken, or he broke it himself."

Re-examining the image of Tam getting into the elevator, Charlie was afraid he was right.

Someone was already in the elevator when Tam got on: a man. Had he been waiting for her? With the axiom about coincidence revolving through her head, Charlie strongly suspected he had been. She could see a black dress shoe and, above it, the lower part of a leg in well-pressed black trousers. She could also see, at waist height above the man's leg, the curl of one side of a silver bar-type handle, and beneath that, the fall of a white cloth that stopped some six inches short of the floor.

Looking at the image, Charlie's mouth went dry.

"What does that look like to you?" Charlie pointed to the handle and cloth.

Everyone except Lena was now gathered around her computer, and they all agreed it looked like a room service cart.

When Lena heard that, her head came up.

"Giselle ordered room service the night she went missing," Lena said.

Tony moved toward her. "Let's look at

that footage of the night Giselle disappeared again."

Lena brought the footage up, and they all watched as room service was delivered to Giselle in her room after Lena had left for the airport. It would have been a riveting moment, except the waitress who brought the meal on the cart was obviously not Destiny and, since Charlie insisted that the killers were a mixed-gender couple, obviously not who they were looking for.

A video hour later (fast-forwarded through in a matter of minutes), a waiter showed up with an empty cart and knocked on Giselle's door, presumably to pick up the remains of the meal. The door opened, and he pushed his cart inside, then reappeared with it piled with dirty dishes some ten minutes later. After that, there was no activity until just before midnight, when Giselle walked out of the room, dressed for a night on the town, and headed toward the elevator.

"Pause that, right there," Charlie said suddenly. "Can you enlarge it?"

Then, as Lena did both of those things, Charlie pointed to something barely visible below the sleeve of Giselle's sequined T-shirt, which had ridden up a bit when Giselle swung her arm forward as she walked: "Look. Did Giselle have a tattoo?"

"No," Lena breathed as they all stared at the image, a curved line of dark blue ink that was only visible in that one frame. "She didn't." A second later, Lena said what Charlie, and presumably the rest of them, had just remembered, "But Destiny Sherman did." She stared hard at the woman on the monitor. "My God, that's not Giselle. That's Destiny Sherman. She's wearing Giselle's clothes, and a wig."

Charlie remembered the wigs on the shelves in Destiny Sherman's room with a little thrill of horror.

"How did I not see that before?" Lena couldn't tear her eyes away from the monitor. "If she's wearing Giselle's clothes, whatever happened to Giselle had already happened."

"None of us saw it." Tony's voice was briskly businesslike. "Let's go back to the last place where we're sure it's Giselle and take it from there."

Lena rewound to when Giselle opened the door to let the waiter in to pick up the used dishes. The camera recorded the door opening and the waiter pushing his cart inside, but showed no glimpse of whoever was inside the room opening the door.

The shot before that, where the waitress delivered the food, showed Giselle opening the door then stepping out of view to allow the waitress in.

"Are we sure that's Giselle?" Tony asked. The footage showed Giselle's face, so determining her identity wasn't difficult.

"Yes," Lena and Buzz answered at the same time.

"Okay. Then that" — Tony tapped the screen — "is the last time we're sure Giselle was present and unharmed." At his direction, Lena once again fast-forwarded through events until Destiny Sherman left the room dressed as Giselle. Then they fast-forwarded through more footage until Lena returned to the room shortly thereafter.

"It had to be either the waitress who delivered the food or the waiter who picked up the dishes," Buzz said. "One of them did something to her, and then managed to get her out of the room."

"It was the waiter," Charlie said. "The primary will be a male."

Michael said, "She has to be stuffed in that cart. The way the white cloth hangs down to the floor you could hide almost anything, especially if you knew you were going to be putting unconscious girls in it and modified it so they'd fit."

He was right. Charlie was sure of it. There really wasn't any other viable possibility.

Her heart hammered as she repeated Michael's observation to the others. Then a thought struck her and she added, "Tam mentioned an enclosed space and silver wheels. A room service cart fits."

"Do we have the other victims' hotel bills?" Tony asked. When Lena answered in the affirmative, he said, "Check them for room service charges on the night each victim was last known to be in her hotel."

"Yes," Lena cried a moment later. "There are room service charges for all of them."

"Then we've got our guy." Tony pointed at the man on the screen. "I need an identity. *Stat.*"

"Oh, God." Lena sounded sick as she stared at the picture of the waiter leaving the room with the cart piled high with dirty dishes and the white cloth billowing toward the floor. "Oh, God. Then Giselle's inside there."

"We need a name," Tony repeated, and they all went to work on identifying the waiter.

Unfortunately, that wasn't as easy as they'd first thought it was going to be. There was no clear shot of the waiter's face. As if conscious of the camera's location, he kept his face deliberately turned away.

"He's about six feet, one-eighty, average

build, short dark hair," Buzz reported after a thorough search of all pertinent footage. "That's all we've got, boss."

"He almost certainly works for Acer Staffing Solutions. They provide waitstaff for the Conquistador and the other victims' hotels," Lena said. "Eleven of our top suspects work for Acer."

"How many of them match the description?" Charlie asked, and Lena started pecking away at her computer keys again.

"Okay." Tony was on the phone with his contact at the ME's office. "Thanks."

He disconnected and told them, "They've finished preliminary tox screens on two of the victims. Both had Zolpidem tartrate in their systems. I'm going to extrapolate that they all do." He looked around at their frowning faces, and translated that to "Ambien."

"Yo. Sleeping pills: the old school date rape drug. That would explain why the last thing those two girls remembered was falling asleep in their hotel room," Michael said to Charlie, who barely remembered not to nod.

"This is how it has to be going down: the victims order room service, the unsub, who presumably has picked them out as possible victims earlier and knows their room numbers, puts Ambien in their food in the kitchen, the victims eat, fall asleep, and when he goes to their rooms, supposedly to pick up the dishes, he grabs the victims and takes them out in the cart. Then they end up starring in his death porn." Buzz sounded savage. "Destiny Sherman must have been inside the cart when he took it in to pick up the unconscious victims. She stayed behind to come out later in their clothes to fool the security cameras."

"We only have footage of that happening one time," Charlie warned. "Although it's a solid theory."

"The reason we only have footage of that happening one time is because nobody started looking for the other victims in time to keep the footage from being recorded over," Lena retorted.

"It doesn't explain what happened to Ms. Green," Tony said. "She didn't order room service, and he didn't come to her room. He appears to have been waiting for her in the elevator."

"Tam went downstairs again." Charlie went cold all over as she thought about it. "If she encountered this guy, she may have had some sort of psychic flash about him. You've seen how she knows things. Maybe he spotted it. Maybe she said something to him."

"That fits with what we know," Tony agreed.

"Which means he was working at the Conquistador yesterday," Charlie told Lena with a quick upsurge of excitement. "Screen for that."

A moment later Lena said, "I'm down to two names. They meet the physical description, they're employed by Acer Staffing, they were working at the Conquistador the night Giselle disappeared, they're locals, they have or have access to four-wheel-drive vehicles, and one's an amateur improviser and the other is a clown. And, both were working at the Conquistador yesterday. On the negative side, neither lives in the grid and neither is named Joe."

"Names and addresses," Tony said.

"Robert Thomas Dobson, Jr. and Cory Bobbins Hill." Lena picked up her phone. "I'll text them to you, along with their addresses."

Tony nodded. "Find out if they're at work today."

Lena made a call, then said, "Neither one of them is scheduled to work today."

"Okay. Let's go check 'em out." Tony was moving toward the door. "Charlie, you're

with me. Kaminsky, you're with Crane.
We've got Dobson, you've got Hill."

CHAPTER THIRTY-TWO

The small ranch house in the Las Vegas suburb of Henderson was shaded by a single bushy olive tree. The woman who answered the door was young, with short blond hair and a baby on her hip. She shook her head in response to Tony's request to speak to Robert Dobson.

"He owns the house, but he doesn't live here anymore. We've been renting here for over two years. I think he couldn't afford the mortgage when the economy tanked, but he couldn't sell it, so . . ." Her voice trailed off. She frowned, looking first Tony and then Charlie, both of whom were standing on the small concrete stoop, over curiously. "You're part of that serial killer hunter team from the FBI, aren't you? I saw you on TV." Her eyes widened. "Is he involved in that?"

Tony shook his head. "We're just doing a routine check to see if any of the people who work in the hotels saw anything that could help us," he lied with perfect aplomb, while Charlie cringed inwardly at the thought of what being recognized might do to their ability to find their quarry and Michael, who'd been vocal about his opinion that Charlie should have stayed back in the safety of the FBI office, said, "Think she's going to run and call our boy the second she's out of sight?"

"He and his wife moved in with his mother, and then they got a divorce so I think it's just him and his mother now. I have her address, if that helps," she volunteered breathlessly.

"It would," Tony agreed, and smiled at her.

"I'll be right back. I'm Kelly Sims, by the way." She returned his smile. Charlie could see that she was impressed with Tony's good looks.

"Special Agent Tony Bartoli, Dr. Charlotte Stone," Tony made the introductions which, since Kelly had already recognized them, there seemed no reason not to do. "Nice to meet you, Kelly."

"You too." Kelly smiled at him again and disappeared inside. A minute later she was back, offering Tony a scrap of paper with an address scribbled down on it. "We have to forward his mail sometimes."

Tony thanked her, and they left.

"Do you think she'll call Dobson and tell him we're looking for him?" Charlie punched the address into the GPS as he backed out of the driveway.

"I don't know. We're not going to get there faster than she can call, so let's hope she doesn't." Tony sounded as calm as always.

"If he lost his house, got a divorce, and had to move in with his mother more than two years ago, any or all of those could be the trigger event we're looking for."

"Fits the time frame," Tony agreed. Following the prompting of the GPS, they pulled onto the expressway.

"Babe, you remember that breakfast we had with the voodoo priestess?" Michael asked musingly from the backseat. "Wasn't the waiter's name — ?"

"Bob!" Charlie gasped as the memory of the waiter who had stared at Tam's cleavage exploded into her consciousness. Tony looked at her with surprise. Burningly conscious that he wouldn't have heard Michael's question, she added, "Bob was the name of the waiter who brought Tam and me our check at the hotel's breakfast buffet. I just remembered it."

"Way to recover," Michael applauded drily.

"Robert Thomas Dobson. Cory Bobbins Hill. Either one of them could be a Bob." Tony was quick on the uptake, as always.

"Yes." Charlie got more excited as she thought about it. "Tam charged our breakfast to her room. *He would know her room number.* She told him she was a psychic, told him a bunch of stuff about himself. Nothing about his being a serial killer, but she's always accurate, and maybe it was enough to spook him."

"Or maybe she saw him again when she made that quickie trip downstairs and said something else to him then," Michael suggested.

Charlie repeated that, and Tony nodded. He was already on the phone. "Kaminsky, did you get those pictures of Dobson and Hill yet?"

"The Conquistador doesn't have their pictures because they aren't employees of the hotel. Acer Staffing doesn't keep the pictures they do have of them on file: the only copies are on the employees' badges, which the employees keep. So I requested a download from the DMV and I'm waiting for it to come through," Lena replied. "You find Dobson?"

"Dobson's moved. We're heading for his new address now," Tony replied. "What about you?"

"We just got here. It doesn't seem like anybody's home. But we looked in all the windows, the house doesn't have a basement, and the detached garage was open. There's nothing out of the ordinary anywhere in sight, and if he's murdering women or holding them prisoner he's not doing it here."

"Tony." Charlie fought to stay calm as the GPS warned that they would be exiting left in two miles and she took a good look at the device's map. *"Dobson's new address is in the grid."*

An excited sound from the other end of the phone let them know that Lena had heard.

"Yeah," Tony acknowledged. "Meet us there." He gave Lena the address. "Better get a search warrant. And get some backup on the scene, too. Tell them to get there, but hang back until we give the word."

Lena acknowledged that, and Tony disconnected.

"This has got to be him." Charlie's palms felt damp. She'd done a good job of keeping her anxiety tamped down until now, when the denouement was at hand. But she was afraid, terribly afraid, of catching the killer only to find that they were too late, and Tam and Giselle were dead. At the thought of them suffering the fate Carmela Lynch and the others had suffered, she felt sick. *Please God, not Tam.* And not Giselle, either. "He meets all the criteria."

"Serial killer hunting as a science." Tony glanced at her. "We wouldn't be anywhere close to finding this guy without you."

"Sounds like Dudley's about to start kissing your hand again," Michael said sardonically. "If he does, pardon me while I throw up."

Aggravation was a pretty good antidote to fear, Charlie discovered. She barely managed not to glare at the phantom menace. Instead she told Tony, "We haven't caught him yet."

It was only as she finished speaking that she discovered she'd primly clasped her hands in her lap.

The good news was, they'd found their killer: Robert Thomas Dobson, Jr., Bob the waiter from the hotel buffet. The bad news was, he wasn't home.

There was ample incriminating evidence in the house, such as a tangle of jewelry (trophies, Charlie identified them as) that included a necklace identical to one in the picture of a victim, various implements of restraint and torture, and a prescription bottle full of Ambien.

The most damning thing they found was the body of his mother, stored in a basement freezer. Whether she'd been murdered or died of natural causes was impossible to determine, but it appeared that she'd been in there for some time. The neighbors said they thought she'd moved to Florida. Her latest Social Security check, unopened, lay in a pile of mail on the kitchen table.

"Where is *Giselle*?" Lena practically quivered with tension as she, Tony, and Charlie came together again in the small, perfectly ordinary-looking living room after having been all through the house and outbuildings.

Tony's eyes, red-rimmed from lack of sleep, were the only giveaway to the direness of the situation. His voice was as deliberate as always, and his lack of emotion was calming. "There's a BOLO out for Dobson and his car. The neighborhood is being staked out, so if he comes home we'll get him. We've got a list of his friends, known associates, and the places he frequents. We'll find him."

"If he hasn't killed Giselle — and Tam —

already, he'll do it just as soon as he finds out that we've identified him." Lena cast a haunted look out the front window of the modest split level. It was after six, and the setting sun threw the shadow of the house over the small front yard with its sun-crisped grass. "All it's going to take is for CNN or somebody to find out that we're here at his house, and it's game over."

It was probably game over anyway, was Charlie's worst fear. The logical place for Bob Dobson to be at that moment was his kill site. She thought of Tam, and her insides twisted. Tam might be a formidable psychic, but she was as human as anyone else. She could be frightened, and hurt, and killed just like Giselle, just like the other victims. Just like Holly, all those years ago.

Charlie took a steadying breath.

Please let us figure this out in time.

"You okay, babe?" Her expression must have changed, because Michael was looking at her with concern. The funny thing was, she'd been looking at him with concern all day, monitoring his ongoing flickering. That synchronicity struck her as funny, and she smiled.

"Goddamn it." Michael's swearing struck her as funny, too, and her smile widened. "You're getting punch drunk. You need food, and you need rest."

"We *need* to find the kill site." Charlie's reply was acerbic. She was talking to Michael, but as soon as she said it she realized what she had done and shifted her gaze to Lena.

Who visibly winced.

"His mother owned three other properties in addition to this one." Buzz came up to them in time to hear that last. "I've got the addresses. They're all in the grid." He looked at Tony. "I texted them to you."

Like Lena, he was giving off desperate vibes. Charlie supposed she was, too. Tony — and Michael — were the only ones who were not, but they all knew the truth: with every minute that passed, the chances grew slimmer that Tam and Giselle were alive.

"Let's go check these places out." Tony was looking at his phone. "Crane, you and Kaminsky take the two to the west. They're fairly close together. Charlie and I will take the other one."

The place they were looking for was in a rural area, its nearest neighbor maybe a quarter of a mile away, hidden from the narrow blacktop road by an overgrown tangle of trees and brush. A battered black mailbox with its lid hanging down was planted at the end of a gravel driveway. Nothing could be seen of the building at the end of the driveway until the Lexus had crunched its way up past the rim of scrub trees only to be confronted by a rusty red farm gate attached to a sagging, tumbledown wire fence that at least once upon a time appeared to have enclosed the property. The gate was secured with a chain and a padlock, blocking the car's access. Beyond the gate, a graveled yard or parking area surrounded a trio of long, low, concrete structures with corrugated metal roofs. The gray paint was peeling, the roofs were rusty, and dusty bushes and stunted trees crowded between the buildings in untamed profusion. The whole impression was of some kind of commercial enterprise that had been abandoned long since.

Tony braked, surveying the buildings as he slid the car into park. His eyes were bloodshot from lack of sleep, his jaw was dark with stubble, and his tie was crooked. All in all, he looked almost as tired as Charlie felt.

Tonight they were going to have to sleep, all of them, or they would be useless. But how could they, if Giselle and Tam were still out there?

The thought brought anguish with it.

"Looks like I'm climbing the fence," Tony said with resignation. He glanced at her, said, "Stay put until I see what's up," and got out of the car.

"This place is isolated as hell." From being stretched out comfortably in the backseat, Michael sat up, frowning as he looked out the windows. He, on the other hand, looked as fresh as an undead daisy, which was the advantage of needing neither food nor sleep. "Want to have another one of those conversations about why you need to find a new line of work?" he asked.

"Not unless you want to tell me why you ended up in Spookville," Charlie retorted, keeping an uneasy eye on Tony's progress. "Because I've been thinking about it, and I don't think that what I've heard you confess to so far is enough to send you there."

"Think about it all you want to," Michael said. "I'm done talking about my past."

She was not, but this wasn't the moment to have the conversation they were absolutely going to have. "You've almost stopped flickering. Tam's grounding spell must've been strong."

Pain combined with pride in her friend's abilities to stab her to the heart.

"What happened to her is not your fault," Michael said quietly. That he could read her

531

mind so well should not have been a surprise, she knew.

"Isn't it?" She gave a wobbly little laugh. "She wouldn't have come to Las Vegas if it wasn't for me."

"You wouldn't have asked her to come if it wasn't for *me,* so if you've got to blame somebody, I'm your huckleberry."

Charlie turned sideways in her seat to see Michael better — he was scanning their surroundings with an intent expression while they spoke — and as she did she spotted a large sign propped against the fence to the left of the gate. From its position, she got the impression that at some time in the past it might have been attached to the gate.

Faded and peeling, what had once been fancy scrolled letters hand-painted on wood said *Shelbourne Kennels.* The name was encased in a delicate pink and beige illustration of a clamshell.

Charlie's eyes widened and her pulse accelerated as she looked at it. What had been a niggle of uneasiness about their surroundings increased a hundredfold.

"Michael. Look over there by the gate."

He followed her gaze and saw the sign. His expression told her that he instantly realized the significance. "Shit. Better warn Dudley."

Charlie was already scrambling out of the car. The baking heat hit her like a wall even though, where she stood, where the car was parked, there was shade from the tangle of trees that shielded the buildings from the sight of the road. Dust and the smell of car exhaust hung in the air. Having climbed over it, Tony was just swinging to the ground on the other side of the gate.

Urgently, she called, "Tony! Look at the sign!" and pointed. Michael, who'd gotten out, too, growled, "Tell him to get his ass back over here or you're leaving without him," as Tony turned to look at the sign, one hand shielding his eyes.

A silver Ford Escape crunched up the driveway behind them.

Charlie's pulse jumped. She turned toward it so fast that she could feel the breeze of her ponytail whipping around. Tony turned to look, too, she saw, while Michael moved in front of her, planting himself between her and whoever was in the car.

Bob Dobson's vehicles do not include a Ford Escape. That was the semi-reassuring thought that ran through her head as the window rolled down even before the car stopped. A man's hand emerged from the window to wave at them.

"Agent Bartoli! Dr. Stone! I've got a tip

for you!"

The voice didn't ring any bells, but the tone and message were reassuring. The sound of a car door opening told her what was happening because Michael's broad back was blocking her view. Muttering, "You know you can't actually stop anything from getting to me, right?" then she stepped out from behind him.

It took her a second to recognize the stocky man with the light brown brush cut and cherubic face as Andrew Hagan, the Conquistador's head of security. He strode toward them, still dressed for work in a navy blazer and khaki slacks. She was standing right in his path but it wasn't her he was focused on. He was heading toward Tony, talking as he came.

"Those missing women you're looking for? I think I might know where —"

At his words her heart sped up with excitement, but then just as Hagan reached her, pain sliced through her head. At the suddenness of it she staggered back to lean against the warm, curved side of the car. Her hands went instinctively to her temples, and she watched him walk on by through a shimmering haze that allowed no sound to penetrate. Michael said something to her, too, but she couldn't make out the words.

What she heard instead was, "I'm in a kennel. An abandoned kennel. It's the waiter —" The words were cut off abruptly by a bloodcurdling scream.

It was Tam's voice. *In her head.*

Charlie was still bent almost double with pain, but there was no mistaking what she'd heard. Tam's voice, she realized with a thrill of horror, was attached to Hagan. *Does that mean Tam's dead?* But there was no time for speculation about that or anything else. Battling through the wooziness, the disorientation, the blinding headache that made her want to drop to her knees, Charlie pulled herself together enough to scream a warning.

"Tony, look out! He's got Tam!"

Through the befuddling haze that still clouded her vision, she saw Tony grabbing for his gun —

Two shots exploded. Charlie's heart leaped into her throat. She screamed, jumped — and watched thunderstruck as two bright red blossoms of blood appeared on the front of Tony's shirt.

Hagan shot Tony.

She was still processing the thought as Tony dropped like a stone.

CHAPTER THIRTY-THREE

"No!" Charlie screamed, and instinctively started toward where Tony lay crumpled on the ground.

"Charlie, get in the car!" Michael leaped in front of her, effectively blocking her path before she'd gone more than a couple of steps, even though she knew, *knew,* she could run through him.

"I'm a doctor, I —"

"Go," he yelled, right in her face. He grabbed at her, but he was as ephemeral as sunlight and couldn't connect. The electric charge of his touch was urgent, familiar.

Charlie's eyes widened as Hagan pivoted toward her. The golden rays of the dying sun glinted off the pistol, big and ugly and black, in his hand. Beyond Hagan, Tony lay unmoving . . .

Michael charged Hagan with a roar.

Charlie had an instant of crystal clarity: if she ran toward Tony, she would be dead in seconds. If she ran into the trees, she would be dead almost as fast. They were too sparse and thin to offer any real cover.

She turned and dove inside the car door she had left open, grabbing for the gearshift even as she hit leather, yanking it into reverse at the same time as she scrambled over the console, righted herself, and slammed her foot onto the accelerator. Her heart thumped. Her pulse raced. Her mouth was sour with fear —

Boom!

The windshield shattered, peppering her with BB-like balls of glass. Charlie screamed like a banshee and crushed the pedal to the floor as the car shot backward, bouncing over the uneven ground, dislodging a flock of blackbirds that flew skyward in a great cloud.

Tam — a flock of birds — Tony . . .

Her heart convulsed with pain, but she couldn't think about any of it now. Her entire focus had to be on surviving. Scrubby tangles of bushes and trees flashed past. Yanking the wheel, she barely managed to avoid smashing into the Escape. The open passenger door hit the edge of the Escape's front fender with a crash and was torn off as the Lexus blasted through. On the other side, the copse of trees scraped terrifyingly close. The screeching sound of bark on metal filled the air as she yanked the car back onto the driveway. Dust and leaves flew up around it like a whirlwind. Stomping the gas for all she was worth, she was half turned in the seat, looking out the rear windshield and steering like a NASCAR driver as the car careened toward the road.

Boom!

The rear window exploded just as something stung the top of her shoulder. It was only as she felt the hot slide of blood against her skin that she realized she'd been shot. Horror washed over her in an icy wave. Adrenaline pumped through her veins.

Oh God oh God please God.

"Duck!" Michael was in the car with her, roaring, throwing himself protectively in front of her as she screamed, and drove, and —

She didn't even feel it when the next bullet hit her in the head.

The pain in her head was unreal. It was debilitating. She was dizzy-sick with it. Her head felt like it was made of concrete. It was so heavy that it drooped forward to loll against her chest like a top-heavy flower after a hard rain.

Her arms were stretched taut above her

head. They ached almost unbearably.

The top of her shoulder burned and stung.

She was upright, hanging from her wrists, her toes just brushing the floor.

Her arms hurt so because they were bearing her weight.

A lightning vision of Carmela Lynch hanging by her handcuffed wrists from a black metal grid set into a ceiling popped into her head.

That was her now.

The horror of it made her eyes snap open. Her heart started to pound. She sucked in a shuddering breath.

"Stay quiet," Michael warned. "Don't move."

His voice was the most welcome thing she had ever heard. She turned her head, just a little, to find him standing there beside her, looking at her with a combination of fury and frustration that she knew had to do with his inability to help her. His face was hard and tight. His blue eyes blazed. Then he stepped out of view, walking around her to, she thought, check out her restraints. She found herself staring miserably down at a poured concrete floor. It came in and out of focus, but she could see well enough to tell that where she was, the concrete had been built up into a rectangular platform that was maybe eighteen inches higher than the rest of the floor: a stage. Away from the center part, which was directly beneath her, the sides sloped slightly down toward a shallow gulley surrounding the platform, punctuated by a metal drain. There were brown stains on it and in the gulley that she thought were dried blood. Remembering how Carmela and Alicia and Kim and the others had died, Charlie shuddered. The place was an abattoir, and she was the next in line for slaughter.

Her stomach knotted in reaction.

"Babe, I know you're hurt. I know you're scared. But you're moving around too much. Try to stay still." Michael was beside her again. His voice was calm, reassuring. But the diamond-bright glitter in his eyes and the hard set of his jaw told her that calm was the last thing he was feeling. She wet her lips as she looked at him. His eyes went murderous. But his voice soothed: "Close your eyes. Imagine we're on a beach somewhere, taking that vacation we should have taken. You think of that, and I'll try to come up with a way to get you out of here."

He moved away from her again.

Charlie willed herself to stay limp, to let her weight drag on her arms. Closing her eyes was beyond her, but she let her lids droop to veil them. She found herself looking at the floor again: somewhere she'd lost her shoes. The tips of her pink-manicured toes barely pressed against the concrete. She was fully dressed otherwise. Her pants were coated with dust, and ugly dark splotches stained her blouse. Dark red drops spattering on the floor around her feet flummoxed her for a moment. Then she realized that the drops were blood — her blood — and that she was bleeding.

I got shot.

Panic surged through her like a jolt of electricity at the thought. Its one positive purpose was that it burned away the fog obscuring her brain.

Lena and Buzz know where we are. They'll come.

The question — the one she really didn't want to think about — was, would they come in time?

"I'll be right back, babe." She knew Michael: as calm as he was deliberately keeping his voice, the raging fear for her that lay beneath his words was intensifying. That he was so afraid underlined for her more graphically than anything else could have done how dire her situation was. "Keep playing like you're unconscious."

Don't leave me.

But she didn't dare say it out loud, and keeping him beside her wouldn't have helped a thing anyway. So she got a grip, kept her mouth shut, and let him go.

"You goddamned psychopath, what'd you have to go and kidnap the redhead for? That's what put them onto you!" The voice — it was close, too close — made her insides quiver. It belonged to Hagan, Charlie was almost sure. She didn't dare lift her head and look. Staying quiet and still was requiring more and more of her energy. She was sick, in pain, afraid. Her wrists and shoulder joints hurt so badly that it was all she could do not to push her toes harder against the floor to try to take some of the weight off them, to relieve some of the pressure, but she was afraid that doing so might draw attention.

"*She* was on to me! She's a psychic! I waited on her at the buffet, and she told me she knew everything about me. Then she came back down later because she'd forgotten to pick up her credit card from the tray and when I gave it to her she told me she saw me surrounded by a bunch of angry, crying women! What was I supposed to do?" The voice of Bob the waiter came from in front of her, to the right. Maybe twelve feet away.

She didn't dare look.

"Who pays attention to a fucking psychic?" Hagan snapped. "There's no such thing as psychics! They're not real!"

Charlie heard the clomp of footsteps, saw a pair of men's brown dress shoes and the lower third of a pair of well-pressed khaki trousers walk past — Hagan — and held her breath.

He kept going.

Bob said, "This one is! She was working with the FBI! With *him.*"

Charlie couldn't help it: something about the tone of that last made her shoot a cautious glance toward Bob. What she saw when she did caused her heart to clutch.

He was aiming a vicious kick at Tony, who lay slumped on the concrete floor by the door as if he'd been carried inside and unceremoniously dumped. The *thump* as Bob's shoe connected with Tony's back made her wince inwardly. What was more frightening was that Tony didn't even flinch.

Oh, God, was he dead? She wondered frantically. His shirt and jacket were shiny red with blood, but not a lot of blood had pooled beneath him, which terrified her because she was afraid it meant that he'd already almost bled out. His eyes were closed, he was limp and motionless, and his skin was the grayish pale color of death or impending death.

No, Charlie raged. Then, *Please let him not be dead.*

A semi-calming thought reared its head: *If he were dead, I'd be able to see his spirit.*

Unless, of course, she couldn't. She couldn't see all of the newly, violently dead. Only those who didn't go immediately into the light.

As decent and upright as Tony was, the light would have come for him right away, she was sure.

She risked another glance. Tony lay maybe ten feet away from the edge of her platform, totally inert. If he was breathing she couldn't tell it, but she refused to allow herself to think that he was dead.

Saying another silent prayer for Tony, she forced herself to focus, and snuck more quick glances at her surroundings: they were inside a building, one of the three that made up the abandoned kennel, presumably. This one was about the size of a three-car garage, with an open space in the middle, which was where she was, and floodlights (currently dark) and camera equipment set up on tripods near the front wall, which was maybe twelve feet away. Cages, big ones, dog run–type cages with rusty wire walls that reached the ceiling, were attached to the walls in rows along either side of her. Most of them seemed to be full of boxes and assorted junk. One held old mattresses: she didn't even like to think what they had possibly been used for. The walls and floor were concrete block and poured concrete, respectively. There was a single metal door near Tony, and a few grimy windows that had been boarded up. The lighting was sparse and functional. It was hot — the rumble she could hear was a single, window-mounted air-conditioning unit that apparently didn't work very well — and smelled of ancient urine.

"You just keep on imagining that vacation." Michael was back. He was all hard-eyed and tight-mouthed and badass, and his powerful body was practically the poster child for formidable masculine strength. Simply having him there beside her made her feel safer, which was stupid, she knew. Ectoplasm equaled no help in this world.

Their eyes met for the briefest of seconds.

I know there's nothing you can do, she absolved him silently.

"I've got you," he said, his voice grim.

"Anyway, what's it to you if I kill her?" Bob moved away from Tony, out of Charlie's sight. The quick glance she'd gotten was enough for her to recognize him: the thirty-ish, dark-haired, good-looking, cleavage-ogling waiter from the breakfast buffet. His attire of jeans and a casual shirt reminded her that he'd had the day off. *If I kill her* — his turn of phrase had almost gotten past her. Hope fluttered: was Tam not yet dead? "You're Dynasty Film's *silent* partner, remember? You don't want to know."

"You're right, I don't want to know," Hagan responded viciously. "I *was* Dynasty Film's silent partner until you went and fucked it up. Only it looks like I can't be a silent partner anymore because you're going to ruin us both. You couldn't just make porn? You had to go murdering fucking women and filming it and screwing the whole thing up? You stupid fuck."

"We're making a lot of money off those snuff films. You said yourself, the international market is huge. And who are you calling a stupid fuck? I don't have to take that shit from you." Bob was bristling.

"I call it like I see it, stupid fuck. If I hadn't come over to warn you and been in here today when these assholes pulled up and gone out and circled around behind them and gotten the drop on Mr. Special Agent over there, your ass would be busted right now. And you'd be dragging me into it, I've got no doubt."

"Fuck you!"

A splashing sound made Charlie frown. Or, rather, start to frown. Frowning hurt so much it distracted her. She almost whimpered. The pain in her head came back like a baseball bat descending on her cranium. She'd been shot: not just in the shoulder but in the head. *Right, I remember.* The impact had been enough to knock her unconscious, but — she wasn't dead, and her senses seemed to be intact, so it obviously wasn't too bad. She thought the bullet had grazed the left side of her forehead, up near her hairline, maybe deflecting off her skull. She was bleeding; now that she thought about it, she could feel the warm stickiness of blood in her hair, see the occasional fresh drop splat near her feet.

Something to worry about later. If I live long enough.

"So where's your girlfriend?" Hagan's question struck Charlie as almost too casual in tone for the circumstances.

"Barbie?" Bob sounded nervous. "She's not my girlfriend. She's my stepsister. My mom and her dad were married for about five years a long time ago."

"Whatever." Hagan's tone brushed that aside. "I thought her name was Destiny."

"I called her Barbie, from when we were kids. My mom used to make me play dolls with her. Destiny had Barbie, and she wanted me to have Ken, but I stuck with G.I. Joe instead. So I ended up calling her Barbie, and she called me Joe."

"So where is she?" Hagan asked with barely concealed impatience. "We're about to get this mess cleaned up. We don't want her out there, some damned loose end shooting off her mouth."

"Oh." Bob hesitated. "You don't have to worry about that. She's dead."

"She's dead?" There was no mistaking the surprise in Hagan's voice. "Did you kill her? You turn your own stepsister into a snuff film, you sick fuck?"

"No!" Bob's voice quivered. "At least — that's not why. The last girl I took scratched her or something, so she beat the hell out of her. Beat her up too bad for me to use her. It pissed me off, so I . . ."

His voice trailed off.

"You killed her," Hagan finished for him, talking over more of the splashing sounds that were starting to worry Charlie a lot. "That's one thing you did right, anyway. Come on, help me spread this stuff around. We need to get this wrapped up before someone comes looking for the damned agent."

"Wait a minute, you're not going to just kill the girls, are you?" Bob sounded like he was reacting to something he was seeing that he didn't much like. "That's a total waste. The FBI bitch is already hanging up there. We can do her quick, then do the others right after. The cameras are right there. It won't take long, and we'll have three more movies we can post to the site."

Three more movies? Charlie's eyes widened as she registered the implication of that. She couldn't stop herself from risking a look toward where Bob and Hagan were talking, which was behind her and to her left.

The first thing she saw was Tam's red hair fanned out against the dull gray floor.

She caught her breath. Her heart leaped with thanksgiving.

Tam lay curled on her side in a corner of one of the dog runs, her pink jumpsuit in shreds. She was unmoving, and her hair obscured her face, but Charlie was almost positive she was unconscious rather than dead. In the same run, lying curled up next to her, was a small, black-haired woman Charlie instantly realized had to be Giselle. Like Tam, she looked battered and unconscious, but *alive.*

Thank you, God. Lena would be ecstatic. For one brief moment, unblemished joy coursed through Charlie's veins.

Then reality hit again, and terror came rushing back with it.

It wasn't like Tam and Giselle had just been rescued. They were still going to die. The only difference was that she and Tony, if he was still alive, were now going to die along with them.

Even more horribly than any of them could have dreamed.

That splashing sound? That was Hagan sloshing some kind of clear liquid through the wire gate at Tam and Giselle. Charlie couldn't see the container, but she could smell the liquid: gasoline.

As she identified it, her heart started to slam against her breastbone. Her blood ran cold. The room seemed to spin. Of all the ways she could think of to die, burning to death ranked right up there with the worst.

"Quit looking over there. Keep your head down. The last thing you want to do is draw their attention." Michael's tone was fierce. He was back where she could see him again, standing beside her on the platform study-ing the spot above her head where the cuffs were secured. His mouth compressed and his nostrils flared as he did so, which Charlie, with a pang of fear that told her how much she had secretly counted on him for rescue, took as a silent acknowledgment of defeat. What he said next put the seal on it: "Where the hell are Pebbles and Bam-Bam?"

"We're out of time," Hagan replied to Bob curtly. He gestured at the can Bob was holding. "Pour some of that on the floor, then throw the rest of it on those boxes over there. I don't want to leave any evidence behind."

Charlie's mouth went dry as Bob did as he was told. Something she did — a spasmodic jerk, say, from the stress of discovering that she, Tony, Tam, and Giselle were about to be barbecued alive — made something above her head give a metal-on-metal clank.

Bob looked her way. And met her eyes.

Charlie froze with horror.

"Why, hello there, pretty girl." Putting the gas can on the ground, Bob walked toward her. He was smiling. His all-American good looks coupled with that sharklike smile made the hair stand up on the back of her neck. His eyes — they were a soft gray — had a gleam in them that she'd seen before: that of a predator locking on to prey. They

were the eyes of a monster.
This is what a serial killer looks like.
She went cold all over.

Chapter Thirty-Four

"Fuck," Michael groaned.

"We don't have time for you to start messing around." Hagan's voice was impatient. Charlie didn't look his way. She was too busy staring in mortal terror at Bob, who had stopped in front of her and was looking her over like a slab of meat.

She sucked in a sickened breath as he put his hand on her breast, feeling the size and shape of it through the layers of her blouse and bra. Somewhere — where he'd gone she couldn't have said; all her attention was focused on the madman in front of her — she could hear Michael cursing a blue streak.

"Nice boobies," Bob leered, and squeezed. Fear and revulsion surged inside her in equal measure. Her chest knotted. Her stomach churned.

"The FBI is on the way. They know who you are. Killing us will just make things go worse for you." Now that playing possum had failed to work, the only weapon left to her was her words. Charlie was proud of how calm and sure she sounded. No one would guess that her blood had congealed with terror or that her throat was threatening to close up.

"Nah," Bob said. He fondled her, watching her face with avid attention. She knew what he was doing: feeding off her helplessness, her loathing. "When you've killed as many women as I have, if the cops get you, nothing can make things go worse."

"Hey, Bobby." Hagan walked into view. Bob turned his head to look at him. Hagan was holding a gun: without another word he jerked it up and fired.

Bob's head exploded.

Blood sprayed like a scarlet fountain. Charlie screamed, what was left of Bob hit the ground in front of her. Hagan stepped over the corpse and met her gaze.

"I got a real problem with leaving loose ends," he told her almost apologetically, and pointed his gun at her face.

Charlie gasped. Her life flashed before her eyes. Cold sweat poured over her in a wave. As time seemed to suspend and everything shifted into a kind of horror movie slow motion, she watched Hagan's eyes narrow, watched his knuckle whiten as it contracted on the trigger.

The thought that petrified her was: *I won't hear the next* bang, *because I'll be dead.*

Galvanized, she screamed like a steam whistle, tried to kick him — and then, silent and deadly, Tony leaped on him from behind, sending Hagan, who yelled in surprise, to the ground. Tony viciously punched him, straddling his back to keep him down. Heart in throat, Charlie watched as Hagan bucked, trying to throw him off — and then Tony locked his arms around Hagan's head and gave it a brutal twist. The sharp little crack that she knew was Hagan's neck snapping was followed almost instantly by the thunderclap-loud *bang* she'd thought she wouldn't be alive to hear.

Hagan's gun had fired. But the bullet had missed her. The bad guys were dead. And Tony? Shaking, breathing like she had been running for miles, Charlie looked down at the security man's corpse and the FBI agent who had just saved her life, calling to him fearfully, "Tony?"

Tony slowly got to his feet. The relief she felt as he did was so profound she was weak with it. His face was ashen and his clothes were soaked with blood, but his eyes were bright and alive as they met hers.

Something about the look in his made hers widen. She knew who he was, knew what had happened, even before he replied with a dry, "Not quite, babe."

"*Michael?*" It might be Tony's body, but what she was seeing in his eyes was Michael's soul. Even as fear for him over the consequences he might suffer began to rear its ugly head, she was dizzyingly grateful to have been saved.

"Yeah." He looked beyond her and his face changed. "Holy shit."

His tone coupled with a funny *whoosh*ing sound behind her made every muscle in her body tighten with dread.

"What is it?" She tried to swivel around, tried to see what was happening behind her even as he crouched beside Bob's body, but she saw nothing wrong. A wave of heat coupled with a crackling sound gave the lie to that. She knew what was happening instinctively, viscerally, even before the smell reached her nostrils: *fire.*

"*Michael.*" Charlie's heart sped up until it felt like it would pound its way out of her chest. Then Michael/Tony was back beside her, a set of keys in his hand as he reached above her head.

"I got you, babe," he said as he had before, and she felt the warm strength of his hand gripping her wrists an instant before he freed her.

She dropped. Her knees refused to support her, and she folded until she was crouching on the hard concrete floor. Bob's headless body and the pulpy mess of his head were right in front of her. Hagan, his head twisted at an unnatural angle, was just a little to the right. Her stomach convulsed as she looked at them, but there was no time.

"Get up." Michael/Tony was beside her, hauling her to her feet. For a second his arm wrapped around her and she leaned against him as her knees rebelled against carrying her weight, watching aghast as flames raced around the room, licking over the trail of gasoline. Then her eyes flew to her friend and Lena's sister trapped and unconscious in the wire cage.

"Tam. Giselle," she cried. The fire would reach them soon.

"Get out of here." He pushed her away from him, and she stumbled toward the only door. The fire was growing as it ran around the edge of the room; the door would be blocked in a matter of minutes. *"Go.* I'll get them."

With a glance that made sure she could move on her own, he ran toward the women in the cage, racing the fire toward them. The flames were growing taller, orange and red peaks that leaped toward the ceiling, and the heat and smell were intense. Charlie took one look at what was happening and stumbled after him. Her legs were wobbly, and her feet felt like they were made of pins and needles, but there was no way she was leaving them to get out — or not — on their own.

She reached Michael as he locked both hands on the gate of the dog run and literally tore it off its hinges. Flinging it aside, he spotted her.

"I told you to leave."

He screamed it over his shoulder as he leaped inside the dog run and she followed him in. At the same time the flames found the mattresses. The roar as they went up was the scariest thing Charlie had ever heard.

"Tam, Tam, wake up!" Charlie screamed by way of an answer. Having reached her friend, she frantically shook her.

"Go. I'll get her." Michael scooped up Giselle and flung her over his shoulder in a fireman's carry. He turned toward Tam. No way was he going to be able to bend down and get her, too, without losing Giselle.

"Tam!" Charlie shrieked.

"Wh— what?" Tam blinked and sat up.

"Get up! Stand up!"

Michael reached Tam's side, and between the two of them he and Charlie managed to haul her upright. She swayed, clearly not fully conscious, but Charlie steadied her as Michael heaved her over his shoulder. He staggered a little under the weight of both of them, and Charlie was reminded that this was Tony's body, not Michael's, and that it was badly wounded, to boot.

Carrying both women, with Charlie still unsteady on her feet beside him, he lurched, not ran, toward the door. It was the only way out. And the fire was racing them for it.

"What's happening?" Tam was groggy, out of it, as she tried to lift her head to look around. Still, she recognized Charlie. "Oh, thank God! I attached my voice to those terrible men. You heard it, and came. I prayed you would."

"Stay still," Charlie yelled at her, putting a comforting hand on her back. The fire was roaring now, consuming the mattresses, the boxes, all the junk in the dog runs, barreling toward them in a giant blazing wall. If it beat them to the door, they were dead. The air was super-heated, so hot it hurt to breathe it in, and the smell of burning was almost overwhelming.

A tiny line of flames racing ahead of the main conflagration shot in front of them just as they were within reach of the door. Charlie reached across it — the doorknob was hot — and yanked open the door.

Michael shoved her through it into the darkness outside and leaped out behind her, knocking her to the gravel and falling with her as a huge shaft of fire shot out over their heads.

A moment later the building was fully engulfed in flames. The crackling roar of it reminded Charlie of a freight train. They'd stumbled, crawled, walked, and been carried, variously, far enough away so that they weren't being showered with sparks any longer and their skin wasn't crisping in the heat. Tam was sitting up, blinking bemused at the enormous column of fire that was leaping toward the sky. Giselle was still unconscious, curled in the gravel. Michael was on his feet, leaning against the outer wall of one of the other buildings. Head aching, knees weak, Charlie leaned against the wall beside him, looking at him rather than the flames.

Tony's physical body might be beside her, but it was Michael who was actually there.

"No more fucking serial killers." He was

breathless, wheezing. The look he gave her was fierce enough that it should have made her cower away from him. Instead she smiled, and pressed her hand to his warm, bristly cheek. She was so glad to be alive, but also still so frightened. For him, and for Tony, too.

Tony was grievously wounded, maybe even dead. Michael — she didn't know what would happen to Michael now.

"You just saved all of us," she told him, and kissed him, her lips pressing gently against his, careful because of the extent of his physical injuries. He wrapped an arm around her waist and pulled her close to his side and bent his head and kissed her back.

Not gently at all.

Sirens filled the air, but she barely heard them.

All of a sudden his head came up, and he shoved her away from him with enough force so that she fell to her knees in the gravel.

Even as she hit the ground he screamed, the sound guttural, agonized.

"Michael?" Her heart in her throat, she looked up just in time to watch his spirit being jerked out of Tony's body. Tony crumpled to the ground like a suit of empty clothes. Michael, all six-foot-three powerful

golden inches of him, went flying up through the air like he weighed nothing.

Then he vanished, the darkness swallowing him up like he'd never been there at all. Fear turned her blood to ice. Her pulse thundered in her ears.

"Michael!" Charlie cried, scrambling to her feet and running toward the spot where he'd disappeared. She was too late: there was nothing there.

"I love you," she screamed after him, in case he could still hear. "I love you."

A whole cavalcade of fire trucks and police cars and other vehicles with, she was sure, Lena and Buzz in there somewhere, came zooming up the driveway. Charlie barely noticed. She didn't care. She stood there in the darkness for a long moment, her heart pounding, her senses reaching out, searching —

Michael was gone. Charlie could sense it, feel his absence like a tangible thing.

Had a hunter gotten him? Or was it something else?

She had no way of knowing. But her heart bled.

Tears sliding down her cheeks, she did the only thing that was left for her to do. She dropped to her knees by Tony's limp body, and took his pulse.

He was alive. Numbly, she began to administer first aid.

Michael hurtled through darkness so absolute that it didn't even allow for the possibility of light.

All around him was nothingness.

It was icy cold.

He could feel it filling him.

It was changing him.

No, it was bringing out more of what was already inside him.

Making him into more of what he really was.

Something born of the dark.

And violence.

All he knew was rage and pain.

Then he heard a whisper.

The tiniest thread of a whisper, twining itself around his cold, dead heart.

A woman's voice: *I love you.*

Lost in the great Eternal Nowhere, he carried those words with him into the dark.

CHAPTER THIRTY-FIVE

Two weeks later, Charlie was on her way home. Her plane had landed at Lonesome Pine Airport about half an hour before. At the moment she was in a taxi, looking out at the familiar streets of Big Stone Gap. It was late afternoon, and the town was alive with golden sunlight and the warm bright colors of autumn.

She'd spent the time sitting by Tony's bedside in the hospital in Las Vegas. His wounds were severe, but the doctors had said he would recover fully. Earlier today, he'd been released. He was going to his parents' house for another two weeks, when the doctors promised he'd be ready to return to work. He'd asked Charlie to come with him.

She had elected to go home instead.

In telling him of her decision, she'd told him the truth, or at least, as much of the truth as she'd felt he could handle: while there wasn't someone currently in her life, there had been someone that she had cared for very much, and she was still getting over him.

She couldn't properly move on — to Tony or anyone — until her heart had fully healed.

Tony had said he understood, and was prepared to wait.

Tam was fine, and had gone home to California.

Lena had fallen on Giselle like a prospector on a newly discovered gold mine, staying with her in the hospital until Giselle had recovered and then flying home with her. The sisters were back in their respective apartments now, but they were tight.

Buzz was getting the cold shoulder from both of them, but he was so happy Giselle was alive, he said he could live with that.

For a little while, at least.

So it was kind of a happy ending all around.

Except for Charlie.

So far, her ending was the opposite of happy.

It had happened exactly the way she had feared. She had fallen in love with her ghost, he had been snatched away, and now her heart was broken.

Tam had tried her best, but there was no doing anything about it. Michael was gone.

All that was left for Charlie to do was get over it.

But it was hard. Unbelievably, gut-wrenchingly hard.

That was why, when the taxi turned the corner there by the First Baptist Church, she willed herself not to even look in its direction. It was a modest, white-painted brick building with a tall steeple, a hedge of bushy green viburnum, and a graveyard off to the side.

In that graveyard was a small white cross, with M. A. Garland painted on it in crude black letters, along with the dates of his birth and death.

Michael's grave.

Just knowing it was there tore at her heart.

She wasn't going to look, but something, some instinct or maybe a movement caught in her periphery vision, made her risk a glance.

What she saw made her eyes widen and her lips part.

A man — a tall, well-built, tawny-haired man — stood in the graveyard looking down at Michael's grave.

"Stop," she practically screeched at the driver. "I'm getting out."

When he did, parking by the curb, she all but fell out the door.

The man stood with his back to her.

He was about six three and powerfully built.

He wore jeans and boots and a black leather motorcycle jacket.

His tawny hair was cut too short.

Still —

"Michael?" Her heart pounded so hard it felt like it was trying to beat its way out of her chest. The sweet scent of the viburnum swirled around her. As she hurried toward him, she stumbled over the soft green grass.

He didn't turn, didn't seem to have heard. Sunlight gilded the bright strands of his hair.

She reached him, put a tentative hand on his muscular, leather-clad arm.

Her breath caught.

He was solid. He was real. *Alive.*

He turned a little as she touched him, and looked down at her.

He had a square jaw, broad cheekbones and forehead, a straight nose, and a beautifully cut mouth. He was, in fact, an absolutely gorgeous guy.

She went dizzy with excitement.

"Michael!"

He was looking down at her with an interested expression, like he had no idea who she was, like he had never seen her before in his life.

Then she noticed two things that sent her stomach plummeting right down to her toes.

He had a small scar at the side of his mouth.

And his eyes weren't Michael's heart-stopping sky blue.

They were hazel.

A hard knot formed in her chest.

"Who are you?" she breathed.

ACKNOWLEDGMENTS

Oh, gosh, where to start? Peter, without you as my on-call media specialist I would forever dwell in the dark ages. Christopher, you have been an invaluable resource for ideas, words, phrases, and advice. Doug, you do everything I can't, or don't want, to do. Then there's my wonderful editor, Linda Marrow, whose instincts are always spot-on, and my agent, Robert Gottlieb of Trident Media Group, who does such an excellent job for me. My thanks to Gina Centrello, Libby McGuire, Kim Hovey, Anne Speyer, and the entire fantastic team at Ballantine Books. I couldn't do it without any of you!

ABOUT THE AUTHOR

Karen Robards is the *New York Times* and *USA Today* bestselling author of forty-five books and one novella. The mother of three boys, she lives in her hometown of Louisville, Kentucky.